U0078817

-修訂五版-

商用英文

黃正興　編著

English
for
Business

三民書局

修訂五版序

　　臺灣是個經濟發展需要依賴貿易為主的國家。臺灣對外貿易依存度 (Taiwan Degree of Dependence on Foreign Trade)，也就是進出口總值佔 GDP 比重幾乎都超過百分之百。可見貿易對臺灣的重要性。

　　為順應貿易及科技時代的來臨，臺灣在面臨 WTO 時代的挑戰，必須非常重視貿易並做好貿易，要做好貿易尤重人才的培育，人才的養成尤需優秀的教科書。本書提供最有系統的貿易流程、貿易交易書信流程、貿易書信架構訓練，尤其輔以有系統的文法與貿易知識訓練，形成一套紮實的訓練體系，條理分明且淺顯易懂。各章節頗值一讀再讀，若能熟能生巧、靈活運用，非常有助於造就優秀的貿易人才。

　　貿易上，關稅一直是個熱門話題。關稅為各國作為國家財政的稅收、保護國內產業、救濟貿易失衡等功用。為幫助瞭解關稅的基本稅率，本書在新版特別於第十二章「商業知識」之「關務」中增列「如何查關稅？」，多一項網路知識，以多增一技之長。

　　在拓展客源技能上，網路是個重要的新武器，臺灣經貿網 (Taiwantrade) 不可忽視。本書在新版第七章「商業知識」增列「臺灣經貿網 (Taiwantrade)」，詳述此網站之功能，在國際貿易交易時，買賣雙方可由此平臺獲得雙方的資訊並完成交易。網路時代的巨量交易，此網厥功甚偉，精通此網，獲另一技也。

　　由於科技的進步，網路傳播溝通的進步，以往溝通為主的電報 (Cable)、電傳 (Telex) 與傳真 (Fax)，在增訂四版的第二十三章，漸漸已不為商業實務界所使用，故於新版時將予刪除。

　　本書自出版至今，由於頗具國際性、實用性、尤其具系統性，承蒙各界採用為教科書或參考書，特此致上謝忱。

黃正興 謹誌

自序

子曰：「工欲善其事，必先利其器。」追求學問所使用之「器」甚為重要。本書為針對「如何學好商用英文」而編的利器；一方面依照教育部所訂的課程標準，另一方面注重理論與實務的配合。在理論上，本書尤重技巧之傳授，以綱要式條列重點，使知如何去做，如何去寫，如何去表達；在實務上，則輔以各種狀況之範例及圖表，以收立竿見影之效，此為本書特色之一。

其二為，注重寫作技巧之闡釋，以三段式論法(簡介、資訊、行動)，為訓練之架構。

其三為，每一章後面的練習皆經特別設計：問答題，以測驗對整章的瞭解程度；文法練習，自成一體系，將商用英文常用之文法予有系統的複習；句型練習，實用靈活，使達熟能生巧；填充練習，以評量對範例文章之理解程度，可收「立即增強印象」之效果。

尤具特色為實務探討，對實務運作常見之話題予以剖析，值得一讀。

本書有疏漏之處，尚祈方家讀者，不吝指正。

黃正興 謹誌

CONTENTS 目次

英文文法目次

英文句型目次

實務探討目次

商業知識目次

Photo Credits

Shutterstock: p. 27 信頭範例圖、p. 45 信封範例圖。

作者提供：p. 46 信紙的摺法 、 p. 126 目錄 、 p. 127 價目表 、 p. 217 信用狀 1 、 p. 218 信用狀 2 、 p. 219 信用狀 3、p. 273 商業發票 1 、 p. 274 商業發票 2、p. 275 海運提單、p. 276 保險單、p. 277 裝箱單 1、 p. 278 裝箱單 2 、 p. 279 重量容積證明書 、 p. 280 海關發票 、 p. 281 檢驗證明 、 p. 282 產地證明 、 p. 428 廣告(A)、 p. 429 廣告(B)。

圖表文件目次

Chapter One

Introduction to Business English

商用英文緒論

 **Outline**

1. Definition	定義
2. Coverage	內容
3. Purpose	目的
4. Key Writing Skill	寫作技巧的關鍵
5. International Trade Procedure	國際貿易流程圖

1. Definition

Business English is English used in business. It deals mainly with business communication, especially the correspondence concerning international trade.

商用英文即應用在商業的英文，主要涉及商業的通訊，尤其是國際貿易相關的事物。

2. Coverage

In addition to grammar and business writing, Business English covers international trade practice, business terms, business knowledge, e-mail, etc.

除了文法及商用英文寫作，商用英文包括國際貿易實務、貿易條款與術語、商業知識、電子郵件等。

3. Purpose

The purpose of learning Business English is to obtain basic letter writing skills, trade knowledge, know-how, business terms, and to be able to apply them in the fields the learners are going to be devoted to.

學習商用英文之目的在獲得基本的商用書信寫作技巧、商業知識、技能和商業術語,使能應用於所從事之行業。

4. Key Writing Skill—Three-paragraph Structure

In Business English letter writing, it is essential that the structure of the body should be divided into three major paragraphs as follows:

在商業書信寫作,重要的是要將書信的主體分成三個主要的段落如下:

⑴ 簡介 (INT, Introduction):信的起頭

⑵ 資訊 (IFM, Information):信之本文

⑶ 行動 (ACT, Action):要求對方採取的行動

茲舉例說明如下:

HOPE COSMETICS CO., LTD.

No. ××, Linsen N. Rd., Zhongshan Dist.,

Taipei, Taiwan

August 12, **20..**

Y&K IMPORTS, INC.

×× Palisades Boulevard,

Palisades Park, NJ 07650

U.S.A.

Dear Sirs,

INT ← We are pleased to receive your letter of August 1, **20..** concerning our cosmetics.

IFM ← As requested, we enclose our latest catalogue and price list for your reference. We are sure that our products are excellent in quality and reasonable in price.

ACT ← As there are many rush orders currently, we would suggest you place your order without delay. We look forward to hearing from you soon.

Sincerely yours,

Delen Lin

Delen Lin

Manager

Enc.

信文中譯：

敬啟者：

簡介——我們很高興收到你們 **20..** 年 8 月 1 日關於我們化妝品的來信。

資訊——如所請求，我們附上最新目錄及價目表以供參考。我們確信我們的產品品質最優，價格最公道。

行動——因目前有很多訂單，我們建議你們立即開出訂單。我們期待很快得到回音。

谨上

附件

5. International Trade Procedure

★國際貿易流程圖：

出口商　　　　　　　　　　　　　　　　　　　　進口商
① 尋找客戶 4.4　　　Looking for Customers　　4.1 尋找客戶 ②

進出口商請求有關機關，如國貿局、外貿協會及雜誌刊物等介紹客戶

③ 招攬生意 5.4　　　　Trade Proposal　　　　5.1 招攬生意 ④

進出口商由有關機關所獲得的資訊直接與對方連絡

⑤ 徵信調查 6.1　　　Credit Enquiries　　　6.2 徵信調查 ⑥

進出口商可經由各種媒介，如有關機關、報章雜誌及各種刊物作徵信調查

⑦ 促銷 11.1　　　Promotion/Enquiries　　9.1 詢問 ⑧

主動發出促銷函　　　　　　　　直接向出口商發出詢問函

⑨ 寄目錄及價目 9.6　Replies/Quotation Request　10.2 請求報價 ⑩

依所請寄出目錄、價目或樣品　　請求依所提數量及規格報價

⑪ 報價 10.4　　Quotation/Counter-offer　10.7 還價 ⑫

洽商工廠後提出報價　　　　　　如認為價格或條件不妥可還價

⑬ 接受 10.9 Acceptance/Order 12.2 訂單 ⑭

可接受或拒絕 如接受時可開出訂單

⑮ 確認 12.4 Sales Confirmation/Opening L/C 14.2 開信用狀 ⑯

開狀銀行

向國貿局及簽證銀行申請進口許

發出銷售確認書確認訂單 可證 IL (Import Licence)，並向開

(sales confirmation) 狀銀行申請開立信用狀且預繳保

證金

⑰ 收到信用狀 14.3 L/C Receipt/Shipping Instruction 14.2 裝船指示 ⑱

通知銀行

―――――― 發出裝船指示，指示包裝及運送細節

確認由通知銀行轉來的信用狀

⑲ 備貨／出貨

與工廠配合準備出貨 (Shipment)

出口簽證

向國貿局及簽證銀行辦理各項出口簽證手續

申請出口許可證 EL (Export Licence)

洽訂船位

向船公司洽訂船位，簽裝貨單 S/O (Shipping Order)

接洽保險

向保險公司申請保險

出口報關

向海關申請出口報關

⑳ 裝船通知 Shipping Advice 14.3

發出裝船明細，包括船名、開航日、預訂到達日等

貨物裝船

把貨物送到貨櫃場或碼頭等

㉑ 押匯　14.7 Negotiation　　　Import Customs Clearance 14.8 進口清關 ㉒

押匯銀行　寄貨運單據　　　　　　　　　付款　開狀銀行

具備文件向押匯銀行押匯，領取貨款　　繳交餘款並贖回貨運單據

㉓ 寄文件副本 14.7　　　　　　　　　　14.8 進口報關

寄貨運單據文件副本給進口商　　　　　辦理報關並繳交關稅

㉔ 追蹤　Follow-up Letters 11.4.1, 11.4.2, 21.1, 21.2　　　　提貨

向進口商追蹤看是否貨已安全
到達，並詢問是否有新訂單

取提單 B/L (Bill of
Lading) 向船公司換
小提單 D/O (Delivery
Order) 並提貨

㉕ 調整 20.1 (B)　Adjustment/Complaint　20.1 (A) 抱怨／再訂單 ㉖

處理進口商所提之抱怨　　　　　驗貨之後如不滿意，提出抱怨；
　　　　　　　　　　　　　　　　如滿意則可再下訂單

✎ Exercise

A. Questions 問答題

1. What is Business English?

2. What does Business English cover?

3. What is the purpose of studying Business English?

4. What is the structure of a three-paragraph business letter?

B. Business Insight 實務探討

◆ 第一印象

在做國際貿易生意時，進出口雙方可能都沒見過面，這時只靠雙方通信往來以瞭解對方。所以，寄出或發出的信件即代表公司，要使生意成交，就必須使對方留下深刻的印象。英文裡有一句名言 "First impression is lasting." 即是此意。貿易公司從業人員尤須注意商用英文書信之格式及寫作技巧。

C. Grammar Practice 文法練習

★ 英文基本句型 (Basic Sentence Patterns)：

英文基本句型有五種。

1. S. + V.	He smiles.
2. S. + V. + C.	I am a businessman.
3. S. + V. + O.	She delivered the goods.
4. S. + V. + I.O. + D.O.	They sent us a letter.
5. S. + V. + O. + C.	We chose him our president.

Notes:

S.: Subject	主詞	O.: Object	受詞
V.: Verb	動詞	I.O.: Indirect object	間接受詞 (表人)
C.: Complement	補語	D.O.: Direct object	直接受詞 (表物)

Selection：寫出下列句子所屬句型的代碼

_____ 1. The prices go up every day owing to the war.

_____ 2. It pays to be polite.

_____ 3. Will you please show me the way to the station?

_____ 4. The king stripped him of all his honors.

_____   5. Mr. Wilson painted the factory green.

_____   6. He stood the candle on the floor.

_____   7. My prediction has come true.

_____   8. The rose smells sweet.

_____   9. I will set all his troubles right.

_____   10. Please forward me any letter that may come.

D. Pattern Practice 句型練習

★請求，將感激……：

> Please send us...
>
> Would you please send us...
>
> If you should..., we would be very grateful.
>
> We would appreciate it if you could...
>
> We would appreciate your...

1. 請寄來你們公司最近的目錄及價目表。

_____

2. 我們將感激，如果你們能郵寄來有關貴公司五金產品的目錄。

_____

E. Business Terms 解釋名詞

1. S/O   2. B/L   3. D/O   4. IL   5. EL

F. Blank-filling 填充練習

Dear _____ ,

We are _____ to _____ your letter _____ August 1, **20..**
_____ our cosmetics.

As _____ , we _____ our latest _____ and _____ list for
your _____ . We _____ sure that our _____ are excellent in
_____ and _____ in price.

As _____ are rushing _____ , we would _____ you _____
your order _____ delay. We _____ forward to _____ from
you _____ .

_____ yours,

Enc.

No. 1 網路：網路行銷 (Internet Marketing)

在網路行銷中，除了要留意產品 (Product)、價格 (Price)、促銷
(Promotion)、通路 (Place) 4P 外，還必須注意 4C。其 4C 分別為顧客經驗
(Customer Experience)、顧客關係 (Customer Relationship)、溝通
(Communication)、社群 (Community)。

網路行銷是最近熱門的銷售方式，經由數位科技方式來行銷產品及服

務則稱為數位行銷 (Digital Marketing)。網路行銷方法包括搜尋引擎行銷 (SEO)、展示型廣告 (Advertising)、社群行銷 (Social Media Marketing)、會員行銷 (Member Marketing) 等。網路行銷已成為企業行銷策略成功的重要關鍵所在。網路行銷方法類型如下：

附註：SEO (Search Engine Optimization) 搜尋引擎優化，當使用者在輸入關鍵字時，能在網路上使自己 (被搜尋者) 的產品、服務、形象等特色出現前幾名搜尋結果之方法，稱為 SEO。根據資料顯示，絕大多數的使用者會點擊前兩個搜尋引擎出現的結果，因此只要你的網站內容夠好，打對關鍵字，透過搜尋引擎優化，就有機會獲得更多的曝光，吸引到潛在的消費者。所以說，SEO=Visibility (能見度)，此為新式的網路行銷方法。

Chapter Two

Letter Formats—
Parts of a Letter, Styles, Punctuation, and Mailing

書信格式——
書信要點、樣式、標點符號及郵寄

 **Outline**

1. The Seven Principal Parts of a Business Letter	書信七個主要部分
2. Additional Seven Parts of a Business Letter	書信另外七大部分
3. Typing Styles	打字格式
4. Punctuation	標點符號
5. Mailing	郵寄

1. The Seven Principal Parts of a Business Letter

The seven principal parts of the structure of a letter are as follows:

書信結構七個主要部分如下：

⑴ Letterhead	信頭
⑵ Date	日期
⑶ Inside Name and Address	收信人之姓名及地址
⑷ Salutation	稱謂
⑸ Body	信文
⑹ Complimentary Close	結尾敬語
⑺ Signature and Official Position	簽名及職稱

＊書信七個主要部分圖示：

Letterhead

_____(1)_____

Date

_____(2)_____

Inside Name
and Address

_____(3)_____

Salutation

_____(4)_____

Body

_____(5)_____

Complimentary
Close

_____(6)_____

Signature and
Official Position

_____(7)_____

茲將此書信七大部分分別說明如下：

(1) Letterhead (信頭)：

A letterhead shows a company's personality. The information shown in the letterhead includes a company's name, address, trademark, telephone number, etc.

信頭代表公司的性質，包括公司名字、地址、商標、電話號碼等。

＊ 公司的種類有無限公司、有限公司、兩合公司及股份有限公司等四種 (公司法第 2 條)。以公司股東之償還債務責任 (liability) 來分，分為有限與無限兩種。有限即是公司股東之償還債務責任有限，依各國之不同，所表示的字亦有不同，茲舉例如下：

　　　　a. 英制：Co., Ltd. (Company Limited)

　　　　b. 美制：Inc. (Incorporated)

　　　　c. 澳制：Pty (Proprietary Limited)

　　臺灣現今仍採用英制系統較多，故公司名後皆有 Co., Ltd.。

⑵ Date (日期)：

There are four ways of expressing a date:

表達日期的方式有下列四種：

Style 方式	Order 次序	Example 範例	
1) English way (英式)	day, month, year	23rd May, **20..**	
2) American way (美式)	month, day, year	May 21, **20..**	
3) Chinese way (中式)	year, month, day	中華民國　年　月　日	
4) Simple way (簡式)	free	3/Apr/**20..**	17/4/**20..**
		May/6/**20..**	5/16/**20..**
		20../Jun/9	**20..**/6/12

由上表可知英式日期的寫法是由小而大，中式則由大而小，美式則屬折衷。簡式雖方便但容易混淆，如 5/6 可能是 5 月 6 日，也可能是 6 月 5 日。

英文序數茲列表如下：

1st	11th	21st	31st
2nd	12th	22nd	
3rd	13th	23rd	
4th	14th	24th	
5th	15th	25th	
6th	16th	26th	
7th	17th	27th	

8th	18th	28th
9th	19th	29th
10th	20th	30th

* st 代表 first 取後兩字母

　nd 代表 second 取後兩字母

　rd 代表 third 取後兩字母

　th 代表除上述 st, nd, rd 外的其他數字之序數

(3) Inside Name and Address (收信人之姓名及地址)：

The inside name and address are placed at the head of the letter, below the date and over the salutation.

收信人之姓名及地址置於信的左上部位，其寫法如下：

Mr. Mike Lee	人名
President	頭銜
Y&K IMPORTS, INC.	公司名
×× Palisades Boulevard,	門牌及街道名
Palisades Park, NJ 07650	城市，州省名及郵遞區號
U.S.A.	國名

收信人之姓名置於公司名及地址之上；地址以三行為原則，置於公司名之下。

◎相關項目說明如下：

A. Courtesy title (禮貌稱呼)：

英文裡常用的禮貌稱呼有如下：

稱呼	全銜	中譯
Mr.	Mister	先生
Mrs.	Mistress	太太；夫人
Ms.	Miss or Mistress	小姐或太太

Ma'am	Madam	女士；夫人
Messrs.	Messieurs	先生 (複數)
Mmes.	Mesdames	女士 (複數)
Esq.	Esquire	紳士
Prof.	Professor	教授
Dr.	Doctor	博士或醫生
Col.	Colonel	上校
Rev.	Reverend	牧師
Sir*		爵士 (冠於姓名之前)

* Sir 冠於姓名之前為「爵士」之意；有別於稱謂的 Dear Sir, 為「敬啟者」之意。

B. The structure of official title (職稱架構)：

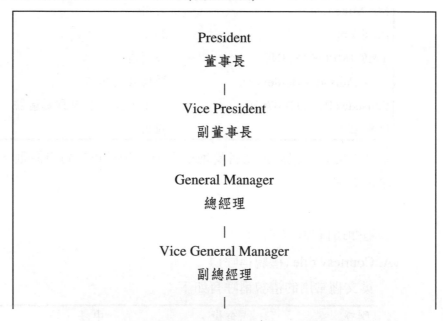

President
董事長

|

Vice President
副董事長

|

General Manager
總經理

|

Vice General Manager
副總經理

|

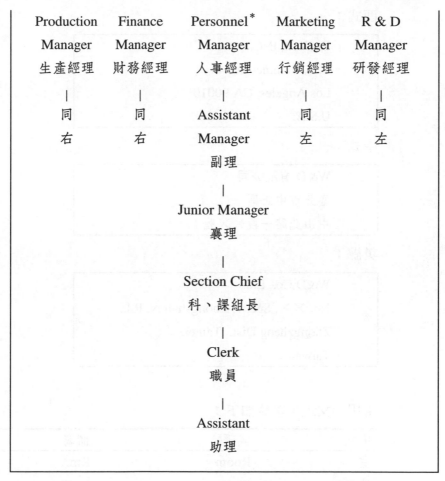

Production	Finance	Personnel[*]	Marketing	R & D
Manager	Manager	Manager	Manager	Manager
生產經理	財務經理	人事經理	行銷經理	研發經理
|	|	|	|	|
同	同	Assistant	同	同
右	右	Manager	左	左
		副理		

Junior Manager

襄理

Section Chief

科、課組長

Clerk

職員

Assistant

助理

* Personnel (人事)，現稱為 Human Resources (人力資源，簡稱 HR)。

C. Address (地址)：

中式地址的寫法和西式的寫法是不同的，西式是由小而大，而中式則由大而小；號碼之寫法亦有所不同，如「8 巷」的英文為 Lane 8，號碼置於後。茲舉例說明如下：

西式：

> EatWell, INC.
>
> ××Summer Drive,
>
> Los Angeles, CA 90010
>
> U.S.A.

中式：

> W&D 有限公司
>
> 臺北市中正區
>
> 中山北路一段××號

英譯：

> W&D Co., Ltd.
>
> No. ××, Sec. 1, Zhongshan N. Rd.,
>
> Zhongzheng Dist., Taipei,
>
> Taiwan

常用中文地址英譯如下：

中文	英譯	簡寫
室	Room	Rm.
樓	Floor	F., Fl.
大樓	Building	Bldg.
弄	Alley	Aly., Ally.
巷	Lane	Ln.
街	Street	Str., St.
段	Section	Sec.
路	Road	Rd.

路	Drive	Dr.
大道	Boulevard	Blvd.
區	District	Dist.
村	Village	Vil.
鄉	Township	
鎮	Town	
市	City	
縣	County	
州	State	
省	Province	Prov.

* 用法注意：

1. 英文地址的門牌號碼前，不必加 No.，之後也不必加逗點，如：100 Park Road，非 No. 100, Park Road。

2. 地址以三行為原則，但是中文地址有時甚長，則不在此限。

3. 國名須單獨一行，如為國內信函，則可省去國名。

⑷ Salutation (稱謂)：

The common salutations are as follows:

常用的稱謂如下：

稱謂	用於
Dear Sir	一般個人 (男女皆可)
Dear Sirs	公司行號
Dear Madam	女士
Mesdames	女士 (複數)
Ladies and gentlemen	先生女士們
Dear Mr. ...	先生
Dear John	約翰

一般商業書信的稱謂剛開始以 Dear Sir 及 Dear Sirs 稱呼最普遍。在一段時間之後，雙方較為熟稔時，可改稱姓，如 Dear Mr. Brown 或只稱名字，如 Dear Mike 等。

＊ 用法注意：

1. 西方人士名字一般有三部分：

	First name,	Middle name,	and Last name
如：	Mike	E.	Brown

其中 First name 代表「名」，Middle name 代表「中間名」，一般以簡寫表示即可，Last name 即代表「姓」。

2. Mr. 後不可接名，而要接姓，例如：不能用 Mr. Mike，而必須用 Mr. Brown 或只稱呼 Mike。中式用法稱人名麥克先生並無不妥，此為中西用法不同之處。

3. 不能連名帶姓：Dear Mr. James Wang (×)

4. 不要重複稱呼：Dear Mr. E. Blue, Esq. (×)

＊ Matching (配對題)：

Inside name and address	Salutation
＿＿＿＿＿ 1. LINTON IMPORTS, INC. × ×× 35th Avenue, Seattle, Washington 98125 U.S.A.	a. Dear Sirs　　　（正式） b. Dear Sir　　　（正式） c. Dear Madam　（正式）

	2. Ms. Alice Black		
	Vice President	d. Dear Manager	(正式)
	LINTON IMPORTS, INC.		
		e. Dear Ms. Black	(較熟)
	3. The Manager		
	LINTON IMPORTS, INC.	f. Dear Mr. Wang	(較熟)
	4. Mr. Scott Wang	g. Dear Alice	(最熟)
	President		
	LINTON IMPORTS, INC.	h. Dear Scott	(最熟)

⑸ **Body (信文)：**

> a. Introduction————————INT
> b. Information————————IFM
> c. Action————————ACT

信文可分三段：簡介、資訊、行動。

1) 簡介 (INT)：

　　信的起頭，即來龍去脈交待，如感謝收到來信或提到某項產品等。

2) 資訊 (IFM)：

　　信之本文，把要旨寫於此，如要求寄目錄、報價或推銷產品等。

3) 行動 (ACT)：

　　要求對方採取的行動，交待於此，如敬候早日回覆或早日下訂單等。這與中文之寫作要領「三段論法」及「起承轉合」不謀而合，只是商業書信在結尾時是採「行動」，並非要「結論」。在意義上，商業書信較積極，因在其「行動」中具期待與要求對方採取行動之意味在。

⑹ Complimentary Close (結尾敬語)：

結尾敬語跟稱謂一樣，都是一種禮貌的用法。

一般常用的結尾敬語有如下：

Faithfully yours,

Sincerely yours,

Truly yours,

With best regards,

Best wishes,

結尾敬語的用法，可配合稱謂，依正式及非正式分下列三種：

分類	稱謂	結尾敬語
Formal	Dear Sir(s)	Yours sincerely
正式	Dear Madam	Yours faithfully
	Dear Manager	Yours truly
		Yours respectfully
Informal	Dear Mr.	Sincerely
非正式		
Friendly	Dear Mike	With best regards
親切		Best wishes
Family	Dad	With love
家庭	Mom	

* 用法注意：

1. 結尾敬語：較正式時，可用 Sincerely yours 或 Yours sincerely；較不正式時，亦可用 Sincerely 一個字即可。Faithfully, Truly, Respectfully 等字的用法亦同。

2. 結尾敬語的寫法要注意：第一個字大寫，第二個字小寫。

* Matching (配對題)：

Salutation	Closing
_____ 1. Dear Madam	a. Best regards, *Carol Lee* Carol Lee
_____ 2. Dear Mike	b. Yours faithfully, *Richard Wang* Richard Wang
_____ 3. Dear Mrs. Watson	c. Yours sincerely, *Wilson Soong* Wilson Soong
_____ 4. Dear Sirs	
_____ 5. Dear David	d. Sincerely, *Lara Yen* Lara Yen
_____ 6. Dear Manager	

⑺ Signature and Official Position (簽名及職稱)：

商業上，簽名的後面或下一行須加上職稱，以示慎重負責並利辨別。

一般簽名可分為下列五種：

1) 有頭銜者 (With Title)：可簽有頭銜者自己的名字

| Sincerely yours, | OR | Sincerely yours,
for W&D Co., Ltd. |

Allen White

Allen White

Manager

Abe Carson

Abe Carson

Sales Manager

2) 公司董事自己簽名 (Directors)：可簽公司自己的名字

Faithfully yours,

W&D, Inc.

W&D, Inc.

3) 得到授權的代簽 (With Authorization)：經理或董事長等，因有事不在時，得授權由其代理人代簽，但須註明 per pro. 或 p.p. 即 per procurationem (經由代理) 之意。茲舉例如下：

Sincerely yours,

per pro. V&J Co., Ltd.

Lisa Lee

Jack Milton

Manager

4) 未得到授權的代簽 (Without Authorization)：經理或董事長等，因有事不在，但未授權由其代理人代簽，此時有重要文件要發出時，則須有公司人員負責代簽，須註明 (for) 為某人代簽，如下例：

Yours sincerely,

for Export Manager

Bill Brown

Cliff Wilson

5) 私人祕書簽名 (Private Secretary)：醫生 (doctor)、律師 (lawyer)、會計師 (CPA: certified public accountant) 等的私人祕書的簽名，須先列出自己的名字及是誰的祕書，並簽自己的名字，如下例：

Yours faithfully,

Lilly Lin

Lilly Lin

Secretary to Dr. Mike Thompson

2. Additional Seven Parts of a Business Letter

Letterhead

_____(1)_____

Ref.

_____(8)_____

Date

_____(2)_____

Inside name
and Address

_____(3)_____

Attention

_____(9)_____

Salutation

_____(4)_____

Subject Heading

_____(10)_____

Body

_____(5)_____

Complimentary
Close

_____(6)_____

Signature and
Official Position

_____(7)_____

Initial Identification   - (11) -

Enc.   - (12) -

c.c.   - (13) -

P.S.   - (14) -

茲將書信另外七大部分，分別說明如下：

⑻ Ref./Reference (檔案編號)：

商業上來往信件甚多，可將發出的信件編個號碼，以利查詢。檔案編號的方法可依下列方法來做：

1) 數字：12345

2) 英文字母：ABCDE

3) 主題：TOY, ENQUIRY

4) 地區：US, CNA, JAP

5) 部門：SHOE DEPT

6) 承辦人的英文代號：JK/cw

7) 綜合：CAR DEPT C-65

⑼ Attention (承辦人)：

將承辦人的名字列出，以利信件的發送及責任歸屬。

⑽ Subject Heading (主題)：

將主題列出，使讀者能一開信，便一目了然，知道此信是關於何種主題。

⑾ Initial Identification (鑑別符號)：

鑑別符號目的在鑑別信件之發信人或單位。一般分成兩個部分：前部為口授者之英文名縮寫，後部為祕書或打字員之名字縮寫，如 JK/cw 代表口授者為 Jack King；祕書為 Carol Wang。

⑿ Enc./Encl./Enclosure (附件)：

信內有附帶文件時，須打出此字以提醒注意。

⒀ c.c./Carbon Copy (副本抄送)：

有副本送某單位時，可打出 c.c. 後接送達的單位，以利收信人知悉。

⒁ P.S./PS/Postscript (附啟)：

當信寫好後，發現漏了某些資料時，可在信後打出 P.S.，然後寫出欲補充的話。

* Continuation page (續頁)

續頁用空白紙，頁首需包括三項：收信人或公司名、頁碼及日期，如：

a. 橫式

| Mr. Mike Lee | −2− | May 1, **20..** |

b. 直式

Page 2
May 1, **20..**
Mr. Mike Lee

3. Typing Styles

⑴ Full-Block Style: 齊頭式
Full-Block Form, Open
Punctuation

①
② ____
③ ____
____
____
④ ____
⑤ ____
____
____ .
____
____
____ .
⑥ ____
⑦ ____

⑵ Semi-Block Style: 半齊頭式
Semi-Block Form, Mixed
Punctuation

①
② ____
③ ____
____
____
④ ____ : (,)
⑤ ____
____
____ .
____
____
____ .
⑥ ____ ,
⑦ ____

(3) Modified-Block Style: 改良齊平式　　(4) Indented Style: 斜列式

　　Modified-Block Form,　　　　　　　　Indented Form,

　　Mixed Punctuation　　　　　　　　　Closed Punctuation

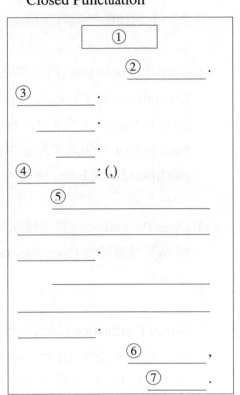

* 說明 1：書信架構

　　① Letterhead　　　　⑤ Body

　　② Date　　　　　　　⑥ Complimentary Close

　　③ Inside Address　　　⑦ Signature

　　④ Salutation

* 說明 2：打字格式

　　①與②間空 2 行　　③與④間空 1 行　　⑤與⑥間空 2 行

　　②與③間空 1 行　　④與⑤間空 2 行　　⑥與⑦間空 2 行

　　信文行間不空行，段落間空 2 行。

4. Punctuation

There are three ways of doing punctuation in a business letter:
英文信上的標點符號有三種：

⑴ Closed Punctuation (閉式標點符號)：Date, Inside Address, Salutation, Complimentary Close 及 Signature 各行後面加上適當標點符號，如逗點 (Comma)(,)、句點 (Period)(.) 或冒號 (Colon)(:) 者，稱為 Closed Punctuation。閉式標點多半配合 Indented Form, Semi-Block Form 及 Modified-Block Form 使用。

⑵ Open Punctuation (開式標點符號)：前述各項每一行後面都不加任何標點符號者稱為 Open Punctuation。開式標點多配合 Full-Block Form 使用。

⑶ Mixed Punctuation (混合式標點符號)：前述各項除了 Salutation 後面用逗號 (,) 或冒號 (:) 及 Complimentary Close 後面用逗號 (,) 外，其餘都不加標點符號者稱為 Mixed Punctuation，現在大都採用混合標點法。

茲將各打字類型及標點符號用法列表如下：

Style	Indented	Punctuation
Full-Block	No	Open
Semi-Block	No	Mixed
Modified-Block	Part	Mixed
Indented	All	Closed

5. Mailing

(1) 信封的寫法
(2) 郵遞指示及注意事項
(3) 信紙的摺法

⑴ 信封的寫法：

1) 發信人名稱和地址

2) 郵票

3) 收信人名和地址

4) 郵遞指示及注意事項

⑵ 郵遞指示及注意事項：

1) 郵遞指示：

Via Airmail   航空信

By express   快遞

Special Delivery   限時專送

Registered   掛號

2) 注意事項：

Attention of...　專陳……(人)

Confidential　機密

Photo Inside　內附照片

Printed Matter　印刷品

Private　私函

Personal　親啟

Please don't fold.　請勿摺疊。

Sample of No Value　貨樣贈品

Urgent　急件

(3) 信紙的摺法：

1) 大型信封：

使用大型信封時，信紙的摺疊先由下向上摺 1/3，然後再向上摺，與上端平行，成三等分。如下圖：

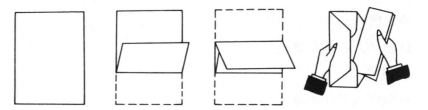

2) 小型信封：

使用小信封時，信紙的摺疊法為先由下端向上對摺，再從右向左摺 1/3，然後再由左向右摺 1/3，再將六摺的信紙裝入信封中。

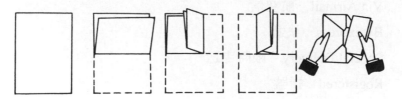

3) 開窗信封 (Window Envelope)：

開窗信封即在信封的中央留一個窗口覆以透明紙。使用這種信封時，摺疊信紙必須將收信人姓名、地址摺於外面，使其裝入信封後，收信人姓名及地址可在窗口露出。使用開窗信封可免在信封上重打收信人姓名、地址，增加效率。

✎ Exercise

Questions 問答題

1. What are the seven principal parts of a business letter?
2. What information is usually included in the letterhead?
3. What are the ways of expressing companies with limited liability?
4. What are the ways of expressing a date?
5. Give three examples of salutation.
6. Give five examples of courtesy title.
7. What is the structure of the official position of a company?
8. What is the framework of the body of a business letter?
9. Give three examples of complimentary close.
10. Give three examples of the types of signature.

Business Terms 解釋名詞

| 1. TM | 2. c.c. | 3. Ref. | 4. Inc. | 5. Co., Ltd. |
| 6. p.p. | 7. Pty | 8. Enc. | 9. P.S. | 10. Messrs. |

C. Business Insight 實務探討

◆ 書信格式

書信的格式，影響書信給人的第一印象，所以必須保持其整齊、清新的原則，看起來美觀，使人一目了然，留下深刻印象。各主要部分，皆有一定的位置，如此才能易於參考與查詢；有時書信格式，雖因時代的需要及情況的不同而有所變更，然而各部分皆有其功能，以顯示一封信的重要資訊。

D. Grammar Practice 文法練習

★句子的種類 (Kinds of Sentences)：以句子結構連接詞來分類。

---

1. 簡單句 (Simple Sentence)：沒連接詞。

   e.g. I need a sample.

2. 複句 (Complex Sentence)：用從屬連接詞，如 when, where, what, as, if, unless, although, after, before, since, until, whether, etc.。

   e.g. I know where the buyer is.

3. 合句 (Compound Sentence)：用對等連接詞，如 and, or, nor, but, so, etc.。

   e.g. Mr. Brown is rich, but he is not happy.

4. 複合句 (Compound-complex Sentence)：用至少一個從屬連接詞及一個對等連接詞。

   e.g. It is true that he eats much, but he is not fat.

Selection：寫出下列句子所屬句子的種類的代號

_____ 1. John was well paid as he had done the work well.

_____ 2. The president started to speak, and all was still.

_____ 3. Jerry is not mistaken, nor am I.

_____ 4. The boss must have left before you arrive, but he may come back soon.

_____ 5. After Joe left us, Lisa moved to Tokyo, and we wrote her very often.

_____ 6. The salesperson asked if anyone had a question.

_____ 7. The production inspector arrived late, but he finished his work on time.

_____ 8. A healthy person, as a general rule, is optimistic.

_____ 9. The factory and the warehouse have been under construction for five
years.

_____ 10. The manager bought a piece of land with a view to building a villa.

E. Pattern Practice 句型練習

★如果：

> If you..., please...
>
> If you..., we would be very thankful.
>
> If you should..., we would be much obliged.

1. 如果有我們可效勞的地方，請不要客氣跟我們連絡。

_____

2. 如果你們需要其他資料，請直接寫信給我們外銷部門。

_____

No. 2 網路：網路銀行 (Online Banking)

網路銀行定義

　　所謂「網路銀行」指的是客戶端電腦經由網路與銀行電腦連線，不用親赴銀行櫃檯即可直接取得銀行所提供之各項金融服務 (例如：帳務查詢、掛失、轉帳、繳費、申請、電子郵件通知等服務)。簡單的講就是銀行藉由網路為平臺，提供客戶即時性、方便性的電子金融服務。

申辦網路銀行

　　網路銀行之功能與實體銀行 (郵局) 是一樣的，申請的辦法亦與銀行 (郵局) 開戶的程序一樣。需本人持存摺、印章、身分證至申辦者的已開戶

銀行 (郵局) 辦理，亦可由代理人辦理，代理人亦須提供其印章和身分證。

網路銀行功能

　　各家的介面都不一樣，不過功能都大同小異，包括交易明細、活期轉定存、定存設定與解約、外幣轉換與定存、基金、信用卡帳目查詢等。

存入和提領現金

　　要至銀行櫃臺辦理。因此，若需要查詢每一筆進出的資料，申辦「網路銀行」的功能即可查詢每一筆存入和提領的紀錄。

Chapter Three

The Seven C's in Writing English Business Letters—
Completeness, Clearness, Correctness, Concreteness, Conciseness, Courtesy, Consideration

商用英文七個 "C"——
完整、清晰、正確、具體、簡潔、禮貌、周全

 **Outline**

1. Completeness	語意完整
2. Clearness	措辭清晰
3. Correctness	內容正確
4. Concreteness	敘述具體
5. Conciseness	字句簡潔
6. Courtesy	禮貌周到
7. Consideration	設想周全

1. Completeness

Writing a letter without giving complete information will give rise to doubt and misunderstanding.

完整性以避免疑慮及誤會。

Ex. 1: Date

Inc.　Thank you for your letter.

Com.　Thank you for your letter of March 28.

Ex. 2: Order Number

Inc.　We have received your goods.

Com.　We have received your sporting goods on our Order No. 234.

2. Clearness

Using clear words and structures, instead of vague, obscure, and ambiguous ones, is essential to good business letter writing.

清晰為好書信之要件。

Ex. 1: Word

Unc.　We will ship the computers ordered biweekly.

Clr.　We will ship the computers ordered two times a week.

Ex. 2: Structure

Unc.　The toys were packed in our opinion poorly.

Clr.　In our opinion, the toys were packed poorly.

Ex. 3: Structure

Unc.　We have received your 10 umbrellas orders.

Clr.　We have received your 10 orders for umbrellas.

Ex. 4: Structure

Unc.　The manager told Mr. Lee that he had received his check.

Clr.　The manager told Mr. Lee that he had received Mr. Lee's check.

3. Correctness

In respect of correctness, there are four approaches:

正確性，可由四方面來看：

(1) Correctness of Statement　　　　　　　説明正確

(2) Accuracy of Numerical Expression　　　正確數據

(3) Correct Use of Commercial Terms　　　正確商語

(4) Grammatical Correctness　　　　　　　文法正確

Ex. 1:　Correctness of Statement

Avoid: Our bikes are certainly the best on the market.

Use:　　Our bikes are superior in quality and attractive in design. They are enjoying good market.

Ex. 2:　Accuracy of Numerical Expression

Avoid: The loan limit is US$100.

Use:　　The loan limit is US$100 or less.

Ex. 3:　Correct Use of Commercial Terms

Avoid: We offer US$2.50 FOB Taipei.

Use:　　We offer US$2.50 FOB Keelung.

Ex. 4:　Grammatical Correctness

Avoid: Please sent us you catalogue.

Use:　　Please send us your catalogue.

4. Concreteness

To give an exact picture in any statement is to the point.

提供具體的說明為要。

Ex. 1: Adjective

Inc.   Our prices are the best.

Con.   Our prices are the lowest on the market.

Ex. 2: Adjective

Inc.   Our sweaters are very good.

Con.   Our sweaters are soft, light, and attractive.

Ex. 3: Noun

Inc.   We expect to receive your reply.

Con.   We expect to receive your early confirmation of the order.

Ex. 4: Date

Inc.   You will receive our samples in due time.

Con.   You will receive our samples before June 10.

Ex. 5: Number

Inc.   We will make shipment under your L/C.

Con.   We will make shipment under your L/C No. BC-01.

5. Conciseness

Simple and concise words and sentences, instead of long and tedious ones, will make the letter clear and effective.

簡潔用語措辭可達簡明之效。

The following are lists of words and phrases to be avoided using and suggested using:

下表左欄為避免用的字；右欄為建議用字：

（1）Words

Avoided using	Suggested using
apparent	clear
approximately	about
ascertain	find out
commence	begin
contribute	give
demonstrate	show
endeavor	do
equivalent	equal
expedite	hasten
modification	change
participate	take part
procure	get

（2）Phrases

Avoided using	Suggested using
at an early date	early
at all times	always
at this moment in time	now
be in a position to	can
by means of	by
cost price	cost
for the reason that	as, because
in view of the fact that	since
in spite of the fact that	although
in the amount of	for
in the case of	if

| under separate cover | separately |
| with reference to | about |

The following are examples of making long sentences short:

Ex. 1: From clauses to phrases

Avoid: Please check the letter of May 1 so that you may know all the facts.

Use: Please check the letter of May 1 for all the facts.

Ex. 2: From long clauses to short ones

Avoid: We take the liberty of writing you with request that you would be kind enough to introduce to us some exporter of shavers in your country.

Use: Please introduce to us some exporters of shavers in your country.

Ex. 3: From passive voice to active voice

Avoid: It is understood that you will arrive next week.

Use: We understand that you will arrive next week.

Ex. 4: Use connectives

Avoid: Thank you for the letter. You wrote your letter on January 20.

Use: Thank you for your letter of January 20.

6. Courtesy

Courtesy is the major element for winning customers. There are five ways for improving courteous elements in business communication.

禮貌為贏得顧客的要素；其方法有五如下：

⑴ Polite Words or Expressions (禮貌用法)

　　e.g. thank you, please, pardon, excuse me, request, regret, etc.

Thank you for your letter of May 2.

We request your immediate payment.

We regret to inform you that you have to pay before July 10.

⑵ Use of Passive Voice (被動用法)

Avoid: You made a serious mistake.

Use:　A serious mistake was made.

⑶ Use of Positive Words (積極字眼)

Avoid: We do not think you will be dissatisfied.

Use:　We are sure that you will be satisfied.

⑷ Use of Mitigation (緩和用法)

e.g. We are afraid...

We would say...

We suggest that...

It seems to us that...

Avoid: We cannot allow any delay in shipment.

Use:　We are afraid that we cannot allow any delay in shipment.

⑸ Use of Subjunctive Mood (假設語氣)

e.g. Would you please...

We should be grateful if you would...

We would appreciate it if you could...

Use: We should be grateful if you would send us your latest catalogue.

7. Consideration

Trying to be in the customers' shoes is essential in business communication.

The proper use of the "You-Attitude" is necessary. Pay attention to use "You" more often than "We."

設想周全，多為對方考量，多用 "You"，少用 "We"。

The following are some examples:

Ex. 1:　Use "You" instead of "We."

Avoid: We are pleased to announce that we will offer you a 5% discount.

Use:　　You will be pleased to know that we will offer you a 5% discount.

Ex. 2:　Use "Your" instead of "Our."

Avoid: We insist on receiving our payment soon.

Use:　　Your immediate payment is requested.

✎ Exercise

A. Questions 問答題

1. What are the seven C's in the skills of writing business letters?

2. What will happen if a letter is written without giving complete information?

3. Why should people use simple and concise words, instead of long and tedious ones, in a business letter?

4. Why is courtesy very important in business letter writing?

B. Business Insight 實務探討

◆ 七個 C

商用英文寫作技巧中的七個 "C"：完整、清晰、正確、具體、簡潔、禮貌、周全，在平時處理實務時，尤須牢記在心。以正確性來看，有一個實例可知其重要性：在臺北有一家貿易公司的經理決定到美國去，預定 11 月 12 日可到舊金山，他請秘書去電通知，並請對方到機場接機，但對方並未到機場；原來，祕書把日期寫成 12/11，在英國為 11 月 12 日，但是在美國，則為 12 月 11 日；日期放的次序，英美用法不同，最好把月份拼出，如 DEC/11 或 NOV/12 以求正確。發文時，可要多方考量，以避免不必要的差錯。

C. Grammar Practice 文法練習

★英文八大詞類 (Eight Parts of Speech)：

詞類	縮寫	中譯	說明	例子
1. Noun	n.	名詞	名稱、名字	car、son
2. Pronoun	pron.	代名詞	代替名詞	it、he
3. Adjective	adj.	形容詞	形容名詞及代名詞	nice、good
4. Verb	v.	動詞	動作、狀態等	eat、see
5. Adverb	adv.	副詞	修飾動、形、副、整句	badly、surely
6. Preposition	prep.	介系詞	形成介系詞片語作形、副用	in、on、at
7. Conjunction	conj.	連接詞	連接字、片語、子句等	and、or、but
8. Interjection	interj.	感嘆詞	表喜、怒、哀、樂等	Oh! Wow!

Selection：寫出下列畫線字所屬詞類的代碼

_____ 1. Bill possesses moral strength.

_____ 2. What would you order this time?

_____ 3. Pollution is a big problem.

_____ 4. This is the material for our garments.

_____ 5. Oh! What a high price it is!

_____ 6. Wow! How beautiful the flower is!

_____ 7. The airplane arrived after we left.

_____ 8. Our product is delicately made.

_____ 9. Oh! What a sight was that!

_____ 10. How often does your buyer come?

D. Pattern Practice 句型練習

★因為：

As..., ...   Because..., ...   Since...

1. 因為我們的品質優越，我們的產品在美國很受歡迎。

_____

2. 因為我們的家具款式很多，我們寄上目錄以供參考。

_____

No. 3 網路：電子資料交換 (EDI)

　　電子資料交換 (Electronic Data Interchange)，是利用電腦應用系統互相傳遞商業資料，由一臺電腦運用標準規定及統一資料格式，將資料傳送到另一臺電腦。EDI 的標準規定使電腦間傳輸的資料能夠自動接收和處理。現廣泛為全球關貿網路所使用。

Chapter Four

Looking for Customers

尋找客戶

 **Outline**

The sources which can help an exporter/importer find his customers are as follows:　　　　　　　　進出口商請求協助介紹客戶

1. Advertisement　　　　　　廣告
2. Recommendation　　　　　推薦
3. Various Trade Organizations　各種貿易機構
4. Show/Fair/Exhibition　　　　展覽

Structure

1. Introduction:	Source
2. Information:	Self-introduction
	POP *
	Trade reference
3. Action:	Await reply

* POP: Point of Purchase，原意為買點，又引申為賣點及海報製作。這裡為進出口商之買點或賣點之意。

1. Advertisement

Example 4.1　進口商請雜誌公司登廣告

January 10, **20..**

Importer Magazine Co., Ltd.
Taipei, Taiwan

Dear Sirs,

From the TAITRA we understand that you are rendering the service of introducing foreign importers to the local exporters and manufacturers.

We are one of the leading importers of bicycles in the U.S. with branch offices in 10 major cities of the world, such as London and Tokyo, and as the business expansion requires we are quite interested in importing bicycles from Taiwan.

If you should kindly publicize our interest in your magazine, we would be very grateful. Your early reply in this matter would be highly appreciated.

Sincerely yours,

---

* TAITRA: Taiwan External Trade Development Council，中華民國對外貿易發展協會 (原先簡寫為 CETRA，現為 TAITRA)。

信文中譯：

敬啟者：

　　從外貿協會，知悉貴公司有提供服務，介紹國外的進口商給國內的出口商及製造商。

　　本公司為美國具領導地位的腳踏車進口商，在世界十個主要城市，如倫敦及東京，都有分公司。由於業務的擴展，本公司有意進口臺灣的腳踏車。

　　如蒙將我們的意向刊登於你們的雜誌上，我們將非常感激。期待對此事早日函覆。

　　　　　　　　　　　　　　　　　　　　　　　　　　　謹上

---

2. Recommendation

Example 4.2　澳洲進口商請雜誌公司登廣告

September 2, **20..**

The Trade Weekly News
The World Trade Center
Taipei, Taiwan

Dear Sirs,

Through the courtesy of the TAITRA, we come to know that you are in a position to help the foreign importers get in touch with the local exporters. With this in mind, we are writing to request your kind assistance.

As one of the most reputable importers of electronic products in

Australia, we have been engaged in this line of business for over twenty years and have been enjoying good reputation for our products in the market here. We are anxious to find suitable and dependable suppliers for our electronic products.

We would, therefore, appreciate it very much if you should kindly make our request public in one of your publications.

Thank you in advance in this matter.

Sincerely yours,

Bill Linton

Bill Linton
Manager

信文中譯：

敬啟者：

　　經由外貿協會，得知貴公司能幫助國外進口商與國內出口商取得聯繫。秉記此意，本公司寫信請求貴公司的協助。

　　本公司為澳洲電子產品最有名望的進口商之一，已從事此業超過二十年，且在本地市場享有卓越產品信譽。本公司盼能尋得電子產品適當及可靠的供應商。

　　如蒙發布本公司之所請於你們的出版刊物，將感激不盡。

　　對此事，先予致謝。

謹上

Example 4.3　進口公司請求客戶介紹出口商

February 23, **20..**

Formosa Shoes Co., Ltd.

No. ××, Sec. 2, Zhongshan N. Rd.,

Zhongzheng Dist.,

Taipei, Taiwan

Dear Sirs,

For the past five years, we have been importing your shoes and we have been quite satisfied with your quality and service.

As now our business is expanding rapidly, and we are planning to include glassware items in our range, we should therefore be very much obliged if you would recommend some friends of yours who are able to supply glassware to us. For your information, our initial order will be around US$20,000.

We appreciate your kind cooperation in the past and are looking forward to hearing from you again soon.

Sincerely yours,

信文中譯：

敬啟者：

　　過去五年來我們一直進口你們的鞋類，對品質及服務均十分滿意。

　　今因業務拓展迅速，擬將玻璃器皿列入產銷項目，如蒙推薦一些供應玻璃器皿的廠商，將不勝感謝。順便告知，初期的訂單約在美金二萬元左右。

　　本公司感激你們過去的合作並候速回音。

謹上

---

3. Various Trade Organizations

Example 4.4　出口公司請求美國洛杉磯商會介紹客戶

March 3, 20..

The Chamber of Commerce
of Los Angeles
Los Angeles, CA 90010
U.S.A.

Dear Sirs,

We are a twenty-year-old manufacturer of furniture in Taiwan and in the past years have been exporting our products to Canada and South America, winning good reputation for our first-rate furniture.

As we are now planning to extend our market to your country, especially on the west coast, we would appreciate it very much if you should kindly supply us with a list of reliable business firms in the Los Angeles area who are interested in importing our furniture.

For the convenience of your checking our credit standing, we refer you to the following bank for further details:

The Bank of Sunshine, Neihu Branch,

Taipei, Taiwan

Your kind assistance in this matter would be highly appreciated.

Sincerely yours,

信文中譯：

敬啟者：

　　本公司為臺灣具有二十年歷史之家具製造商，在過去幾年裡，已外銷產品至加拿大及南美，為本公司第一流的產品獲得良好的商譽。

　　因今打算拓展我們的市場到貴國，尤其是西岸，如蒙提供一張包括在洛杉磯地區有意進口我們家具的績優公司的名單，我們將非常感激。

　　為了便於徵信，請參考下列的銀行：

　　陽光銀行，臺北內湖分行

　　本公司將非常感激貴公司對此事的協助。

謹上

Example 4.5   美國出口商請求外貿協會介紹客戶

March 1, **20..**

The TAITRA

No. ××, Sec. 1, Keelung Rd.,

Xinyi Dist., Taipei, Taiwan

Dear Sirs,

We are interested in developing our trade in your market and would be grateful if you could kindly introduce us to the related importers in your country.

As a manufacturer of leather goods, we have been established for over ten years and have won good reputation for our unique design and excellent quality.

For information about our credit standing, please refer to the following:

    The Bank of Sunshine

    Los Angeles Branch,

    Los Angeles, CA 90010

    U.S.A.

Your kind assistance in this matter would be highly appreciated.

Sincerely yours,

James Joyce

James Joyce

Manager

信文中譯：

敬啟者：

　　本公司有意拓展貿易到貴國的市場，如蒙引介本公司給貴國的相關進口商，將感激不盡。

　　本公司為皮貨的製造商，已成立超過十年了，且已贏得獨特設計及卓越品質的好名聲。

　　關於本公司的信用狀況資料，請參考下列：

陽光銀行

洛杉磯分行，

洛杉磯，加州 90010

美國

貴公司對此事之協助，本公司十分感激。

謹上

4. Show/Fair/Exhibition

Example 4.6　出口商寫給曾參觀展覽的商業團體

April 12, **20..**

The Italian Business

Association

Milan, Italy

Dear Sirs,

It has been our honor and pleasure to meet your group in the yearly Sporting Goods Exhibition held in Taipei.

We are one of the leading and reputable exporters and manufacturers of sporting goods in Taiwan, and our products have been exported to the U.S., Canada, and Australia. As we are developing our market to Europe, especially Italy, we should be grateful if you would kindly send us a list of importers in your country who are interested in importing our first-rate sporting goods.

Your early sending us the above list would be much appreciated.

Sincerely yours,

信文中譯：

敬啟者：

　　非常榮幸在臺北舉行的本年度運動器材展覽會裡會見你們的團體。

　　本公司是臺灣具領導地位及名望的運動器材出口商及製造商，我們的產品已外銷至美國、加拿大及澳洲。因本公司欲拓展市場到歐洲，尤其是義大利，如蒙寄來一張貴國有意進口我們第一流運動器材的進口商名單，將感激不盡。

懇請於最快時間惠予寄達為盼。

謹上

✏ Exercise

A. Questions 問答題

1. What are the sources which can help an exporter/importer find his customers?

2. What are the trade organizations which can help an exporter/importer develop his trade in Taiwan? Give two examples.

3. Why does a company supply trade references?

4. When a company introduces itself, what are the points to be included?

B. Business Terms 解釋名詞

1. POP　　　　2. P.O.B.　　　3. TAITRA　　　4. Co., Ltd.

5. Sec.　　　　6. Chamber of Commerce

C. Business Insight 實務探討

◆ 尋找客戶

　　每家貿易公司各有其客戶來源的管道，有些來自廣告，有些來自貿易展覽，有些來自客戶及貿易機構的推薦，有些來自進出口商名錄，有些甚至由舊公司所挖角過來的。一般新成立的公司必須有其成長及發展的空間，否則不久便會被淘汰。因此，新公司對於客戶的招攬，便無所不盡其極。例如，每次貿易展覽，買賣雙方皆擠滿現場，皆希望把握良機，促成交易以招攬更多的客戶。

D. Grammar Practice 文法練習

★片語 (Phrases)：

不含主詞和述詞，兩字以上連在一起，作某一詞類之用，共有七種。

1. 名詞片語：I don't know what to do.
2. 形容詞片語：The man sitting there is Abe.
3. 副詞片語：The customer left at once.
4. 動詞片語：He stood up and went out.
5. 介詞片語：Lisa sat in front of me.
6. 連接詞片語：Max as well as I is here.
7. 感嘆詞片語：My God! We did it.

Selection：寫出下列畫線字所屬片語詞類的代碼

_____ 1. The samples on the table are ours.

_____ 2. The clerk parked his car in the garage.

_____ 3. Goodness me! We won the game.

_____ 4. The man with a blue necktie is Tommy.

_____ 5. The speaker has been talking for two hours.

_____ 6. Lucy and Linda ran very gracefully.

_____ 7. Jane sat in front of us.

_____ 8. To tell a lie is wrong.

E. Pattern Practice 句型練習

★感謝：

We thank you for...

Thank you for...

We appreciate...

We are much obliged to...

We are grateful for...

1. 我們感謝收到你們 2 月 14 日的來信關於我們的雨傘產品。

_____

2. 我們感謝你們 8 月 25 日由航空寄來的化妝品樣品。

_____

F. Blank-filling 填充練習

Dear _____ ,

From the _____ , we _____ that you are _____ the service of _____ foreign _____ to the _____ exporters and _____ .

We are _____ of the _____ importers of _____ in the U.S. with _____ offices in 10 major cities _____ the world and are _____ in _____ bicycles from _____ .

If you _____ kindly _____ our _____ in your _____ , we _____ be very _____ .

Sincerely _____ ,

G. Letter-writing 書信寫作

As an importer of toys in the U.S., write your letter to the Taiwan Chamber of Commerce to ask them to recommend potential exporters.

No. 4 網路：關貿網路 (Trade-Van)

　　「關貿網路股份有限公司」成立於 1996 年，著重於提升通關自動化服務，使 EDI (Electronic Data Interchange 電子資料交換) 發揮最大效用。目前已有超過數萬家客戶，所提供的服務有通關網路服務、電子商務服務、全球運籌服務、政府專案服務、金融保險服務、財產管理服務、電子報稅服務等。

Chapter Five

Trade Proposal

招攬生意

 **Outline**

The sources for an exporter/importer to find his customers are as follows:

進出口商尋找客戶之來源

1. Advertisement/Directories　　　廣告進出口商名錄
2. Recommendation　　　　　　　推薦
3. Various Trade Organizations　　各種貿易機構
4. Show/Fair/Exhibition　　　　　展覽

1. Advertisement/Directories

Example 5.1　　進口商由雜誌廣告得知出口商

May 23, **20..**

W&D Co., Ltd.

No. ××, Sec. 1, Zhongshan N. Rd.,

Zhongzheng Dist.,

Taipei, Taiwan

Dear Sirs,

We learn from the recent issue of the magazine that you are exporters of handbags of various kinds and would like to establish a business relationship with you.

We are an importer with 30-year history and as we are now in the process of contracting our orders for the coming new season, we would appreciate receiving your latest catalogue and best price list.

Please let us hear from you in a couple of days.

Sincerely yours,

信文中譯：

敬啟者：

　　本公司由最近一期的雜誌得知貴公司為各種手提袋的出口商，故有意與貴公司建立商業關係。

　　本公司為具有三十年歷史的進口商；因我們正簽訂我們新一季的訂單，將感激收到你們最近的目錄及最低的價目表。

　　盼近日內得到回音。

謹上

2. Recommendation

Example 5.2　出口商由朋友介紹得知進口商

August 25, **20..**

Harry Imports Co., Ltd.
No. ××, Sec. 3, Neihu Rd., Neihu Dist.,
Taipei, Taiwan

Dear Sirs,

It is through the recommendation of W&D, Inc. that we come to know your company and are writing to you with a view to introducing our excellent quality jewelry to you.

As we have been exporting considerable quantities of jewelry to South East Asian countries, we are sure that you will be interested in importing our first quality jewelry, such as earrings and pendants.

Enclosed please find our detailed brochures and price list for your reference.

We look forward to receiving your comments.

Sincerely yours,

Enc.

信文中譯：

敬啟者：

　　經由 W&D 公司的推薦，本公司得知貴公司，今寫此信以推薦我們優良品質的珠寶給你們。

　　因本公司已出口大量的珠寶到東南亞國家，相信你們會有意進口我們第一品質的珠寶，例如耳環及墜子。

　　隨函附上我們詳細的小冊子及價目表以供參考。

　　懇請及早函覆高見。

謹上

附件

3. Various Trade Organizations

Example 5.3　進口商由外貿協會得知出口商

July 15, **20..**

JOYCE LEATHER, INC.
×× Greenfield Ave.,
Los Angeles, CA 90025
U.S.A.

Dear Sirs,

We are indebted to the TAITRA for your name and address and are writing to you with the purpose of establishing a business relationship with your company.

We are old and well-established importers of all kinds of leather goods and, with our large sales organizations, are in a position to import large quantities of your leather goods.

Please send us your related brochure for our further evaluation.

We look forward to hearing from you soon.

Sincerely yours,

Tony Wang

Tony Wang

Import Manager

信文中譯：

敬啟者：
　　感激外貿協會提供你們的名字及地址。本公司致函貴公司目的在與你們建立商業關係。
　　本公司是老牌且營運健全的進口商，進口各種皮革貨品，有龐大的銷售組織，能大量進口你們的皮貨。
　　請寄來相關的資料以供進一步評估。
　　期待收到回音。
　　　　　　王湯尼
　　　　　　進口部經理　　謹上

＊註解：

除了外貿協會可提供資訊外，商會、銀行、領事館或進口商名錄等，皆可獲得
進出口商資料。

4. Show/Fair/Exhibition

| Example 5.4　出口商由展覽中得知進口商 |

September 3, **20..**

Mr. Mike Wilson
President
W&S Imports, Inc.
×× Broadway,
New York, NY 10010
U.S.A.

Dear Mr. Wilson,

It was our pleasure to meet you at the Taipei Hand Tool Show and to
introduce our products to you. As we know you are quite interested in
importing hand tools from Taiwan and as we have been exporting these
items for more than ten years, we are in a position to supply you with our
solid and heavy-duty tools at very competitive prices.

We enclose our new catalogues and price lists for our whole range of
products, including those newly-developed items for your reference.

If you need any further information about our products, please feel free to contact us.

Sincerely yours,

Enc.

信文中譯：

威爾森先生，你好！

　　本公司很榮幸在臺北手工具展覽會上遇見你，並介紹我們的產品給你。如我們所知，貴公司有意進口臺灣手工具。本公司已經出口這些項目超過十年，能以最有競爭性的價格，供應堅固而耐用的手工具給你們。

　　隨函附上本公司整系列產品的新目錄及價目表，包括最新開發的項目，以供參考。

　　如果你需任何關於我們產品的更詳細資料，請隨時跟我們聯絡。

謹上

附件

 Exercise

A. Questions 問答題

1. What are the sources for an exporter/importer to find his customers?

2. Why does an exporter write a trade proposal?

3. Why does an importer write a trade proposal?

4. What does an exporter usually enclose in a trade proposal?

B. Business Insight 實務探討

◆ 招攬生意

進出口商由各種媒介,如展覽、報章雜誌、相關機構等來源,得知對方的名字和地址時,就可主動寫信給對方。當然,像這種信並不一定會得到回音,有時等了很久仍無消息。所以,公司裡必須要有健全的檔案管理制度。在發出一封信後的某一段時間內,像是兩星期或一個月後,就必須開始追蹤 (follow up),另寫一函,以確定前封信已收到,並徵求其高見,以促成交易的契機。

C. Grammar Practice 文法練習

★子句 (Clauses):

子句含有主詞和動詞,為構成句子的一部分。子句的種類可依結構和功能分類。

1. 以結構來分以下兩種:

---

1. 對等子句 Coordinate Clause (用於合句):
   兩個子句以對等連接詞 (and, or, so, but 等) 連接。
   e.g. You are old, but I am young.

2. 主要子句與從屬子句 Main Clause and Subordinate Clause (用於複句):
   兩個子句以從屬連接詞 (when, what, where, if, as 等) 連接起來,其中以從屬連接詞所引導的叫作從屬子句,另一個表達主要意思的叫主要子句。
   e.g. If he comes tomorrow, I will let you know.
   　　　　從屬子句　　　　　主要子句

---

2. 以功能來分，可分下列三種：

---

1. 名詞子句 (Noun Clause)：名詞子句其功能等於名詞

   e.g. I don't know what you said.

     That he will come is true.

2. 形容詞子句 (Adjective Clause)：形容詞子句其功能等於形容詞

   e.g. This is the book which I like.

     The man whom you talked about is Robert.

3. 副詞子句 (Adverbial Clause)：副詞子句其功能等於副詞

   e.g. I was reading when you came in.

     If you work hard, you will succeed.

Selection：寫出下列畫線字所屬從屬子句的代碼

_____ 1. What he said is right.

_____ 2. As you are tired, you had better rest.

_____ 3. It never rains, but it pours.

_____ 4. The house in which he lives is very large.

_____ 5. Whether he will go or not depends on the manager.

_____ 6. If he comes, please let me know.

_____ 7. Anne asked if the airplane would arrive on time.

_____ 8. This is the book which I mentioned about.

D. Pattern Practice 句型練習

★附上：

We enclose...

We are enclosing...

Enclosed is/are...

Enclosed please find...

...is/are enclosed.

1. 隨信附上我們最近的電子產品目錄及價目表以供參考。

_____

2. 隨信附上我們毛衣產品的式樣卡及樣品以供選擇。

_____

E. Blank-filling 填充練習

_____ Sirs,

We learn _____ the recent issue _____ the magazine _____
you _____ exporters _____ handbags and _____ like to
_____ a business _____ with _____.

We _____ an _____ with 30-year history and _____ we
_____ now _____ the _____ of _____ our orders
_____ the _____ season, we would _____ _____ your
latest _____ and _____ list.

Please _____ us _____ from _____ in a _____ of _____.

_____ yours,

F. Letter-writing 書信寫作

As an exporter of sweaters in Taiwan, write your letter to W&S, Inc., U.S.A., recommended by the magazine to make a trade proposal.

商業知識

No. 5 網路：Skype 的功能

　　Skype 是語音通訊的即時通訊軟體，利用 P2P (點對點技術) 的技術讓用戶可以互相聯絡，尤其是雙方網路順暢時，音質相當清晰，甚至可能超過一般電話。凡是 Skype 與 Skype 之間的通話一律免費。

Chapter Six

Credit Enquiries and Replies

徵信調查

 **Outline**

1. The Sources of Making Credit Enquiries 徵信來源
2. Requesting References and Reply 索備詢資料及回函
3. Credit Enquiry and Reply 徵信及回函

1. The Sources of Making Credit Enquiries

(1) Trade references supplied by the customer 顧客提供資料

(2) The customer's bank 顧客的銀行

(3) Various trade associations 貿易機構

(4) Credit agency 徵信社

2. Requesting References and Reply

Example 6.1　Enquiry from the Exporter　出口商請進口商提供備詢人

March 5, **20..**

Dear Sirs,

We thank you for your order of February 20. As it is your first with us, we would like to say how pleased we were to receive it.

Our terms of payment for this order are on an open account basis. When customers open new accounts, it is our practice to ask them for trade references. Please send us the names and addresses of two other suppliers with whom you have dealings. We shall be glad if you send us the information soon.

Meanwhile, we have put your order in hand with dispatch. We will deliver the goods immediately after we hear further from you.

Sincerely yours,

信文中譯：

敬啟者：

　　感謝貴公司 2 月 20 日的訂單。由於這是我們第一次合作，我們想表達我們很高興收到你們的第一張訂單。

　　此訂單的付款條件是賒銷。當顧客開新帳戶時，我們慣例要求顧客提供貿易備詢資料。請你們寄來跟你們有交易的其他二家供應商的名字及地址。如果你們儘速寄來此資料，將非常感激。

　　同時，我們已即刻處理了你們的訂單。在收到進一步消息後，本公司就會立即出貨。

謹上

Example 6.2　Reply from the Importer　進口商提供備詢資料

March 15, 20..

Dear Sirs,

We thank you very much for your letter of March 5 asking us to supply you with our reference.

As requested, we are now sending you the references of two of the suppliers who have done business with us for your checking our credit standing as follows.

K&O Trading Co., Ltd.

No. ×, Sec. 1, Zhongxiao E. Road, Zhongzheng Dist.,

Taipei, Taiwan

Ideal Exports, Inc.

No. ×, Sec. 1, Neihu Road, Neihu Dist.,

Taipei, Taiwan

Please write to them directly for the details of our standing. We are sure that they would be very willing to be of any assistance to you. Meanwhile, we are looking forward to receiving our orders soon.

Sincerely yours,

信文中譯：

敬啟者：

感謝你們 3 月 5 日的來函要求本公司提供我們的備詢資料。

如所請，本公司寄上二家與我們做過生意的供應商，以供查核我們的信用狀況如下：

K&O 貿易有限公司
臺北市中正區忠孝東路一段××號

理想出口公司
臺北市內湖區內湖路一段××號

請直接去函以查詢我們的信用狀況。本公司確信他們將很樂意協助貴公司。同時，期待迅速收到所訂購的貨物。

謹上

---

3. Credit Enquiry and Reply

Example 6.3　Enquiry from the Exporter　出口商向備詢人徵信

March 20, **20..**

Dear Sirs,

We have received a request from W&D, Inc. in New York for supplies of our tennis rackets on open account. They have given us your name as a reference.

We should be grateful if you would let us know, in your opinion, whether they are reliable in their dealing and prompt in their payment, and whether they are able to meet their commitment to credit up to US$200,000.

Any information you supply will be treated in strict confidence.

Sincerely yours,

信文中譯：

敬啟者：

　　本公司已獲紐約 W&D 公司請求以賒銷方式供應網球拍。該公司提供貴公司作為備詢人。

　　如蒙示知該公司是否信用可靠、付款迅速及是否可容賒銷達美金二十萬元，將不勝感激。

　　任何貴公司所提供之資訊，本公司將以極機密方式處理。

謹上

Example 6.4　Reply from the Referee (Favorable Reply)

備詢人回函 (有利)

March 25, **20..**

(Confidential)

Dear Sirs,

We are pleased to inform you that the company referred in your letter of March 20, **20..** has placed regular orders with us for the past five years and has been trustworthy and reliable.

As far as our knowledge goes, they meet their commitments punctually and a credit you mention would seem to be safe.

We hope this information will be of help to you.

Sincerely yours,

信文中譯：

(機密)
敬啟者：
  本公司樂於告知，貴公司 **20..** 年 3 月 20 日來函所提及的公司在過去五年來，固定向本公司採購，信用可靠。
  據本公司所知，該公司付款準時；依所提之賒購，應可放心。
  盼此資訊能有所助益。

謹上

Example 6.5 Reply from the Referee (Unfavorable Reply)
     備詢人回函 (不利)

March 25, **20..**

(Confidential)

Dear Sirs,

We are writing in connection with the credit standing of the firm referred to in your letter of March 20, **20...**

The firm was a well-reputed one but went bankrupt last month. This seems to be a case in which caution is necessary.

This information is strictly confidential and is given without any responsibility on our part.

Sincerely yours,

信文中譯：

(機密)

敬啟者：

　　本公司回覆貴公司 **20..** 年 3 月 20 日來函所提公司之信用狀況。

　　該公司以往為有名望之公司，但已於上月宣告破產。此事宜小心為是。

　　此資料極機密；本公司不負任何責任。

謹上

✎ Exercise

A. Questions 問答題

1. What are the sources from which an exporter/importer can make credit enquiry about his customer?

2. Give two examples of various trade organizations in Taiwan.

◆ 徵信調查

　　理論上，進出口公司應該先做好徵信工作，確定對方信用可靠後，才開始建交做生意。然而在實務上，由於一般皆以信用狀作為付款條件較為可靠，且時間緊迫，寄目錄、價目、樣品、報價、討價還價等，一連串的來來往往通訊後，緊接著就要催開信用狀，準備出貨，所剩時間已不多。但是，最好仍須盡速做好徵信工作。另外，如果付款條件是付款交單 (D/P)、承兌交單 (D/A)、賒銷 (O/A)、寄銷 (On Consignment) 等時，就絕對必須做好徵信工作。

C. Grammar Practice 文法練習

★句子 (Sentences)：

Subject (主詞) + v.i. (不及物動詞)
Subject (主詞) + v.t. (及物動詞) + O. (受詞)

＊ 用法注意：

1. 一個句子原則上一定要有一個主詞與動詞，並表達一個完整意思。

2. 動詞用法有兩種：及物 (v.t.) 和不及物 (v.i.)

3. 及物動詞 (transitive verb)，即動詞後一定要加受詞，如 take, send, find 等。

4. 不及物動詞 (intransitive verb)，即動詞後不能加受詞，如 look, go, agree 等。如要接受詞，則後必須接介詞，如：

　　e.g. He usually looks at the map.

　　　　 He goes to school every day.

　　　　 Jack agrees with me.

5. 有些動詞可為及物與不及物，如 put, make, order, sell 等，其用法需查字典。

    e.g. We sent.   (錯，因 send 是及物動詞要接受詞)

          We sent him a letter.   (對，因有受詞 him 及 a letter)

True or False (T or F)：如果句子對的用 T，錯的用 F

_____ 1. Our friends enjoyed very much.

_____ 2. Any person who is interested.

_____ 3. Because of the weather conditions.

_____ 4. The secretary knows me.

_____ 5. Sam looks the new samples.

_____ 6. The customers were told.

_____ 7. The firm is liable for this damage.

_____ 8. Mr. Gonzales is going New York.

_____ 9. My boss agrees me to go abroad.

_____ 10. We will ship on time.

D. Pattern Practice 句型練習

★分開寄上，另外寄上：

> Under separate cover, we are sending...
>
> Under separate post, we are sending...
>
> By separate cover, we are sending...
>
> By separate post, we are sending...

1. 由郵政包裹分開寄上一系列我們最流行的運動器材樣品以供參考。

2. 另外由快遞寄上我們最近推出的羊毛內衣樣品以供促銷。

E. Blank-filling 填充練習

Dear _____ ,

We _____ you _____ your order _____ February 20. _____ it _____ your _____ with _____ , we _____ like to _____ how _____ we _____ to receive _____ .

As our _____ of payment for this _____ are _____ account and _____ _____ open new _____ , it _____ our _____ to ask _____ for _____ references. Will you _____ send us the _____ and _____ of two other _____ _____ whom you _____ dealings.

We _____ be _____ if you _____ us the _____ soon.

Sincerely _____ ,

F. Letter-writing 書信寫作

You are an exporter of hardware from Taiwan. Write your letter to an importer to ask for trade references.

No. 6 網路：網路人力銀行
(Internet Websites of Manpower Bank)

　　隨著網路的發達，網路人力銀行已成為眾多求職者找工作最主要的管道之一。許多公民營的網路人力銀行為求職和求才者服務，例如：台灣就業通、104 人力銀行、1111 人力銀行、yes123 求職網等。而各地公立就業服務中心於全省均有服務機構可登記求職。

求職求才網站：

1. 勞動部勞動力發展署：

   https://www.wda.gov.tw/

2. 104 人力銀行：

   https://www.104.com.tw/

3. 1111 求職人力銀行：

   https://www.1111.com.tw/

4. yes123 求職網：

   https://www.yes123.com.tw/

Chapter Seven

Agreement on General Terms and Conditions of Business

交易條件及一般條款

Outline

1. To state the parties who sign the agreement.　　　買賣雙方
2. To list the general terms of quotation and acceptance.　報價條款
3. To regulate the steps to be taken when an order is placed.　訂單步驟
4. To regulate the terms as to quality, packing, marking,　其他條款
   payment, shipment, and insurance, etc.
5. To submit the ways of settling claims.　　　　索賠方式
6. To include other details, such as rate of exchange, etc.　其他細節

AGREEMENT ON GENERAL TERMS AND CONDITIONS OF BUSINESS AS PRINCIPAL TO PRINCIPAL.

THIS AGREEMENT entered into between PIZA CO., LTD. No. ××, Sec. 3, Xinsheng S. Rd., Da'an Dist.,Taipei, Taiwan, hereinafter referred to as SELLER, and WATSONS IMPORTS, INC. ×× Blue Drive, San Francisco, CA 90012, U.S.A. hereinafter referred to as BUYER, witnesses as follows.

(1) Business:

Both SELLER and BUYER act as principal not as agents.

(2) Commodities:

Commodities in business and their units to be quoted are specified in each specific price list and quotation.

(3) Quotations and Others:

Unless otherwise specified in written forms, all quotations and offers submitted by either party to this Agreement shall be in U.S. dollars on CIF San Francisco basis.

(4) Firm offers:

All firm offers shall be subject to a reply within the period stated in respective correspondence.

(5) Orders:

Any business concluded by the internet shall be confirmed in writing without delay, and orders thus confirmed shall not be cancelled unless by mutual consent.

(6) Payment:

Payment shall be made by BUYER by usual negotiable and irrevocable letter of credit in the favor of SELLER, to be opened 30 days before shipment, covering 100% of the invoice value against a full set of shipping documents.

(7) Shipment:

All commodities sold in accordance with this Agreement shall be shipped within the stipulated time. The date of Bill of Lading is taken as conclusive proof of the day of shipment. Unless expressly agreed to, the port of shipment is at SELLER's option.

⑻ Marine Insurance:

All shipments shall be covered All Risks for a sum equal to the amount of the invoice plus 10 percent, if no other conditions are particularly agreed to. All policies shall be made out in U.S. currency and payable in San Francisco.

⑼ Quality:

Quality to be guaranteed equal to descriptions of the commodities and/or as the sample shows.

⑽ Inspection:

Commodities, unless otherwise specified, will be inspected in accordance with normal practice of suppliers.

⑾ Packing & Marking:

All shipment shall be packed in standard export cartons and be marked WTS.

⑿ Damage:

Seller shall ship all commodities in good condition and Buyer shall assume all risks of damage, deterioration, or breakage during transportation.

⒀ Claims:

Claims, if any, shall be submitted by e-mail within fourteen days after arrival of commodities at destination. Certificates by recognized surveyors shall be sent by mail without delay. All claims which cannot be amicably settled between SELLER and BUYER shall be submitted to arbitration.

(14) Arbitration:

The arbitration board shall consist of two members; one to be nominated by SELLER and one by BUYER, and should they be unable to agree, the decision of an umpire selected by the arbitration shall be final, and the losing party shall bear the expenses thereto.

(15) Exchange Rate:

The price offered in U.S. dollars is based on the prevailing official exchange rate in Taiwan between the U.S. dollar and the New Taiwan dollar. Any devaluation of the U.S. dollar to the New Taiwan dollar at the time of negotiating draft shall be for BUYER's risks and account.

In witness hereof, PIZA CO., LTD. have hereunto set their hands on the 2nd day of May, **20..**, and WATSONS IMPORTS, INC. have hereunto set their hands on the 22nd day of May, **20...** This Agreement shall be valid on and from the 1st day of June **20..** and any of the articles in this Agreement shall not be changed and modified unless by mutual written consent.

SELLER   BUYER
PIZA CO., LTD.   WATSONS IMPORTS, INC.

Jerry Wang   *David Smith*
‾‾‾‾‾‾‾‾‾‾‾‾‾‾‾‾‾‾   ‾‾‾‾‾‾‾‾‾‾‾‾‾‾‾‾‾‾
President   President

信文中譯：

> 　　*皮賽有限公司* (以下簡稱賣方)，地址：臺灣臺北市大安區新生南路三段××號，與華生進口公司 (以下簡稱買方)，地址：美國加州舊金山藍道××號，茲訂立本合約書，證明下列各事項：
>
> ⑴ 交易形態：當事人雙方均為法律上的本人，非代理人。
>
> ⑵ 貨物：買賣的貨物及報價單位，如附表。
>
> ⑶ 報價：除非有書面規定，本合約書任何一方提出的報價，均按美金計算，而且以 "CIF San Francisco" 為基準。
>
> ⑷ 穩固報價：所有穩固報價，均須在個別通信所載的期限內回覆。
>
> ⑸ 訂單：憑網路成交的買賣，應迅速用書面確認；訂單經確認後，除非經雙方同意，不得取消。
>
> ⑹ 付款方式：買方應以通常，可讓購，不可撤銷信用狀付款：此項信用狀應以賣方為受益人，於裝運前 30 天開出，規定憑全套貨運單據支付發票全額金額。
>
> ⑺ 出貨：所有憑本合約書售出的貨物，都必須在約定的期間內發出。提單日期，應視為出貨日的決定證據。除非有明確規定，出貨港由賣方選擇。
>
> ⑻ 海上保險：如未特別約定其他條件，所有出貨，均應投保全險，保險金額等於發票金額加一成。所有保險單應載明投保美金，在舊金山理賠。
>
> ⑼ 品質：賣方應保證，所裝貨物在品質及狀況方面，與說明及／或樣品相符。
>
> ⑽ 檢驗：除非另有規定，貨物將依供應商通常方式實施檢驗。
>
> ⑾ 包裝及刷麥：所有貨物須以標準外銷紙箱包裝，並刷上 WTS 為麥頭。
>
> ⑿ 損壞：賣方應運出情況良好的貨物；買方則須負擔貨物在運輸中損壞，變質或破損的危險。
>
> ⒀ 索賠：如須索賠，應於貨物到達目的地 14 日內，用郵件提

出；認可的公證行所簽發的證明書，應速即郵寄。買賣雙方不能友好解決的所有索賠事件，應交付仲裁。

⒁ 仲裁：仲裁庭包括兩人，其中一位由賣方指定，另一位由買方指定，如兩人的意見不能一致時，則以仲裁人所選評判人的決定為準，而敗方須負擔費用。

⒂ 匯兌風險：以美金報價的價格，乃以現行臺灣美金對新臺幣的公定價格為準；在押匯時，如美金對新臺幣有任何貶值，則此項風險歸買方負擔。

為證明上述約定，皮賽有限公司於 **20..** 年 5 月 2 日在本合約書簽字；華生進口公司於 **20..** 年 5 月 22 日在本合約書簽字，本合約書自 **20..** 年 6 月 1 日起生效，除非經雙方書面同意，本合約書中任何條款不得變更或修改。

賣方　　　　　　　　　　　　　　　　買方
皮賽有限公司　　　　　　　　　　　　華生進口公司
王傑瑞　　　　　　　　　　　　　　　大衛・史密斯
董事長　　　　　　　　　　　　　　　董事長

Exercise

A. Questions 問答題

1. What are the details usually included in an agreement on general terms and conditions of business?

2. Will an agreement on general terms and conditions of business be signed before or after starting doing business?

3. Is an agreement on general terms and conditions of business very important for both the buyer and the seller? Why or why not?

B. Business Insight 實務探討

◆ 先訂遊戲規則

在國際貿易上，買賣雙方，對於以後生意經營的模式與方法，要訂下規則，以避免不必要的糾紛。此規則或契約，由買方或賣方擬定皆可；先由一方擬定，然後郵寄給對方審閱後再簽署生效。然而，在國際貿易實務中，由於在臺灣一般交易付款皆以信用狀為主，而交易條件皆以Incoterms 所規定為規則的依據，所以，除非另有規定，否則為爭取時效，就不必先定規則，可直接進行詢價、報價等，而把重要條款列於報價單或訂單上，一樣可達到互相規定的效用。

* Incoterms: 國貿條規，例如：FOB、CFR、CIF 等，為 International commercial terms 之縮寫。

C. Grammar Practice 文法練習

★時態 (Tense)：

英文的時態可分以下十二種：

	簡單式	完成式	進行式	完成進行式
現在	I live ①	I have lived ④	I am living ⑦	I have been living ⑩
過去	I lived ②	I had lived ⑤	I was living ⑧	I had been living ⑪
未來	I will live ③	I will have lived ⑥	I will be living ⑨	I will have been living ⑫

Selection：寫出下列時態所屬類型的代碼

_____ 1. Initial negotiations took place yesterday at Montreal.

_____ 2. Ms. Gelera is giving a long speech at the Hilton Hotel.

_____ 3. On international shipments, all taxes are paid by the recipient.

_____ 4. We have accepted the proposal the committee submitted.

_____ 5. Joe has been discussing the topic with the manager for two hours.

_____ 6. We will be talking with you about the orders tomorrow morning.

_____ 7. By June, they shall have been living in Sydney for ten years.

_____ 8. Recent changes in policies have affected our sales.

_____ 9. Some staff had been informed of a rise in salary before last week.

_____ 10. Grace was waiting for checking in at Narita International Airport at 7:00 last night.

D. Pattern Practice 句型練習

★相信：

We believe...

We trust...

We assure...

---

1. 我們相信我們的運動器材產品品質優越、價錢公道。

_____

2. 我們相信你們會對我們的紡織品完全滿意。

_____

No. 7 網路：臺灣經貿網 (Taiwantrade)

　　臺灣經貿網是由中華民國經濟部國際貿易局委託中華民國對外貿易發展協會 (TAITRA) 於 2002 年設立的 B2B 經貿網站。

　　該網站運用各種方式整合國內外市場資訊，供臺灣企業交流資訊，且經由經濟部暨外貿協會駐外單位收集國外企業的商業資訊。因此，本經貿網定位為「臺灣貿易整合總入口網站」，以促進線上交易為主要核心。本網站主要功能為：

1. 商業資訊提供：即時將採購洽談、推銷洽談等資訊提供給企業界。
2. 企業網站建立：可於臺灣經貿網中建立個人企業網站及刊登企業資料和新產品，以利招攬客戶，促進行銷。
3. 經貿資訊提供：公布重要的經貿資訊、定期提供資訊給國內供應商及國外買主、更新商業動態給廠商等，以利國內外生意的拓展。

NOTE

Chapter Eight

Terms and Conditions

條款及條件

Outline

1. Commodity	商品名稱
2. Quality Terms	品質條件
3. Quantity Terms	數量條件
4. Price Terms	價格條件
5. Packing and Marking	包裝及麥頭
6. Insurance Terms	保險條件
7. Delivery Terms	交貨條件
8. Payment Terms	付款條件

國際貿易交易的條款有統一的交易規則，國際交易秩序才會一致，才不會混亂，誤導。此統一的交易規則，即是 T.O.T. (Terms of Trade)，包括商品名稱、品質、數量、價格條款、包裝及麥頭、保險、交貨及付款條款等，分別說明如下：

1. Commodity

常用的商品用字有 goods, merchandise, products, ware, cargo 等。

⑴ Goods (貨物，貨品，商品，原料)

Canned goods	罐頭品
Capital goods	資本財

Consumer goods	消費品
Cotton goods	棉織品
Household goods	家庭用品
Luxury goods	奢侈品
Inflammable goods	易燃品
Processed goods	加工品
Sporting goods	運動用品
Standard goods	標準品
Sundry goods	雜貨

(2) Merchandise (商品，集合名詞)

General merchandise	雜貨

(3) Products (產品，製品)

Agricultural products	農產品
Industrial products	工業製品
Fishery products	漁產品
Commercial products	商業品

(4) Ware (手工藝品，製品，物品)

Bambooware	竹器
Brassware	銅器
Ceramicware	陶瓷器
Earthenware	瓦器
Glassware	玻璃製品
Hardware	五金
Kitchenware	廚具
Silverware	銀器

| Tableware | 餐具 |
| Woodenware | 木器 |

⑸ Cargo (貨物，保險界運輸界用語)

Bulk cargo	大宗貨物
Bulky cargo	超大貨
General cargo	雜貨

⑹ Others (其他)

Toys	玩具
Umbrellas	雨傘
Stoves	爐子
Shoes	鞋子
Bicycles	腳踏車

2. Quality Terms

一般品質條件有以下四種：

⑴ 樣品為準 (Sale by sample)：以買方或賣方所提供樣品為依據，一般常用之。

⑵ 標準品為準 (Sale by standard)：以各公會所訂標準為準，以農產品為主，如黃豆等。

⑶ 檢驗規格為準 (Sale by grade)：以政府或民間工商團體所訂的等級為準，如 JIS*、CNS*等。

⑷ 平均品質為準 (Sale on FAQ* or GMQ*)：以中等平均品質為準。

* JIS: Japanese Industrial Standards	日本工業標準
CNS: National Standards of the Republic of China	中華民國國家標準
FAQ: Fair Average Quality	良好平均品質
GMQ: Good Merchantable Quality	適銷品質

3. Quantity Terms

一般常用的數量單位如下：

Bag	包	Gross	籮、12 打
Bale	包、綑	Head	頭
Bundle	束	Pack	包
Case	箱	Pair	雙
Carton	紙箱	Piece	個、件
Coil	捲 (電線用)	Reel	捲、線捲
Deca-	十個	Ream	令 (紙張用)
Dozen	打	Roll	捲
Dozen pair	打、雙	Set	套、組、臺、部
Each	件、條	Sheet	張
Great Gross	大籮、12 籮	Unit	部

4. Price Terms

一般國際貿易上作為價格基礎的價格條件，是以 Incoterms 所規定為準；實務上，以 FOB、CFR 或 CIF 為最普遍，茲說明如下：

⑴ 以出口地為交貨地的條件

　　1) EXW　　　　　　　　　　　　　　工廠交貨價
　　　(Ex Works, Ex Factory, Ex Mills)

　　2) FAS　　　　　　　　　　　　　　船邊交貨價
　　　(Free Alongside Ship)

　　3) FOB　　　　　　　　　　　　　　船上交貨價，離岸價格
　　　(Free On Board)

　　4) FCA　　　　　　　　　　　　　　向運送人交貨價
　　　(Free Carrier)

　　5) CFR　　　　　　　　　　　　　　運費在內價
　　　(Cost and Freight)

6) CIF 運保費在內價

(Cost, Insurance, and Freight)

7) CPT 運費付訖價

(Carriage Paid To)

8) CIP 運保費付訖價

(Carriage and Insurance Paid To)

(2) 以進口地為交貨地的交貨條件

9) DAP (Delivered at Place) (...named place of destination) 目的地指定地點未卸貨價。 DAP 於 Incoterms 2010 取代了 Incoterms 2000 下列三項：

① DAF (Delivered At Frontier) 邊境交貨價

② DES (Delivered Ex Ship) 目的港船上交貨價

③ DDU (Delivered Duty Unpaid) 未稅價，稅未付訖價

10) DAT (Delivered At Terminal) 目的地指定港站或地點已卸貨價。 Terminal 指包括所有海關管制的貨站，如機場、海港、邊境等。 DAT 於 Incoterms 2010 取代了 Incoterms 2000 ： DEQ (Delivered Ex Quay) 目的港碼頭交貨價。

11) DPU (Delivered at Place Unloaded) 目的地卸貨後交貨價。Place 可以是任何地方，DPU 卸貨地不限於海港、機場、邊境等終點站，賣方只要確保指定目的地可以從運輸工具卸貨並交給買方即可。 也就是說，賣方的運輸、風險、責任、負擔範圍更大，所以在排列的次序上也略有變更。 DPU 要排在 DAP 的後面。 DPU 於 Incoterms 2020 取代了 Incoterms 2010 ： DAT(Delivered at Terminal) 目的地指定港站或地點已卸貨價。

12) DDP (Delivered Duty Paid) 完稅價，稅訖交貨價

* FOR (Free On Rail) 鐵路交貨價及 FOA (FOB Airport) 機場交貨價 ， 現在已經取消。

價格條款 (Price Terms) 的價格由低至高，列如下圖：

```
Cost EXW FOR FAS FOB CFR CIF│DES    DEQ    DDU    DDP    2000 年
$2   $3   $4   $5   $6  $7.4 $7.7│(DAP) (DAT) (DAP) (DDP) 2010 年
                                │[DAP] [DPU]        [DDP]  2020 年
────────────────────────────────────────────────────────────────→
出口國                          │進口國
```

5. Packing and Marking

⑴ 包裝 (Packing)

國際貿易上的進出口貨物，由於大部分都須經長途運輸，經手人甚多，故包裝尤其重要。現代雖有貨櫃運輸，較方便，也較安全，但包裝仍不可忽視，才能確保貨物的安全到達。一般常用的包裝材料有如下：

Bale	包、綑	Carton	紙箱
Barrel	鼓形桶	Crate	板條箱
Basket	簍	Drum	大桶
Bottle	瓶	Keg	小桶
Can	罐	Sack	大布袋
Wooden case	木箱	Tin	罐、罐頭
Cask	桶	Tub	桶

⑵ 麥頭 (Shipping Mark)

麥頭即是標示在包裝材料外的標誌，可分主麥及側麥兩方面來看：

1) 主麥 (Main mark)：包括主標誌、目的港、箱號、原產國標誌等。

2) 側麥 (Side mark)：品質標誌、重量體積標誌、注意標誌等。

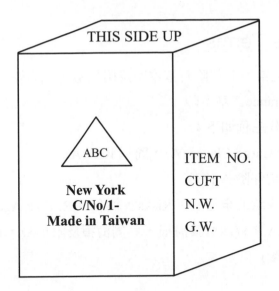

* 常用的注意標誌如下：

This side up　此端向上

This end up　此端向上

Handle with care　小心搬運

Use no hook　請勿用鉤

Keep cool　放於涼處

Keep dry　保持乾燥

Inflammable　易燃貨物

Fragile　當心易碎

Explosives　易爆貨物

Keep upright　豎立安放

CUFT　才 (材) 積

N.W.　淨重 (Net Weight)

G.W.　毛重 (Gross Weight)

6. Insurance Terms

在國際貿易上常用的保險有基本險及附加險，說明如下：

⑴ Basic Insurance　基本險

基本險可分三種如下：

1) Institute Cargo Clause (A)，簡稱 ICC (A)

協會貨物保險 A 條款

即是舊條款的全險 (All Risks，簡稱 A.R.，或 Against All Risks，簡稱 A.A.R.) (保單獨海損，共同海損及附加險，但不含兵險及罷工暴動險)

2) Institute Cargo Clause (B)，簡稱 ICC (B)

協會貨物保險 B 條款

即是舊條款的水漬險 (With Average，簡稱 W.A.) (保單獨海損及共同海損)

3) Institute Cargo Clause (C)，簡稱 ICC (C)

協會貨物保險 C 條款

即是舊條款的平安險 (Free from Particular Average，簡稱 FPA) (只保共同海損不保單獨海損)

以上 ICC (A)、ICC (B)、ICC (C) 均不包括兵險 (War Risks) 或罷工暴動險 (SRCC)。因此，如要獲這種危險保障，須另加保。

⑵ Additional Insurance　附加險

如偷竊遺失險，破損險，鉤損險等。

兵險 (W.R. = War Risks)

罷工暴動險 (SRCC = Strikes, Riots, and Civil Commotions)

偷竊遺失險 (TPND = Theft, Pilferage, and Non-delivery)

破損險 (Breakage)

鉤損險 (Hook Hole)

7. Delivery Terms

⑴ 交貨時間

　1) 即期交貨

　　① Immediate delivery is required.

　　② Prompt delivery is essential.

　2) 定期交貨

　　① Shipment is to be made in September.

　　② Shipment is required before July 31.

　3) 以某一定點為準

　　① Shipment is to be made within 35 days after receipt of L/C.

　　② Shipment will be made within 40 days after receipt of your L/C.

⑵ 交貨方法

　1) 可否分批

　　① Partial shipments are not allowed.

　　② Partial shipments are allowed.

　2) 可否轉船

　　① Transhipment is prohibited.

　　② Transhipment is not permitted.

3) 分幾次出貨

① Shipment in equal separate lots.

② Shipment to be spread equally over three months.

8. Payment Terms

分付款方式及付款工具說明。

(1) 付款方式

國際貿易的付款方式，依時間的先後可分為以下三種：

1) 預付貨款 (Payment In Advance)

① CWO (Cash With Order) 　　　　　訂貨付現

② CIA (Cash In Advance) 　　　　　預付現金，等於 CWO

③ Anticipatory L/C 　　　　　預支信用狀

2) 裝貨付款 (Payment On Shipment)

① CAD (Cash Against Documents) 　　　　　現金交單

② Sight L/C 　　　　　即期信用狀

3) 延期付款 (Deferred Payment)

① COD (Cash On Delivery) 　　　　　貨到付現

② D/P (Documents Against Payment) 　　　　　付款交單

③ D/A (Documents Against Acceptance) 　　　　　承兌交單

④ On Consignment 　　　　　寄售

⑤ Open Account 　　　　　賒銷

⑥ By Installments 　　　　　分期付款

(2) 付款工具

1) Remittance: 匯付 (順匯)

① M/T (Mail Transfer)　　　　　　信匯

② D/D (Demand Draft)　　　　　　票匯

③ Personal Check　　　　　　　　私人支票

2) Drawing: 發票 (逆匯)

① Clean Bill　　　　　　　　　　光票

② Documentary Bill　　　　　　　跟單匯票

＊順匯：由債務人發票予債權人 (付款)

＊逆匯：由債權人發票予債務人 (收款)

✏ Exercise

A. Questions 問答題

1. What is T.O.T.?

2. What are the common terms of price?

3. What are the common terms of insurance?

4. What are the common terms of payment?

5. What are the terms of payment commonly used in trade business in Taiwan?

B. Business Insight 實務探討

◆ T.O.T. 是什麼？

　T.O.T. 是 "Terms of Trade" 的縮寫，也就是貿易條款。一般貿易條款可分為單位、數量、包裝、品質、報價、運送、付款、保險、索賠、仲裁等。這些條款皆為交易前，所定遊戲規則中的重要項目；可以先定，也可以在報價、訂單、或交易契約中訂定，以避免不必要的糾紛，或有糾紛時可作為索賠或處理的依據。

C. Grammar Practice 文法練習

★時態 (Tense)──簡單式 (Simple Tense)：

---

1. 現在簡單式 (Simple Present Tense)：用於表現有的事實、狀態、動作或習慣、真理等。

   e.g. I live in Tainan.

   　　 I take a walk in the morning.

2. 過去簡單式 (Simple Past Tense)：表過去的事實、狀態、動作或習慣經驗等。

   e.g. I lived in Singapore last year.

   　　 Joe went to Japan last month.

3. 未來簡單式 (Simple Future Tense)：表示未來將發生的動作或狀態等。

   e.g. I will live in Canada next year.

   　　 Lucy will send you the catalogue next week.

Selection：選出最適當的答案

_____ 1. Linda _____ a very good work on that project last month.

　　　 (A) did　　　　 (B) do　　　　 (C) will do　　　 (D) does

_____ 2. I am afraid I _____ late for the meeting.

　　　 (A) is　　　　 (B) was　　　　 (C) will be　　　 (D) be

_____ 3. Contracts must be read thoroughly before they _____.

　　　 (A) were signed　 (B) are signed　 (C) will be signed (D) signed

_____ 4. If it _____ fine tomorrow, I will go shopping with you.

　　　 (A) be　　　　 (B) is　　　　 (C) will be　　　 (D) were

_____ 5. Carl said he _____ me next week.

　　　 (A) calls　　　 (B) called　　　 (C) will call　　 (D) would call

_____ 6. Neither the CEO nor the president _____ opposed to our plans.

　　　 (A) are　　　　 (B) be　　　　 (C) is　　　　 (D) were

_____ 7. Jimmy _____ the mail in a few minutes.

(A) will deliver　(B) delivering　(C) delivered　(D) delivers

D. Pattern Practice 句型練習

★請即函覆：

> We expect to...
>
> We are waiting to/for...
>
> We await...
>
> We look forward to...

1. 我們期待儘速得到你們的回音。

_____

2. 煩請儘速函覆，以便及早開始生產。

_____

E. Business Terms 解釋名詞

1. EXW	2. FOR	3. FAS	4. FOB
5. CFR	6. CIF	7. FCA	8. FOA
9. DES	10. DDP	11. TLO	12. FPA
13. W.A.	14. A.A.R.	15. SRCC	16. TPND
17. CWO	18. D/P	19. COD	20. DPU

No. 8 書信：存證信函 (Certified Mail)

　　存證信函的目的在將意思表示通知對方，以發生法律效力。

　　民法第 95 條第一項規定：「非對話而為意思表示者，其意思表示，以通知達到相對人時，發生效力。」一旦對方確實收受後，寄件人 (公司法人) 已經握有證據，就算日後對簿公堂，也有存證信函可以佐證。

　　存證信函可以使用郵局印好的存證信函用紙或「其他同格式紙張」(例如：將存證信函紙影印) 書寫。

　　存證信函的功用，在於備作證據以便日後發生紛爭，甚至對簿公堂時，得以證明有利於己之事實。因此，在法律上是否因寄件人的意思表示而發生了法律上特定的效果，是應特別注意。

　　可存證的地方，在國內有郵局、法院、公證人 (notary public)、律師事務所等。在國外，以法院及律師事務所為主。

Chapter Nine

Trade Enquiry and Reply to Enquiry

詢問函及回函

Outline

1. The Characteristics of an Enquiry

The characteristics of an enquiry are being simple, being clear, and being concise.

詢問函之特色為簡單、明瞭、扼要。

2. The Details Which a Buyer Usually Enquires About

A buyer usually enquires about general information, a catalogue, a price list, a sample, a quotation, an estimate, specification, new items, and so on.

買方常詢之事項包括一般資訊、目錄*(如附圖)、價目表*(如附圖)、樣品、報價、估價、規格、新項目等。

3. The Outline of an Enquiry

⑴ State the source from which the buyer learns the name and address of the seller.

⑵ Describe the specifications of the products the buyer intends to make an enquiry about.

⑶ Request any information available.

⑷ Await the seller's reply along with details.

4. The Ways of Beginning an Enquiry

There are five ways of starting an enquiry:

⑴ Source   如 From...   來源

⑵ Recommendation   如 Through...   推薦

⑶ Self-introduction   如 We are...   自介

⑷ Direct approach   如 Please send...   直接

⑸ Indirect approach   如 Last year...   間接

5. Examples of an Enquiry

Example 9.1   Source   來源

January 23, 20..

Dear Sirs,

We have seen your advertisement in the magazine and are interested in importing your stuffed toys.

We are one of the large importers of toys in the U.S. and believe that if your prices and quality are satisfactory, we may be able to place very substantial orders. If you should send us your latest catalogue and price list, we would be very grateful.

When replying, please state your discount for large orders and your earliest delivery date.

Sincerely yours,

信文中譯：

敬啟者：

　　本公司在雜誌看到你們的廣告，頗有意進口你們的填充玩具。

　　本公司是美國最大的玩具進口商之一，相信若你們的價格及品質令人滿意，本公司能夠下相當大的訂單。如果貴公司能寄來最近的目錄及價目表，將非常感激。

　　請回覆說明大量訂單的折扣及最早交貨日期。

謹上

*A Catalogue (目錄)：

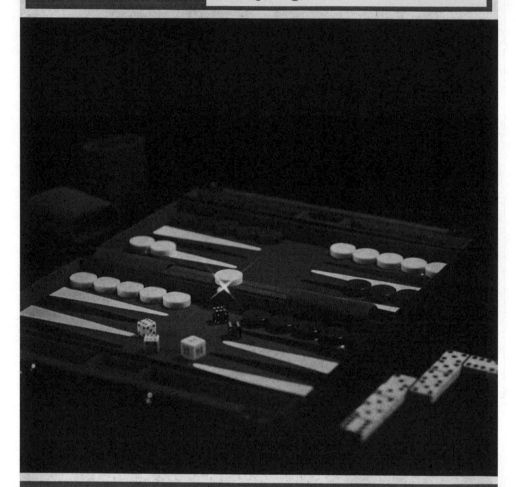

GAME SETS

Backgammon　Chess
Rummy　Dominoes
Mahjong　Go Game

Manufacturer & Exporter
R. HANSE CO., LTD.
No. XX, Lane 519, Sec. 3,
Neihu Road, Neihu Dist.,
Taipei, Taiwan

* A Price List (價目表)：

R. HANSE CO., LTD.

No. ××, Lane 519, Sec. 3,   TEL: (02)2531-××××

Messrs Y & K Corp.   Neihu Road, Neihu Dist.,

Taipei, Taiwan

Pricelist   Date: Dec. 14, **20..**

Item No.	Descriptions	Unit	Unit Price FOB Taiwan	Packing & Cuft
5522	16" × 81/2" × 2" Rummy Brown Vinyl Case.	set	US$6.70	12 sets/2.5'
5500	-do- but Brown Vinyl Case With Two Strips.	set	US$6.80	12 sets/2.5'
5503	-do- but Brown Vinyl Case With Two Strips.	set	US$6.80	12 sets/2.5'
5510	-do- but Brown Vinyl Case With Two Dark Brown & One Ivory Strips.	set	US$6.80	12 sets/2.5'
5531	-do- but Brown Corduroy Case.	set	US$6.80	12 sets/2.5'
5580	-do- but Black Imitation Alligator Case.	set	US$6.80	12 sets/2.5'
5570	-do- but Jacquard Case.	set	US$6.80	12 sets/2.5'
5021	15" × 5" × 3" Rummy Brown Vinyl Case.	set	US$6.10	12 sets/1.9'
5000	-do- but Brown Vinyl Case With Two Strips.	set	US$6.20	12 sets/1.9'
5010	-do- but Brown Vinyl Case With Two Dark Brown & One Ivory Strips.	set	US$6.20	12 sets/1.9'
5031	-do- but Brown Çorduroy Case.	set	US$6.20	12 sets/1.9'
5080	-do- but Black Imitation Alligator Case.	set	US$6.20	12 sets/1.9'

REMARKS:

1. Payment: By irrevocable letter of credit at sight in our favor.

2. Shipment: Within 40 days after receipt of L/C.

3. Minimum Order: US$1,500.00

4. Cost of sample:

   a. For small items: By mail, the above FOB price plus mail charge.

   b. For larger items: By air cargo.

Manufacturer & Exporter

Backgammon Rummy Mahjong Chess Dominoes Go Game

Example 9.2   Recommendation   推薦

February 12, **20..**

Dear Sirs,

Mr. Smith recommended your name to us as a major supplier of hardware in Taiwan. We are writing to you with the purpose of establishing a business relationship with you.

We are reputable importers of hardware and general merchandise in Canada, with strong sales networks in all major cities in Canada and the U.S. As we are expanding our business rapidly, we would like to include hardware as one of our main promotion items this year.

We would therefore appreciate it very much if you should send us your latest catalogue along with your price list for our reference.

Yours sincerely,

信文中譯：

敬啟者：

　　史密斯先生推薦貴公司為在臺的主要五金供應商。我們寫此函，意在跟你們建立商業關係。

　　本公司是加拿大著名的五金及雜貨進口商，在加拿大及美國的主要城市皆有完整的銷售網路。因本公司業務拓展迅速，有意列五金為本年度促銷的項目。

　　如貴公司能寄來最近的目錄以及價目表以供參考，將不勝感激。

謹上

Example 9.3　Self-introduction　自介

March 15, 20..

Dear Sirs,

We are one of the leading importers and wholesalers in Australia. As your electronic parts have been highly recommended by the consumers here, we are much interested in importing your electronic products.

As our annual demand for electronic products has been huge, we are writing to you with a view to understanding your intention in cooperating with us for developing the market here.

In order to help us know more about your range of products, we would be grateful if you should send us your illustrated catalogue with your most competitive price.

Sincerely yours,

信文中譯：

敬啟者：

　　本公司為澳洲居首位的進口商及批發商，因在此消費者非常推薦你們的電子零件，本公司有意進口你們的電子產品。

　　因本公司每年對於電子產品的需求量甚大，故去此函，以瞭解貴公司是否有意合作開發此地市場。

　　為使能更瞭解貴公司的產品，如蒙惠寄有附圖說明的目錄，連同最有競爭性的價格，將不勝感激。

謹上

Example 9.4　Direct Approach　直接

April 30, **20..**

Dear Sirs,

Please send us your latest catalogue and price list for your full range of kitchenware as we are expecting to place more orders for the new items for the new season to come.

We look forward to hearing from you soon.

Yours sincerely,

信文中譯：

敬啟者：

　　因本公司正準備下一季新產品訂單，請惠寄貴公司整系列廚具之最新目錄及價目表。

　　期待盡快得到回信。

謹上

Example 9.5　Indirect Approach　間接

May 18, **20..**

Dear Sirs,

Several years ago we imported a big quantity of your DIY furniture, but as the demand for it fell to the minimum, we really had a hard time selling it.

We are now, however, in a better position to sell more of your products as we have since then established our own strong sales networks and therefore stand a good chance of dominating the market in our country.

If you should provide any pertinent information which you think might be of use to us for our promotion, we would be very grateful.

Sincerely yours,

＊ DIY: do-it-yourself 自己動手做；自助

信文中譯：

敬啟者：

幾年前本公司曾大量進口貴公司的自助家具,因當時需求量已跌到谷底,本公司頗難促銷。

然而,今因本公司已建立堅強銷售網,尤能銷售貴公司之產品,能成功地掌握本地市場。

如蒙惠予提供任何有助於促銷之資訊,將感激不盡。

謹上

6. The Techniques of Writing an Enquiry

(1) Express clearly what the buyer intends to know.

(2) Give more information about the descriptions, making it easier for the seller to reply.

(3) Make it a three-paragraph letter, which is easier to understand.

(4) Use polite expressions, such as please, grateful, etc.

(5) Pay attention to the use of P.O.P., such as substantial quantities, leading importers, large orders, etc.

7. The Outline of Replying to an Enquiry

(1) Thank the buyer for his enquiry.

(2) Supply the information required.

(3) Use selling points properly and assure best cooperation.

(4) Expect to receive orders soon.

8. The Ways of Replying to an Enquiry

(1) If the seller has the information in hand (如果有資料可提供):

1) Thank the buyer for his enquiry.

2) Enclose the details requested.

3) Offer more service.

(2) If the seller does not have the information in hand (如果沒資料):

1) Thank the buyer for his enquiry.

2) Say sorry for not being able to supply information.

3) Say when the information will be available or recommend other sources the buyer can contact.

9. Examples of a Reply

Example 9.6　Information Available　如果有資料可提供

June 14, **20..**

Dear Sirs,

Thank you very much for your letter of May 20, **20..** showing interest in importing our hardware products. We are glad to say that we have our own factory. We are in a position to offer you our best quality products.

Enclosed please find our latest catalogue and price list for your initial reference. We are sure that our excellent quality products and our competitive prices will win your full confidence in us.

As the market demand has been increasing these days, we would appreciate your early orders without delay.

Sincerely yours,

Enc.

信文中譯：

敬啟者：

　　感謝貴公司 20.. 年 5 月 20 日來信顯示對進口本公司的五金產品有興趣。本公司樂於告知本公司有自己的工廠。本公司能提供最佳品質之產品。

　　隨函附上本公司最近的目錄及價目表以供初步參考。本公司確信最優品質產品及有競爭性的價格,將獲貴公司十足的信心。

　　近因市場需求一直攀升,如蒙惠予儘速下訂單,將不勝感激。

謹上

附件

Example 9.7　Information not Available　如果沒資料

July 26, **20..**

Dear Sirs,

We are pleased to receive your letter of June 20, **20..** concerning our furniture products. We thank you very much for your interest in doing business with us.

However, we are sorry to inform you that due to some unexpected reasons we are now not able to supply you at this moment with the DIY furniture you mentioned. Nevertheless, we would like to refer you to Smith Furniture Co., Ltd., who we are sure will be able to help you in this matter.

If we can be of any further service, please feel free to contact us.

Sincerely yours,

信文中譯：

敬啟者：

　　本公司高興收到貴公司 **20..** 年 6 月 20 日來信，關於本公司的家具產品。感謝貴公司有興趣跟我們做生意。

　　然而，本公司遺憾告知，因某意料之外之理由，本公司此刻無法供應貴公司所提的自助家具。然而，本公司願意推薦貴公司與史密斯家具有限公司聯絡。本公司相信他們會在此事上幫助貴公司。

　　如能有再度效勞之處，請不吝來函聯絡。

謹上

Example 9.8　Information Available　如果有資料可提供

July 27, **20..**

Dear Sirs,

We welcome your enquiry and thank you for your interest in our products. A copy of our illustrated catalogue and price list along with our shoe samples is being sent under separate cover to you today.

As soon as you receive our reference submitted, we are sure that you will agree that our products are excellent in quality and reasonable in price.

We look forward very much to the pleasure of receiving an order from you.

Sincerely yours,

信文中譯：

敬啟者：

　　本公司歡迎貴公司的詢問函並感謝你們對本公司產品的興趣。本日另函寄出一份附圖說明的目錄及價目表，連同鞋子樣品。

　　在收到本公司寄出的資料時，確信貴公司會同意本公司的產品是品質優越，價錢公道的。

　　期待能有榮幸收到貴公司的訂單。

謹上

Example 9.9　Information Available　如果有資料可提供

August 6, 20..

Dear Sirs,

In reply to your letter of April 30, **20..**, we are pleased to enclose the current catalogue and price list of our kitchenware for your kind reference.

Due to the heavy demand for our kitchenware, we would ask you to place your order immediately.

Your early reply would be highly appreciated.

Sincerely yours,

Enc.

信文中譯：

敬啟者：

　　敬覆你們 **20..** 年 4 月 30 日來函，本公司很高興附上我們目前廚具的目錄及價目表，以供參考。

　　由於廚具的大量需求，請貴公司立即下訂單。

　　若早日收到回音將感激不盡。

謹上

附件

10. The Techniques of Writing a Reply

（1）Express thanks for the buyer's enquiry. Show P.O.P., such as large market, heavy demand, excellent quality, competitive prices, etc.

（2）Refer to future action, encouraging the buyer to place an order.

✎ Exercise

A. Questions 問答題

1. What are the characteristics of an enquiry?

2. What does a buyer usually enquire about in an enquiry?

3. What is the outline of an enquiry?

4. What are the ways of starting an enquiry?

5. What are the techniques of writing an enquiry?

6. What is the outline of a reply to an enquiry?

7. What are the ways of replying to an enquiry?

8. What are the techniques of writing a reply?

B. Business Insight 實務探討

◆ 老闆，你們一斤賣多少錢？

　　詢價函就如早期菜市場裡，顧客詢價模式「老闆，你們一斤賣多少錢？」的延伸。在國際貿易上，買方也是要詢問對方一斤賣多少錢；只是數量上使用雙方都能接受的單位。而貨幣上，也大部分用美金，很少使用臺幣。而方式上，皆以書面為之，較正式。另外，買方在詢價時，要盡量將所要買的產品規格詳細列出，如有數量，也一併告知，以易於賣方報價及估價。

C. Grammar Practice 文法練習

★時態 (Tense)──完成式 (Perfect Tense)：

---

1. 現在完成式 (Present Perfect Tense)：

   表示到目前為止所完成的動作或狀態。

   e.g. I have lived in Taipei for ten years.

2. 過去完成式 (Past Perfect Tense)：

   表示過去某時間以前完成的動作或狀態。

   e.g. I had lived in Taipei for ten years before I went to Japan.

3. 未來完成式 (Future Perfect Tense)：

   表示到未來某時間將完成的動作或狀態等。

   e.g. By next June, I will have lived here for twenty years.

Selection：選出最適當的答案

_____ 1. Ms. Smith _____ in a good business plan to the director.

(A) had handed   (B) has handed

(C) has been handed   (D) hands

_____ 2. The president of the corporation _____ in Copenhagen for the meeting.

(A) has arrived   (B) had arrived

(C) has been arrived   (D) had been arrived

_____ 3. On the ninth of next month, they _____ for us for ten years.

(A) have worked   (B) worked

(C) will have worked   (D) had worked

_____ 4. I heard that my CEO _____ abroad.

(A) has gone   (B) had been gone

(C) will have gone   (D) had gone

_____ 5. The secretary _____ her work before she went to the airport.

(A) has finished   (B) is finished

(C) had finished   (D) will have finished

____   6. Barbara ____ to Sydney several times.

(A) had been   (B) goes   (C) has been   (D) had gone

____   7. Robert ____ to Toronto five times before he moved to Montreal.

(A) has been   (B) went   (C) has gone   (D) had been

____   8. Mr. Jackson ____ in New York for six years by next August.

(A) have lived   (B) had lived

(C) have been living   (D) will have lived

D. Pattern Practice 句型練習

★關於：

As to..., S. + V.

Concerning..., S. + V.

Regarding..., S. + V.

With/In reference to..., S. + V.

With respect to..., S. + V.

With/In regard to..., S. + V.

As regards..., S. + V.

---

1. 關於所提到的玩具樣品，我們將於下星期一用航空包裹寄出。

_____

2. 關於所要求的目錄、價目表及樣品，我們已於昨天用航空寄出。

_____

E. Blank-filling 填充練習

Dear _____ ,

We have _____ your _____ in the _____ _____ and are _____ in _____ your _____ toys.

We are _____ of the largest _____ of _____ in the _____ and _____ that if your _____ and _____ are _____ , we may _____ able _____ _____ _____ orders.

If you _____ send _____ your _____ _____ and _____ _____ , we would _____ very _____ .

_____ yours,

F. Letter-writing 書信寫作

As an importer of stationery in Taiwan, write your letter of enquiry to an importer to enquire about details of his products.

No. 9 書信：關於 E-mail 的法律效用

　　一般重要文件以送達為生效要件。依行政程序法第 68 條規定：「文書依法規以電報交換、電傳文件、傳真或其他電子文件行之者，視為自行送達。」E-mail 雖然具有法律效用，但若為重要的事情，簽紙本合約仍較有保障。發函主要目的是意思表示之送達，故重點有二：

1. 意思表示之內容：若告訴對方欠債還錢，產生相關之法律效果。

2. 送達：對方若沒收到就沒有法律效果。

　　電子郵件之送達以對方當事人承認為限生其效力。原因是你無法證明內容如何，對方有無收到，對方否認就等於沒有。甚至有些合約中會規定某些重要事情一定要用書面通知，否則不具效力。何況通常 e-mail 中都只會寫一些簡單的東西，但是有關東西有問題的瑕疵擔保、沒有按時付錢的遲延利息等，最好雙方 e-mail 來確認，並請對方簽回確認 (countersign)。

　　通常大公司都會有嚴格的簽署合約流程，以避免可能的爭議發生，因此紙本合約是有其存在的價值。

Chapter Ten

Offer and Acceptance

報價及接受

 **outline**

1. The Elements of a Request for a Quotation

In writing a request for a quotation, a buyer should pay attention to the following points:

(1) to state the name of the commodity

(2) to give details of descriptions

(3) to mention the quantity he has in mind

(4) to state the price terms required

(5) to make the delivery date clear

(6) to request favorable terms if possible

Example 10.1　A Request for Quotation for Shoes　請求鞋子的報價

* 寫作技巧 (A) Direct Approach　直接法開場：

June 12, **20..**

Dear Sirs,

Please send us a quotation for the supply of 12,000 pairs of leather shoes, Item No. SH-012, as shown in your catalogue. We require shoes of the finest quality and will need a shoe sample for our evaluation. Please quote the price on the basis of CIF New York and delivery will be around the end of September.

If you can give us a really competitive quotation, we expect to place a large order.

Sincerely yours,

信文中譯：

敬啟者：

　　請貴公司寄下報價單，報 12,000 雙皮鞋，編號 SH-012，如目錄所示。本公司需要最好品質鞋子，並需要一隻鞋樣品以便評估。請報 CIF 紐約的價格，交貨時間約在 9 月底。

　　如蒙報確實有競爭性的價格，本公司預期可下一大訂單。

謹上

Example 10.2　A Quotation Request for Hand Tools
　　　　　　　請求手工具的報價

---

* 寫作技巧 (B) Indirect Approach　間接法開場：

May 23, **20..**

Dear Sirs,

You have previously supplied us with your hand tools, and we have been quite satisfied with your quality.

As we are in great demand for hand tools at this moment, we therefore should be glad if you would quote us your lowest CIF San Francisco prices for 1,000 pieces each of Article No. CK-03, CK-04, and CK-05.

Delivery would be required around late July. If your prices are competitive enough, we will place regular orders.

As the matter is urgent, we should like to have the information by the end of this week.

Sincerely yours,

信文中譯：

敬啟者：

　　貴公司以前曾供應本公司手工具，且本公司對你們的品質非常滿意。

　　因目前正大量需要手工具，本公司將感激如果貴公司能報編號 CK-03，CK-04，CK-05，每項各 1,000 組的 CIF 舊金山最低價錢。

　　本公司需要在 7 月底前交貨。如果貴公司價格夠競爭性，本公司會下固定訂單。

　　因此事急迫，盼在本星期內收到回信。

謹上

2. The Elements of a Satisfactory Quotation

The elements of a satisfactory quotation include:

(1) to thank the buyer for his enquiry

(2) the details of prices, discounts, and terms of payment

(3) the terms of quotation, such as FAS, FOB, etc.

(4) a promise of the date of delivery

(5) the validity

(6) to hope the quotation will be accepted

Example 10.3　A Reply to a Quotation Request for Shoes
　　　　　　　回覆鞋子報價

＊ 寫作技巧 (A) Quotation Letter　直接在信上報價：

June 19, **20..**

Dear Sirs,

We thank you very much for your enquiry of June 12, and as requested, send a shoe sample under separate cover today. For the quantity you mentioned in your letter, we are pleased to quote our best CIF New York price as follows:

Item No.	Quantity	Unit	Price
SH-012	12,000	pairs	US$100.00
			CIF New York

All our shoes are of the finest quality, and we guarantee delivery will be made before the end of September.

We hope you will find both our sample and price satisfactory and look forward to receiving your initial order.

                                    Sincerely yours,

信文中譯：

　　感謝貴公司 6 月 12 日詢問，依函我們本日另寄一隻鞋樣品。於信上所提到的數量，本公司很高興報最好的 CIF 紐約價格如下：

編號	數量	單位	價格
SH-012	12,000	雙	美金 100.00
			CIF 紐約

本公司鞋子品質最優且保證在 9 月底前交貨。
盼貴公司對本公司的樣品及價格會滿意，並期待收到初訂單。

                                    謹上

Example 10.4   Reply to a Quotation Request for Hand Tools
回覆手工具報價

---

* 寫作技巧 (B) Quotation Form Enclosed   附上報價單：

May 29, 20..

Dear Sirs,

Replying to your enquiry of May 23 for a further supply of our hand tools, we are pleased to say that we are in a position to supply you with our best quality products.

Enclosed please find our Quotation No. HT-66 based on CIF San Francisco. You may rest assured that the prices we offered are the best on the present market.

We assure that delivery can be made around late July provided your L/C reaches us before the end of June.

We trust you will find our quotation satisfactory and look forward to receiving your order.

Sincerely yours,

Enc.

信文中譯：

敬啟者：

　　敬覆你們 5 月 23 日詢問函，關於再度訂購本公司的手工具，本公司樂於表示能供應最佳品質的產品給貴公司。

　　隨函附上本公司的報價單 HT-66 號，報價以 CIF 舊金山為基礎。貴公司可放心本公司所報的價格是市面上最好的。

　　如貴公司的信用狀在 6 月底前抵此，本公司保證可在 7 月底左右出貨。

　　本公司相信貴公司會滿意我們的報價，並期待收到訂單。

謹上

附件

PIZA CO., LTD.

No. ××, Sec. 3, Xinsheng S. Rd., Da'an Dist.,

Taipei, Taiwan

May 29, **20..**

QUOTATION

No. HT-66

Messrs.

WATSONS IMPORTS, INC.

×× Blue Drive

San Francisco, CA 90012

U.S.A.

Dear Sirs,

We have pleasure of offering you the commodities as follows:

Item No	Descriptions	Unit	Quantity	Unit Price	Amount
				CIF San Francisco	
CK-03	Hand tool set	set	1,000	US$6.15	US$6,150
CK-04	-do-	set	1,000	US$6.25	US$6,250
CK-05	-do-	set	1,000	US$5.34	US$5,340

1) Payment: At sight draft under irrevocable L/C

2) Terms: CIF San Francisco

3) Packing: To be packed in standard export cartons

4) Shipment: Within 35 days after receipt of your L/C

5) Minimum Order: US$2,000

6) Validity: 90 days but subject to our final confirmation

PIZA CO., LTD.

William Wang

William Wang

Manager

信文中譯：

報價單

HT-66 號

敬啟者：

本公司很開心提供手工具報價如下：

項目	規格	單位	數量	單價	小計
				CIF 舊金山	
CK-03	手工具	組	1,000	美金 6.15	美金 6,150
CK-04	同上	組	1,000	美金 6.25	美金 6,250
CK-05	同上	組	1,000	美金 5.34	美金 5,340

1) 付款條件：以即期匯票的不可撤銷信用狀

2) 條款：CIF 舊金山

3) 包裝：須用標準的外銷紙箱包裝

4) 出貨：在收到信用狀後 35 天內

5) 最少訂量：美金 2,000.00

6) 有效日期：90 天，但需經我們最後確認

皮賽有限公司

王威廉

經理

3. The Styles of a Quotation

There are two styles of a quotation: a quotation letter and a quotation form.

The advantages and disadvantages of each are as follows:

STYLE	ADVANTAGE	DISADVANTAGE	FUNCTION	EXAMPLE
Quotation letter	Convenient; economical	Not proper for too many items; important details may be omitted	For fewer items	Ex 10.3
Quotation form	Available for more items; essential details will be included	Not so economical	For more items	Ex 10.4

報價單有兩種格式，報價信和報價單，各有其優缺點如下：

種類	優點	缺點	用途	範例
報價信	方便、經濟	項目不多、容易遺漏重點	項目少時用	Ex 10.3
報價單	項目可多、細節易把握	較不經濟	項目多時用	Ex 10.4

4. Quotation Subject to Conditions of Acceptance

賣方在報價時，有時必須考慮物價波動及存貨有限等問題，所以在報價時，必須訂些規定以保護自己，同時可激勵買方早日下訂單。茲列舉常用的條件如下：

⑴ For acceptance within seven days.　七天內有效。

⑵ This offer is made subject to the final confirmation of the seller.
須經賣方最後確認。

⑶ The offer is subject to acceptance within ten days.　須於十天內確認。

⑷ The prices quoted will apply only to orders received before June 1.
適用於 6 月 1 日前訂貨。

⑸ The offer is made subject to the goods being unsold when the order is placed.　訂貨時貨還在為限。

5. Firm Offer

A firm offer is an offer made when a seller promises to sell certain goods at a stated price which is valid within a certain period.　穩固報價即是有期限的報價。

Example 10.5　A Quotation Request　請求報價

November 5, **20..**

Dear Sirs,

We are writing in connection with your handicrafts advertised on the internet and are interested in importing your products.

As one of the reputable importers in Europe, we are thinking of a large order for various ranges of your products. We would therefore appreciate very much receiving your representative range of samples for our further estimation.

If your prices compare favorably with those of other suppliers, we shall send you an order.

Sincerely yours,

信文中譯：

敬啟者：

　　本公司寫信來是關於你們在網路所刊登的手工藝品廣告，有意進口你們的產品。

　　本公司為歐洲著名進口商，本公司正考慮下相當大的訂單訂各種系列的產品。因此如蒙寄來貴公司具代表性的樣品，以供進一步評估，將感激不盡。

　　如果貴公司的價格優於其他供應商，本公司會寄上一張訂單。

謹上

Example 10.6　A Firm Offer　穩固報價

November 11, **20..**

Dear Sirs,

We acknowledge receipt of your letter of November 5 concerning our range of handicraft items.

We have made a good selection of samples and sent them to you today by air parcel. Their fine quality, attractive design, and exquisite workmanship will, we are sure, convince you that our products are really of good value.

Enclosed is our best quotation for your reference. Please note that as there is a heavy demand for our products, we will make you a firm offer for delivery by the end of December.

Please take advantage of the offer and place an order without delay.

Sincerely yours,

Enc.

＊ firm offer：穩固報價，即是有期限的報價。

信文中譯：

敬啟者：

感激貴公司 11 月 5 日的來信關於我們手工藝品系列的產品。

本公司已選了一些樣品且本日已由航空小包寄上。相信本公司優良的品質、吸引人的樣式及精細的手藝將使你深信本公司的產品是有價值的。

隨函附上本公司最好的報價單以供參考。請注意到，因我們的產品需求量很大，本公司報穩固報價，限於 12 月底前交貨。

請利用此報價並立即下一訂單。

謹上

附件

6. Counter-offer

When a buyer receives an offer with which he is not satisfied either in price, delivery, packing, terms of payment or others, he may make a counter-offer.

買方對於賣方前所發出的報價內容如有不滿意時，可提出還價，即是反要約。

Example 10.7   A Counter-offer   反要約

June 26, **20..**

Dear Sirs,

We are glad to receive your letter of June 19, **20..** quoting your price for your shoe Item No. SH-012 and informing us of the sending of your sample shoe.

This morning we received your sample submitted and are quite satisfied with your quality; however, we are sorry to tell you that the price you offered is very much higher than that of your competitor. We regret not being able to give you an immediate order, but shall consider it if you will reduce your price, say, by 20%.

As this is a very competitive market, we will have to offer our products at a very low price and therefore would appreciate your acceptance in this matter.

Sincerely yours,

信文中譯：

敬啟者：

　　高興收到貴公司 **20..** 年 6 月 19 日來函，報鞋子編號 SH-012 號價格並通知已寄出鞋子樣品。

　　今早收到貴公司寄來的樣品，對品質十分滿意。然而，遺憾告知，貴公司所報的價格比競爭者的價格要高出很多。抱歉不能下立即訂單，但如果你們能減價，如 20%，我們會考慮的。

　　因這是個非常競爭的市場，我們必須低價提供我們的產品；因此，如果你們接受減價，將不勝感激。

謹上

Example 10.8　Refusing a Counter-offer　拒絕反要約

June 30, **20..**

Dear Sirs,

Thank you for your letter of June 26, **20..**, from which we are sorry to learn that you find our price too high.

In fact, we have already quoted you our best price based on the quantity you mentioned, and our quoted price leaves us with only a small profit margin. To reduce the price any further would make it hard for us to accept your order.

We appreciate your market situation and wish we could help in this respect.

Sincerely yours,

信文中譯：

敬啟者：

　　感謝貴公司 **20..** 年 6 月 26 日來信；從來函本公司很遺憾得知貴公司認為我們的價格太高。

　　事實上，本公司是依據所提到的數量來報最好價錢，所報的價格我們只賺很少的利潤。再減價的話，便無法接受你們的訂單。

　　本公司瞭解貴地的市場狀況，但對於此事愛莫能助。

謹上

Example 10.9　Accepting a Counter-offer　接受反要約

June 30, **20..**

Dear Sirs,

We are obliged for your letter dated June 26, **20..** asking for a better price for our shoe Item No. SH-012 and are sorry to learn that you find our price too high.

Considering the quality of the shoes offered, we do not feel that the price we quoted is high, but bearing in mind the special character of your market, we have decided to offer you a special discount of 10%. We make this allowance because we should like to do business with you.

We hope this revised offer will enable you to place an order.

Sincerely yours,

信文中譯：

敬啟者：

感謝貴公司 **20..** 年 6 月 26 日來信，要求鞋子編號 SH-012 較佳價錢。遺憾貴公司認為價格太高。

鑑於所報鞋子的品質，本公司毫不認為所報價格太高，但顧慮到貴地市場之特性，決定報特別 10% 折扣。本公司允諾此折扣，因盼能成交。

期盼此修正報價能助貴公司下訂單。

謹上

7. Acceptance of a Quotation

If the price and other related details are satisfactory to the buyer, the buyer will then accept the quotation and place an order.

如果價格及其他條款令買方滿意的話，買方會接受報價並依所報的條款下訂單。

Example 10.10　Acceptance of a Quotation　接受報價

July 1, **20..**

Dear Sirs,

In answer to your letter of June 12, **20..**, enclosing your quotation and a jewelry sample, we are pleased to acknowledge receipt of them.

As the pricc and the quality of your jewelry seem quite satisfactory, we are glad to enclose our Purchase Order No. JD-01 for ten items of your range of jewelry.

We require delivery before the end of August. Please confirm the order as soon as possible.

Sincerely yours,

Enc.

信文中譯：

敬啟者：

　　敬覆貴公司 **20..** 年 6 月 12 日來函，附來的報價單及珠寶樣品，本公司已收到。

　　因貴公司珠寶價格及品質頗令人滿意，本公司樂意附上訂單 JD-01 號，訂 10 項珠寶系列。

　　本公司要求在 8 月底前交貨。請儘速確認訂單。

謹上

附件

✐ Exercise

A. Questions 問答題

1. What are the elements of a request for a quotation?

2. What are the elements of a satisfactory quotation?

3. What are the styles of a quotation?

4. Give two examples of condition of acceptance in a quotation.

5. What is a firm offer?

6. What is a counter-offer?

7. What will a buyer do if a quotation is accepted?

B. Business Insight 實務探討

◆客人，我們一斤賣三塊錢

報價給客人時，在國際貿易市場上的報價，不同於市場上的報價，因光報單位及價錢是不夠的，如我們一斤賣三塊錢，但未考慮是否要包括送貨到指定地的費用、保險或佣金等；雖然有些市場會有幫客人免費送貨服務，但在國際貿易上，則因運送地點、方式、風險、產品類別、品質、原料、款式等的不同而有不同的報價。所以，當賣方收到詢價時，除了自己先計算出成本、利潤外，以上各種不同的變數皆要仔細考慮，以便報出合理的價格，達成生意的成交。

C. Grammar Practice 文法練習

★時態 (Tense)──進行式 (Progressive Tense)：

＊公式：be + Ving

> 1. 現在進行式：現在還在做。
>   e.g. I am learning English.
>   Jack is making a report.
> 2. 過去進行式：表過去某時正在做。
>   e.g. Judy was making a speech when the general manager arrived.
>   Tom was leaving for airport when he heard the good news.
> 3. 未來進行式：表未來某時將在做。
>   e.g. Edward will be meeting the customers at this time tomorrow.
>   Allen will be having dinner with us at 6:30 tomorrow night.

Selection：選出最適當的答案

_____ 1. The President of France _____ with the Minister of Trade when the reporter cut in.

　　(A) is meeting 　　　　　　　(B) was meeting

　　(C) will be meeting 　　　　　(D) was met

_____ 2. Nancy _____ a report when you phoned her last night.

　　(A) making 　　　　　　　　(B) is making

　　(C) was making 　　　　　　(D) will be making

_____ 3. It _____ hard when Abe got to the airport.

(A) is raining   (B) raining

(C) will be raining   (D) was raining

_____ 4. By the time you arrive, the manager _____ his demonstration.

(A) will be finishing   (B) is finishing

(C) is finished   (D) was finishing

_____ 5. Ms. Wood, the CEO, _____ dinner with us at 7:00 tomorrow night.

(A) is having   (B) will be having

(C) was having   (D) having

_____ 6. Mr. Webber _____ your phone call when John handed him a box.

(A) is answering   (B) answering

(C) will be answering   (D) was answering

D. Pattern Practice 句型練習

★保證，確信：

> We assure...
>
> We are sure...
>
> We guarantee...

1. 我們保證我們的五金產品，品質最優、價格最公道。

_____

2. 我們確信我們的成衣款式最新、質料最好。

_____

E. Blank-filling 填充練習

Dear _____,

Will you _____ send _____ a _____ for the _____ of 20,000 _____ of _____ shoes, Item No. 112, as _____ in your _____.

We _____ shoes _____ the finest _____ and will _____ a _____ sample _____ our _____. Please _____ the price _____ the _____ of CIF _____ with _____ around the _____ of _____.

If your _____ are really _____, we expect _____ place a _____.

_____ yours,

F. Letter-writing 書信寫作

You are an importer of machinery. Write your letter asking for a quotation for 1,000 sets of automatic stamping machines.

No. 10 書信：PDF 的功能

　　PDF 是可攜式文件格式 (Portable Document Format)，為目前常用的電子文件，在各個不同的電腦平臺與作業系統間均可以互相傳遞及閱覽。現今，許多的專業文件均用 PDF 作為製作的標準。

　　PDF 的優點在於跨平臺，且保留文件原有格式 (layout)，能免授權 (royalty-free) 開發 PDF 相容軟體。

Chapter Eleven

Sales Promotion and Follow-up

促銷及追蹤

1. The Four Elements of a Good Sales Letter   促銷函四要素
2. The Structure of a Sales Letter   促銷函的結構
3. The Appeals of a Sales Letter   促銷函的訴求
4. The Elements of a Follow-up Letter   追蹤函的要素

1. The Four Elements of a Good Sales Letter

The four elements of a good sales letter are as follows:

(1) to cause attention   引起注意

(2) to arouse interest   產生興趣

(3) to create desire   激發慾望

(4) to prompt action   刺激行動

＊ 以上四要素簡稱為 "AIDA"。

Example 11.1   Offer of Microwave Oven   微波爐提議

May 1, **20..**

Dear Sirs,

Attention ←	It is our honor to offer you one of our best selling items of microwave oven－MIK.
Interest ←	Since you are one of our most regular customers, we would like to share the best selling oven of the year－MIK with you. The oven has been popular in our area; we are sure it will sell well in your country.
Desire ←	With its unique design and attractive function, the oven takes much shorter time than ordinary ovens do. Enclosed please find our relative brochure and price list. You will note that we allow you a 10% discount for your promotion.
Action ←	We hope you will take full advantage of this exceptional offer.

Sincerely yours,

Enc.

信文中譯：

敬啟者：

很榮幸提供我們最暢銷的產品之一——微波爐 MIK。

因你們是我們最固定的顧客，我們想分享給你們本年度最暢銷的微波爐——MIK。此微波爐在此地區很暢銷；我們確信它也會在貴國暢銷。

由於具獨特設計及吸引人的功能，我們的微波爐花的時間比一般微波爐要少。隨函附上相關的小冊子及價目表。你們將會注意到我們允許你們 10% 折扣以利促銷。

希望你們能充分利用此難得的機會。

謹上

附件

Example 11.2　Offer of Stationery　文具提議

October 1, **20..**

Dear Sirs,

We have the pleasure of sending you by separate post some samples of B pen, a newly-developed item.

You may be aware from the price list enclosed that we can offer the prices from 5% to 10% lower than those of other brands. Besides the low prices, you may rest assured that our products are of the finest quality and of the best workmanship, as shown in our samples.

With these advantages, we feel sure you will find a ready sale for this excellent pen and look forward to receiving your order soon.

Sincerely yours,

Enc.

信文中譯：

敬啟者：

　　本公司很榮幸另函寄上一些新開發出來的 B 筆樣品。

　　從所附上的價目表貴公司會察覺到所報的價錢比其他廠牌要低5% 到 10%。除了低的價錢外，本公司保證產品品質最優，手藝最好，如樣品所示。

　　具此優點，本公司確信此筆可以迅速銷售，並盼速開訂單。

謹上

附件

Example 11.3　Offer of Super-Paint　超級油漆提議

September 2, **20..**

Dear Sirs,

You may be interested in the new "Super" paint we have just introduced to the market. A sample has been sent to you today by air parcel.

"Super" is the result of our long-term careful research. It is made from a special formula and has great superiority over other paints in luster and adhesion. It has the quality to expand without the cracks and therefore will give longer protection.

"Super" is available in twenty basic colors and as you can see from the enclosed price list, its prices are surprisingly low.

We will keep the prices open for only 21 days, so please make use of this special offer immediately.

Sincerely yours,

Enc.

信文中譯：

敬啟者：

　　貴公司可能對本公司剛上市的新「超級」油漆會有興趣。本日已由郵政包裹寄上一罐樣品。

　　「超級」是我們長期小心研究之結果。它是由特別的配方所製成；在光澤及附著力方面尤優於其他品牌。它具有延展性使不易龜裂，因此可提供較長的保護。

　　「超級」可提供 20 種基本顏色，且由附上的價目表可看出，它的價錢出奇地低。

　　此價錢僅有效 21 天，所以請立即利用此特別的報價。

謹上

附件

2. The Structure of a Sales Letter

The structure of a sales letter will include:

(1) an attractive opening　　　　　　　　吸引人的開場白

(2) an explanation of the products　　　　解釋產品

(3) stressing the selling points　　　　　加強賣點

(4) an effective close　　　　　　　　　有效結尾

3. The Appeals of a Sales Letter

Sales letters can appeal to the following points:

(1) self-esteem: dress, shoes, necktie, cars, etc.

(2) economy: gas stove, car, bicycle, air conditioner, etc.

(3) health: glasses, medicine, sporting goods, etc.

(4) safety: mobile phones, cars, helmet, etc.

(5) future prospects: employment center, schools, etc.

(6) caution: equipment, kitchenware, etc.

(7) convenience: furniture, electric items, etc.

4. The Elements of a Follow-up Letter

The elements of a follow-up letter are as follows:

(1) to refer to previous correspondence

(2) to show sincere interest in doing business again

(3) to assure advantages of the products and service

(4) to induce immediate action

Example 11.4.1　A Follow-up Letter (A)　追蹤函 (A)

August 23, **20..**

Dear Sirs,

Not having heard from you since we sent you our brochure of kitchenware, we are wondering whether you require further information before deciding to place an order.

Our kitchenware has space-saving advantages. It is specially designed for any kitchen where economy of space is important. The neat and tidy appearance along with its attractive display boxes appeal greatly to consumers.

As you may not have received our brochure and our price list, we are enclosing a new copy for you. Please take this special opportunity and place your order right away.

Sincerely yours,

Enc.

信文中譯：

敬啟者：

　　自從本公司寄給貴公司廚具的小冊子後都沒收到回音。不知是否貴公司在決定下訂單前，需要更進一步的資料。

　　本公司的廚具有節省空間的優點。它是為任何廚房裡需考量空間經濟者所設計的。整齊而清潔的外表連同吸引人的展示盒非常吸引消費者。

　　貴公司可能尚未收到本公司的小冊子及價目表，隨函附上一份新的資料。請利用此特別的機會馬上下一張訂單。

謹上

附件

Example 11.4.2   A Follow-up Letter (B)   追蹤函 (B)

September 1, **20..**

Dear Sirs,

Further to our letter of August 15, **20..** enclosing our catalogue and price list for our electric items, we are writing again to make sure if the reference submitted has reached your side and to know if you are interested in our products.

As our electric products have been in great demand in these few months, we are finding it hard to meet the demand for the market. In order to expand our market in your area, we are offering you special prices for orders received before the end of this month.

Please acknowledge receipt of our brochure submitted and take advantage of the special offer immediately.

Sincerely yours,

Enc.

信文中譯：

敬啟者：

　　追溯本公司 **20..** 年 8 月 15 日寫給貴公司的信；信上附本公司電器項目的目錄及價目表。本公司寫此信以瞭解貴公司是否收到所寄出之資料，並想知道貴公司是否對本公司的產品有興趣。

　　因本公司的電器產品在最近幾個月來，需求量一直很大，難以應付市場需求。為了擴展貴地區的市場，本公司對於本月底前收到的訂單，提供特別的價格。

　　收到所提供的資料請回函告知並速採用此特別的報價。

謹上

附件

✐ <u>Exercise</u>

A. Questions 問答題

1. What are the four elements of a sales letter?
2. What is the structure of a sales letter?
3. What are the appeals of a sales letter?
4. What are the elements of a follow-up letter?

B. Business Insight 實務探討

◆ 叫賣

促銷信函在某方面，就有如商場的叫賣。在叫賣時，除了要注意裝修好自己的門面招牌外，尤其要注意叫賣的技巧與產品的品質，也就是要強調自己的賣點 (selling point)。把自己公司或自己產品的特色表達出來，表達時就要依照推銷的要素：引興趣、促慾望、傳信心等來執行。例如：推銷成衣就要抓著客戶的心理，瞭解其需求背景，靈活運用叫賣的技巧——以「新款式」引興趣，「低價位」促購買慾，「品質優」傳信心，「市場大」而催其購買，達到叫賣購買的目標。

C. Grammar Practice 文法練習

★時態 (Tense)──完成進行式 (Perfect Progressive Tense)：

* 公式：have + been + Ving

---

1. 現在完成進行式：從過去一直到現在仍在進行。

   e.g. I have been trying to telephone Wayne before he leaves the office.

2. 過去完成進行式：從過去一直到過去某時仍在進行。

   e.g. I had been typing letters for two hours when you arrived.

3. 未來完成進行式：從過去某時開始到現在仍在進行，未來將繼續。

   e.g. By June, I shall have been living in New York for seven years.

Selection：選出最適當的答案

_____ 1. Jesse _____ talking about his sales campaign all the morning.

   (A) had been   (B) have been

   (C) has been   (D) will have been

_____ 2. By 8:00 tonight, George _____ driving for three hours on the freeway.

   (A) will have been   (B) has been

   (C) did   (D) had been

_____ 3. The Ranes, Inc. _____ doing business with us for over ten years.

   (A) had been   (B) did

   (C) will have been   (D) has been

_____ 4. The sales team _____ talking for one hour when the bell rang.

   (A) has been   (B) had been

   (C) did   (D) will have been

_____ 5. Roy _____ staying in Taiwan for one year by September.

   (A) has been   (B) had been

   (C) will have been   (D) will be

　　6. The designer ＿＿ waiting for two weeks before your samples arrived.

　　　(A) has been　　　　　　　　(B) had been

　　　(C) will have been　　　　　(D) will be

D. Pattern Practice 句型練習

★能夠：

---

can

be able to

be in a position to

---

1. 我們現在能夠提供廣大系列的鞋類產品。

_____

2. 我們相信我們能夠以最有競爭性的價格提供我們的手工藝品。

_____

E. Blank-filling 填充練習

Dear _____ ,

We take the _____ of _____ you one _____ our _____ selling _____ of _____ , which is newly _____ .

With its _____ design and _____ function, the _____ cooks _____ and takes much _____ time than ordinary _____ do.

Enclosed _____ find our _____ brochure and _____ list. You

will _____ that we _____ you a _____ discount for your _____.

We _____ you will _____ full _____ of this _____ offer.

Sincerely _____,

Enc.

As an exporter of microwave ovens in Taiwan, write a sales letter to promote your products.

No. 11 租稅：臺灣與他國的所得稅協定 (Tax Treaty)

所得稅協定定義

　　我國所得稅協定政策是為避免雙重課稅、防杜逃漏稅及增進實質關係而訂定。所簽訂之所得稅協定是遵照 OECD 稅約範本，並考量雙方之政治、財政、經濟及貿易狀況為基礎的。

所得稅協定簽訂國家

　　我國已與許多國家或地區簽訂所得稅協定 (含全面性租稅協定及海空互免單項協定)。其中有避免所得稅雙重課稅及防杜逃稅協定。

＊ 關於與我國簽訂所得稅協定國家，請參見附錄四及附錄五。

參考資料：

財政部全球資訊網

Chapter Twelve

Orders and Reply to Orders

訂單及回覆

1. The Styles of an Order

There are two styles of an order:

(1) Order Letter: it is clear and accurate.

(2) Order Form: it is convenient and efficient.

Example 12.1　　Order Letter　訂單信

December 12, **20..**

Dear Sirs,

We are much obliged for your letter of December 1, **20..** along with your catalogue, price list, and doll samples.

As we find your terms attractive and your quality satisfactory, we are pleased to place the following order.

Item No.	Descriptions	Quantity	Unit Price
			FOB Keelung
3456	Stuffed Toy	3,000	US$5.00
3345	-do-	2,000	US$5.10
3458	-do-	1,000	US$5.20

We require shipment of the above goods before the end of January and as soon as we receive your confirmation, we will open the relative L/C.

　　　　　　　　　Sincerely yours,

* do 為 ditto 之縮寫,代表同上。

信文中譯:

敬啟者:
　　感謝 **20..** 年 12 月 1 日來信目錄價目表,以及洋娃娃樣品。
　　因本公司認為你們的條款具吸引力且品質令人滿意,很高興下下列的訂單:

項目編號	規格	數量	單價
			FOB Keelung
3456	填充玩具	3,000	美金 5.00

| 3345 | 同上 | 2,000 | 美金 5.10 |
| 3458 | 同上 | 1,000 | 美金 5.20 |

　　我們需要這批貨在 1 月底前出貨，而一收到你們的確認書，會立即開出相關的信用狀。

謹上

Example 12.2　Order Letter with Order Form　訂單信附訂單

June 1, **20..**

Dear Sirs,

We thank you for your letter of May 29, **20..** and enclose our Order Form No. 411 for three of your hand tool items. Please make sure strict quality control is maintained.

Please acknowledge the order and confirm that you will be able to deliver the goods by the end of July **20...**

Sincerely yours,

Enc.

* 本文為回覆 Example 10.4

信文中譯：

敬啟者：

　　感謝貴公司 **20..** 年 5 月 29 日的來信。附上訂單 411 號訂三項你們的手工具項目。請保證維持嚴格的品質管制。

請確認此訂單並保證可在 7 月底前出貨。

謹上

附件

2. The Structure of an Order

(1) Thank the seller for supplying product information.

(2) Enclose the order form.

(3) Requirements: quality, delivery, etc.

(4) Please confirm the order soon.

WATSONS IMPORTS, INC.

×× Blue Drive

San Francisco, CA 90012

U.S.A.

June 1, **20..**

ORDER FORM

No. 411

Messrs.

PIZA CO., LTD.

No. ××, Sec. 3, Xinsheng S. Rd., Da'an Dist.,

Taipei, Taiwan

Dear Sirs,

We take pleasure in placing the following order with you:

Item No.	Descriptions	Unit	Quantity	Unit Price	Amount
					CIF San Francisco
CK-03	Hand tool set	set	1,000	US$6.15	US$6,150.00
CK-04	-do-	set	1,000	US$6.25	US$6,250.00
CK-05	-do-	set	1,000	US$5.34	US$5,340.00
					TOTAL: US$17,740.00

1) Payment: At sight draft under irrevocable L/C

2) Terms: CIF San Francisco

3) Packing: To be packed in standard export cartons

4) Shipment: Before end of July **20..**

5) Remarks: Samples of each quality to be airfreighted to us for approval
  before shipment

WATSONS IMPORTS, INC.

Bill Watson

Bill Watson

Manager

信文中譯：

訂單

411 號

敬啟者：

本公司很高興開出下列的訂單給貴公司：

項目編號	規格	單位	數量	單價	小計
					CIF 舊金山
CK-03	手工具	組	1,000	美金 6.15	美金 6,150.00
CK-04	同上	組	1,000	美金 6.25	美金 6,250.00
CK-05	同上	組	1,000	美金 5.34	美金 5,340.00
					總計美金 17,740.00

1. 付款：以即期匯票的不可撤銷信用狀
2. 條款：CIF 舊金山
3. 包裝：須用標準的外銷紙箱包裝
4. 出貨：在 **20..** 年 7 月底前
5. 附註：出貨前每樣品質的樣品必須空運運來以便作最後的核准

　　　　　華生進口公司

　　　　　比爾・華生

　　　　　經理

3. The Details of an Order

The details included in an order are:

(1) order number

(2) order date

(3) the buyer and the seller

(4) the commodity

(5) the specifications; the descriptions

(6) the quantity

(7) the unit

(8) the price terms

(9) the price

(10) the packing

(11) the terms of payment

(12) the delivery

4. Placing an Order

(1) When an order is placed, the buyer's obligations are as follows:

    1) to accept the goods supplied

    2) to pay for them

    3) to check the goods immediately

(2) When an order is confirmed, the seller's obligations are as follows:

    1) to deliver the goods exactly as ordered

    2) to guarantee the goods

Example 12.3　Placing an Order　下訂單

December 13, **20..**

Dear Sirs,

Thank you very much for your letter of December 1, **20..** enclosing your quotation, together with your power tool samples, which were sent under separate cover.

As we are expanding our market and have decided to include your range of power tools in our promotion items, we are enclosing our Order Form No. 413 for delivery before the end of February **20...** This is a trial order and if the shipment is found satisfactory, more orders will follow.

Please confirm the order so that we may open the relative L/C without delay.

Sincerely yours,

Enc.

信文中譯：

敬啟者：

　　非常感謝貴公司 **20..** 年 12 月 1 日的來信，附來報價單連同分開郵寄寄來的電力工具樣品。

　　因我們正擴展市場且已決定將貴公司的電力工具列為促銷項目，所以附上我們訂單 413 號，在 2 月底前交貨。這是一張試訂單，而如果出貨令人滿意的話，更多的訂單會隨後而至。

　　請確認此訂單，如此可立即開出相關的信用狀。

謹上

附件

WATSONS IMPORTS, INC.

×× Blue Drive

San Francisco, CA 90012

U.S.A.

December 13, **20..**

ORDER FORM

No. 413

Messrs.

PIZA CO., LTD.

No. ××, Sec. 3, Xinsheng S. Rd., Da'an Dist.,

Taipei, Taiwan

Dear Sirs,

We take pleasure in placing the following order with you:

Item No.	Descriptions	Unit	Quantity	Unit Price	Amount
				CIF San Francisco	
PT-01	Power tool set	set	100	US$10.00	US$1,000.00
PT-02	-do-	set	100	US$11.00	US$1,100.00
PT-03	-do-	set	100	US$12.00	US$1,200.00
				TOTAL:	US$3,300.00

1) Payment: At sight draft under irrevocable L/C

2) Terms: CIF San Francisco

3) Packing: To be packed in standard export cartons

4) Shipment: Before end of February **20..**

5) Remarks: Samples of each quality to be airfreighted to us for approval
before shipment

WATSONS IMPORTS, INC.

Albert Smith

Albert Smith

Manager

信文中譯：

訂單

號碼 413

敬啟者：

本公司很高興開出下列的訂單給貴公司：

項目編號	規格	單位	數量	單價	小計
					CIF 舊金山
PT-01	電力工具	組	100	美金 10.00	美金 1,000
PT-02	同上	組	100	美金 11.00	美金 1,100
PT-03	同上	組	100	美金 12.00	美金 1,200
				總計	美金 3,300

1. 付款：以即期匯票的不可撤銷信用狀
2. 條款：CIF 舊金山
3. 包裝：須用標準的外銷紙箱包裝
4. 出貨：在 **20..** 年 2 月底前
5. 附註：出貨前每樣品質的樣品必須空運運來以便作最後的核准

華生進口公司

艾伯特‧史密斯

經理

5. Confirming an Order

When an order is placed, it should be confirmed by the seller.

The structure of a sales confirmation letter is as follows:

⑴ Thank the buyer for the order.

(2) Confirm it by enclosing a sales confirmation.

(3) Guarantee the buyer's requirements to be fulfilled.

(4) Ask for early opening the L/C.

Example 12.4　Sales Confirmation　確認訂單

June 16, 20..

Dear Sirs,

Order No. 411

We thank you very much for your Order No. 411 for our hand tool items and are pleased to confirm the order as per our enclosed Sales Confirmation No. 003 for the amount of US$17,740.00.

We guarantee that we will spare no efforts in keeping strict quality control. You may rest assured of our best service and on-time delivery.

We would appreciate your early opening the covering L/C.

Sincerely yours,

Enc.

＊ 本文為回覆 Example 12.2

信文中譯：

敬啟者：

訂單 411 號

感謝貴公司的訂單 411 號，訂我們的手工具項目。

很高興確認訂單，如附上的銷售確認書 003 號所示，金額為美金 17,740.00。

保證會不遺餘力來維持嚴格品管。確信本公司最好的服務及準時交貨。

若能儘早開出相關的信用狀，本公司將感激不盡。

謹上

附件

PIZA CO., LTD.

No. ××, Sec. 3, Xinsheng S. Rd., Da'an Dist.,

Taipei, Taiwan

June 16, **20..**

SALES CONFIRMATION

No. 003

Messrs.

WATSONS IMPORTS, INC.

×× Blue Drive

San Francisco, CA 90012

U.S.A.

Dear Sirs,

We take pleasure in confirming your Order No. 411 dated June 1, **20..** as follows:

Item No.	Descriptions	Unit	Quantity	Unit Price	Amount
				CIF San Francisco	
CK-03	Hand tool set	set	1,000	US$6.15	US$6,150.00
CK-04	-do-	set	1,000	US$6.25	US$6,250.00
CK-05	-do-	set	1,000	US$5.34	US$5,340.00
				TOTAL: US$17,740.00	

SAY: US DOLLARS SEVENTEEN THOUSAND SEVEN HUNDRED AND FORTY ONLY.

1) Payment: At sight draft under irrevocable L/C

2) Terms: CIF San Francisco

3) Packing: To be packed in standard export cartons

4) Shipment: Before end of July **20..**

5) Remarks: Samples of each quality to be airfreighted to the buyer for approval before shipment

PIZA CO., LTD.

William Wang

William Wang

Manager

* Sales Confirmation (銷售確認書，簡寫為 S/C) 實務上又稱為 Proforma Invoice (預估發票或形式發票，簡寫為 P/I)。

信文中譯：

銷售確認書
003 號

敬啟者：

　　本公司很樂意確認貴公司訂單 411 號，日期為 **20..** 年 6 月 1 日，如下：

項目編號	規格	單位	數量	單價	小計
					CIF 舊金山
CK-03	手工具	組	1,000	美金 6.15	美金 6,150.00
CK-04	同上	組	1,000	美金 6.25	美金 6,250.00
CK-05	同上	組	1,000	美金 5.34	美金 5,340.00
				總計	美金 17,740.00

合計：美金壹萬柒仟柒佰肆拾元整。

　　1. 付款：以即期匯票的不可撤銷信用狀
　　2. 條款：CIF 舊金山
　　3. 包裝：須用標準外銷紙箱包裝
　　4. 出貨：在 **20..** 年 7 月底前
　　5. 附註：出貨前每樣品質的樣品必須空運給買方以便作最後的核准

　　　　　　　　皮賽有限公司
　　　　　　　　王威廉
　　　　　　　　經理

6. Declining an Order

A seller will decline an order on the following conditions:

(1) when he is not satisfied with the buyer's terms

(2) when the goods are not available

(3) when the buyer's credit is doubtful

The plan of the letter is as follows:

(1) regret not being able to supply the goods ordered

(2) propose an alternative product if one is available

(3) hope to do business in the future

Example 12.5　Declining the Order　拒絕訂單

January 20, **20..**

Dear Sirs,

Bobby Handbags

We are very glad to receive your order of January 10, **20..** for 1,000 sets of our "Bobby" handbags, but since you make delivery before February 20, **20..** a firm condition, we deeply regret that we can't supply you with the goods before the stipulated time.

This is due to the overall shortage of leather material here, which has nearly suspended our production line. To our knowledge, the supply of material will not continue until the end of March. If you could wait till then, we would be glad to supply the goods ordered.

We regret the inconvenience caused and hope to have any opportunity to serve you.

Sincerely yours,

信文中譯：

敬啟者：

保比手提袋

很高興收到你們 **20..** 年 1 月 10 日訂單，訂 1,000 個我們「保比」手提袋，但因貴公司列 **20..** 年 2 月 20 日前出貨訂為主要條款，本公司遺憾無法在規定的時間前供應貨品。

由於全面性的皮革原料短缺，幾乎使本公司的生產線中斷。據所知，原料供應要到 3 月底才會持續。如果貴公司能等至那時，本公司將很樂意供應訂貨。

遺憾引起不便，並期望有機會為貴公司服務。

謹上

7. Cancelling an Order

A buyer is legally entitled to cancel the order on the following conditions:

(1) if the order is not confirmed by the seller

(2) if wrong goods are delivered

(3) if the goods are not delivered by the agreed time

(4) if the quantity delivered does not match that ordered

(5) if the goods arrive damaged

Example 12.6　Cancelling the Order　取消訂單

May 25, **20..**

Dear Sirs,

Order No. CK-023

We are referring to our Order No. CK-023, L/C No. HOB-1234 for 10,000 pieces of umbrella, which you promised to ship before the end of April.

As we have received no information regarding the delivery of the order from you, nor have we heard any explanation. We are supposed to deliver the goods ordered to our customers in these few days, but we can't. Your non-delivery has caused us much inconvenience.

Such being the case, we cannot choose but cancel the order and will ask you to compensate for what we lose.

Sincerely yours,

信文中譯：

敬啟者：

訂單 CK-023 號

追溯本公司訂單 CK-023 號，信用狀 HOB-1234 號，關於 10,000 支雨傘；此批貨貴公司應允在 4 月底前出貨。

因未收到關於訂單出貨的消息，也沒有得到任何解釋。近日本公司應交貨給顧客，但交不出。貴公司未交貨已引起本公司諸多不便。

情況既然如此，本公司毫無選擇的餘地，只得取消訂單並要求賠償損失。

謹上

8. Supplier's Counter-offer

If a seller receives an order which he can't meet for some reasons, he may take one of the following steps:

(1) he may send a substitute

(2) he may make a counter-offer

(3) he may regretfully decline the order

Example 12.7　Seller Sends a Substitute　賣方送來替代品

March 23, **20..**

Dear Sirs,

Thank you very much for your letter of March 15, **20..** enclosing your Purchase Order No. 567 for ten of our textile items.

We are very glad to confirm the order and are enclosing our Sales Confirmation No. TX-012 for the items ordered. As you stress immediate delivery being an urgent matter and as we don't have Item No. WD-01 women's dresses in stock, we will send you WD-02 instead. We are sending you a sample of WD-02 by express for your final approval.

Please confirm your comment on this.

As all the other items are available and are now ready for shipment, please confirm acceptance of the above item and also open the related L/C soon.

Sincerely yours,

Enc.

信文中譯：

敬啟者：

　　感謝貴公司 **20..** 年 3 月 15 日來信附來訂單 567 號，訂 10 項我們的紡織品。

　　本公司樂意確認此訂單並附上銷售確認書 TX-012 號，包括所訂的項目。因貴公司強調立即交貨的重要性，且因沒有 WD-01 女裝服飾存貨，本公司將寄上 WD-02 以為替代。另用快遞寄上一件 WD-02 樣品以供最後核准。請確認對此事的高見。

　　因所訂其他項目皆備妥，且正準備出貨，請確認接受上述項目並立即開出相關信用狀。

謹上

附件

9. Seller's Follow-up Letter

Example 12.8　A Seller's Follow-up Letter　賣方的追蹤函

February 12, **20..**

Dear Sirs,

It has been over two months since you placed your last order in December **20..** and we are still waiting for your order for this season.

Our electronic products have been selling well. This is as a result of our paying attention to strict quality control and improving our service to our customers. We trust our new products will be of interest to you and enclose our latest catalogue and price list of our new items for your reference.

We expect to hear from you in a very short time.

Sincerely yours,

Enc.

信文中譯：

敬啟者：

　　自從貴公司在 **20..** 年 12 月下上一張訂單後已經有二個月了。本公司仍等候貴公司本季的訂單。

　　本公司的電子產品一直很暢銷。此因注重嚴格品管及提升顧客服務所致。相信貴公司會對新產品有興趣，附上最近新產品目錄及價目表，以供參考。

祈盼速回音。

謹上

附件

 Exercise

1. What are the two styles of an order?

2. What are the details of an order?

3. What are the obligations of a buyer when an order is placed?

4. What are the obligations of a seller when an order is confirmed?

5. What should a seller do after receiving an order from the buyer?

6. On what conditions will a seller decline an order?

7. On what conditions will a buyer cancel an order?

8. What are the supplier's counter-offers?

9. When does a seller write a follow-up letter?

Business Insight 實務探討

◆ 成交了！

　　成交即是在完成一件交易，交易完成時買方即是下訂單，又稱下單。下訂單時，應該把所需要的產品名稱、規格、數量、包裝、保險等重要明細一併列入。賣方在收到訂單後必須要與工廠再連絡，看所訂的貨是否可以準時出貨。如果可以時，必須向買方確認，表示可以接單，並寄出銷售確認書以為確認；買方再依此銷售確認書，向開狀銀行開出信用狀。

C. Grammar Practice 文法練習

★語態 (Voice)——被動語態 (Passive Voice)：

＊ 公式：be + p.p. + (by)

---

1. 簡單式　be + p.p.
2. 完成式　have + been + p.p.
3. 進行式　be being + p.p.
4. 完成進行式　沒有被動

   e.g. 主動　Judy manages the store.

      被動　The store is managed by Judy.

Selection：選出最適當的答案

_____ 1. The material _____ by W&D Company.

   (A) is supplied　　(B) supplies　　(C) be supplied　　(D) supplying

_____ 2. The shipping samples you mentioned _____ to you today.

   (A) are being sent　　　　　(B) were sending

   (C) are sending　　　　　　(D) was sent

_____ 3. We _____ that his quality is good and dependable.

   (A) were told　　　　　　　(B) will be told

   (C) have been told　　　　　(D) told

_____ 4. Your letter of June 25 _____ today with our careful attention.

   (A) has received　　　　　　(B) received

   (C) is receiving　　　　　　(D) has been received

_____ 5. An order for 10,000 pairs of shoes _____ right away.

   (A) will place　　　　　　　(B) will be placed

   (C) will be placing　　　　　(D) placed

D. Pattern Practice 句型練習

★由於：

> Due to + N., S. + V.
>
> Owing to + N., S. + V.
>
> Because of + N., S. +V.
>
> Because + S. + V., S. + V.

1. 由於我們使用大量生產，我們才能夠降低成本。

　　_____

2. 由於訂單大量湧入，我們請求你們早日下訂單。

　　_____

E. Blank-filling 填充練習

Dear _____ ,

We _____ you _____ your letter _____ May 29, **20..** and _____ our Order _____ No. 411 _____ three of your _____ tool items. Please _____ sure _____ quality _____ is _____ in _____ up the _____ .

Please _____ the _____ and _____ that you will _____ able to _____ by the _____ of _____ **20...**

　　　　　　　　_____ yours,

F. Letter-writing 書信寫作

You are an exporter of textiles. Write your letter to place an order.

No. 12 關務：A. 關稅 (Customs)
B. 稅則分類 (Tariff Classification)
C. 如何查關稅？

A. 關稅 (Customs)

　　關稅乃外國產品貨物經過陸海空海關邊境時，政府對其課徵之稅賦。政府可對進口或出口貨課徵關稅，以作為國家財政的歲收、保護國內產業、調節國內物價及救濟貿易失衡等，例如：課徵反傾銷稅。目前以課徵進口關稅為主。關稅依課徵方式可分為：

1. 從價稅 (ad valorem tariff)：

　是以進口產品價格一定百分比課徵關稅；

2. 從量稅 (specific tariff)：

　是以進口產品之單位或數量為計算基礎而課徵一定數額之關稅；

3. 混合稅 (mixed tariff)：

　是以從價和從量混合課徵關稅。

B. 稅則分類 (Tariff Classification)

　　指將世界上所有作為商品之有形物質及無形資產財 (如電腦軟體)，加以有系統的分門別類與編號，俾作為各國進出口統一採納課關稅之依據。稅則分類編號如下列表格，以鮮蘋果為例：

0	8	0	8	1	0	0	0	0	0	2
1	2	3	4	5	6	7	8	9	10	11
﹂章﹁		﹂節﹁		﹂目﹁		﹂款﹁		﹂項﹁		檢查號（電腦作業）
Chapter		Heading		Sub-heading		Division（海關課稅之用）		Item（統計號別之用）		
1. HS 號別 (前面 6 碼)										
2. 中華民國海關稅則號別 (8 碼)										
3. 中華民國商品標準號列 (10 碼)										

1. HS 號別 (調和商品分類制度，國際商品統一分類制度)：

　The Harmonized Commodity Description and Coding System

2. 中華民國海關稅則號別：

　Customs Tariff of the Republic of China

3. 中華民國商品標準號列：

　Standard Classification of Commodity of The Republic of China Code

C. 如何查關稅？

來源：關港貿單一窗口網站

方法：

1. 內容查詢

2. 分章查詢 (含歷程)

3. 稅則分章查詢

程序：

1. 上網輸入 (key in)「稅則稅率綜合查詢作業」網站。

2. 輸入前項 B 範例稅則分類的中文貨名 「鮮蘋果」 或稅則號別「08081000002」。

3. 即可看到「稅則稅率查詢」內容。

4. 再按「稅則號別 (08081000002)」即可得知關稅稅率。

參考資料：

黃立、李貴英、林彩瑜。《WTO 國際貿易法論》。臺北市：元照。

施智傑。《海關解讀》。臺北市：商鼎。

關港貿單一窗口網站

Chapter Thirteen

Sales Contract

銷售契約

Outline

1. To State the Parties Who Sign the Contract　　簽約雙方
2. To List the Details of the Goods, such as Commodity,　產品細節
   Quality Standard, Quantity, etc.
3. To Regulate the Shipment Date　　交貨日期
4. To Agree to the Terms of Payment　　付款條件
5. To State the Responsibility of Insurance　　保險責任
6. To Mention the Methods for Settling Claims　　索賠處理
7. To Include Arbitration and the Governing Laws　　仲裁及法源

SALES CONTRACT

This CONTRACT is made this ＿＿＿＿ day of ＿＿＿＿, **20..** by PIZA CO., LTD. (hereinafter referred to as SELLERS), whose registered office is situated at ＿＿＿＿, who agree to sell, and WATSONS IMPORTS, INC. (hereinafter referred to as BUYERS), whose registered office is situated at ＿＿＿＿, who agree to buy the following goods on the terms and conditions set forth below:

1. COMMODITY: Men's cotton underwear

2. QUALITY: 100% cotton

         New style

         Size: Medium and small

         Weight: Light

         Color: White

3. QUANTITY: 10,000 (ten thousand) each size

4. UNIT PRICE: US$4.00 per piece CIF San Francisco

Total amount: US$80,000 (Say US Dollars Eighty Thousand Only) CIF San Francisco

5. PACKING: One piece in a polybag, 100 pieces to a carton.

6. SHIPPING MARK:

SAN FRANCISCO

NO. 1-UP

7. SHIPMENT: To be shipped on or before December 31, **20..** subject to acceptable L/C reaches SELLERS before the end of October **20..** and partial shipments allowed; transhipment allowed.

8. PAYMENT: By a prime banker's irrevocable sight L/C in SELLERS' favor for 100% value of goods.

9. INSURANCE: SELLERS shall arrange marine insurance covering

ICC (B) plus TPND and war risk for 110% of the invoice value and provide for claim, if any, payable in San Francisco in US currency.

10. INSPECTION: Goods are to be inspected by an independent inspector and whose certificate of inspection of quality and quantity is to be final.

11. FLUCTUATIONS OF FREIGHT AND INSURANCE PREMIUM: The prices mentioned herein are all based upon the current rate of freight and/or war and insurance premium. Any increase in freight and/or insurance premium rate at the time of shipment is to be for BUYERS' risks and account.

12. CLAIMS: In the event of any claim arising in respect of any shipment, notice of intention to claim should be given in writing to SELLERS promptly after arrival of the goods at the port of discharge and opportunity must be given to SELLERS for investigation. Failing to give such prior written notification and opportunity of investigation within twenty-one (21) days after the arrival of the carrying vessel at the port of discharge, no claim shall be allowed.

13. FORCE MAJEURE: Non-delivery of all or any part of the merchandise caused by war, blockade, revolution, insurrection, civil commotion, riots, mobilization, strikes, lockouts, act of God, severe weather, plague or other epidemic, destruction of goods by fire or flood, obstruction of loading by storm or typhoon at the port of delivery, or any other cause beyond SELLERS' control before shipment shall operate as a cancellation of the sale to the extent of such non-delivery.

14. ARBITRATION: Any disputes, controversies or differences which may arise between the parties, out of, or in relation to or in connection with this contract may be referred to arbitration. Such arbitration shall take place in Taipei, Taiwan and shall be held and shall proceed in accordance with the government arbitration regulations.

15. PROPER LAW: The formation, validity, construction, and the performance of this contract are governed by the laws of the Republic of China.

IN WITNESS WHEREOF, the parties have executed the contract in duplicate by their duly authorized representative as on the date first above written.

BUYER	SELLER
WATSONS IMPORTS, INC.	PIZA CO., LTD.
_____	_____
Manager	Manager

信文中譯：

銷售契約

　　本契約由皮賽有限公司——總公司設於……(以下簡稱賣方)，與華生進口公司——總公司設於……(以下簡稱買方) 於 **20..** 年月日訂定，雙方同意按下列條件買賣下列之貨：

1. 商品：男用棉內衣

2. 品質：100% 棉

　　　新款

　　　尺寸：中及小

　　　重量：輕

　　　顏色：白色

3. 數量：每種尺寸各 10,000 件

4. 單價：每件美金 4.00 CIF 舊金山；總金額美金 80,000 CIF 舊金山

5. 包裝：每一件裝一塑膠袋；100 件裝一外銷紙箱

6. 裝船麥頭：

SAN FRANCISCO

NO. 1-UP

7. 裝運：**20..** 年 12 月 31 日前裝運，但以可接受之信用狀於 **20..** 年 10 月底前開到賣方為條件，容許分批裝運及轉運。

8. 付款：憑一流銀行的不可撤銷的即期信用狀付款，信用狀以賣方為受益人，並照貨物金額百分之百開發。

9. 保險：賣方應洽保水險，投保 B 款險並加保遺失竊盜險及兵險，保險金額按發票金額的 110% 投保，並須規定如有索賠應在舊金山以美金支付。

10. 檢驗：貨物須經一家獨立公證行檢驗，其出具品質及數量檢驗證明書應為最後認定標準。

11. 運費和保險費的變動：契約中所列價格全是以目前運費率及／或兵險和水險保險費率為準。裝運時運費率及／或保險費率如有增加，應歸由買方負擔。

12. 索賠：對於貨物有索賠情事發生時，請求索賠通知必須於貨物抵達卸貨港後即刻以書面提示賣方，並且必須給賣方有調查的機會，倘若運送船隻到達卸貨港後 21 天內沒有提示這項預先的書面通

知以及提供調查機會,則索賠應不予受理。

13. 不可抗力:因戰爭、封鎖、革命、暴動、民變、民眾騷擾、動員、罷工、停工、天災、惡劣氣候、疫病或其他傳染病、火災水災損壞貨物、暴風雨或颱風在交貨港阻礙裝船,或在裝船前有賣方無法控制之事故發生,而致貨物的全部或一部分未能交貨,這未交貨部分的契約應予取消。

14. 仲裁:有關本契約買賣雙方間所引起的任何糾紛、爭議或歧見,可付諸仲裁。這項仲裁應於臺灣臺北舉行,並應遵照政府仲裁法規處理及進行。

15. 適用法:本契約的成立,效力,解釋以及履行均受中華民國法律管轄。

　　本契約書一式兩份業經雙方法定代理人訂定,於前文日期簽署。

買方　　　　　　　　　　　　　　　賣方
華生進口公司　　　　　　　　　　　皮賽有限公司
經理　　　　　　　　　　　　　　　經理

✎ Exercise

A. Questions 問答題

1. What are the essential points of a sales contract?

2. What are the two parties concerned in this contract?

3. What is the commodity the buyers intend to buy?

4. What are the specifications of the commodity?

5. What is the quantity?

6. What are the terms of trade?

7. In case of a claim, what should be given to sellers?

B. Business Insight 實務探討

◆ 訂約要慎重

買賣契約的訂定是需要慎重處理的，一般是較大筆的買賣才要正式簽約。雖然訂貨買賣只需下訂單，並寄發銷售確認書確認妥當，或經過對簽後，生意即已成交。嚴格來說，這也算一種契約，但較大筆的交易或公家機關的進出口買賣，則較慎重，需要正式的簽約手續儀式。所以，契約在初擬階段時，就必須慎重，審核其條文，例如交貨、運送、付款等重要細節，皆不可忽視。

C. Grammar Practice 文法練習

★語氣 (Mood)──假設語氣 (Subjunctive Mood)：

一般常用的有三種：

---

1. 可能的未來：

   e.g. If you work hard, you will succeed.

2. 與現在事實相反：

   e.g. If I had a car, I would be happy.

3. 與過去事實相反：

   e.g. If I had been there, I would have helped you.

Selection：選出最適當的答案

_____ 1. If Bill _____ for the position, he would be hired in an instant.

　　(A) applied　　　　　　　　　(B) would apply

　　(C) had applied　　　　　　　(D) applies

_____ 2. _____ you not reminded me, I would have forgotten the issue.

　　(A) Did　　　　(B) Should　　　　(C) If　　　　(D) Had

_____ 3. Paul _____ to the meeting if he had had time.

    (A) comes   (B) would have come

    (C) came   (D) is coming

_____ 4. If it _____ , you will get wet.

    (A) rained   (B) rains

    (C) had rained   (D) should have rained

_____ 5. If he _____ now, he will catch the airplane.

    (A) started   (B) starts

    (C) had started   (D) should start

_____ 6. If Jack _____ then, he would have caught the airplane.

    (A) set off   (B) has set off

    (C) had set off   (D) should set off

_____ 7. It's time we _____ the store. It's already 10 o'clock.

    (A) had closed   (B) closed   (C) have closed   (D) closing

_____ 8. You didn't ask me; otherwise, I would _____ you the whole story.

    (A) have told   (B) tell

    (C) have been told   (D) had told

_____ 9. Anyone is welcome _____ they act respectfully during the meeting.

    (A) provide that   (B) provided if

    (C) providing that   (D) providing if

D. Pattern Practice 句型練習

★確認：

> We confirm...
>
> We make sure...
>
> Please confirm...
>
> Please make sure...

1. 請確認你們最好的價格，並用航空寄來玩具樣品。

_____

2. 請確認你們到臺北的時間，我們可以到機場接你們。

_____

No. 13 關務：非關稅貿易障礙
(Non-customs Trade Barriers)

　　非關稅貿易障礙，即通常採取行政手段或數量限制的方式，但較易為專斷使用，例如：對進口貨另課國內稅捐、數量限制和防衛協定 (safeguard agreement) 等。數量限制為最普遍之防衛協定策略。數量限制乃是各國用以支解國際貿易之工具，嚴重侵蝕了最惠國待遇原則，使各國政府在貿易政策上可運用比關稅更大的取捨權限。因為關稅的調整，必須經過複雜而漫長之修法途徑才有可能，但數量限制有行政命令即可。

參考資料：

黃立、李貴英、林彩瑜。《WTO 國際貿易法論》。臺北市：元照。

NOTE

Chapter Fourteen

Letter of Credit Transaction

信用狀交易

 **Outline**

1. What is a L/C?

A L/C means a letter of credit. It represents the credit of the importer. It is a written document opened at the request of importer and sent to the exporter permitting the latter to be able to obtain payment when the conditions specified are fulfilled.

信用狀代表進口商的信用，它是書面的文件，應進口商之請而開，允許出口商在完成它所規定的條款即可獲得付款。

2. The Parties Concerned in a L/C Transaction

The parties concerned in a L/C transaction are:

(1) Applicant for Credit (開狀申請人)　　即 buyer (買方)，又稱 accountee (被記帳人)

(2) Opening bank (開狀銀行)　　又稱 issuing bank

(3) Beneficiary (受益人)　　即 Seller (賣方)

(4) Advising bank (通知銀行)　　轉知信用狀的銀行

(5) Negotiating bank (押匯銀行)　　讓出口商押匯的銀行，一般為出口商的往來銀行

(6) Confirming bank (保兌銀行)　　應開狀銀行之請，就所開信用狀承擔保證兌現之銀行

(7) Paying bank (付款銀行)　　即信用狀規定匯票的被發票人可能是開狀銀行或其他銀行

(8) Reimbursing bank (歸償銀行)　　即對押匯銀行償還其款項之銀行

3. The Kinds of L/C

信用狀分類如下：

⑴ 依可否片面撤銷分

1) Revocable L/C	可撤銷信用狀	在受益人未押匯以前，買方可隨時片面予以修改或撤銷
2) Irrevocable L/C	不可撤銷信用狀	不可任意撤銷

⑵ 依有無保兌分

1) Confirmed L/C	保兌信用狀	經開狀銀行以外的另一財力雄厚銀行保證兌現
2) Unconfirmed L/C	未保兌信用狀	未經保兌

⑶ 依匯票期限分

1) Sight L/C	即期信用狀	受益人憑即期匯票 (Sight Draft) 押匯取款
2) Usance L/C	遠期信用狀	憑遠期匯票 (Usance Draft) 取款

⑷ 依可否押匯分

1) Negotiation L/C	可押匯信用狀	可向付款銀行以外的銀行請求押匯
2) Straight L/C	直接信用狀	信用狀只能向信用狀規定的銀行押匯

⑸ 依是否須附單據分

1) Clean L/C	光票信用狀	押匯時，不必附上單據

2) Documentary L/C	跟單信用狀	須附單據

(6) 依可否轉讓分

1) Transferable L/C	可轉讓信用狀	可轉給他人使用
2) Non-transferable L/C	不可轉讓信用狀	不可轉讓

(7) 依主從分

1) Master L/C	主信用狀	進口商開給出口商的信用狀
2) Back-to-Back L/C	背對背信用狀	出口商依主信用狀開給工廠或供應商的信用狀，又稱 Local L/C

(8) 依用途分

1) Traveler's L/C	旅行信用狀	供旅行使用
2) Commercial L/C	商業信用狀	供貿易商業用

(9) Standby L/C	擔保信用狀	供擔保用

(10) Red Clause L/C	紅條款信用狀	受益人在未押匯前即可預支款項

4. L/C Examples

＊ L/C 範例 1：Sunshine National Bank

Irrevocable
Documentary
Letter of Credit

Sunshine National Bank

International Banking Department
P. O. Box XX
Seattle, Washington 98124

THIS IS A CONFIRMATION OF THE CREDIT OPENED BY TELEX UNDER EVEN DATE. [X]	DATE OF ISSUE 19 June 20..	CREDIT NO. OF ISSUING BANK 55046	CREDIT NO. OF ADVISING BANK

ADVISING BANK:

MAIL TO

Star Commercial Bank
No. XX, Fuxing North Road,
Zhongshan Dist.,
Taipei, Taiwan

ACCOUNT PARTY:

Watsons Imports, Inc.
XX Blue Drive, San Francisco, CA 90012
U.S.A

BENEFICIARY:

PIZA CO., LTD.
No. XX, Sec. 3, Xinsheng S. Rd.,
Da'an Dist., Taipei, Taiwan

AMOUNT: US$4,689.60

(FOUR THOUSAND SIX HUNDRED EIGHTY NINE AND 60/100 US DOLLARS)

DEAR SIRS: WE HEREBY ISSUE THIS LETTER OF CREDIT IN YOUR FAVOR, WHICH IS AVAILABLE AGAINST YOUR DRAFT AT ___sight___ DRAWN ON ___Sunshine National Bank, Seattle, Washington___ BEARING THE CLAUSE: "DRAWN UNDER THE SUNSHINE NATIONAL BANK DOCUMENTARY CREDIT NUMBER ___55046___", ACCOMPANIED BY THE FOLLOWING DOCUMENTS:

[X] SIGNED COMMERCIAL INVOICE IN ___4___ COPIES

[X] SPECIAL CUSTOMS INVOICE

[X] FULL SET OF CLEAN "ON BOARD" OCEAN BILLS OF LADING
ISSUED TO THE ORDER OF [X] SUNSHINE NATIONAL BANK [ ] SHIPPER, BLANK ENDORSED.
NOTIFY: G&A Customs Brokers, XX Parkroad, Seattle, WA 98101, U.S.A.
Attn: Melisa

[ ] ORIGINAL AIR WAYBILL MARKED FREIGHT _____ CONSIGNED TO
NOTIFY:

[ ] INSURANCE POLICY OR CERTIFICATE COVERING WAR RISKS

[ ] CERTIFICATE OF INSPECTION IN DUPLICATE

[X] CERTIFICATE OF ORIGIN

[ ] CERTIFICATE OF WEIGHT AND MEASUREMENT IN DUPLICATE

[X] PACKING LIST IN TRIPLICATE

[X] Beneficiary's certificate that all cartons, containers, and items are marked MADE IN
EVIDENCING SHIPMENT OF: /TAIWAN as per US Customs Regulations and that the Packing and Marking /requirements of the Federal Trade Commission have been complied with

Adult Games Of Taiwan Origin as per Order 21180

FOB VESSEL TAIWAN PORT

SHIPMENT FROM: Taiwan Port		PARTIAL SHIPMENTS	TRANSHIPMENTS
SHIPMENT TO: Seattle, Washington		Not Allowed	Not Allowed
SHIPMENT MUST BE EFFECTED NOT LATER THAN: 17 August 20..	EXPIRY DATE FOR NEGOTIATION IN THE COUNTRY OF BENEFICIARY:		17 August 20..

SPECIAL CONDITIONS:

Ship via American Rapid Lines

DRAFTS AND DOCUMENTS MUST BE PRESENTED FOR NEGOTIATION WITHIN 10 DAYS FROM DATE OF SHIPMENT.

WE HEREBY ENGAGE WITH DRAWERS AND/OR BONA FIDE HOLDERS THAT DRAFTS DRAWN AND NEGOTIATED IN CONFORMITY WITH THE TERMS OF THIS CREDIT WILL BE DULY HONORED ON PRESENTATION AND THAT DRAFTS ACCEPTED WITHIN THE TERMS OF THIS CREDIT WILL BE DULY HONORED AT MATURITY. THE AMOUNT OF EACH DRAFT (OR TRANSFER, IF TRANSFERRED) MUST BE ENDORSED ON THE REVERSE HEREOF BY THE NEGOTIATING (TRANSFERRING) BANK. THE ADVISING BANK IS REQUESTED TO NOTIFY THE BENEFICIARY WITHOUT ADDING THEIR CONFIRMATION.
THE AMOUNT OF EACH DRAFT MUST BE ENDORSED ON THE REVERSE OF THIS CREDIT BY THE NEGOTIATING BANK.

VERY TRULY,

Foster

AUTHORIZED SIGNATURE

INDICATIONS OF ADVISING BANK

THIS IS AN IRREVOCABLE LETTER OF CREDIT OF THE ABOVE MENTIONED ISSUING BANK AND IS TRANSMITTED TO YOU WITHOUT ANY RESPONSIBILITY OR ENGAGEMENT ON OUR PART

PLACE, DATE, NAME, AND SIGNATURE OF ADVISING BANK

FORM M44 REV. 10-73

＊L/C 範例 2：Australia Banking Group Limited

EAST MELBOURNE AREA
P.O. BOX XX, ABBOTSFORD
VICTORIA. AUSTRALIA.

Date ....30th MAY 20...

This credit is forwarded to the Advising Bank
by airmail.

IRREVOCABLE DOCUMENTARY CREDIT Advising Bank	Issuing Bank's No. 6926/3298	Advising Bank's No.

Star Commercial Bank
No. XX, Fuxing North Road,
Zhongshan Dist.,
Taipei, Taiwan

Applicant

Watsons Imports, Inc.
XX Wall Street
Fitzroy 3065
Victoria
Australia

Amount

Beneficiar

R. HANSE CO., LTD.
No. XX, Lane 519, Sec. 3,
Neihu Road, Neihu Dist.,
Taipei, Taiwan

US$3,917.12 THREE THOUSAND NINE
HUNDRED AND SEVENTEEN DOLLARS
AND TWELVE CENTS. UNITED STATES
CURRENCY.

Expiry Date 15 AUGUST 20.. in the
Country of the Beneficiary

Dear Sirs,

　　We hereby inform you we have opened our irrevocable credit in your favour available for payment/acceptance of
your draft(s) at **60 DAYS** sight drawn on AUSTRALIA BANKING GROUP LTD.
LOS AGENCY, **XX** WILSHIRE BOULEVARD, LOS ANGELES, U.S.A.
accompanied by the following documents (at least in duplicate unless otherwise specified)

Invoice(s)
Full set of clean "on board" ocean bills of lading made out to shipper's order and endorsed in blank.
* Insurance Buyer's care

Evidencing Shipment of GAME SETS AS PER SALES CONFIRMATION R-5002 AS PER
ORDER NO 29521.

Latest Shipment Date 15 August 20..

From	TAIWAN (F.O.B.)	Partial Shipments	ALLOWED
To	MELBOURNE AUSTRALIA	Transhipment	NOT ALLOWED

Special Conditions

We undertake that drafts drawn and presented in conformity with the
terms of this credit will be duly honoured.
INSTRUCTIONS TO THE NEGOTIATING BANK
The amount of each drawing must be endorsed on the reverse hereof.
Drafts are to be forwarded to the drawee bank together with the
reimbursement claim.
All documents are to be despatched in two sets by consecutive airmails
to the issuing branch.

Remarks, Date and Signature of Advising Bank

Yours faithfully,

(Authorised Signature (No. 2462)

Countersignature

*L/C 範例 3：Global Shine Bank

GLOBAL SHINE BANK, BARCELONA BRANCH

×× AMOUR AVE, BARCELONA, SPAIN

ADV. BANK:　COMMON BANK, TAIPEI BRANCH

ISSUE OF A DOCUMENTARY CREDIT

SEQUENCE OF TOTAL1/1

FORM OF DOCUMENTARY CREDIT　　　　IRREVOCABLE

DOCUMENTARY CREDIT NUMBER　　　　RS-CH2083

DATE OF ISSUE　　　　　　　　　　**20..0817**

DATE AND PLACE OF EXPIRY　　　　　**20..0930**

APPLICANT:

RANES INDUSTRIAL CO., LTD.

×× OAK STONE STREET,

BARCELONA, SPAIN

BENEFICIARY:

THIRD TRADING COMPANY

No. ××, PARK ROAD, NEIHU DIST.,

TAIPEI, TAIWAN

CURRENCY CODE, AMOUNT　　　　　　US$240,519.00

AVAILABLE WITH...BY...　ANY　BANK　IN　TAIWAN　BY NEGOTIATION

DRAFTS AT　30 DAYS AFTER　B/L　DATE

DRAWEE　ISSUIG BANK FOR FULL INVOICE VALUE

PARTIAL SHIPMENTS　　　　　　　　　PROHIBITED

TRANSSHIPMENT　　　　　　　　　　　PROHIBITED

LOADING ON BOARD/DISPATCH/TAKING IN CHARGE AT/FROM　KEELUNG

FOR TRANSPORTATION TO　　　　　　　BARCELONA

LATEST DATE OF SHIPMENT　　　　　　**20..0920**

DESCRIPTION OF GOODS AND/OR SERVICES

WOODEN TOYS MW5006: 4160pcs MW5421: 3750pcs

AS PER SALES CONFIRMATION NO.: TCH-GB00259

SHIPPING MARK: RANES (IN DIAMOND)/BARCELONA/NO. 1-UP

DOCUMENTS REQUIRED

1. SIGNED COMMERCIAL INVOICE IN TRIPLICATE

2. SIGNED PACKING LIST IN DUPLICATE

3. INSURANCE POLICY OR CERTIFICATE IN DUPLICATE, ENDORSED IN BLANK, FOR 110 PERCENT OF FULL CIF VALUE, COVERING ALL RISKS AND WAR RISKS OF I.C.C. DATED 1/1/**20..** SHOWING CLAIMS, IF ANY, ARE TO BE PAID AT DESTINATION IN THE SAME CURRENCY OF THE DRAFT

4. FULL SET OF CLEAN ON BOARD OCEAN BILLS OF LADING MADE OUT TO ORDER OF SHIPPER MARKED FREIGHT PREPAID AND NOTIFY APPLICANT.

5. BENEFICIARY'S CERTIFICATE ACCOMPANIED WITH THE RELATIVE COPY CERTIFYING THAT ALL SHIPPING DETAILS HAVE BEEN FACSIMILED TO APPLICANT WITHIN 2 DAYS AFTER SHIPMENT EFFECTED

CHARGES:

ALL BANKING CHARGES OUTSIDE OPENING BANK AND REIMBURSING/
PAYMENT CHARGES ARE FOR A/C OF BENEFICIARY

PERIOD FOR PRESENTATION:

15 DAYS AFTER THE DATE OF SHIPMENT

CONFIRMATION INSTRUCTIONS:　WITHOUT

INSTRUCTIONS TO THE PAYING/ACCEPTING/NEGOTIATING BANK

1. EACH DRAWING BE ENDORSED ON THE REVERSE BY NEGOTIATING BANK.

2. ALL DOCUMENTS MUST BE SENT TO US IN ONE COVER BY COURIER SERVICE.

SENDER TO RECEIVER INFORMATION

THIS IS THE OPERATIVE INSTRUMENT, NO MAIL CONFIRMATION WILL FOLLOW.

END OF MESSAGE

5. The Details of a L/C

依上述 L/C 範例 1、L/C 範例 2 和 L/C 範例 3 回答下列有關細節：

(1) The opening bank is _____

(2) The advising bank is _____

(3) The applicant is _____

(4) The amount is _____

(5) The beneficiary is _____

(6) Is it revocable? _____

(7) Is it a usance L/C? _____

(8) What is the tenor of the L/C? _____

(9) What does the buyer order? _____

(10) What are the documents required for _____
　　 negotiation?

(11) What is the expiry date? _____

(12) What is the latest shipment date? _____

(13) Are partial shipments allowed? _____

(14) Are transshipments allowed? _____

(15) What is the exporting port? _____

(16) What is the importing port? _____

(17) What is the special instruction on _____
　　 the use of shipping company?

此參考解答 1 是依據 L/C 範例 1 作答如下：

(1) The opening bank is — Sunshine National Bank, Seattle, Washington

(2) The advising bank is — Star Commercial Bank, Taipei, Taiwan

(3) The applicant is — Watsons Imports, Inc. San Francisco, U.S.A.

(4) The amount is — US$4,689.60

(5) The beneficiary is — Piza Co., Ltd.

(6) Is it revocable? — No, it is irrevocable.

(7) Is it a usance L/C? — No, it is a sight L/C.

(8) What is the tenor of the L/C? — The tenor of the L/C is "at sight."

(9) What does the buyer order? — Adult Games of Taiwan Origin as per Order 21180

(10) What are the documents required for negotiation? — The documents required are as follows:

1. Signed commercial invoice in 4 copies

2. Special customs invoice

3. Full set of clean "on board" ocean bills of lading

4. Certificate of origin

5. Packing list in triplicate

6. Beneficiary's certificate that all cartons, containers, and items are marked MADE IN TAIWAN as per US Customs Regulations and that the Packing and Marking

	requirements of the Federal Trade Commission have been complied with
(11) What is the expiry date?	August 17, 20..
(12) What is the latest shipment date?	August 17, 20..
(13) Are partial shipments allowed?	No, not allowed.
(14) Are transshipments allowed?	No, not allowed.
(15) What is the exporting port?	Taiwan port
(16) What is the importing port?	Seattle, Washington
(17) What is the special instruction on the use of shipping company?	Ship via American Rapid Lines.

此參考解答 2 是依據 L/C 範例 2 作答如下：

(1) The opening bank is	Australian Banking Group Limited, Abbotsford, Victoria, Australia
(2) The advising bank is	Star Commercial Bank, Taipei, Taiwan
(3) The applicant is	Watsons Imports, Inc. Victoria, Australia
(4) The amount is	US$3,917.12
(5) The beneficiary is	R. HANSE CO., LTD. Taipei, Taiwan
(6) Is it revocable?	No, it is irrevocable.
(7) Is it a usance L/C?	Yes, it is a usance L/C.
(8) What is the tenor of the L/C?	60 days
(9) What does the buyer order?	Game sets as per sales confirmation R-5002 as per order No. 29521
(10) What are the documents required for negotiation?	The documents required are as follows:

1. Invoices
2. Full set of clean "on board" ocean bills of lading

(11) What is the expiry date? August 15, 20..

(12) What is the latest shipment date? August 15, 20..

(13) Are partial shipments allowed? Yes, they are allowed.

(14) Are transshipments allowed? No, they are not allowed.

(15) What is the exporting port? Taiwan port

(16) What is the importing port? Melbourne, Australia

(17) What is the special instruction on the use of shipping company? N/A (Not applicable) / No special instruction.

此參考解答 3 是依據 L/C 範例 3 作答如下：

(1) The opening bank is Global Shine Bank, Barcelona Branch, Spain

(2) The advising bank is Common Bank, Taipei, Taiwan

(3) The applicant is RANES INDUSTRIAL CO., LTD. ×× Oak Stone Street, Barcelona, Spain

(4) The amount is US$240,519.00

(5) The beneficiary is Third Trading Company

(6) Is it revocable? No, it is irrevocable.

(7) Is it a usance L/C? Yes, it's a usance L/C.

(8) What is the tenor of the L/C? 30 days after B/L date

(9) What does the buyer order? Wooden toys MW5006: 4160 pcs / MW5421: 3750 pcs

(10) What are the documents required for negotiation? The documents required are as follows:

1. Signed commercial invoice in triplicate
2. Signed packing list in duplicate
3. Insurance policy or certificate in duplicate
4. Full set of clean on board ocean bills of lading
5. Beneficiary's certificate accompanied with the relative copy certifying that all shipping details have been facsimiled to applicant within 2 days after shipment effected

(11) What is the expiry date? September 30, 20..

(12) What is the latest shipment date? September 20, 20..

(13) Are partial shipments allowed? No, not allowed.

(14) Are transshipments allowed? No, not allowed.

(15) What is the exporting port? Keelung

(16) What is the importing port? Barcelona, Spain

(17) What is the special instruction on the use of shipping company? N/A (Not applicable) / No special instruction.

6. The Process of a L/C Transaction

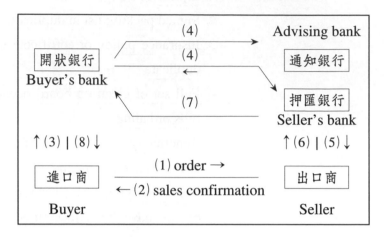

信用狀交易流程說明：

(1) 進口商下訂單給出口商。

(2) 出口商確認訂單，發出銷售確認書，以便進口商開信用狀。

(3) 進口商備妥文件向開狀銀行預繳保證金，申請開出信用狀。

(4) 開狀銀行將信用狀寄給通知銀行或押匯銀行。

(5) 通知銀行將信用狀轉給出口商。

(6) 出口商在出貨後備貨運單據向押匯銀行押匯，取得貨款。

(7) 押匯銀行將貨運單據寄給開狀銀行，請求歸償。

(8) 開狀銀行請進口商來繳餘款，並取得貨運單據，辦理提貨手續。

7. The Process of a D/P D/A Transaction

D/P: Documents against payment　　付款交單

D/A: Documents against acceptance　承兌交單

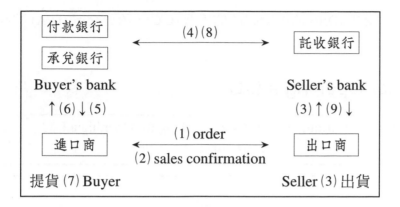

D/P D/A 流程說明：

(1) 進口商下訂單給出口商。

(2) 出口商確認訂單，發出銷售確認書。

(3) 出口商即可備貨。出貨後，備貨運單據，向託收銀行 (賣方銀行)，請求託收。(託收即委託賣方銀行向買方銀行收款之意)

(4) 託收銀行將貨運單據寄給買方銀行，請求執行付款交單 (D/P) 或承兌交單 (D/A)(依買賣雙方約定)。

(5) 買方銀行請買方來付款 (pay) ／ 承兌 (accept)。

(6) 買方銀行在買方付款 ／ 承兌後，將單據交給買方。

　　＊註解：

　　1. 如果要付款的即是付款交單 (D/P) ； 如果只要承兌的即是承兌交單 (D/A)。

　　2. 承兌為承諾兌現之意，即只要在匯票正面簽名，承諾匯票到期時付款。

(7) 買方取得貨運單據，即可辦理提貨手續。

(8) 如為付款交單，買方付款後，買方銀行將貨款，扣除手續費及其他費用，匯至賣方銀行；如為承兌交單，買方銀行要等匯票到期，買方來付款後，才能匯款。

(9) 賣方銀行在扣除手續費及其他費用後，將匯款轉交給賣方。

所以，付款交單 (D/P) 的風險高於信用狀 (L/C)，承兌交單 (D/A) 的風
險又高於付款交單。

8. Asking for Opening a L/C

Example 14.1   Confirming the Order and Asking for Opening a L/C
確認訂單並請求開信用狀

13th March, **20..**

Dear Sirs,

Thank you for your Order No. EP-001 for our electronic products.

We are glad to confirm the order and enclose our Sales Confirmation No.
CK-12, the total amount of which is US$20,000.

We would appreciate it if you should open a L/C in our favor as soon as
possible.

Sincerely yours,

Enc.

信文中譯：

敬啟者：
　　感謝貴公司訂單 EP-001 號，訂購我們的電子產品。
　　很高興確認訂單並附上銷售確認書 CK-12 號，總金額為美金

20,000 元。

懇請於最快時間惠予開出以我們為受益人之信用狀為盼。

謹上

附件

9. Opening a L/C

Example 14.2 Opening a L/C 開出信用狀

March 20, **20..**

Dear Sirs,

We are glad to receive your letter of March 13 enclosing your Sales Confirmation No. CK-12.

As requested, we have opened today a letter of credit through Sunshine National Bank for the total amount of US$20,000.

Please ship the goods by American Rapid Lines before the middle of April and pay special attention to quality and packing.

We expect to receive the orders soon.

Sincerely yours,

信文中譯：

敬啟者：

　　高興收到貴公司 3 月 13 日來信附來銷售確認書 CK-12 號。

　　如所請，本公司本日已經由陽光國家銀行開出一張信用狀，總金額為美金 20,000 元。

　　請在 4 月中旬前經由 American Rapid Lines 運出這批貨物並特別注意品質及包裝。

　　期待盡快收到所訂購的貨物。

謹上

10. Confirming Receipt of a L/C

Example 14.3　Confirming Receipt of a L/C　確認收到信用狀

April 10, **20..**

Dear Sirs,

Order No. EP-11

We thank you for your L/C No. DK-035 for your Order No. EP-11, amounting to US$25,000, which has reached us today.

As arranged, the electronic products will be shipped per s.s. President Nick V-61 sailing from Keelung on/about April 20, with ETA Los Angeles around May 20.

We assure best quality control will be kept while filling your above order.

Sincerely yours,

信文中譯：

敬啟者：

<u>訂單 EP-11 號</u>

感謝本日收到貴公司依訂單 EP-11 號所開的信用狀 DK-035，金額為美金 25,000 元。

如所安排，此批電子產品預定於 4 月 20 日左右，裝在尼克總統輪船 V-61，由基隆港運出，預定到達洛杉磯在 5 月 20 日左右。

本公司保證在準備訂貨時，將維持最佳品質管制。

謹上

11. Urging Opening a L/C

Example 14.4　Urging Opening a L/C　催開信用狀

April 21, **20..**

Dear Sirs,

Further to our letter of April 10, **20..** enclosing our Sales Confirmation No. VB-51 for your Order No. TR-02, totalling US$30,000, we wonder if you have received the above letter and if the relative L/C has been opened.

As the order is scheduled to be shipped via American Rapid Lines around

May 1, **20..**, please confirm immediately the opening of the L/C.

Please reply by return e-mail.

Sincerely yours,

信文中譯：

敬啟者：

　　追溯本公司 **20..** 年 4 月 10 日去函，附上銷售確認書 VB-51 號，確認訂單 TR-02 號，總數為美金 30,000 元，不知貴公司是否已收到上述之信及已開出相關的信用狀。

　　因此訂單預定於 **20..** 年 5 月 1 日左右由 American Rapid Lines 運出，請立即確認開出信用狀。

　　請儘速以郵件回覆。

謹上

12. Buyer's Request for D/P Payment

Example 14.5　Buyer's Request for D/P Payment
　　　　　　買方請求以付款交單付款

June 1, **20..**

Dear Sirs,

We are pleased to inform you that the hardware we ordered on our Order

No. HD-90 has arrived at our side safe and sound. As the quality of your products seems quite satisfactory, we are planning to place further orders.

Due to the restriction of foreign exchange in our country, we wonder if it is possible for you to grant us D/P terms for our future orders. If so, we would be in a position to place even larger orders.

We look forward to hearing favorably from you.

Sincerely yours,

信文中譯：

敬啟者：
　　本公司高興通知訂單 HD-90 號所訂購的五金已安抵這邊。因貴公司產品品質十分令人滿意，本公司打算下更多訂單。
　　由於本國的外匯管制，不知貴公司是否願意對以後的訂單允許以付款交單條款交易。如果願意的話，本公司將能下更大的訂單。
　　期盼佳音。

謹上

13. Asking for L/C Payment

Example 14.6　Asking for L/C Payment　要求信用狀付款

June 8, 20..

Dear Sirs,

We acknowledge with thanks receipt of your letter dated June 1, **20..**, concerning your request for the change of the terms of payment.

We appreciate your satisfaction in our products and understand your situation well. However, it has been our policy to do business on L/C terms and when closer business relationship is established, we will consider accepting D/P terms.

As the case stands, we would appreciate it if you should accept L/C as terms of payment and confirm your orders soon.

Sincerely yours,

信文中譯：

敬啟者：

感謝收到貴公司 **20..** 年 6 月 1 日來信，請求變更付款的條件。

感激對本公司產品滿意且十分瞭解貴公司的情況。然而，本公司的政策是以信用狀做生意，而在建立良好關係後，會考慮接受付款交單付款。

根據目前情況，如蒙接受信用狀付款並且迅速確認訂單，將不勝感激。

謹上

14. Sending Copies of Shipping Documents After Negotiation

Example 14.7   Sending Copies of Shipping Documents After
Negotiation   押匯後寄出裝運單據副本

September 12, **20..**

Dear Sirs,

We are pleased to inform you that the garments ordered on your Order No. GM-021 were shipped via s.s. President Nick V-234 sailing on September 9.

Enclosed please find the relative copies of shipping documents, including invoice, packing list, bill of lading, etc. for your reference. We trust that the goods will reach you in good condition.

For your information, we have already negotiated your L/C for the above order today and are looking forward to receiving further orders from you.

Sincerely yours,

Enc.

信文中譯：

敬啟者：

　　本公司很高興通知貴公司訂單 GM-021 號所訂購的成衣已裝運
9 月 9 日開航的尼克總統輪船 V-234。

　　隨函附上相關的裝運單據副本，包括發票、裝箱單、提單等以供
參考。相信此批貨物將安然抵達貴國。

　　另外，本公司已辦妥上述訂單之信用狀的押匯手續，且期盼收到
貴公司後續訂單。

謹上

附件

---

15. Import Customs Clearance and Reordering

Example 14.8　Import Customs Clearance, Import Redemption of
Documents, Picking Up Goods and Reordering
進口清關、贖單、提貨與續下單

October 10, **20..**

Dear Sirs,

With reference to your letter of September 12, **20..**, we take pleasure in
informing that the 1,000 pieces of garments on our Order No. GM-021
were cleared from customs and were also delivered to our Los Angeles
warehouse for further examination and distribution.

Under the initial inspection of our relative department, up to this
moment, the quality has been found to be satisfactory. Also, as the

market demands, we are, therefore, willing to place a repeat order for another 1,000 pieces of garments, the details of which are listed in the enclosed Order Sheet No. GM-022. Please confirm the order early so that we may open the relative L/C.

As the matter is urgent, please confirm the order before this week and we will open a L/C. We expect to hear from you soon.

Sincerely yours,

Enc.

信文中譯：

敬啟者：

敬覆貴公司 **20..** 年 9 月 12 日來函，本公司樂於示知，訂單號碼 GM-021 訂 1,000 件成衣已由海關清關，並運往本公司洛杉磯倉庫作進一步檢驗與配銷。

經由本公司相關部門初步檢驗，到目前為止，產品品質是令人滿意。另外，由於市場之需求，本公司樂於再下一張訂單，訂 1,000 件成衣。其細節如附上之訂單號碼 GM-022。請早日確認訂單，以便可開出相關信用狀。

由於事出緊急，請於本星期內確認，而本公司將開出信用狀。敬候速回音。

謹上

附件

✎ Exercise

A. Questions 問答題

1. What is a L/C?

2. What are the parties concerned in a L/C transaction?

3. What are the kinds of L/C? Give three kinds.

4. What are the details of a L/C? Give three examples.

5. Draw a chart to show the process of a L/C transaction.

B. Business Insight 實務探討

◆ 信用狀可靠嗎?

信用狀到目前來說,在國際貿易實務上,是最可靠的付款辦法之一。因它的交易,牽涉到四邊關係者的互相信用:買方、賣方、買方銀行、賣方銀行等,四邊互相信用才能使交易完滿達成。其實在國際上,因信用狀而引起的糾紛,也時有所聞,例如在德國科隆,就曾發生一家著名銀行,因財務問題而倒閉,也就影響它所開出的信用狀,使得此家銀行開出的信用狀交易造成各關係人的損失。然而,一般而言,信用狀仍不失其在現代國際貿易中所佔的重要角色。

C. Grammar Practice 文法練習

★連綴動詞 (Linking Verbs):

連綴動詞是用來連繫主詞與補語間的關係。其後不接副詞;因為它要形容的不是句中的動詞,而是動詞前的那個主詞,所以要用形容詞。所以,只能接形容詞或名詞於其後,作為補語,屬不完全不及物動詞。常用的連綴動詞 (含感官動詞) 有:

> be, keep, lie, stand, remain, seem, appear, look,

become, grow, get, make, feel, sound, taste, smell

e.g. Ms. Smith feels happy.

The pineapples taste sweet.

Selection：選出最適當的答案

_____ 1. The trip you have described sounds _____ .

(A) excited   (B) excitedly   (C) exciting   (D) excite

_____ 2. Debby appears _____ at the news.

(A) happy   (B) happily   (C) being happy   (D) be happy

_____ 3. The new manager asked us to keep our office _____ .

(A) cleanly   (B) to clean   (C) cleaning   (D) clean

_____ 4. The counter samples appear _____ to the buyer.

(A) well   (B) good   (C) nicely   (D) brightly

_____ 5. The project manager's report sounds _____ to all.

(A) interested   (B) interesting   (C) interestingly   (D) to interest

_____ 6. Your way of solution to the problem seems _____ .

(A) correctly   (B) correcting   (C) correct   (D) to correct

_____ 7. The silk material feels _____ and is good for the market.

(A) soft   (B) softly   (C) soften   (D) to be soft

D. Pattern Practice 句型練習

★以便：

...so that we may...

...so that we can...

...in order that we may...

...in order that we can...

1. 請寄來汽車零件樣品，以便我們展示給顧客看。

_____

2. 請儘速確認訂單，以便我們可早些採購所需原料。

_____

E. Business Terms 解釋名詞

1. Irrevocable L/C
2. Usance L/C
3. Back-to-Back L/C
4. Standby L/C
5. D/P
6. D/A

F. Blank-filling 填充練習

_____ Sirs,

Thank _____ _____ your Order No. 111 _____ our _____ products.

We _____ glad _____ confirm the _____ and _____ our _____ _____ No. 12, the _____ amount _____ which _____ US$30,000.

We _____ appreciate _____ if you _____ open an _____ in _____ favor as _____ as _____ .

Sincerely _____ ,

_____

G. Letter-writing 書信寫作

You are an exporter of electronic products. Write your letter to confirm the importer's order and ask him to open a L/C soon.

No. 14 關務：通關方式
(Kinds of Customs Clearance)

通關種類，依照查驗的方式可分為以下三種：

㈠ **C1 通關**

　　免審免驗通關，也就是免審核文件及免查驗貨物。出口貨物可立即出口；進口貨物則完成繳稅後持放行通知和原提貨單提貨即可。

㈡ **C2 通關**

　　文件審核通關，此種方式業者需補送報關文件，經海關審核無誤後，貨物可免驗放行。

㈢ **C3 通關**

　　貨物查驗通關，也就是必須查驗貨物及審核書面文件無誤後才可放行。

附註：以上通關方式為進出口貿易大宗貨物所採用。對於完稅價格新臺幣五萬元以下的進口包裹，必須透過 EZ WAY 易利委 APP 進行報關手續。

參考資料：

財政部關務署網站

NOTE

Chapter Fifteen

Marine Cargo Insurance

海上貨物保險

1. Why is Insurance Necessary in Trade?

In international trade, it usually takes time for the goods to be transported from one place to another. During the transportation, in order to provide against any damage or accident, the goods usually have to be insured.

在國際貿易上，由於貨物出口地到進口地要經一段時間，其間難免會遇到天災人禍等意外危險而遭受損失，所以貿易上一般貨物皆須保險。

2. The Types of Loss

損害的類型可分兩種：

(1) Total loss　全損

所投保的貨物全部毀損，又稱 "Total Loss Only" (TLO)。

⑵ Partial loss　分損

部分損壞，又稱海損 (Average)。海損分兩種，茲說明如下：

1) General average　共同海損

當船於航行中遇有緊急危險如暴風雨等，需將某些貨物故意丟入海中，以解救船隻時，所丟貨物的損失由所有此船貨主共同來分擔。平安險即只保共同海損。

2) Particular average　單獨海損

當船於航行中由於意外所引起的單獨損失稱之。水漬險不僅保共同海損，尚包含單獨海損。

3. The Types of Insurance

保險的種類，原則上可分下列兩種：

⑴ Basic Insurance　基本險

基本險可分三種如下：

1) Institute Cargo Clause (A)，簡稱 ICC (A)

協會貨物保險 A 條款

即是舊條款的全險 (All Risks，簡稱 A.R.，或 Against All Risks，簡稱 A.A.R.) (保單獨海損，共同海損及附加險，但不含兵險及罷工暴動險)

2) Institute Cargo Clause (B)，簡稱 ICC (B)

協會貨物保險 B 條款

即是舊條款的水漬險 (With Average，簡稱 W.A.) (保單獨海損及共同海損)

3) Institute Cargo Clause (C)，簡稱 ICC (C)

協會貨物保險 C 條款

即是舊條款的平安險 (Free from Particular Average，簡稱 FPA)

(只保共同海損不保單獨海損)

以上 ICC (A)、ICC (B)、ICC (C) 均不包括兵險 (War Risks) 或罷工暴動險 (SRCC)。因此，如要獲這種危險保障，須另加保。

(2) Additional Insurance　附加險

1) Wars Risks	兵險
2) Strikes, Riots, and Civil Commotions	罷工、暴動、民變 (SRCC)
3) Theft, Pilferage, and Non-delivery	偷竊、盜竊、遺失 (TPND)
4) Fresh Water and Rain Damage	淡水、雨水損
5) Breakage	破損
6) Leakage	漏損
7) Hook Hole	鉤損
8) Oil Damage	油汙
9) Contamination with Other Cargoes	汙染
10) Sweat and Heat, etc.	汙濕、發熱等

4. Insurance Policy and Certificate of Insurance

In most cases, an exporter, when having the shipment insured, will receive an insurance policy; while if there are regular shipments an insurance policy for larger amount will be taken out. After each shipment, a certificate of insurance will be issued for negotiation.

出口商在出貨如需保險貨物時，可向保險公司索取要保書 (proposal form)，辦妥手續後可領取保險單，但如果出口商的客戶出口的次數很多時，出口商可保一張大的保單，每次出貨時只要向保險公司申報，然後開出保險證明即可押匯。

5. Floating Policy and Open Policy

⑴ Floating Policy　流動保單

A floating policy, usually with a larger sum, will cover a number of shipments. After each shipment, a certificate of insurance will be issued.

當出口商有固定貨物出口時，可保一張金額大而整數的流動保單，如美金五萬元等。每次出貨只要在一表格上宣告，保險公司即發給保險證明，直到金額用完，再開新的保單。此流動即表所剩金額一直在變動或源源流長之意。

⑵ Open Policy　預約保單

An open policy has the same function as that of the floating policy. It is open in the sense of the total amount; it extends a period of usually a year.

又稱「開口保單」，與流動保單功能類似，總金額不限，每次出貨金額有限，期限一般為一年，此比流動保單更富彈性，所以更受歡迎。

6. Lloyd's

Lloyd's is, especially active in marine insurance, a London corporation of insurers, who issues most kinds of policy.

位於倫敦的勞合社為世界保險業的中心，起源於十七世紀的一間咖啡屋，主人叫做愛德華‧勞依茲 (Edward Lloyd)，生意人常聚於此。一些有錢的人開始共同以自己財產為某些船隻航行擔保，在一張紙上寫上各種擔保之風險，最後他們在卷後簽名為 underwriters，引申為保險業者，此為保險業之起源。

7. Examples

Example 15.1　Enquiry for Insurance Rate　詢問保險率

September 21, **20..**

Dear Sirs,

Please quote us your lowest rate for marine insurance, ICC (B) plus TPND and war risks, on a shipment of bicycles, valued at US$32,000 by the s.s.* Pre. Jeff V-651 sailing from Keelung to Los Angeles. The ship is scheduled to leave Keelung around September 25, **20..**, and we hope to have your early reply.

Sincerely yours,

* s.s. = steam ship 汽船。

信文中譯：

敬啟者：

　　請報最低的水險費率，保基本 B 類險，另加偷竊盜竊遺失險及兵險。貨物為一批腳踏車，價值美金 32,000 元，將裝在傑夫總統輪船 V-651，由基隆運到洛杉磯。此船隻預定於 **20..** 年 9 月 25 日左右離開基隆；希望能儘速收到回函。

謹上

Example 15.2　Reply from Insurance Company　回覆保險公司

September 22, **20..**

Dear Sirs,

We acknowledge with thanks receipt of your letter of September 21, **20..** enquiring about marine insurance rate to cover a shipment of bicycles from Keelung to Los Angeles. In compliance with your request, we hereby quote you our lowest rate at 1% to cover ICC (B) plus TPND and war risks. Please note that this is the lowest rate we are able to offer and there will be no rebate.

Please confirm early so that we may issue the policy in time.

Sincerely yours,

信文中譯：

敬啟者：

　　感激收到你們 **20..** 年 9 月 21 日來信詢問水險費率，含括一批腳踏車，由基隆運往洛杉磯。遵照你們所請，我們在此報給你們最低的費率 1%，包括基本 B 類險，另加偷竊盜竊遺失險及兵險。請注意，這是我們能報的最低費率，而且沒有回扣。

　　請儘早確認，如此我們才能及時開出保單。

謹上

✎ Exercise

A. Questions 問答題

1. Why is insurance necessary in international trade?

2. What are the types of loss?

3. What are the types of insurance?

4. What are the three kinds of basic insurance?

5. What are the examples of additional insurance?

6. What is A.R.? What is W.A.? What is FPA?

7. What is the difference between an insurance policy and a certificate of insurance?

8. What is a floating policy?

9. What is Lloyd's?

B. Business Insight 實務探討

◆ 保不保險？

保不保險？這句話包含兩個意思：一為，要不要保個險？另一為，這事可不可靠？由此涵義可知，保個險是可以增加可靠性的。海上保險最早起源於十七世紀的英國，當時業務集中在勞合社 (Lloyd's)，它為英國保險業者所組成的一個機構。原來當時英國海運興盛，生意人常聚在咖啡廳 (coffee house) 裡聊天。其中最有名的一家是 Mr. Edward Lloyd 所開。閒聊中，富有的商人常聯合起來，為某些船隻或航行擔保，被保者繳保費，而萬一有損失時，由保者共同來承擔；以共同的力量，來擔保大家的安全或少數人的損失，此即保險的精義，具有同舟共濟之意。現在對於做任何事情是否妥當也稱保不保險？

C. Grammar Practice 文法練習

★不定詞 (Infinitive)：

不定詞形式固定，不受主詞的人稱及數的限制，故稱不定詞，可作名詞、形容詞及副詞等。

---

1. 名詞：

　　e.g. To see is to believe. (眼見為憑)

　　　　To get up early is good for the students.

　　　　(→"To see" 與 "To get up early" 皆當名詞用)

2. 形容詞：

　　e.g. Mr. Nelson has a lot of things to do this morning.

　　　　(→"to do" 形容 "things"，作形容詞用)

3. 副詞：

　　e.g. I am glad to see you here.

　　　　(→"to see you" 修飾 "glad" 作副詞用)

下列的字只能接不定詞 (不可接動詞加 ing)：

---

agree, be able, be going, care, expect, have, hope, like, pretend, promise, need, ought, try, used, want, wish

---

Selection：選出最適當的答案

_____ 1. He _____ examine the blueprints carefully.

　　(A) asked to

　　(B) was asked

　　(C) was asked to

　　(D) being asked to

_____ 2. Bob wants you _____ this project quickly.

    (A) finish

    (B) finishing

    (C) to be finished

    (D) to finish

_____ 3. The merchandise is known _____ .

    (A) to be damaged

    (B) to damage

    (C) damaging

    (D) be damage

_____ 4. Computers are _____ stolen from the factory.

    (A) said having

    (B) saying to

    (C) said to have been

    (D) said be

_____ 5. The president agreed _____ us a paycheck today.

    (A) give

    (B) giving

    (C) having to give

    (D) to give

_____ 6. The manufacturers promised _____ the hardware on time.

    (A) to shipping

    (B) shipping

    (C) to be shipped

    (D) to ship

D. Pattern Practice 句型練習

★因此／如此：

...so...	因此 (自然之結果)
...so that...	如此；因此 (人為之結果)

1. 我們公司一向保持嚴格的品管，因此我們的產品風評很好。

_____

2. 我們降低我們的電腦價格，如此你們有機會可大量採購。

_____

E. Business Terms 解釋名詞

1. TLO　　　　2. Average　　　3. ICC (A)　　　4. A.R.

5. W.A.　　　　6. FPA　　　　7. SRCC　　　　8. TPND

F. Blank-filling 填充練習

Dear _____ ,

Please _____ us your _____ rate _____ marine _____ ,
ICC (B) _____ TPND and war _____ , _____ a shipment of
_____ , valued _____ US$30,000 _____ the s.s. President Jeff
_____ from _____ to _____ .

The _____ is _____ to leave _____ around _____ and we
_____ to have your _____ reply.

　　　　　　　　　　Sincerely _____ ,

G. Letter-writing 書信寫作

As an exporter, write your letter to an insurance company to enquire about the rate of insurance for a shipment of motorcycles.

商業知識

No. 15 關務：關稅之核定依據
(Base for Customs Valuation)

　　從價課徵關稅之進口貨物，其完稅價格 (Duty-Paying Value, DPV) 以該進口貨物之交易價格 (Transaction Value, TV) 作為計算根據 (關稅法第 29 條)。目前 WTO 採用的交易價格是以起岸價格 (CIF) 為關稅核課基礎。

參考資料：

全國法規資料庫網站

Chapter Sixteen

Ocean Transportation

海運運輸

Outline

1. The Container Service

Containers are metal boxes specially made for the efficiency and convenience of transportation. They are of standard length ranging from ten to forty feet; in international trade there are two common sizes: twenty feet and forty feet.

貨櫃為金屬的容器，有助於增進運輸效率與便利。長度由十英尺到四十英尺，在貿易上，常用的有二十英尺及四十英尺兩種。

2. Liners and Tramps

Liners are ships sailing at regular times and on regular routes; tramps are ships that have no regular times or routes.

定期船有固定船期及航線；不定期船則無固定船期及航線。

＊如何找船、裝船：

⑴ 如果以定期船運輸，出口商可由船公司或船務代理所印發的船期表或報紙，選擇適當的船隻向船公司洽訂艙位，即是簽 S/O (Shipping Order) 裝貨單或 Booking Note 訂艙單。

⑵ 出口商出貨時，憑此 S/O 將貨物交給船長，貨物裝上船後，大副簽發大副收據 M/R (Mate's Receipt) 交出口商。

⑶ 出口商拿此大副收據 M/R 向船公司換領提單 B/L。

3. Shipping Conference

A shipping conference is a system or association formed by some shipping lines on some sea routes, offering regular liners and offering better rate system to its members.

運費同盟為各船公司所組成，有固定的船隻、航行固定的航線，為其會員提供較優的運費費率。目前有歐洲運費同盟、澳洲運費同盟等。

4. Chartering of Ships

When goods are shipped in large quantities, it is advantageous to hire or charter a whole ship. This is the chartering of ships. The contract signed between the shipper and the shipping company is called a charter party (C/P).

大宗散裝貨出口時，貨主可傭船較有利。傭船即把整艘船租下，貨主與船公司訂的契約叫傭船契約。

5. Ways of Container Service

There are four ways of container service in accordance with the loading and unloading of the goods:

依裝貨與卸貨，貨櫃運輸可分下列四種方式：

⑴ CY to CY (出口商整櫃裝→進口商整櫃拆)　　　　　　　　　整裝整拆

⑵ CY to CFS (出口商整櫃裝→進口商併櫃拆)　　　　　整裝併拆

⑶ CFS to CY (出口商併櫃裝→進口商整櫃拆)　　　　　併裝整拆

⑷ CFS to CFS (出口商併櫃裝→進口商併櫃拆)　　　　　併裝併拆

　* CY: Container Yard，貨櫃集散場，即整裝或整拆

　　CFS: Container Freight Station，貨櫃集散站，即併裝或併拆

　　FCL: Full Container Load，整裝整拆 (歐洲地區用) = CY

　　LCL: Less Than Container Load，併裝併拆 (歐洲地區用) = CFS

6. Examples

Example 16.1　An Enquiry for Freight　詢運費

April 2, **20..**

Dear Sirs,

We shall be pleased if you will quote us the lowest freight rate for 2,000 bales of cotton yarn, weighing 150 kilos each, to be shipped to Hamburg from Keelung before June 30, **20...**

Please also inform us of the names of vessels sailing from Keelung to Hamburg direct before the deadline mentioned.

Your early reply will be appreciated.

Sincerely yours,

信文中譯：

敬啟者：

　　將感激如果你們能報最低的運費率。貨物為 2,000 綑的棉紗，重量每綑 150 公斤，將於 **20..** 年 6 月 30 日前由基隆運往漢堡。

　　請也示知在上述截止日期前由基隆開往漢堡的直航船隻的名稱。

　　將感激收到你們儘早回覆。

謹上

Example 16.2　A Reply about the Freight　回詢運費

April 4, 20..

Dear Sirs,

Thank you very much for your enquiry of April 2, **20..** concerning the ocean freight to Hamburg for 2,000 bales of cotton yarn. We are pleased to inform you that the freight rate is as follows:

US$75.00 per cubic meter (CBM) or 1,000 kilos

The rate is the agreed minimum freight rate.

As to the vessels for the above line, there are two regular liners:

s.s. Sun Maru sailing around May 1, **20..**;
s.s. Moon Maru sailing around June 2, **20..**

We hope to have the pleasure of dealing with your shipment.

Sincerely yours,

信文中譯：

敬啟者：

　　感謝你們 **20..** 年 4 月 2 日詢問函，關於 2,000 綑的棉紗運到漢堡的海運運費。我們很高興通知運費費率如下：

　　美金 75.00 元，每立方公尺或 1,000 公斤

　　此費率為公認的運費同盟的最低費率。

　　至於上述航線的船，有兩艘固定船隻：

　　太陽丸輪船約於 **20..** 年 5 月 1 日開航

　　月亮丸輪船約於 **20..** 年 6 月 2 日開航

　　希望能有榮幸處理你們的出貨。

謹上

Example 16.3　An Enquiry for the Chartering of Ships　詢傭船

May 23, **20..**

Dear Sirs,

We have 6,000 metric tons of rice packed in bags for shipment from Keelung to Cape Town and wish to charter a ship for the above shipment.

We should be grateful if you would arrange a vessel and quote us the best charter rate.

We should add that the vessel must be lying on the berth at Keelung on or before August 1, **20..** ready to load the cargo.

Your early reply in this matter would be highly appreciated.

Sincerely yours,

信文中譯：

敬啟者：

　　我們有 6,000 公噸的袋裝米，將由基隆運往開普頓；我們希望能傭船。

　　將感激，如果你們能安排一艘船，並報給我們最低的傭船費。

　　另外，我們希望船隻必須在 **20..** 年 8 月 1 日或之前停泊在基隆港，準備裝貨。

　　將感激你們對此事的早日回覆。

謹上

Example 16.4　A Reply about the Chartering　回詢備船

May 25, **20..**

Dear Sirs,

We thank you for your letter of May 23, **20..** enquiring about the chartering of our ships and are glad to inform you that we have found a ship which we think would serve you well. The ship is s.s. Tigris Maru, with a cargo capacity of about six thousand registered metric tons.

We confirm the ship will be lying on the berth at Keelung and ready to load the cargo before August 1, **20...**

Please confirm if the ship is satisfactory to you.

Sincerely yours,

信文中譯：

敬啟者：

感謝你們 **20..** 年 5 月 23 日來信，詢問關於僱我們的船隻。我們高興通知我們已幫你們找到一艘，可為你們服務很好的船隻。此為底格里斯九輪船，載貨容積約 6,000 註冊公噸。

確信此艘船將於 **20..** 年 8 月 1 日前會停泊在基隆港準備裝貨。

請確認是否此船令你們滿意。

謹上

✏ Exercise

A. Questions 問答題

1. What is the container service?

2. What are liners?

3. What are tramps?

4. What is a shipping conference?

5. What is the chartering of ships?

6. What is a C/P?

B. Business Insight 實務探討

◆ 海運運輸

進出口貿易所運送的貨物，十之八九都由海運運送。在早期，海上貨物運輸，皆是散裝運送，費時又費力；但在貨櫃 (container) 運輸流行暢通之後，運送速度已大為提升，費用也大為降低，增加了運送的效率，促進了國際貿易的發展。

C. Grammar Practice 文法練習

★動名詞 (Gerund)：動名詞即是動詞加 ing 當作名詞用。

e.g. Doing business is interesting.

It is no use crying over spilt milk.

He likes swimming.

I am fond of talking with him.

We have to finish packing today.

必須用動名詞的字

avoid, enjoy, mind, finish, complete, go on, keep, give up, stop, be used to

* stop 後亦可接不定詞，然意思不同，表示停下來而去做某事之意。

e.g. He stopped smoking. （他停止抽煙。）

He stopped to smoke. （他停下來抽煙。）

Selection：選出最適當的答案

_____ 1. The foreman is tired of _____ the workers.

(A) to lead   (B) leading   (C) lead   (D) to leading

_____ 2. The museum is worth _____ for all people.

(A) to visit   (B) to visiting   (C) visiting   (D) visit

_____ 3. I heard that Graham's _____ the order.

(A) getting   (B) to get   (C) to getting   (D) get

_____ 4. Clyde is _____ the situation very well.

(A) handle   (B) to handle   (C) to handling   (D) handling

_____ 5. By the time we got to the airport, the wind had stopped _____.

(A) blowing   (B) to blow   (C) to blowing   (D) be blowing

D. Pattern Practice 句型練習

★建議：

> We suggest S. + V.
>
> We propose S. + V.

1. 我們建議你們下一張試訂單，如此你們可看看我們卓越的運動器材。

_____

2. 我們建議你們月底前確認訂單，如此我們才可在 8 月中出貨。

_____

E. Business Terms 解釋名詞

1. S/O   2. M/R   3. C/P   4. B/L

5. CY   6. CFS   7. FCL   8. LCL

9. Booking Note   10. Shipping Conference

F. Blank-filling 填充練習

Dear _____ ,

We _____ be _____ if you will _____ us the _____ freight

rate _____ 2,000 bales _____ cotton _____ , _____ 150

kilos _____ , to _____ shipped to _____ from _____ before

_____ .

Your _____ quotation will be _____ .

_____ yours,

G. Letter-writing 書信寫作

As an exporter, write your letter to a shipping company to enquire about the
freight rate for a shipment of computers.

No. 16 關務：關稅之核定程序
(Procedures for Customs Audit)

完稅價格之核定程序可分以下三種：

㈠ 先放後核：為加速進口貨物通關，海關得按納稅義務人應申報之事項，先行徵稅驗放，事後再加審查 (關稅法第 18 條一項)。

㈡ 先核後放：進口貨物未經海關依前項規定先行徵稅驗放，且海關無法即時核定其應納關稅者，海關得依納稅義務人之申請，准其檢具審查所需文件資料，並繳納相當金額之保證金，先行驗放 (關稅法第 18 條二項)。

㈢ 事後稽核：海關於進出口貨物放行之翌日起兩年內，對納稅義務人實施之 (關稅法第 13 條)。

參考資料：

全國法規資料庫網站

No. 17 貿易：配額 (Quota)

配額是指政府在某一期間內對特定商品的進口或出口進行數量或金額上的控制，其目的在於調整收支和保護國內工農業生產，是非關稅貿易障礙措施之一。早期，在我國，配額制度最普遍用於紡織業，引起很多分配等問題。

Chapter Seventeen

Shipping Documents

貨運單據

1. The Types of Shipping Documents

There are two major types of shipping documents:

貨運單據可分兩大類如下：

(1) Fundamental Shipping Documents   基本貨運單據

The fundamental shipping documents can be classified into three categories:

基本貨運單據可依下列三方面來分類：

1) In sale (在交易方面)

    Commercial Invoice   商業發票

2) In transportation (在運輸方面)

   ① Ocean Bill of Lading   海運提單

   ② Air Waybill (AWB)   空運提單

　　　③ Parcel Post Receipt　　　　　　　　　　　郵政包裹收據

　　3) In insurance (在保險方面)
　　　① Insurance Policy　　　　　　　　　　　　保險單
　　　② Certificate of Insurance　　　　　　　　保險證明

(2) Subsidiary Shipping Documents　輔助貨運單據
　　The following examples are common subsidiary shipping documents:
　　常用的輔助貨運單據如下：
　　1) Shipment details (出貨明細類)
　　　① Packing List　　　　　　　　　　　　　裝箱單
　　　② Weight/Measurement List　　　　　　　　重量容積單

　　2) Related to invoice (發票類)
　　　① Consular Invoice　　　　　　　　　　　領事發票
　　　② Customs Invoice　　　　　　　　　　　海關發票

　　3) Certificate/Report (證明／報告類)
　　　① Certificate of Origin　　　　　　　　　產地證明書
　　　② Inspection Certificate　　　　　　　　　檢驗證明書
　　　③ Fumigation Certificate　　　　　　　　　熏蒸證明書
　　　④ Health Certificate　　　　　　　　　　健康證明書
　　　⑤ Survey Report　　　　　　　　　　　　公證報告

2. Examples of Shipping Documents

項目	範例編號
1.商業發票	17.1.1 和 17.1.2
2.海運提單	17.2
3.保險單	17.3
4.裝箱單	17.4.1 和 17.4.2
5.重量容積證明書	17.5
6.海關發票	17.6
7.檢驗證明	17.7
8.產地證明	17.8

⑴ 商業發票 (Commercial invoice)

商業發票 (Commercial invoice)，簡稱發票 (Invoice)。

出口商在運出貨物時，必須開出商業發票，以說明所出貨的明細，並作為押匯或收款之憑證。

⑵ 海運提單 (Ocean Bill of Lading, Marine Bill of Lading)

海運提單為船公司或其代理人所簽發證明收到貨物，並約定將貨物自某一地運至另一地，交給提單持有人的一種物權文件 (Document of Title)。

◎ 提單重要項目如下：(請參閱 17.2 海運提單)

1) Shipper：發貨人；出口商

2) Consignee ：收貨人，通常在此欄填上 "to order" (待指定)；"to order of shipper" (待託運人指定)；但也可以 "to order of...Bank" 表示由某銀行指定。

3) Notify party：被通知人，通常為進出口商、收貨人或其代理人，如
　　報關行等。

4) Bill of Lading No.：提單編號

5) S/O：裝貨單

6) Port of loading：裝貨港

7) Intended vessel & voyage number：預定裝貨船名及航次

8) Port of discharge：卸貨港

9) Marks and Nos：麥頭及件號

10) Quantity：數量

11) Description of goods：品名規格

12) Container number：貨櫃號碼

13) Gross weight：毛重，貨物總重量

14) Measurement：容積；貨物體積

15) Total number of：件數 (大寫)

16) Place of acceptance：收貨地

17) Place of delivery：交貨地

18) Issued：開出 (地點及日期)

(3) 保險單 (Insurance Policy)

　　保險單為證明保險契約成立的正式憑證。出口商在出貨時，如報價
　　條件為 CIF 時，則必須向保險公司保險；如報價條件不含保險時，
　　如 FOB，則須詢問看買方是否有安排或指定保險公司。

◎ 保險單在分類上的不同，有如下各種：

　　1) 依船名是否已確定：

　　　　① Named policy (船名確定保單)

　　　　② Unnamed policy (船名未確定保單)

　　　　　　又分以下兩項：

　　a. Floating policy (流動保單)：固定出貨時用，保單總金額隨出
　　　貨而流動之意。

　　b. Open policy (預約保單)：也為固定出貨時用，總金額為
　　　Open，即不固定。

　2) 依保險金額是否確定：

　　① Valued policy (定值保單)：即保單上載明保險標的物價值。

　　② Unvalued policy (不定值保單)：保單上僅訂最高限度，金額待
　　　日後再予補充。

⑷ 裝箱單 (Packing List)

　裝箱單 (Packing List)，又稱包裝明細 (Packing specification)；此為商
　業發票之補充文件，列明各項產品之包裝詳細情形，以作為檢驗、
　驗貨之憑證。

⑸ 重量容積證明書 (Certificate of Weight and Measurement)

　此為記載每件貨物的重量及容積明細的文件，此文件可由賣方或公
　共丈量人 (public weigher) 開出。

⑹ 海關發票 (Customs Invoice)

　目前貨物銷往美國、加拿大、澳洲、紐西蘭、南非等國時，出口商
　須提出海關發票，其作用如下：

　1) 作進口國海關統計之用。

　2) 作為產地證明。

　3) 作為查核看有無傾銷或運違禁品。

(7) 檢驗證明 (Inspection Certificate)

為防止出口商裝出的貨物不合乎契約規定，進口商常在信用狀中規定要出口商提出檢驗證明，以確保貨物品質及規格完美。

檢驗證明發出的單位如下：

1) 出口商。

2) 同業公會。

3) 公證行。

4) 進口商指定的代理人。

5) 政府機關，如我國的經濟部標準檢驗局等。

(8) 產地證明 (Certificate of Origin)

產地證明可由公會、商會或經濟部標準檢驗局發出；其功能如下：

1) 作享有優惠關稅證明用。

2) 防止貨物來自敵對國家。

3) 防止傾銷及禁貨輸入。

4) 供作海關統計用。

Example 17.1.1　Commercial Invoice 1　商業發票 1

INVOICE

No. #000888　　　　　　　　　　　　　　　Date: 20../1/5

INVOICE of 17,000 pcs of buttons and buckles (貨品名稱)

For account and risk of Messrs. ABC Intermation Corp. (買方)

(國名、地址等)

Shipped by (船公司)　　　　　　　　　　Per (船名)

sailing on or about (開航日期)　　From Taiwan　　to HKG (目的地)

L/C No. FA2035015RG (信用狀號碼)　Contract No. P.I. #A1210F

Marks & Nos.	Description of Goods	Quantity	Unit Price	Amount
ABC	Grey Buttons	5,000	US$0.01	US$50.00
D/NO. 1–24	White Buttons	2,000	US$0.01	US$20.00
MADE IN TAIWAN	Buckles 357	10,000	US$0.01	US$100.00
(麥頭)	(貨物品名及詳細資料)	(貨物數量)	(單價)	(總價)

【範本】

＊公司名義寄件：請在此處蓋上公司大章、小章及發票章。

＊個人名義寄件：請在此處蓋上個人私章，並準備本人身分證影本乙份。

＊請準備 Invoice 一式三份。

＊Please sign your name here and prepare your passport copy.

＊Please prepare the invoice in 3 copies.

Example 17.1.2　Commercial Invoice 2　商業發票 2

R. HANSE CO., LTD.

No. XX, Lane 519, Sec. 3,
Neihu Road, Neihu Dist.,
TEL: (02)2531-XXXX　　　Taipei, Taiwan

INVOICE

No. R- 79016 _____　Date: _____

Messrs. M. Peter Co., Ltd., Sweet Lane, Straford, London

Shipped per　"ELBE MARU" V-534

sailing on or about _____　From Keelung to London

L/C No. UCC/10300 _____　Contract No. _____

Marks & Nos.	Description of Goods	Quantity	Unit Price	Amount
M./134	Backgammon And Chess Sets Sets　CIF London			
	6820 18½' Backgammon	60	US$8.89	US$533.40
	6829 -do-	60	8.89	533.40
London	6062 10½' Backgammon	48	4.53	217.44
C/No. 1-	6063 -do-	48	4.53	217.44
167	6061 -do-	48	4.53	217.44
Made in		———		————
Taiwan		264		US$1719.12

SAY U.S. DOLLARS ONE THOUSAND SEVEN HUNDRED
NINETEEN AND CENTS TWELVE ONLY.

Drawn under Common Bank.
XX North Hill, Stratford, London E15 4QN
Credit number UCC/10300, dated 6th March 20..

As per invoice No. R-2021

Example 17.2　Ocean Bill of Lading　海運提單

Shipper

R. HANSE CO., LTD.

Tel. no.

Consignee (if 'order' state notify party)

TO ORDER

Notify party (only if not stated above: otherwise leave blank)

PIZA CO., LTD.
XX Maple Road, Stratford,
London, E13 2QP

Intended vessel & voyage number | Port of loading
"ELBE MARU" V-534 | **KAOHSIUNG**

Intended port of discharge
SOUTHAMPOTH

World Containers Limited

WCL

Bill of Lading No. | 77570732
Shippers Ref.

S/O No.

L/270

Combined Transport Bill of Lading

Received in apparent good order and condition except as otherwise noted the total number of containers or other packages or units enumerated below for transportation from the place of receipt to the place of delivery subject to the terms hereof. One of the signed Bills of Lading must be surrendered duly endorsed in exchange for the Goods or delivery order. On presentation of this document (duly endorsed) to the Carrier by or on behalf of the Holder, the rights and liabilities arising in accordance with the terms hereof shall (without prejudice to any rule of common law or statute rendering them binding on the Merchant) become binding in all respects between the Carrier and the Holder as though the contract evidenced hereby had been made between them.

SEA FREIGHT: PREPAID

Freight and charges

Origin zone transport charge　XXXXX
Origin zone service charge　PAID ORIGIN
Sea freight　PAID ORIGIN
Destination zone service charge　DUE DESTINATION
Destination zone transport charge　PAID ORIGIN

Details of cargo as declared by shipper			Gross weight	Measurement
Marks and numbers	Quantity and type of packages	Description of goods and container number Container's as indicated supplied by, or on behalf of the Carrier.		
⟨PIZA⟩ diamond LONDON C/No.1-167 MADE IN TAIWAN	167 C'TNS vvvvvvvvvvv	BACKGAMMON AND CHESS SET. (TOYS)		

COPY NOT NEGOTIABLE

CONTAINER NO. SSIU 2045728-167　12.34CBM

Total number of

ONE HUNDRED SIXTY SEVEN CTNS ONLY.

Subject to the conditions on back and to terms of Carrier's applicable tariff.

Place of acceptance

KEELUNG CFS

For Carrier's use

In witness whereof

THREE　(　3　) original Bills of Lading have been signed, one of which being accomplished. the other(s) to be void.
BANG CO., LTD.　For the Carrier

Place of delivery

WCL CONTAINERBASE LONDON EAST

Issued
at................. **Taipei**................ Date
26TH APR.

As Agent(s) only

WCL TPE 4/77

Example 17.3　Insurance Policy　保險單

MARINE CARGO POLICY

Policy No.　KF79188726

ASSURED:　Watsons Imports, Inc.

Invoice No.　Eton A-100

CLAIM, if any, payable at　NEW YORK　in　USD　Currency

CLAIM AGENT:　Amount insured　USD45970.00

BANG CO., LTD.
XX WALL STREET, NEW YORK
TEL: (212)630-XXXX

U.S. DOLLARS FORTY FIVE THOUSAND
NINE HUNDRED SEVENTY ONLY

Ship or Vessel:　　　From　KEELUNG
　S.S. Ever Brown V-100　To　NEW YORK

Sailing on or about:　Transhipped at　BOSTON　To/Thence to _____
　April 8, 20..

L/C No.　S-1540-480

SUBJECT-MATTER INSURED: Marks and Numbers as per Invoice No. specified above.

SPORT SHOES

Q'TY:　2,000 PAIRS　　　　NEW YORK
PACKING:　200 CARTONS　　C/No. 1-200

**Subject to Institute Radioactive Contamination Exclusion Clause
and the following clauses**

Conditions:　INSTITUTE CARGO CLAUSES (A)
　　　　　　INSTITUTE STRIKES CLAUSES (CARGO)

Valued at the same as Amount insured
Place and Date
Signed in　KEELUNG, April 10, 20..　Number of Policies Issued:　2　Copies

President

Tony Wang

Example 17.4.1   Packing List 1   裝箱單 1

R. HANSE CO., LTD.

No. XX, Lane 519, Sec. 3,   TEL: (02)2531-XXXX
Neihu Road, Neihu Dist.,
Taipei, Taiwan

PACKING LIST

No. R-79026 _____   Date: _____

Messrs. W&D Co., Ltd. _____   **MARK & NOS:**

   XX Mainland Street, Vancouver, BC V6B 1A9, Canada

Shipped per "PRES. PIERCE" V-48 _____

sailing on or about May 27, 20.. _____

From Keelung _____   **to** Vancouver _____

Packing No.	Description	Quantity	Net Weight	Gross Weight	Measurement
C/No.1-21 21C'tns	7030 Toy-games, (Backgammon, Tan)	sets @24 5.04	kgs @19 399	kgs @21 441	
22-42	7030 Toy-games (Backgammon, Brown)	@24 504	@19 399	@21 441	
43 1C'tns	Spare parts: 2 doz.		7	8	
43C'tns		1,008	805	890	

Example 17.4.2　Packing List 2　裝箱單 2

PACKING/WEIGHT LIST

No. _____　　　　　　　　　　Date: _____

PACKING LIST of _____　　MARK&NOS:

_____

For account and risk of Messrs. _____

_____

Shipped by _____

per S.S. _____

sailing on or about _____

From _____　to _____

Packing No.	Description	Quantity	Net Weight	Gross Weight	Measurement
	E. & O.E.				

Example 17.5　Certificate of Weight and Measurement
重量容積證明書

No. _____　　　　　　　　　　Date: _____
　　　　　　　　　　　　　　　　　　MARK&NOS:

WEIGHT/MEASUREMENT LIST

Messrs. _____

_____

Shipped from _____ to _____
　per S.S. _____ on _____
　Drawn Under L/C No. _____

Packing No.	Description	Quantity ( )	Weight (kgs)		Measurement
			Net	Gross	

Example 17.6　Customs Invoice　海關發票

DEPARTMENT OF THE TREASURY UNITED STATES CUSTOMS SERVICE 19 U.S.C. 1481, 1482, 1484	**SPECIAL CUSTOMS INVOICE** (Use separate invoice for purchased and non-purchased goods.)	Form Approved. O.M.B. No. 48-R0348

1. SELLER
R. HANSE CO., LTD.
No. XX, Lane 519, Sec. 3,
Neihu Road, Neihu Dist.,
Taipei, Taiwan

2. DOCUMENT NR.*

3. INVOICE NR. AND DATE*
R-79011 MAR 27 20..

4. REFERENCES*

To the order of Seattle Sunshine National Bank

6. BUYER (If other than consignee)
W&D Co., Ltd.
XX Mainland Street, Vancouver,
BC V6B 1A9, Canada

7. ORIGIN OF GOODS
Taiwan

9. NOTIFY PARTY*
W&D Co., Ltd. and G&A Customs Brokers,
XX Parkroad, Seattle, WA 98101, U.S.A.
Attn: Melisa

8. TERMS OF SALE, PAYMENT, AND DISCOUNT
FOB KEELUNG, TAIWAN

Irrevocable Documentary Letter of Credit
at sight

10. ADDITIONAL TRANSPORTATION INFORMATION*
Shipped per "PRES. TRUMAN" V-74
Sailing on: MAR 27 20..
From Keelung to Seattle

11. CURRENCY USED
U.S. CURRENCY

12. EXCH. RATE (If fixed or agreed)

13. DATE ORDER ACCEPTED

14. MARKS AND NUMBERS ON SHIPPING PACKAGES	15. NUMBER OF PACKAGES	16. FULL DESCRIPTION OF GOODS	17. QUANTITY	UNIT PRICE 18. HOME MARKET	19. INVOICE	20. INVOICE TOTALS
◇ W&D ◇ SEATTLE C/NO. 126-209 MADE IN TAIWAN	84 C'tns	Adult games of Taiwan Origin #10PWS (7028) Backgammon set (Spare parts 2 dos) SAY U.S. DOLLARS FOUR THOUSAND FOUR HUNDRED FORTY ONLY.	sets 2,000	US$2.22	FOB KEELUNG US$4,440.00	

a. ☐ If the production of these goods involved furnishing goods or services to the seller (e.g. assists such as dies, molds, tools, engineering work) and the value is not included in the invoice price, check box (21) and explain below.

27. DECLARATION OF SELLER/SHIPPER (OR AGENT)

I declare:
(A) If there are any rebates, drawbacks or bounties allowed upon the exportation of goods. I have checked box (A) and itemized separately below

(B) If the goods were not sold or agreed to be sold. I have checked box (B) and have indicated in column 19 the price I would be willing to receive.

I further declare that there is no other invoice differing from this one (unless otherwise described below) and that all statements contained in this invoice and declaration are true and correct

(C) SIGNATURE OF SELLER/SHIPPER (OR AGENT):

28. THIS SPACE FOR CONTINUING ANSWERS

22. PACKING COSTS	
23. OCEAN OR INTERNATIONAL FREIGHT	
24. DOMESTIC FREIGHT CHARGES	
25. INSURANCE COSTS	
26. OTHER COSTS (Specify Below)	

THIS FORM OF INVOICE REQUIRED GENERALLY IF RATE OF DUTY BASED UPON OR REGULATED BY VALUE OF GOODS AND PURCHASE PRICE OR VALUE OF SHIPMENT EXCEEDS $500 OTHERWISE USE COMMERCIAL INVOICE
* Not necessary for U.S. Customs purposes.

Customs Form 5515 (12-20-76)

Example 17.7　Inspection Certificate　檢驗證明

INSPECTION CERTIFICATE

DATED: _____

TO WHOM IT MAY CONCERN:

THIS IS TO CERTIFY THAT THE UNDER-MENTIONED COMMODITY,
SHIPPED PER S.S. _____ FROM _____
TAIWAN TO _____ SAILING ON OR ABOUT
_____ , IS IN GOOD ORDER
AND HAS BEEN INSPECTED THOROUGHLY BY US AND WE FURTHER CERTIFY THAT
THE COMMODITY DECLARED HEREON WAS INSPECTED AS SATISFACTORY
TO US.

BUYER　　　　　:

COMMODITY　　　:

QUANTITY　　　　:

MARKS & NUMBERS　:

FAR EAST SAFETY EQUIPMENT CO., LTD.

_____

Example 17.8 Certificate of Origin 產地證明

1. Exporter's Name and Address PIZA CO., LTD. No. ××, Sec. 3, Xinsheng S. Rd., Da'an Dist., Taipei, Taiwan	CERTIFICATE NO. 1234 Page of 1/2 CERTIFICATE OF ORIGIN
2. Importer's Name and Address WATSONS IMPORTS, INC. ×× Blue Drive, San Francisco, CA 90012 U.S.A.	(Issued in Taiwan) ORIGINAL/COPY
3. Port of Loading KEELUNG	4. Port of Discharge San Francisco 5. Country of Destination U.S.A.

6. Description of Goods: Packaging Marks and Numbers	7. Quantity/Unit
THIS IS TO CERTIFY THAT THE UNDERMENTIONED COMMODITY IS PRODUCTS OF TAIWAN 　　COMMODITY: 2,000 SETS OF HAND TOOL SETS 　　QUANTITY: 2,000 SETS PACKED IN 100 CTNS 　　SHIPPER: PIZA CO., LTD. 　　　　　No. ××, Sec. 3, Xinsheng S. Rd., 　　　　　Da'an Dist., Taipei, Taiwan 　　BUYER: WATSONS IMPORTS, INC. 　　　　×× Blue Drive, 　　　　San Francisco, CA 90012 　　　　U.S.A. 　　MANUFACTURER: FAR HARDWARE CO., LTD. 　　　　　NO. ××, Zhongshan Rd., 　　　　　West Central Dist., Tainan, Taiwan 　　SHIPMENT: PER S.S. "EVER BROWN" V-321 FROM 　　　　　KEELUNG TO SAN FRANCISCO, 　　　　　SAILING ON/ABOUT AUGUST 12, **20..**	2,000/set
This certificate shall be considered null and void in case of any alteration.	

COMMODITY DESCRIPTION SUPPLEMENT	CERTIFICATE NO. 1234
	Page of 2/2

MARKS:

WATSONS

San Francisco

C/NO. 1-100

MADE IN TAIWAN

Certification

It is hereby certified that the goods described in this certificate originate in Taiwan.

TAIWAN CHAMBER OF COMMERCE

Authorized signature

Date of Certification: FEB 15, **20..**

This certificate shall be considered null and void in case of any alternation.

✎ Exercise

A. Questions 問答題

1. What are the two major types of shipping documents?

2. What are the major shipping documents in transportation?

3. What are the major shipping documents in insurance?

4. Give five examples of shipping documents.

B. Business Insight 實務探討

◆ 裝運單據製作

出口貿易公司在將貨物運出之後，必須要製作單據以便押匯 (Negotiation)。單據的製作須依照信用狀的規定來製作，不能有差錯。一般常用的裝運單據有發票 (Invoice)、裝箱單 (Packing list)、提單 (B/L)、保險單 (Insurance policy) 等；如果是大型的貿易公司，由於皆設有船務部，所以單據製作皆可由公司自己做。而一般規模較小之公司，單據製作則委託報關行 (Customs broker) 來做，較經濟、方便，也較有效率。

C. Grammar Practice 文法練習

★分詞 (Participles)：

分詞的種類	型式	功用	例子
1. 現在分詞 (Present Participle)	V + ing	表主動	a sleeping dog a dining room
2. 過去分詞 (Past Participle)	V + ed	表被動	a broken door a changed plan

e.g. 1. 現在分詞

(1) The girl writing a letter is Alice.

(2) I heard Lucy singing a song in her office.

2. 過去分詞

（1）The secretary handed me a letter written in English.

（2）The buyer tried to make himself understood.

Selection：選出最適當的答案

_____ 1. Mr. Nelson appeared _____ at the news conference.

(A) surprising (B) being surprising

(C) to surprised (D) surprised

_____ 2. The manager found the workers _____ the goods in the wrong way.

(A) packing (B) packed (C) to be packed (D) be packing

_____ 3. The production director wanted the work _____ on schedule.

(A) finish (B) finishing (C) finished (D) be finished

_____ 4. The diplomat seemed _____ to meet his foreign friends.

(A) exciting (B) excited (C) to excite (D) be exciting

_____ 5. The tourists watched the airplane _____ off at the airport.

(A) take (B) took (C) taking (D) taken

_____ 6. The technicians decided to have their garage _____ blue.

(A) painted (B) painting (C) paint (D) be painted

_____ 7. Daniel will get his hair _____ tonight.

(A) to cut (B) cut (C) cutting (D) to cutting

D. Pattern Practice 句型練習

★以供參考：

...for your reference...

...for your information...

...for your evaluation...

...for your examination...

1. 我們由航空包裹寄上我們最新的家具目錄及價目以供參考。

_____

2. 我們附上我們最近開發出來的瓷磚照片及型錄以供參考。

_____

E. Business Terms 解釋名詞

1. B/L	2. AWB	3. S/O	4. Open policy
5. Survey report	6. Invoice	7. Notify party	8. Consignee

No. 18 貿易：歐盟 (European Union—EU) 歐元 (Euro)

　　The European Union (EU) is an economic and political union of 27 member states which are located in Europe. The EU was established by the "Maastricht Treaty" in 1993. The currency officially used in the UN is Euro, signed as €.

　　歐洲聯盟 (簡稱歐盟，英文縮寫 EU)，是根據 1993 年簽署的《歐洲聯盟條約》(也稱《馬斯垂克條約》) 所建立的國際組織，現擁有 27 個會員國。規範歐盟的條約經過多次修訂，目前歐盟的運作方式是依照《里斯本條約》。歐盟所通用貨幣為歐元，符號為「€」。

Chapter Eighteen

Bill of Exchange

匯票

 **outline**

1. What is a Bill of Exchange?

匯票 (Bill of Exchange)，又稱 Draft，簡稱 B/E；依 *Longman Dictionary of Business English*，其定義如下：

A bill of exchange is a written order telling one person to pay a certain sum of money to a named person on demand or at a certain time in the future.

匯票為一書面命令，要求受票人於見票時或在未來某一確定日期，支付一定的金額給一特定人。

2. The Style of Bill of Exchange

＊匯票格式：

BILL OF EXCHANGE
①

Draft No. ___②___   Taipei, ___③___

Exchange For ___④___

At ___⑤___ sight of this FIRST of Exchange (Second the same tenor
⑥

and date being unpaid)

Pay to the order of

BANK OF ××

The sum of ⑦ _____

_____ Value received
⑧

Drawn under ⑨ _____

Irrevocable L/C No. _____ Dated _____

To ___⑩___

_____

_____

⑪

* 說明：

① Bill of Exchange：匯票。

② 匯票號碼。

③ 發票地點及日期。

④ Exchange for：用阿拉伯數字表示匯票金額。

⑤ 填上匯票期限，例如，即期時，"at sight"，90 天到期則 "at 90 days' sight"。

⑥ 其意為：「憑本匯票第一聯 (以票期及發票日期相同之第二聯匯票尚未付
訖為限) 見票 (或見票後……天) 支付臺灣銀行或其指定人……。」

⑦ 填上金額 (以英文字大寫表示)。

⑧ Value received：價款收訖。

⑨ "Drawn under" 後面填上開狀銀行名稱。 "Irrevocable L/C No." 後面填上
信用狀號碼。"Dated" 後面填上開狀日期。本條款稱為 "Drawn Clause"(發

票條款)，在憑 L/C 開發匯票時，都須填上，如非憑 L/C 者，如 D/P 或 D/A 者，不必填寫。

⑩ "To" 後面填上付款人名稱，一般為進口商或付款銀行，依信用狀規定。

⑪ 發票人名字及簽字。

3. The Kinds of Bill of Exchange

匯票從不同的角度來看，有各式的分類如下。

(1) 依匯票的發票人及付款人身分分為：

1) 銀行匯票 (banker's draft or bill)：簡稱 B/D，為銀行向銀行發出的匯票。通常用於順匯。

2) 商業匯票 (commercial draft, Trade bill)：商人向商人或銀行發出的匯票。

(2) 依匯票是否附有貨運單證分為：

1) 跟單匯票 (documentary draft or bill)：附有貨運單證的匯票。這種匯票可向銀行申請押匯，所以又稱押匯匯票。

2) 光票 (clean draft or bill)：未附有貨運單證的匯票。

(3) 依匯票期限分為：

1) 即期匯票 (sight draft or bill, demand draft or bill)：見票 (sight) 即付或要求 (on demand) 即付的匯票。

2) 定期匯票 (time draft or bill) 或遠期匯票 (usance draft or bill)：即將來某一時日付款的匯票，可分為：

① 發票後定期付款匯票：即發票日後一定日期付款的匯票，例如 "ninety days after date"，即以發票日後九十天付款。

② 見票後定期付款匯票：即見票日後一定期間付款的匯票，如 "ninety days after sight"，即以見票日後九十天付款。

③ 定日付款匯票：即以某特定日付款的匯票。

⑷ 依交付單證方式分為：

　1) 付款交單匯票 (documents against payment draft or bill, D/P bill)：付款人付清票款後才交付貨運單證的匯票，又稱為付款押匯匯票 (documentary payment bill)。

　2) 承兌交單匯票 (documents against acceptance draft or bill, D/A bill)：即匯票經付款人承兌 (accept) 後即交付貨運單證的匯票，又稱承兌押匯匯票 (documentary acceptance bill)。

＊匯票範例：

BILL OF EXCHANGE

Draft No.　HW-123 　　　　　　　　　Taipei, August 10, 20..

Exchange for USD4,689.60

At XXX sight of this SECOND of exchange (First the same tenor and date being unpaid)

Pay to the order of

×× COMMERCIAL BANK

The sum of US Dollars FOUR THOUSAND SIX HUNDRED EIGHTY-NINE AND CENTS SIXTY ONLY

Drawn under Sunshine National Bank, Seattle, Washington 98124

L/C No.　55046 　　　　　　　　　Dated　June 19, 20..

To Sunshine National Bank

　　Seattle 　　　　　　　　　Piza Co., Ltd

　　Washington 　　　　　　　*Jake Chang*

---

4. The Parties Concerned with a Bill of Exchange

匯票關係人 (The parties concerned with a bill of exchange)：

drawer　發票人

drawee
payer　} 被發票人 (付款人)

payee　受款人

bearer　執票人

endorser　背書人

endorsee　被背書人；endorsement　背書

holder　持票人

acceptor　承兌人

surety　保證人

paying agent　擔當付款人

referee in case of need　預備付款人

acceptor for honor　參加承兌人

payer for honor　參加付款人

* 註解：

1. holder：持票人。

2. acceptance：匯票的付款人在匯票正面簽名的行為，稱為承兌 (accept)。

3. paying agent：即代替付款人擔當支付票據的人。

4. acceptor for honor：參加承兌人；當遠期匯票被 "drawee" 拒絕承兌時，由另人代付款人承兌的行為，叫做參加承兌 (acceptance for honor)，此人即參加承兌人。

5. payer for honor：參加付款人；包括預備付款人和其他任何人，在匯票遭拒付時，代發票人、背書人等對執票人付款的行為叫做 "payment for honor"。

6. surety：擔保人；票據債務人以外的第三者，在匯票上簽字保證票款的支付的人。

✏ Exercise

A. Questions 問答題

1. What is a bill of exchange?
2. What are the essential parts of a bill of exchange?
3. What are the kinds of bill of exchange?
4. What are the parties concerned with a bill of exchange?

B. Business Insight 實務探討

◆ 匯票製作

匯票的製作，如果是以信用狀出口，須要依據信用狀的指示來做，不能有差錯。一有差錯，在押匯時會構成「瑕疵」，便拿不到錢，故須小心。另外，如果以託收方式出口，即是跟單匯票 (documentary bill)，可分：付款交單 (D/P) 及承兌交單 (D/A) 兩種。在這種狀況下，則出口商在出貨後，必須準備匯票連同相關的裝運單據，提交自己的銀行，請求向對方銀行託收。

C. Grammar Practice 文法練習

★分詞構句 (Participial Construction)：

分詞形成的片語作形容詞或副詞用。

種類	例　　句
現在分詞	Typing rapidly, Miss Haynes made great progress. Arriving at the station, Joe found the train had gone. I met Anita carrying a handbag.
過去分詞	The report made by Helen has ten pages. I saw a mouse caught in a trap. Written with care, the letter looks good.

Selection：選出最適當的答案

_____ 1. _____ at the airport, Alice found the buyer was there.

(A) Arriving   (B) Arrived   (C) To arrive   (D) Have arrived

_____ 2. _____ his work, Roger took a rest.

(A) Finished   (B) To finish   (C) Finishing   (D) Have finished

_____ 3. _____ in good English, the book sells well.

(A) To write   (B) Writing   (C) Be written   (D) Written

_____ 4. _____ by antiques, Bill examined the silver dog carefully.

(A) Fascinating   (B) Fascinated

(C) Fascinate   (D) Be fascinated

_____ 5. _____ his work, Abe left the office early.

(A) Having finished   (B) Finished

(C) To finish   (D) Finish

_____ 6. _____ in good colors, the dress looks attractive.

(A) Dye   (B) Dyeing   (C) Dyed   (D) To dye

D. Pattern Practice 句型練習

★為了：

```
in order to ＋ V. (原形)
in order that ＋ S. ＋ V.
with a view to ＋ Ving
```

1. 為了能確信準時交貨，請及早開出訂單。

_____

2. 為了能跟你們建立親密的商業關係，我們寫信給你們。

_____

E. Business Terms 解釋名詞

1. B/L	2. at sight	3. tenor	4. pay to the order of
5. value received	6. on demand	7. D/P	8. D/A
9. drawer	10. B/D		

No. 19 貿易：世界貿易組織 (WTO)

　　世界貿易組織 (WTO) 是處理國與國間貿易法規的全球性國際組織。它的核心基礎是 WTO 協議。這些協議是由大多數世界貿易國家經開會、談判、簽字和批准通過的。目的在幫助貨物和服務的生產商、出口商和進口商經營生意。

　　WTO 總部設在瑞士日內瓦，功能在執行 WTO 貿易協定，作為貿易談判論壇、處理貿易爭端、監測各國貿易政策、與其他國際組織合作等。我國於 2002 年 1 月 1 日加入 WTO。

Chapter Nineteen

Collection and Payment

託收、討債及付款

Outline

1. Collection by D/P and D/A Terms

Example 19.1　　出口商通知出貨並託收貨款

January 17, **20..**

Dear Sirs,

We take pleasure in informing you that we have shipped the sundry goods on your Order No. CH-034 today by the s.s. President Nick V-546 sailing from Keelung to New York.

Herewith we enclose the following shipping documents for your kind reference:

Commercial invoice
Bill of lading
Packing list
Certificate of weight and measurement
Special customs invoice

As agreed, we have drawn on you at 90 days for US$25,000 through our bankers, ×× Commercial Bank. The original documents along with the draft will be handed to you by our bankers through Sunshine National Bank on your acceptance of the draft.

We shall be glad if you will duly pay the draft.

Sincerely yours,

Enc.

信文中譯：

敬啟者：
　　很高興通知我們本日已將你們訂單 CH-034 號訂的雜貨經由尼

克總統輪船 V-546，由基隆運往紐約。

在此我們附上下列的裝運單據以供參考：

商業發票

提單

裝箱單

重量容積證明書

特別海關發票

為了獲此批貨款，我們已經由我們銀行，××商業銀行，向你們開出金額美金 25,000 元的 90 天匯票。文件正本隨附在匯票上；我們的銀行將經由陽光國家銀行，依承兌匯票的基礎，將文件轉交給你們。

如果你們可以按時承兌匯票，我們將感激不盡。

謹上

附件

2. Settlement of Account

在國際貿易上，貨款的收付大多以信用狀 (L/C)、付款交單 (D/P)、承兌交單 (D/A) 方式辦理，但有些公司在關係密切後，也採用賒帳方式 (Open Account，簡稱 O/A) 交易，這時在帳目的清理就必須用到以下的文件：

⑴ Invoice	發票
⑵ Debit Note (D/N)	借項清單
⑶ Credit Note (C/N)	貸項清單
⑷ Statement of Accounts	對帳單

茲分別說明如下：

⑴ Invoice　發票

＊ 用法說明：

　　1. 當賣方運出貨物時，賣方寄出發票給買方。

　　2. 發票即發貨之憑票，以作為登錄帳目，或作為收款之依據。

＊ 範例如下：

PIZA CO., LTD.

No. ××, Sec. 3, Xinsheng S. Rd., Da'an Dist.,

Taipei, Taiwan

INVOICE

No. HD-201

February 1, **20..**

Messrs.

WATSONS IMPORTS, INC.

×× Blue Drive,

San Francisco, CA 90012

U.S.A.

Item No.	Descriptions	Quantity	Unit Price FOB Keelung	Amount
PT-002	Power tool set 9"	10	US$100.00	US$1,000.00

for PIZA CO., LTD.

_____

E. & O.E.

* E. & O.E.: Errors and omissions excepted. 即錯誤、遺漏不在此限或有錯當查；即保留修改之權利。

⑵ Debit Note (D/N)　借項清單

* 用法說明：

　1. 當要向對方索錢時，寄出借項清單。

　2. 當賣方發票索價太低時，寄出借項清單補收，以為補收款項之依據。

* 範例如下：

PIZA CO., LTD.

No. ××, Sec. 3, Xinsheng S. Rd., Da'an Dist.,

Taipei, Taiwan

DEBIT NOTE

No. 302

March 2, **20..**

Messrs.

WATSONS IMPORTS, INC.

×× Blue Drive,

San Francisco, CA 90012

U.S.A.

Order No.	Descriptions	Amount
HD-098	To 1,000 hardware tool kits	
	KT-01 charged on Invoice	
	No. 234 at $1.00 each	
	Should be $1.50	
	Difference	$500.00
The amount debited to your account		$500.00

for PIZA CO., LTD.

_____

⑶ Credit Note (C/N)　貸項清單

＊ 用法說明：

　　1. 當欠對方錢時，寄給對方貸項清單。

　　2. 當賣方發票索價太高時，寄上貸項清單，使買方抵銷帳目。

　　3. 當買方退貨或退回包裝材料時，寄給買方貸項清單。

＊ 範例如下：

PIZA CO., LTD.

No. ××, Sec. 3, Xinsheng S. Rd., Da'an Dist.,

Taipei, Taiwan

CREDIT NOTE
No. 404

April 4, **20..**

WATSONS IMPORTS, INC.

××Blue Drive,

San Francisco, CA 90012

U.S.A.

Order No.	Descriptions	Amount
CP-362	By 10 hand tool sets DX-99 returned. Charged to you on Invoice No. 236	$400.00
The amount debited to your account		$400.00

for PIZA CO., LTD.

_____

⑷ Statement of Accounts　對帳單

＊用法說明：

1. 對帳單為某段期間內，買賣雙方交易帳目的明細。

2. 對帳單起於前期未付金額。

3. 對帳單內，賣方加上發票、借項清單等的金額；減下已付帳款、貸項清單等的金額。

＊ 範例如下：

PIZA CO., LTD.

No. ××, Sec. 3, Xinsheng S. Rd., Da'an Dist.,

Taipei, Taiwan

STATEMENT OF ACCOUNT

No. ET-630

June 30, **20..**

Messrs.

WATSONS IMPORTS, INC.

×× Blue Drive,

San Francisco, CA 90012

U.S.A.

Date	Item	Debit	Credit	Balance
20..		US$	US$	US$
Jan 1	Account rendered			100.00
Feb 1	Invoice HD-201	1,000.00		1,100.00
Mar 2	Debit Note D. 302	500.00		1,600.00
Apr 4	Credit Note C. 404		400.00	1,200.00
May 15	Check		1,000.00	200.00

for PIZA CO., LTD.

_____

E. & O.E.

3. The Steps of Collection

討債信有雙重意義，一方面要說服買方付錢，一方面又要保住對方的商譽，所以寫信時要特別小心。開始時不必特地寫一封信，只要寄上對帳單即可。其步驟如下：

(1) A first statement of account	第一封對帳單
(2) A second statement of account	第二封對帳單
(3) A form letter	格式信
(4) The first collection letter	第一封討債信
(5) The second collection letter	第二封討債信
(6) The final collection letter	最後一封討債信

4. A Form Letter

Example 19.2　A Form Letter　格式信

(Date)

Dear Sirs,

Your account No.

_____

We are sorry to inform you that your account No. _____, dated _____ has not been settled.

The enclosed statement shows the amount owing to be $_____. We look forward to your early settlement.

Sincerely yours,

Enc.

信文中譯：

敬啟者：

你們的帳號

遺憾通知你們你們的帳號_____、日期_____，尚未清償。

附上的對帳單顯示未付餘額為 $_____，我們期待你們早日清

償。

謹上

附件

5. The Techniques of Writing Collection Letters

⑴討債信的寫法與技巧如存證信函 (certified mail)。

⑵寫作技巧的重點在於：

　1) 寬限期　　　2) 處理的手段

　由此兩方面著眼，期限愈緊，手段愈強，以達到討債目的為主。

6. The First Collection Letter

Example 19.3　The First Collection Letter　第一封討債信

June 30, 20..

Dear Sirs,

Your account No.

<u>345</u>

As you are one of our regular customers, we wonder whether there is any special reason why we have not yet received payment from you for the above account, already two months overdue.

Perhaps you may not have received our statement of account we sent you on April 30, **20..** showing the balance of US$200.00. We are now sending you a new one for your reference.

We hope to receive your payment within the next few days.

Sincerely yours,

信文中譯：

敬啟者：

你們帳號 345 號

因你們是我們固定的顧客，我們不知是否有特別的理由，令我們尚未收到上述帳號的付款；此帳已經過期二個月了。

或許你們可能沒有收到我們的 **20..** 年 4 月 30 日寄出的對帳單，顯示未付餘額為美金 200.00 元。我們現在寄給你們一張新的對帳單以供參考。

希望幾天內收到你們的付款。

謹上

7. The Second Collection Letter

Example 19.4　The Second Collection Letter　第二封討債信

August 1, 20..

Dear Sirs,

Your account No.

　　345
_____

We are writing again to remind you that up to this moment we have not yet received your payment of the sum of $200.00 still owing on your above account.

We regret that we have reached the stage when we must press for immediate payment. If we cannot receive your payment within this month, we are afraid we will have to seek other sources to solve the problem.

We trust you will now attend to this matter without further delay.

Sincerely yours,

信文中譯：

敬啟者：

你們帳號 345 號

　　再度寫信給你們來提示，到目前為止，我們尚未收到你們在帳上仍欠的美金 200.00 元的付款。

　　我們很遺憾我們已到達必須強迫你們付款的階段。如果我們在本月內沒有收到付款，恐怕我們必須尋求其他方式來解決問題。

　　相信你們現在會立即處理此事。

　　　　　　　　　　　　　　　　　　　　　　　　　　　　謹上

8. The Final Collection Letter

Example 19.5　The Final Collection Letter　最後一封討債信

September 15, **20..**

Dear Sirs,

Your account No.

　　345

We note with surprise and disappointment that we have not received any reply to our previous applications for payment of your above account.

Unless your payment of US$200.00 is made or a satisfactory explanation is received before October 10, **20..**, we shall instruct our lawyers to recover the amount due.

Sincerely yours,

信文中譯：

敬啟者：

　　你們的帳號 345 號

　　很驚訝與遺憾得知我們尚未收到任何來信，回覆我們先前請求你們付上開帳戶的款項。

　　除非你們在 **20..** 年 10 月 10 日前支付美金 200.00 元或提出令人滿意的解釋，否則將通知我們的律師來收取所欠的金額。

謹上

9. Payment

Example 19.6　Payment　付款

October 1, **20..**

Dear Sirs,

We are pleased to enclose a banker's draft No. BK-098 for US$200.00 dated October 1, **20..** drawn by the Sunshine National Bank, New York on the Bank of Taiwan in full settlement of your statement of account No. 345.

We shall be pleased if you will send us your official receipt.

Yours sincerely,

信文中譯：

敬啟者：

　　很高興附上由紐約陽光國家銀行向臺銀開出的銀行匯票號碼 BK-098 號，金額美金 200.00 元，日期為 **20..** 年 10 月 1 日，以付清你們對帳單 345 號貨款。

　　如果你們能寄給我們正式的收據，我們將感激不盡。

謹上

✎ Exercise

A. Questions 問答題

1. Among the terms of payment used in international trade, what are the two common methods of collection?

2. What are the common shipping documents used in international trade?

3. What are the documents used in settlement under O/A payment terms?

4. What are the steps of requesting payment?

B. Business Insight 實務探討

◆ 討債

在國際貿易上，尤其在臺灣，由於付款方式皆採用信用狀 (L/C)，所以要討債的機會並不多。除小額的帳款如樣品費等，有時需要討債外，一般付款因有銀行的擔保，較不易出問題。但是，如果交易條件是以賒銷方式 (O/A) 的話，較易造成呆帳，這時就要做好討債的準備，擬好各階段的討債信，以便寄出。所以，在以賒銷方式 (O/A) 交易時，尤其要做好徵信工作，以免以後造成討債上的困擾。

C. Grammar Practice 文法練習

★助動詞 (Auxiliary Verbs)：

與本動詞形成動詞片語，以表示時態 (Tense)、語態 (Voice)、語氣 (Mood)、疑問、或否定等，如 be, have, do, shall, will, can 等。常用的助動詞分類如下：

助動詞	例　　　　子
be 動詞	be, am, are, is, was, were, being, been
have 動詞	have, has, had
do 類動詞	do, did, done, need, dare, used
語氣助動詞	can, could, may, might, shall, should, will, would, must, ought 等。

★常與助動詞搭配使用的片語：

be able to	能	
had better	最好	
should like to	願欲	+ V. (原形)
would like to	願意	
would rather	寧願	
cannot but	不得不	
used to	習慣於 (過去)	
cannot help	不禁	+ Ving
be used to	習慣於	+ Ving

＊ 用法注意：

助動詞後必須接動詞原形。

Selection：選出最適當的答案

_____ 1. Listen! Someone _____ at the door.

(A) knocked　　　　　　　　(B) is knocking

(C) has knocked　　　　　　 (D) will knock

_____　2. The library building is nearly _____.

　　　　(A) completing　　(B) complete　　(C) completed　　(D) completion

_____　3. They _____ be married soon.

　　　　(A) are to　　　(B) are　　　(C) to　　　(D) were to

_____　4. The merchandise shall _____ on time.

　　　　(A) arrived　　(B) to arrive　　(C) arrive　　(D) arriving

_____　5. Mr. Taylor would _____ me at the hotel lobby.

　　　　(A) to meet　　(B) meet　　(C) met　　(D) meeting

_____　6. Lisa had better _____ in her house because of the typhoon.

　　　　(A) staying　　(B) to stay　　(C) stayed　　(D) stay

_____　7. Louis did _____ so.

　　　　(A) said　　(B) say　　(C) says　　(D) saying

D. Pattern Practice 句型練習

★相關的：

> ...related...
>
> ...relative...

1. 我們將感激收到你們的手套樣品及其他相關資料。

_____

2. 我們將感激如果你們寄來雜貨的目錄及其他相關細節。

_____

E. Business Terms 解釋名詞

1. D/P　　　　2. D/A　　　　3. D/N　　　　4. C/N

5. Statement of Accounts　　　6. E. & O.E.

F. Blank-filling 填充練習

Dear _____ ,

We take _____ in _____ that we _____ shipped the _____
goods on your _____ No. CH-11 today _____ the s.s. President
Nick V-546 _____ from Keelung _____ New York.

Herewith we _____ the _____ shipping _____ for your kind
_____ :

Commercial _____
Bill of _____

As _____ , we have _____ on you _____ 60 days _____
US$25,000 through _____ bankers, First _____ Bank.

We _____ be glad if you will duly _____ the _____ on
_____ :

_____ yours,

_____

G. Letter-writing 書信寫作

As an exporter, write your letter to the importer enclosing the related copies of
shipping documents and asking him to accept the bill on the terms of D/A.

No. 20 貿易：國際快遞
(International Express Delivery)

　　目前空運運輸除了郵局與航空貨運公司或貨運承攬商外，最常用的就是國際快遞公司。他們各有其特色與顧客群。

　　航空貨運一般為龐大貨物或大宗貨物。如果是小件或中型貨物如樣品等，一般以郵局的航空包裹或國際快捷郵件寄之。

NOTE

Chapter Twenty

Claims and Adjustments

索賠及調整

 **Outline**

1. What is a Complaint?

When the importer is not satisfied with either the exporter's products or his service, he may make a complaint to the exporter.

進口商對於出口商的產品或服務有不滿時，他可向出口商提出抱怨。

2. What is a Claim?

In international trade, a claim is a demand made to the insurer or the seller. When there is a loss or damage to the goods shipped, the importer can ask for compensation.

在國貿上，在貨物受損時，進口商可向保險公司或出口商要求索賠。

3. What is the Difference between a Complaint and a Claim?

Both "complaint" and "claim" refer to dissatisfaction in either the goods ordered or service rendered. Originally, claim is a word used in insurance and later also commonly applied in trade. An importer will complain first, and if the case is not settled, he will make a claim on the exporter for compensation.

抱怨與索賠皆指對所訂購的貨品和提供的服務不滿。起初，索賠原用於保險上，貿易上現也用之。進口商一般會先抱怨，如未獲解決，便會提出索賠。(補充：原則上抱怨是提出問題並要求解決，而索賠只是解決問題之一種。索賠包括退錢、退貨、賠錢等。另外，如加強包裝、準時出貨、更換貨品等，皆為解決抱怨之道。)

4. The Plan of a Complaint

The plan of a complaint is as follows:

抱怨信計畫如下：

⑴ Regret having to complain.　表遺憾。

⑵ State details of the order and the shipment.　訂單出貨細節。

⑶ Give reasons for the complaint.　抱怨理由。

⑷ Refer to the inconvenience caused.　引起不便。

⑸ Ask for an adjustment.　要求處理。

5. The Common Cases of Complaints

The common cases of complaints are as follows:

常見的抱怨信案例如下：

(1) Wrong goods　　　　　　　　　　　　　錯誤貨品

(2) Poor quality　　　　　　　　　　　　　劣質

(3) Not match the sample　　　　　　　　　與樣品不符

(4) Damage　　　　　　　　　　　　　　　損壞

(5) Bad packing　　　　　　　　　　　　　不良包裝

(6) Quantity　　　　　　　　　　　　　　　數量

(7) Late delivery　　　　　　　　　　　　　延遲交貨

(8) Non-delivery　　　　　　　　　　　　　未交貨

6. Rules for Making a Complaint

When making a complaint, an importer should:

進口商在寫抱怨信時，須把握以下要領：

(1) Make a complaint at once.　立即抱怨。

(2) Supply evidence.　提供證據。

(3) Let the exporter explain the reasons.　讓對方解釋。

(4) Not suggest any reason.　勿猜測原因。

(5) Avoid rudeness.　勿失禮。

7. What is an Adjustment?

An adjustment is a letter written or a step taken by the exporter to deal with a complaint.

「調整」為出口商所寫的信或所採取的步驟，以處理進口商的抱怨。

8. Rules for Making an Adjustment

When dealing with a complaint, an exporter should:

出口商在寫調整函時，須把握以下要領：

(1) Know that the customer is always right.　知道顧客總是對的。

(2) Be glad when the buyer complains.　高興接受顧客抱怨。

(3) Look into the case carefully.　仔細調查此案。

(4) Admit it readily if there is something wrong.　如有錯馬上承認。

(5) Refuse it politely if there is nothing wrong.　如無錯禮貌回絕。

(6) Solve the case satisfactorily.　完滿解決此案。

9. The Plan of an Adjustment

The plan of an adjustment is as follows:

調整函計畫如下：

(1) Regret to cause the trouble.　對所造成的麻煩表示遺憾。

(2) Look into the matter and will take full responsibility.

　　檢視事態並負起全責。

(3) Sorry for inconvenience.　對不方便感到抱歉。

(4) Make an adjustment.　對抱怨做調整。

(5) Hope the adjustment is satisfactory.　希望調整能被滿意。

10. Examples

Example 20.1　Wrong Goods　錯誤貨品

(A) Complaint

January 23, **20..**

Dear Sirs,

Yesterday when we took delivery of the shoes we ordered on our Order No. SH-034, we were surprised to find that the cartons contained 1,000 pairs of women's shoes, whereas our order was for 1,000 pairs of men's shoes.

Please check with your dispatch department and send us the right ones without delay.

Sincerely yours,

信文中譯：

(A)

敬啟者：

昨天當我們收到訂單 SH-034 號所訂的鞋子時，很驚訝發現箱子裝的是 1,000 雙的女用鞋子，然而我們訂單是訂 1,000 雙的男鞋。

請與你們的出貨部門核對一下並立即寄給我們正確的鞋子。

謹上

(B) Adjustment

January 30, **20..**

Dear Sirs,

We hasten to reply to your letter of January 23, **20..** in which you informed us that we shipped 1,000 pairs of women's shoes instead of 1,000 pairs of men's shoes.

Today, we have checked with our dispatch department and were sorry to learn that we made a mistake in your order.

We are sending you 1,000 pairs of men's shoes by air freight today and apologize for the inconvenience caused.

Sincerely yours,

信文中譯：

(B)

敬啟者：

　　我們急忙回覆你們 **20..** 年 1 月 23 日來信；在你們信上你通知我們說我們運出 1,000 雙女用鞋子，而非 1,000 雙男用鞋子。

　　本日已與我們出貨部門洽談,而非常遺憾得知在你們的訂單犯了錯誤。

　　本日經由航空貨運寄給你們 1,000 雙男用鞋子，並對所引起的不便道歉。

謹上

Example 20.2　　Poor Quality　　劣質

(A) Complaint

September 12, 20..

Dear Sirs,

We are writing to inform you that the 12,000 ball pens we ordered from you on our Order No. BP-90 of June 10, **20..** have reached us and have already been distributed to our chain stores for sales promotion.

However, many of our chain stores have returned the pens, stating that 90 percent of the pens leak and fail to write without making blots, as the report shows.

We are enclosing some of the samples for your examination and would demand a satisfactory solution to this problem.

Sincerely yours,

Enc.

信文中譯：

(A)

敬啟者：

　　我們寫信通知你們，**20..** 年 6 月 10 日訂單 BP-90 號訂購的 12,000 枝原子筆已抵此，並已分配至我們的連鎖店以利促銷。

　　然而，很多連鎖店退回這些筆，如報告所示，有 90% 的筆會漏水，且一寫就造成汙漬。

　　附上些樣品以供檢查，並要求對此問題有個圓滿解決。

謹上

附件

(B) Adjustment

September 20, **20..**

Dear Sirs,

Your letter of September 12, **20..** complaining about the pens supplied to your order No. BP-90 has caused a great deal of concern.

We have tested the samples you sent us and agree that they were not perfect. The defects have been traced to a fault in one of the machines and this has been put right.

We are sorry for the inconvenience and are sending you 10,000 ball pens as replacement. Also, we would be much obliged if you should return the faulty ones to us soon.

Sincedrely yours,

信文中譯：

(B)

敬啟者：

你們 **20..** 年 9 月 12 日來信，抱怨我們供應你們訂單 BP-90 號的筆，已引起我們很大的關心。

已試驗過你們寄來的筆且同意這些筆並非良品。這些缺點追根至一部機器的疏失，且此差錯現已修正了。

> 對此不便感到抱歉，並寄給你們 10,000 枝原子筆作為更換品。另外，如果你能將有瑕疵的筆儘速退還給我們將感激不盡。
>
> 謹上

Example 20.3 Not Match the Sample 與樣品不符

⒜ Complaint

March 14, **20..**

Dear Sirs,

When we came to examine the goods received against our Order No. FC-98, we found that the quality was different from what we ordered.

On this order we ordered 200 rosewood dressers, while we received 200 plywood dressers. It's different from your sample, as the attached survey report shows. As there is big difference in price in these two materials, please explain the reason for the mistake.

We look forward to hearing that the matter will be put right soon.

Sincerely yours,

Enc.

信文中譯：

(A)

敬啟者：

　　當檢查依我們訂單 FC-98 號所供應的貨物時，發現品質與我們所訂完全不同。這張訂單，我們訂購 200 臺花梨木化妝檯，然而我們收到 200 臺夾板的化妝檯，與樣品不符合，如附上的公證報告所示。因這兩種質料價格差異極大，請解釋為何會有此差錯。

　　期待得知此事將很快獲得更正。

謹上

附件

(B) Adjustment

March 20, 20..

Dear Sirs,

We very much regret to learn from your letter of March 14, **20..** that you found our dressers different from what you ordered in quality. From what you say, it seems possible that some mistakes have been made in the selection of the materials prepared for your order. We apologize for any inconvenience caused.

As the case stands, we would like to make you an allowance of 20% for the difference in price and expect you will accept our adjustment.

Sincerely yours,

信文中譯：

⒝

敬啟者：

　　很遺憾從你們 **20..** 年 3 月 14 日來信得知你們發現我們的化妝檯
與你們所訂的在品質上不同。

　　從你們所說來看，可能在選擇給你們訂單的原料時，犯了錯。我
們對引起的不便道歉。

　　因情況是如此，願對於價格的差異給你們 20% 的折讓，並希望
你們會接受我們的調整。

謹上

Example 20.4　Damage　損壞

⒜ Complaint

April 21, 20..

Dear Sirs,

We regret to inform you that the 1,000 mirrors on our Order No. RS-01,
as per your invoice No. 031 dated March 2, **20..**, were seriously damaged
when they reached us.

As our enclosed survey report shows, among the 1,000 pieces ordered,
200 were completely broken and 250 were cracked. The damaged
condition has caused us much inconvenience.

As the situation stands, we would appreciate it if you should send us 500 mirrors for replacement.

We expect to hear that the replacement is sent right away.

Sincerely yours,

Enc.

信文中譯：

(A)

敬啟者：

　　遺憾通知你們，我們訂單 RS-01 號所訂的 1,000 個鏡子，如你們 20.. 年 3 月 2 日發票 031 號所示，當到達此地時已嚴重損害。

　　如我們附上的公證報告所示，在所訂購的 1,000 個中，200 個已完全破裂；250 個有裂痕。此損壞的情況已引起我們很大不便。

　　因情況是如此，若你們能寄給我們 500 個鏡子以為更換將感激不盡。

　　期待得知更換品立即寄出。

謹上

附件

(B) Adjustment

April 29, 20..

Dear Sirs,

We regret to learn from your letter of April 21, **20..** that the mirrors shipped to your Order No. RS-01 were damaged when they arrived at your side.

We will certainly take full responsibility and are now looking into the case. Meanwhile, we have sent you today 500 mirrors by airfreight for your replacement and trust they will reach you in a couple of days.

We hope you will be satisfied with our handling and would apologize for any inconvenience caused.

                               Sincerely yours,

信文中譯：

(B)

敬啟者：

　　遺憾從你們的 **20..** 年 4 月 21 日來信中得知依你們訂單 RS-01 號所運出的鏡子在運達你們那邊時遭受損壞。

　　我們當然會負全責並正調查此案。同時，本日已由航空貨運寄給你們 500 個鏡子以利更換，且相信近日內這些鏡子會到達你們那邊。

　　希望你們會對我們的處理方式感到滿意，並為任何不便道歉。

　　　　　　　　　　　　　　　　　　　　　　　　　　　謹上

Example 20.5　Bad Packing　不良包裝

(A) Complaint

May 2, 20..

Dear Sirs,

The 1,000 sets of chinaware you supplied according to our order No. CH-045 were delivered today. We thank you for your prompt shipment.

However, when we unpacked the goods, due to your poor packing, we were not surprised to find that some of them were broken. As this is the second time in two months, we would suggest you improve your method of packing right away.

We are sending you a report and would ask you to send us the replacement soon.

Sincerely yours,

Enc.

信文中譯：

(A)
敬啟者：
　　依我們訂單 CH-045 號所供應的 1,000 組瓷器本日已送達。感謝你們迅速的出貨。

　　然而，當打開這些貨物時，由於包裝不良，我們料到有一些已破損。因這是二個月以來的第二次，我們建議立即改進你們包裝的方式。

　　現寄給你們一張報告且要求你們馬上寄來更換品。

謹上

附件

(B) Adjustment

May 10, 20..

Dear Sirs,

We are very sorry to learn from your letter of May 2, **20..** that some of the chinaware supplied to your order No. CH-045 were broken when delivered.

We have checked with our packing department and have found the packing material not strong enough for export. We will use better packing material next time to ensure safe shipment.

As required, we are sending you a series of chinaware for replacement and regret the trouble we have caused you.

Sincerely yours,

信文中譯：

⒝

敬啟者：

　　很遺憾從你們 **20..** 年 5 月 2 日信中得知有些依你們訂單 CH-045 號所供應的瓷器在到達時已損壞。

　　我們已與包裝部門商討過，而發現所用包裝原料不夠堅固以耐出口。下次我們會用較好的包裝原料以確定貨物能安全到達。

　　如你們所要求，寄給你們一系列的瓷器以利更換並為所引起的麻煩感到抱歉。

謹上

Example 20.6　Quantity　數量

⒜ Complaint

June 1, **20..**

Dear Sirs,

We thank you very much for your prompt delivery of the coffee beans we ordered on March 23, **20...**

The number of bags delivered was 2,000 whereas our order was for 2,200. Obviously, the shipment was 200 bags in shortage as shown in our attached survey report.

Please send the short-shipped 200 bags to us by air soon.

> Sincerely yours,
>
> Enc.

信文中譯：

> (A)
>
> 敬啟者：
>
> 　　非常感謝你們迅速地將我們於 **20..** 年 3 月 23 日所訂購的咖啡豆運達。
>
> 　　所運達的數量是 2,000 袋，然而我們訂的是 2,200 袋。明顯地，這批貨短少 200 袋，如附上的公證報告所示。
>
> 　　請立即由航空寄來此短少的 200 袋。
>
> 謹上
>
> 附件

(B) Adjustment

> June 7, **20..**
>
> Dear Sirs,
>
> We are much concerned to learn from your letter of June 10, **20..** that you received only 2,000 bags of coffee beans instead of 2,200. We checked with our export department and learned that due to a confusion of orders we made the shipment short of 200 bags.

We would like to make an apology for this and are arranging to send the 200 bags by air tomorrow.

We hope this will now settle the matter to your complete satisfaction.

Sincerely yours,

信文中譯：

(B)

敬啟者：

　　從你們 **20..** 年 6 月 10 日來信中得知你們僅收到 2,000 袋咖啡豆，而非 2,200 袋感到擔憂。已與我們的出口部門核對過，而得知由於對訂單有些混亂，我們出的貨短少 200 袋。

　　願為此道歉，並正安排明天由航空運出此 200 袋。

　　希望現在如此解決可令你們滿意。

謹上

Example 20.7　Late Delivery　延遲交貨

(A) Complaint

July 5, **20..**

Dear Sirs,

We regret to have to complain about late delivery of the computers ordered on our Order No. CP-45 of April 5, **20...**

As you promised to ship the goods before the end of April, we placed the order on this understanding. However, we were disappointed to learn that the goods did not arrive here until a few days ago. The delay has caused us much trouble.

Unless we can receive satisfactory explanation from you, we will return the goods for compensation.

Sincerely yours,

信文中譯：

(A)
敬啟者：

　　遺憾必須抱怨關於我們 **20..** 年 4 月 5 日的訂單 CP-45 號所訂購的電腦延遲交貨。

　　因你們答應在 4 月底前出貨，我們瞭解此點才下了訂單。然而，我們很失望得知這批貨到幾天前才到達此地。此延誤已引起我們很大麻煩。

　　除非我們能得到令人滿意的答覆　，否則將退回此批貨物以求賠償。

謹上

(B) Adjustment

July 10, **20..**

Dear Sirs,

Your letter of July 5, **20..** complaining of delay in delivery time has caused us a great deal of concern.

It is our practice to ship the goods ordered on time. However, for your order No. CP-45, due to the fact that there was a great shortage of plastic material for the computers ordered, the production schedule was delayed.

Actually, though we expedited our production immediately when the material was available, a delay in shipping seemed unavoidable.

We apologize for the inconvenience the delay caused.

Sincerely yours,

信文中譯：

(B)

敬啟者：

20.. 年 7 月 5 日來信抱怨延遲交貨已引起我們十分關心。

我們慣例是準時交貨。然而，對於你們訂單 CP-45 號，由於所訂購電腦的塑膠原料有嚴重短缺，生產計畫因而延誤。

其實，當原料獲得時，雖曾立即盡力加速生產，然而延誤似仍不可避免。

為此延誤所帶來的不便感到抱歉。

謹上

Example 20.8　Non-delivery　未交貨

⑷ Complaint

June 20, **20..**

Dear Sirs,

On March 1, **20..** we placed an order for your sunglasses on the mutual understanding that you will ship the goods ordered before April 20, **20...**

However, since the latest shipment date has been over for one month, we have received neither the goods we ordered nor any advice from you.

Please explain the reason why you delay in shipment and state when we may expect our goods.

Sincerely yours,

信文中譯：

(A)

敬啟者：

　　在 **20..** 年 3 月 1 日得知你們會在 **20..** 年 4 月 20 日前出貨，我們下一張訂單訂你們的太陽眼鏡。

　　然而，最後出貨日期已超過一個月了，我們沒有收到所訂的貨物，也沒有得到任何消息。

　　請解釋為何會延遲交貨並說明我們何時可收到我們的貨物。

謹上

(B) Adjustment

June 27, 20..

Dear Sirs,

We hasten to reply to your letter of June 20, **20..** and to apologize for the unfortunate mistake you pointed out.

When you placed your order, we supposed you would require shipment before the end of June and therefore are planning to ship the order on June 29, **20..** via Sea Land.

We apologize for the inconvenience caused by the non-delivery.

Sincerely yours,

信文中譯：

⒝

敬啟者：

　　我們趕快回覆你們 **20..** 年 6 月 20 日來信，並為所指出的令人遺憾的錯誤道歉。

　　當你們下訂單時，我們以為要在 6 月底前出貨，因此我們預定在 **20..** 年 6 月 29 日經由美商海陸航線運出此訂單。

　　為此未運出貨物所帶來的不便感到抱歉。

　　　　　　　　　　　　　　　　　　　　　　　　　　　　　　謹上

✎ Exercise

A. Questions 問答題

1. What is a complaint?

2. What is a claim?

3. What is the difference between a complaint and a claim?

4. What is the plan of writing a letter of complaint?

5. What are the cases of complaints?

6. What are the rules of making a complaint?

7. What is an adjustment?

8. What are the rules of making an adjustment?

B. Business Insight 實務探討

◆ 索賠

　　在生意上，各種糾紛如：品質差、規格不符、數量差異、包裝不良、延遲交貨等，買賣雙方尤須誠心誠意地來處理。如果處理不當或情形較嚴重，則會造成索賠。在索賠時，就必須提出證明，如公證報告 (survey report) 等，以昭信對方，以獲得公平合理的解決。

C. Grammar Practice 文法練習

★名詞 (Nouns)：

名詞是表人、動物、事物、地方或抽象觀念等，以可不可數分以下兩類：

1. 可數名詞：包括普通名詞與集合名詞。

2. 不可數名詞：包括專有名詞、物質名詞與抽象名詞。

分類	包括	例　　　子
可數名詞	普通名詞	cat, boy, dog, etc.
	集合名詞	people, family, fish, etc.
不可數名詞	專有名詞	John, China, Japan, etc.
	物質名詞	air, water, sunshine, etc.
	抽象名詞	duty, love, health, etc.

Selection：選出最適當的答案

_____ 1. His only _____ about his job is that he has to work on Saturdays.

　　(A) complement　(B) compliment　(C) complaint　(D) accompany

_____ 2. All _____ are asked to show up by 10:00 a.m.

　　(A) personal　　(B) personalities　(C) personnels　(D) personnel

_____ 3. Under the new contract, everyone will get a 5% _____ in salary.

　　(A) raise　　　　(B) rise　　　　(C) arise　　　　(D) praise

_____ 4. Sarah was moved to the new _____ by the window.

　　(A) garage　　　(B) office　　　(C) comparison　(D) companion

_____ 5. Call the repair person. The _____ is tearing the papers again.

　　(A) jack　　　　(B) scissors　　(C) woodcutter　(D) copier

_____ 6. _____ affects the buying power of the dollar.

　　(A) Attraction　(B) Inflation　　(C) Prosecution　(D) Competition

_____ 7. We have to adopt a new marketing _____ to sell our new product.

　　(A) delivery　　(B) proceeding　(C) strategy　　(D) protection

D　Pattern Practice 句型練習

★我們以……寄上……：

> We sent...by air parcel.
>
> We sent...by air express.

1. 我們以航空快遞寄上我們的訂單，請儘速確認。

_____

2. 我們以航空包裹寄上我們的罐頭食品樣品，一共五盒，收到時請告知。

_____

E　Blank-filling 填充練習

Dear _____ ,

Yesterday when we _____ delivery _____ the shoes we _____ on our _____ No. 12, we _____ surprised to _____ that the _____ contained 1,200 _____ of women's _____ , whereas our order _____ for 1,200 _____ of men's.

Please _____ with your _____ department and _____ us the right _____ without _____ .

　　　　　　　　Sincerely _____ ,

F. Letter-writing 書信寫作

As an importer, write a letter of complaint to complain about an exporter's shipment of wrong goods.

No. 21 外匯：外匯存底
(Foreign Exchange Reserves)

　　外匯儲備，也稱為外匯存底。是指一個國家貨幣當局持有並可以即時兌換外幣資產。以狹義來說，外匯儲備指一個國家外匯的累積；而以廣義來說，外匯儲備是指以外匯計價的資產，包含現鈔、黃金、國外有價證券等。外匯儲備對於平衡收支和穩定匯率有非常重要的影響力。

＊註解：

　　SDR 為 IMF (國際貨幣基金組織) 會計上記帳的單位。假使將 IMF 視為世界的央行，SDR 就相當於 IMF 創造出來的一種「貨幣」。特殊提款權 (SDR) (Special Drawing Rights) 1969 年由 IMF 所創造。

Chapter Twenty-One

Regaining Lost Customers

挽回顧客

 **Outline**

1. The Importance of Regaining Lost Customers	挽回客戶的重要性
2. The Plan of a Letter Regaining Lost Customers	寫信的計畫
3. The Techniques of Writing a Letter Regaining Lost Customers	寫作的技巧
4. Examples	範例

1. The Importance of Regaining Lost Customers

It is important to find new customers; it is even more important to keep old ones. It is quite often that an old customer may, due to some unexpected reasons, lose contact with the seller. It is the seller's duty to find the reasons and to improve his service in regaining the lost customers.

開發新客戶很重要，但更重要的是維持舊客戶。常常舊客戶因某些原因而沒有與賣家聯絡。賣家的責任是找出原因所在且改善服務，重獲顧客信心。

2. The Plan of a Letter Regaining Lost Customers

The plan of a letter regaining lost customers is as follows:

挽回客戶信的寫作計畫：

⑴ Mention not having received any order for a long time.

坦白提到久未接到訂單。

⑵ Sincerely ask the reason for being so.

誠懇詢問為什麼。

⑶ Send the latest reference and assure best service.

寄上最新的資料，保證提供最好的服務。

⑷ Express thanks for past patronage.

對過去的支持表示謝意。

3. The Techniques of Writing a Letter Regaining Lost Customers

The techniques in writing a letter regaining lost customers are as follows:

挽回客戶信寫作的技巧：

⑴ Be efficient

當顧客久未來信時，約一兩個月左右，不要太長，即要準備寫信。
因時間越久沒連絡，越難把線接上。英文裡 "Out of sight, out of
mind." 即是此理。

⑵ Be polite

語氣要誠懇，就是知道對方已經向別家採購，也要保持穩重，誠懇
請問對方自己改進之道，以獲好感、重獲惠顧。

⑶ Be patient

不斷地把公司最新的資料寄給對方，耐心地保持聯繫。

⑷ Be far-sighted

把眼光看遠，不斷追蹤，並強調提升品質與服務，必能重獲顧客信心。

4. Examples

Example 21.1　To regain a lost customer (A)　挽回客戶 (A)

March 12, **20..**

Dear Sirs,

We have not received either your letter or your order for four months.

It's our policy to have good contacts with our customers. We wonder if there is any special reason for your absence.

We assume that it is quite possible that at this moment you may be in the market for our products. Therefore, we are now sending you our latest catalogue and price list for your reference.

Please inform us of the items in which you are interested so that we may render further service.

Sincerely yours,

Enc.

信文中譯：

敬啟者：

已有四個月沒有收到你們的信或訂單了。

我們的政策是與我們的顧客保持良好的聯繫。不知是否有任何特別理由才使得我們未聯絡。

我們認為很有可能你們此刻會需要採購我們的產品。因此,現在寄上我們最近的目錄及價目表以供參考。

　　請通知我們，你們有興趣的項目，如此可以為你們提供更多的服務。

謹上

附件

Example 21.2　To regain a lost customer (B)　挽回客戶 (B)

June 6, 20..

Dear Sirs,

It has been five months since we shipped your last order on January 20, **20...** We trust the sporting goods have reached you in good condition and would like to know if we can be of further service to you.

We understand that at this moment you may be in great demand for our kitchenware. We are, therefore, sending you our current catalogue and price list for your evaluation.

We would appreciate receiving your early reply.

Sincerely yours,

Enc.

信文中譯：

敬啟者：

　　自從於 **20..** 年 1 月 20 日運出你們上一張訂單後已經過了五個月了。我們相信那批運動器材已安然抵達你們那邊；我們想知道是否可以為你們做更多的服務。

　　我們瞭解此刻你們可能需要採購我們的廚具。因此，寄給你們我們目前的目錄及價目表以供評估。

　　若能及早收到你們的回音將感激不盡。

謹上

附件

✎ Exercise

A. Questions 問答題

1. Why is it important to write a letter regaining lost customers?
2. What is the plan of writing a letter regaining lost customers?
3. What are the techniques used in writing a letter regaining lost customers?
4. What does the seller usually enclose in a letter regaining lost customers?

B. Business Insight 實務探討

◆ 斷了線的風箏

在國際貿易上，由於市場與市場之間競爭激烈，時而會有訂單中斷的狀況。當顧客在採購之後，很久都沒有回音，如斷了線的風箏；這時賣方就要採取緊迫盯人的態度，適時寄出追蹤函，問問看對方對於所運出的貨物是否滿意，是否要購買新的產品，是否需要其他服務。其實在商業上最直接有效的推銷方式，就是直接洽談；然而，在國際貿易上，因路途的關係，可用 e-mail 或通訊軟體往來追蹤。也因如此，才能把斷了線的風箏接上線。

C. Grammar Practice 文法練習

★關係代名詞 (Relative Pronouns)：

關係代名詞是兼有代名詞與連接詞作用的代名詞，故稱之。

關係代名詞	例　　　　　　句
who	I know the man who came yesterday.
whose	The man whose name is John is here.
whom	The girl whom you met is Lucy.
which	The letter which she wrote is on the desk.
that	This is the house that I live in.
what	I know what he said.

Selection：選出最適當的答案

_____ 1. The lady _____ Bob is talking to is Lucy.

(A) who　　　　(B) whom　　　(C) which　　　(D) whose

_____ 2. I saw a house _____ windows were broken.

(A) whose　　　(B) which　　　(C) that　　　　(D) what

_____ 3. Joe has an uncle _____ store is in London.

(A) which　　　(B) that　　　(C) what　　　(D) whose

_____ 4. Robert lives in Keelung, _____ is a large seaport.

(A) where　　　(B) which　　　(C) that　　　(D) whose

_____ 5. The police tried to locate anyone _____ saw the criminal.

(A) which　　　(B) whom　　　(C) who　　　(D) that

_____ 6. David had a bank account, _____ he had opened last week.

(A) what　　　(B) that　　　(C) whose　　　(D) which

_____ 7. The place _____ Judy worked part time last summer is Melbourne.

(A) what　　　(B) where　　　(C) of which　　　(D) whom

_____ 8. Judy told us _____ she knew about Australia.

(A) what　　　(B) that　　　(C) whom　　　(D) which

Pattern Practice 句型練習

★惟限，如果 (在……條件下)：

---

provided (that) S. + V. = on condition that S. + V.

subject to + N.

---

1. 我們可以在 6 月底前出貨，惟限你們的信用狀在 6 月 10 日前到達。

_____

2. 我們可以下訂單訂兩萬臺腳踏車，惟限你們允許我們百分之五的折扣。

_____

Blank-filling 填充練習

Dear _____ ,

We _____ not received either your _____ or your _____ for _____ months. It's our _____ to _____ good contacts _____ our customers. We _____ if _____ is any _____ reason for your _____ .

We are now _____ you our _____ catalogue and price _____ for your _____ .

Please _____ us _____ the items _____ which you _____ interested so _____ we _____ render _____ service.

　　　　　　　　Sincerely _____ ,

F. Letter-writing 書信寫作

You are the exporter of garments. Write a letter to an importer, hoping to regain the lost customer.

No. 22 外匯：順差 / 逆差

(Favorable Balance/Unfavorable Balance)

　　順差是指一國的國際收支帳 (balance of payments) 中收入比支出高或是貿易差額 (balance of trade) 中出口總額高於進口總額。超出的資金可作為外匯存底 (foreign exchange reserves)、外匯基金、國外投資使用等。整體來說，順差是有利的，但超出過多，可能引起國內通貨膨脹。反之則為逆差 (unfavorable balance)。

No. 23 外匯：外匯 (Foreign Exchange)

　　外匯代表購買力，一種在他國購買商品或享受服務的能力。

　　外匯市場是外幣買賣的市場，分為：即期外匯交易 (一般投資人最常用，例如：出國購買外幣現鈔或旅行支票、出口商出口押匯、進口商進口押匯)、遠期外匯交易 (提供投資人外匯避險的管道，例如：進出口商鎖定匯率成本)、外匯換匯交易 (主要用於銀行的資金拆借上，把多餘的幣別換入所需的幣別)。

Chapter Twenty-Two

Establishment of Agency Ship

建立代理關係

 **Outline**

1. The Qualifications of an Agency

When choosing an agency, the exporter/importer/manufacturer will consider the following qualifications:

選擇可靠的代理商，出口商／進口商／製造商必須要考慮的資歷條件如下：

⑴ Reliability and financial soundness   可靠性

⑵ Technical ability in handling the goods to be sold   專業性

⑶ Market relations   市場關係

⑷ Of other competing products   競爭品牌

⑸ Sales outlets   銷售網路

2. The Sources of Finding an Agent

The sources of finding an agent are as follows:

尋找代理商的來源有以下五種：

(1) Government's trade organization, such as　　　政府貿易機關
  the Bureau of Foreign Trade

(2) Embassy, such as the AIT　　　　　　　　大使館

(3) Trade promotion organizations, such as　　貿易發展協會
  the TAITRA

(4) The chamber of commerce, such as　　　　商會
  the Taiwan Chamber of Commerce

(5) The banks　　　　　　　　　　　　　　銀行

  * BOFT: the Bureau of Foreign Trade　　　國貿局

  * AIT: American Institute in Taiwan　　　美國在臺協會

3. An Agency Agreement

Example 22.1　An Agency Agreement　代理商合約書

AN AGENCY AGREEMENT

Suitable for exclusive and sole agents (representing manufacturers overseas)

This Agreement is made this _____ day of **20..** between PIZA CO., LTD. whose registered office is situated at No. ××, Sec. 3, Xinsheng S. Rd., Da'an Dist., Taipei, Taiwan (hereinafter called "the Principal") of the one part and WATSONS IMPORTS, INC. ×× Blue Drive, San Francisco, CA 90012, U.S.A. (hereinafter called "the Agent") of the other part.

WHEREBY IT IS AGREED as follows:

1. The Principal appoints the agent from this date as its Sole Agent in _____ (hereinafter called "the area") for the sale of _____ manufactured by the Principal and such other goods and merchandise (all of which are hereinafter referred to as "the goods") as may hereafter be mutually agreed between them.

2. The Agent will during the term of _____ years (and thereafter until determined by either party giving three months' previous notice in writing) diligently and faithfully serve the Principal as its Agent and will endeavour to extend the sale of the goods of the principal within the area.

3. The Principal will from time to time furnish the Agent with a statement of the minimum prices at which the goods are respectively to be sold and the Agent shall not sell below such minimum prices.

4. The Agent shall not sell any of the goods to any person, company, or firm residing outside the area without consent in writing of the Principal.

5. The Agent shall not during the continuance of Agency constituted sell goods of a similar class or such as would or might compete or interfere with the sale of the Principal's goods either on his own account or on behalf of any other person.

6. Upon receipt by the Agent of any order for the goods the Agent will immediately transmit such order to the Principal who will execute the same by supplying the goods direct to the customer.

7. Upon the execution of any such order the Principal shall forward to the Agent a duplicate copy of the invoice sent with the goods to the customer and in like manner shall from time to time inform the Agent when payment is made by the customer to the Principal.

8. The Agent shall duly keep an account of all orders obtained by him and shall every three months send in a copy of such account to the Principal.

9. The Principal shall allow the Agent the following commissions (based on FOB US dollars _____ ,) in respect of all orders obtained by the Agent in the area.

10. The Agent shall be entitled to commission on the terms and conditions mentioned in the last preceding clause on all export orders for the goods received by the Principal.

11. Should any dispute arise as to the amount of commission payable by the Principal to the Agent the same shall be settled by the Auditors.

12. This Agreement shall in all respect be interpreted in accordance with the Law of the Republic of China.

As Witness the hands of the Parties hereto the day and year first hereinbefore written.

PIZA CO., LTD.   WATSONS IMPORTS, INC.

_____   _____

信文中譯：

代理商合約書

本合約書是於 **20..** 月日由當事人一方皮賽有限公司，位於臺灣臺北市大安區新生南路三段××號 (以下簡稱本人) 與他方當事人華生進口公司，美國加州舊金山藍道××號 (以下簡稱代理商) 所簽訂。茲約定事項如下：

1. 本人茲任命代理商自本日期起為 (以下簡稱代理地區) 之獨家代理以銷售本人所製造之以及以後雙方互相同意之其他貨物及商品 (以下簡稱商品)。

2. 代理商在其年任期內 (以及其後由當事人一方在三個月以前書面通知他方所決定之期間內) 將竭誠為本人服務並努力在代理地區內促銷本人之商品。

3. 本人將經常向代理商提供每種商品最低售價表，代理商不得以低於表定價格出售。

4. 代理商未經本人書面同意，不得將商品之任何部分售與代理地區以外之任何個人、公司或行號。

5. 代理商在本代理合約書有效期間內，不得以自己名義或代表任何其他個人、公司或行號銷售與本人商品類似之商品，因而干擾本人商品之銷售或與之競爭。

6. 代理商接到商品訂單後，應立即將訂單寄交本人，本人如果接受，則將商品直接運交顧客。

7. 本人履行每一訂單後，則將開往顧客之發票副本寄交代理商，並當顧客向本人付款時，以同樣方式隨時通知代理商。

8. 代理商所獲得之一切訂單均應記帳並每隔三個月向本人寄送一份帳單。

9. 代理商在代理地區所直接獲得之一切訂單經本人接受並履行後，由本人給予代理商佣金 (按 FOB 美金計算)。

10. 本人輸往代理地區之一切出口訂單，代理商均得依照上條所述之條件請求支付佣金。

11. 如因本人付給代理商之佣金數目發生爭執時，將以本人之稽核員所決定之數目為準。

12. 一切有關本合約書之解釋，以中華民國法律為準。

茲證明本合約書是雙方當事人於前述之年、月、日簽訂。

皮賽有限公司   華生進口公司

_____   _____

4. Enquiry from a Prospective Agent

Example 22.2   Enquiry from a Prospective Agent   可能的代理商來函

March 10, **20..**

Dear Sirs,

We are indebted to the TAITRA for your name and address and would like to know if you are interested in extending your export business to our country by appointing us as your agents for the sale of your products.

We are a well-established firm with more than 20 years of history and integrity in Taiwan. We not only have our own complete sales networks, but also have very good relations with local enterprises.

We feel confident that if you give us the opportunity to deal in your products, the result will be entirely satisfactory to both of us.

We hope that this will be a forerunner to many years of profitable business to both of us and look forward to hearing from you soon.

Sincerely yours,

信文中譯：

敬啟者：

　　我們感激外貿協會，得知你們的名字及地址。我們想知道是否你們有興趣任命我們作為你們產品的代理商以促銷你們的產品，來拓展你們的出口業務至本國。

　　我們是在臺一家 20 多年歷史與正派經營的健全公司。我們不僅有我們完善的銷售網路，而且與當地企業界有非常好的關係。

　　我們相信如果你們給我們機會來處理你們的產品，結果必能使我們雙方皆完全滿意。

　　我們希望此將是我們雙方長久有利生意的開始，並期待很快得到回音。

謹上

5. Reply from a Manufacturer

Example 22.3　Reply from a Manufacturer　製造商回函

March 20, **20..**

Dear Sirs,

Thank you very much for your letter of March 10, **20..**, in which you show an interest in acting as our agents for the sale of our products in Taiwan.

After completion of our credit files and careful consideration of your proposal, we have now made our decision to accept your proposal and to appoint you as our sole agents in Taiwan district for a period of one year.

For guidance and to help towards pleasant relations between us in our transactions, we have prepared an Agency Agreement in duplicate, which is enclosed for your reference. Any suggestion you may have will be welcome. If you have no objection to any of its articles, please return the duplicate copy duly signed.

It is our strong belief that this agency relationship will prove mutually beneficial and we trust that we will have a satisfactory cooperation in the years to come.

Sincerely yours,

Enc.

信文中譯：

敬啟者：

　　非常感謝你們 **20..** 年 3 月 10 日來信，在信上你們表示有興趣作為我們在臺灣的代理商，來銷售我們的產品。

　　在完成我們的信用調查及謹慎考慮你們的提議後，我們已決定接受你們的提議來任命你們作為我們在臺灣地區的獨家代理商,期限為一年。

為了有個指引並為了幫助在我們交易時能達成愉悅的關係,我們已準備了一份代理商合約書,一式兩份,隨函附上,以供參考。有任何建議歡迎多加提出。如果你們對條款沒有反對意見時,請在合約書上簽名並寄回一份。

我們深信此代理關係將證明對我們雙方皆有利,且相信不久後我們將會有個令人滿意的合作。

謹上

附件

✎ Exercise

A. Questions 問答題

1. What are the qualifications to be considered, when an exporter/importer is trying to find an agency?

2. What are the sources of finding an agency?

B. Business Insight 實務探討

◆ 代理商

代理商,顧名思義,即是代理買賣雙方業務的人或公司。在早期,約於鴉片戰爭前,我國貿易開始興盛時,當時代理與外國作買賣業務的機構或商店,叫作洋辦或洋行。代理商設在進出口兩邊國家皆可。現代的貿易,尤其較具知名度的公司,尤須代理商來作促銷及廣告工作。

C. Grammar Practice 文法練習

★關係代名詞 (Relative Pronouns)──限定與非限定用法 (Restrictive/Non-Restrictive):

分為限定用法 (Restrictive) 及非限定用法 (Non-Restrictive)。

種　類	用　　　法
1. 限定用法	關係子句作限定及形容詞用，其前後不加逗點。 e.g. My brother who is a doctor came to see me. 　　（→有很多兄弟） We want a man who can speak English. 　　（→限定會說英文）
2. 非限定用法	關係子句作補述用，其前後要加逗點。 e.g. My brother, who is a doctor, came to see me. 　　（→只有一個兄弟） We want a man, who can speak English. 　　（→剛好會說英文）

Selection：寫出適當的答案代碼

限定用 R (Restrictive)，非限定用 N (Non-Restrictive)。

_____ 1. The man whom you saw at the jewelry store was Mike Brown.

_____ 2. The house that we bought last month was large.

_____ 3. The man whom we met yesterday is Mr. Smith.

_____ 4. Tom Jones, whom we know, is a big buyer.

_____ 5. These are all the goods that I have kept in stock.

★關係代名詞的省略 (Omission of Relative Pronouns)：

當關係代名詞的先行詞是屬於受格時，則此關係代名詞可省略。

種　類	省略	用　　　法
1. 為受格時	可省	關係代名詞，如為受格時，可省略。 e.g. The house that we bought was large. (可省) 　　The man whom you saw was Jerry. (可省)
2. 介詞 + which	不可省	關係代名詞，如前有介詞時，則不能省略，但如介詞置於後面即可省略。 e.g. This is the house in which I live. (不可省) 　　This is the house (which) I live in. (可省) 　　This is the place where I live. (不可省) (主格)

3. 有補述用法	不可省	有補述用法，即非限制用法，不能省。 e.g. Bob, whom I haven't seen for years, is coming. (whom 不能省)

＊關係代名詞的省略，為較口語化用法，正式場合以不省為宜。

Selection：選出最適當的答案

_____ 1. This is the town _____ Charles lives.

    (A) which　　　(B) in which　　　(C) to which　　　(D) in that

_____ 2. He was the first man _____ came here.

    (A) who　　　(B) that　　　(C) whose　　　(D) whom

_____ 3. Is this the man _____ you are looking for?

    (A) whom　　　(B) who　　　(C) that　　　(D) whose

_____ 4. Mr. Abe Lincoln is the president _____ we respect.

    (A) who　　　(B) which　　　(C) whose　　　(D) ✕

_____ 5. I like the secretary _____ is very responsible.

    (A) who　　　(B) whom　　　(C) whose　　　(D) ✕

_____ 6. The prices _____ you quoted are much too high.

    (A) what　　　(B) ✕　　　(C) in which　　　(D) whose

_____ 7. _____ we ordered has reached us today.

    (A) That　　　(B) Which　　　(C) Where　　　(D) What

D. Pattern Practice 句型練習

★因為情況是如此：

> As the case stands...
>
> As the situation stands...
>
> As such is the case...
>
> Such being the case...

1. 因為情況是如此，我們不得不拒絕接受此批羊毛內衣的交貨。

   _____

2. 因為情況是如此，我們希望你們降低 10% 的價格以利我們促銷。

   _____

E. Blank-filling 填充練習

Dear _____ ,

We are _____ to the TAITRA _____ your name and _____
and would _____ to know _____ you _____ interested
_____ appointing us _____ your agents _____ the _____
of your products. We are a _____ firm with more _____ 20 years
_____ history.

We feel _____ that _____ you give us the _____ to deal
_____ your products, the _____ will be _____ to _____ of
us.

We look _____ to _____ from you soon.

                    Sincerely _____ ,

F. Letter-writing 書信寫作

As an importing agent in Taiwan, write your letter to an exporter to ask for the
rights of representing the sale of his electric products here.

No. 24 外匯：匯率 (Exchange Rate)

何謂匯率 (Exchange Rate)？

匯率是兩國貨幣的兌換比率。經濟是否景氣與匯率的波動有相互變動關係。當景氣好時，許多企業投資意願高、資金需求量變大，利率相對提升，以致於國內投資市場獲利率提高而吸引海外資金流入，促使新臺幣 (對美元) 匯率呈現升值效應。

Chapter Twenty-Three

Circular Letters

通函

Outline

1. What is a Circular?

It is a letter, usually sent in large quantity, to customers or prospective ones, for a promotional purpose or for announcing something.

通函為公司為了某種目的，如業務或廣告等，大量發給顧客或潛在顧客的函件。

2. The Functions of a Circular

通函之功能有下列兩種：

⑴ To inform (通知)：宣布事項，像是開張、遷移啟事等。

⑵ To promote (促銷)：促銷商品或服務。

3. The Features of a Circular

通函之特色有下列兩種：

⑴ simple in style (格式簡潔)：為了能大量發函，格式以簡潔為主。

⑵ clear in meaning (意義清晰)：由於一般通函內容較單純，所以意義也就較清晰。

4. The Kinds of Circulars

通函之種類通常有下列三種：

⑴ Announcing Opening	宣布開張
⑵ Removal	遷移啟事
⑶ Announcing Others	宣布其他事情

Example 23.1   Announcing Opening   宣布開張

May 10, **20..**

Dear Sirs,

We take pleasure in informing you that on May 1, **20..**, we established ourselves as an exporter of General Merchandise.

As we have had very good connections with factories, we are in a position to supply you with our high-grade goods at most competitive prices.

We look forward to the pleasure of serving you.

Sincerely yours,

信文中譯：

敬啟者：

　　榮幸通知，在 **20..** 年 5 月 1 日本公司成立為雜貨出口商。

　　因跟工廠關係很好，我們能以最有競爭性的價格，供應我們高級產品給你們。

　　期待為你們服務的榮幸。

謹上

Example 23.2　Removal　遷移啟事

March 5, 20..

NOTICE OF REMOVAL

Dear Sirs,

We are pleased to inform you that owing to the expansion of our business we have decided to move our office to the following address:

W&D TRADING CO., LTD.

No. ××, Sec. 3,

Nanjing E. Road, Songshan Dist.,

Taipei, Taiwan

Our telephone number remains the same.

Your new patronage will be highly appreciated.

Sincerely yours,

信文中譯：

遷移啟事

敬啟者：

　　　很高興通知，由於業務的擴展，我們已決定將我們的辦公室遷至下列的地址：

　　W&D 貿易有限公司

　　臺灣臺北市松山區南京東路三段××號

　　我們的電話號碼仍沒有變更。

　　我們將非常感激你們重新惠顧。

謹上

Example 23.3　Announcing Others　宣布其他事情——通知漲價

August 12, **20..**

Dear Sirs,

Owing to the rapid and unexpected rise of material which has greatly influenced our production cost, we are sorry to inform you that from and after September 1, **20..** our old price list will be cancelled and replaced by the new one as per the enclosed sheet.

As the demand for our textiles has still been very high, we would suggest you place your order before the old price list expires.

Sincerely yours,

Enc.

信文中譯：

敬啟者：

　　由於原料成本迅速及意外的上漲，如此相當地影響我們的生產成本，我們遺憾通知，從 **20..** 年 9 月 1 日起，我們舊的價目表將取消而由附上的新的價目表取代。

　　因我們的紡織品需求量一直仍很高，建議你們在舊價目表失效前下訂單。

謹上

附件

Example 23.4   Announcing Others
宣布其他事情——通知成立分公司

January 1, 20..

Dear Sirs,

In view of the rapid development of our business in the U.S., we have now decided to open a branch at the following address:

HEALTH SPORTS, INC.
×× West 30th St.,
New York, NY 10001
U.S.A.

Since the new branch will open on January 15, **20..**, we shall be pleased if you will visit our showroom there for our new sports products.

Mr. Ben Wang, our branch manager, will be much willing to serve you.

Sincerely yours,

信文中譯：

敬啟者：
　　鑑於在美國業務的迅速發展，我們現已決定在下列地址成立我們的分公司：

健康運動器材公司

美國紐約州紐約市

西 30 街××號

　因我們的分公司將於 **20..** 年 1 月 15 日開張，我們會很高興如果你們能參觀我們那兒的新樣品間，看我們新的運動產品。

　王班先生是我們分公司經理；他將很樂意來為你們服務。

　　　　　　　　　　　　　　　　　　　　　　　　　　　　謹上

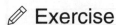 Exercise

A. Questions 問答題

1. What is a circular?

2. What are the functions of a circular?

3. What are the features of a circular?

4. What are the examples of circulars?

B. Business Insight 實務探討

◆ DM 是什麼？

　在行銷上，常用的促銷方式之一，即是 DM (direct mail)，中譯為直接郵寄，也就是所謂的通函或循環信，可作為開發促銷或通知事情之用。在促銷策略上，先看好選擇性的潛在顧客群，即收集情報後，寄予強勢文宣包括產品及服務的型錄及簡介，使之留下深刻的印象，為產品之促銷鋪路。DM 適用於國內外的促銷，在國內，常常在打開信箱時會發現一大堆 DM，來自超市、百貨公司、房屋公司、建築公司、汽車公司、補習班或美髮院等，五花八門，無所不有。在國際貿易上，DM 功用亦頗大，新成立的公司，尤須靠 DM 來打入國際市場。DM 在國際市場拓展上，是一主要尖兵。

C. Grammar Practice 文法練習

★**副詞 (Adverbs)**：副詞修飾動詞、形容詞和整句。

用法種類	例　　句
1. 修飾動詞	John orders much every year. Linda runs fast in the park.
2. 修飾形容詞	The salesperson is very happy. Your report is wonderfully good.
3. 修飾副詞	The accountant learns much quickly. The goods sell very well.
4. 修飾整句	Luckily he survived. Happily she danced on the floor.

Selection：選出最適當的答案

_____ 1. I was _____ busy that I forgot to send the samples to Tony.

(A) hardly　　　(B) too　　　(C) such　　　(D) so

_____ 2. Betty spoke _____ firmly to him about his poor job performance.

(A) most　　　(B) quite　　　(C) quiet　　　(D) little

_____ 3. The director read my letter very _____ .

(A) careful　　　(B) carefully　　　(C) care　　　(D) caring

_____ 4. The report is _____ written.

(A) bad　　　(B) worse　　　(C) badly　　　(D) worst

_____ 5. The inspector _____ opened the carton.

(A) quickly　　　(B) quick　　　(C) quicken　　　(D) quickening

_____ 6. William _____ knows anything.

(A) hard　　　(B) harden　　　(C) hardening　　　(D) hardly

_____ 7. The factory workers sang _____ .

(A) merrily　　　(B) merry　　　(C) happy　　　(D) joy

D Pattern Practice 句型練習

★請通知是否……：

> Please say whether...
>
> Please inform us whether...
>
> Please advise whether...

1. 請通知是否你們願意作我們在中東地區的獨家代理。

_____

2. 請通知是否能於 10 月底前以空運運出 1,000 條 100% 棉質床單。

_____

E Blank-filling 填充練習

Dear _____ ,

We take _____ in _____ that on _____ we established _____ as _____ exporter _____ General Merchandise _____ the address _____ shown _____ the letterhead.

We _____ forward _____ the _____ of _____ you.

Sincerely _____ ,

F. Letter-writing 書信寫作

As a manager of a trading company, write your circular to announce the opening of your business.

No. 25 金融：「境外金融中心」
OBU (Offshore Banking Unit)

　　境外金融中心，也稱為國際金融業務分行，是政府提供免稅或減稅待遇服務、吸引金融機構、貿易商、投資者等來我國所成立的金融單位。

　　簡單來說，註冊在海外的公司即為「境外公司」，是依國際商法註冊之租稅優惠的公司。一般為節稅目的而設立的境外公司，大多登記在英屬維京群島 (British Virgin Islands)、薩摩亞 (Samoa)、模里西斯 (Mauritius) 等免稅天堂地區的外國公司。

　　境外公司擁有開立 OBU 帳戶的資格，只要在免稅天堂地區註冊登記，皆享有雙重免稅優惠，即對我國政府免稅，對公司註冊地的政府也免稅。因此，公司可利用 OBU 帳戶進行海外投資及商務往來的靈活運用。

No. 26 金融：洗錢 (Money Laundering)

定義

洗錢，也稱洗黑錢，指透過非法手段所取得的金錢，經由「洗淨」變為看似合法的資金。洗錢常與毒品交易、恐怖組織、黑道等重大犯罪有所關連，尤以跨國方式最常見。洗黑錢的共通性有高額資金、來歷不明、模糊資金的來源地等。

目的

因為查緝犯罪手段的進步，如果犯罪者直接拿不當的金錢使用，很容易被政府查到。所以常透過洗錢的手法，將不當的金錢偽裝成正當的交易。

方法

因多數政府針對洗錢行為有所管制，犯罪者為了逃避各機關的監視，其洗錢方法是將大筆的金錢分為數個款項，並以他人名義開設其他帳戶，這些帳戶彼此互不相關，之後經由匯款、開立支票等方式轉入犯罪者的名下。

Chapter Twenty-Four

Position Vacant and Position Wanted

求才及求職

Outline

1. How to Write a Want Advertisement

求才廣告之內容，應包括下列各項：

⑴ 徵求人才的公司行號名稱。

⑵ 徵求人才的種類。

⑶ 應徵人 (applicant, candidate) 應具備的資格，如學經歷等。

⑷ 說明待遇、福利等。

⑸ 說明應徵方法。

⑹ 應徵截止日期。

2. Want Ad Examples

Example 24.1.1   A Want Ad 1   徵才廣告 1

A SECRETARY TO MANAGER WANTED

A leading American Trading Company in Taipei requires a female secretary to the manager.

All applicants must be college graduates with a bachelor's degree and have complete understanding of spoken and written English, and accounting. Applicants are requested to apply in their own handwriting personal data including past experience and salary expected and including one recent photo to Personnel Dept., W&D Trading Co., Ltd. All applications will be treated confidentially.

信文中譯：

徵經理祕書

臺北一家著名美國貿易公司徵一經理女祕書。

所有應徵者必須是大學畢業，具學士學位，英文說寫流利，通會計。應徵者必須親筆寫個人資料，包括過去經驗及希望待遇，並附上近照寄至 W&D 有限公司人事部。所有應徵資料將會機密地處理。

Example 24.1.2　A Want Ad 2　徵才廣告 2

IMPORT/EXPORT ASSISTANT WANTED

Energetic young people preferably with at least one year's working experience in import/export field. Good command of English and typing ability are necessary. We provide a challenging and excellent opportunity to develop with the company. Please send your application in English (with name and address in Chinese and English) with full details and recent photo marked "Confidential" to: Personnel Dept., W&D Trading Co., Ltd.

信文中譯：

徵進出口助理

　　年輕充滿活力，最好具至少一年在進出口業工作經驗。必須英文能力強，打字能力好。我們提供具挑戰性及卓越機會與公司一起成長。請備英文應徵函(具中英名字及地址)，包括所有細節及近照，註明「機密」，寄至 W&D 有限公司高林公司人事部。

3. Reference Required for Job Application

⑴ Résumé　履歷表

　　又稱 curriculum vitae，履歷表應包括下列項目：

　　1) 個人資料 (Personal Details)：如姓名、年齡等。

　　2) 應徵職位 (Job Objective)：如祕書、經理等。

　　3) 教育背景 (Education)：包括學歷、科系、主修、副修科目等。

　　4) 經歷 (Work Experience)：把最近的工作寫在上面，一目了然。

5) 出版作品 (Publication)：如果有的話，可擇要列出。

6) 獲獎記錄 (Awards)：在校內或校外、工作上、社會上，曾獲得的獎勵、優良記錄，均可列舉。

7) 備詢人 (Reference)：即推薦人或保證人，可將其姓名、住址、電話、職位及所屬機關名稱寫出，但需先徵求同意。一般用 "Reference will be furnished upon request."(要求即寄) 即可。

Example 24.2.1　A Résumé 1　履歷表 1

AMY CHEN
No. ××, Sec. 3, Zhongshan N. Rd.,
Zhongshan Dist., Taipei
(02)2521-××××

OBJECTIVE

To obtain a position in finance with particular interest in banking, and consulting or multinational investments, utilizing my economic and accounting background in a domestic or international environment.

EDUCATION

NATIONAL ×× UNIVERSITY

Bachelor of Law degree in Economics, **20...**

Course work included International Economics, Accounting, Monetary and the Banking System, Statistics.

OVERSEAS STUDY: English program in ×× University for one month.

HONORS: Dean's List; Scholarship to ×× University.

ACTIVITIES: The Guitar Club; Student Association of Economics Department, ×× University.

×× FIRST HIGH SCHOOL

HONORS AND ACTIVITIES: Principal's List; Music Club.

EXPERIENCE

TUTOR: taught junior high school students in Math and English subjects. January **20..**–March **20..**

PROMOTION SERVICE: helped and consulted customers in the supermarket. July **20..**–September **20..**

DAY CAMP COUNSELOR: Taipei. June **20..**–July **20..**

PERSONAL

Born: January 15, **20...** Interest in guitar, music and current events.

Traveled through the U.S. and Japan. Reference available upon request.

Example 24.2.2　A Résumé 2　履歷表 2

John Smith

×× Spring Ridge Drive,

Berkeley Heights, NJ 07922

OBJECTIVE

To obtain a position in finance or international trade with particular interest in banking, consulting, multinational investments and trading, utilizing my business and economic background in a domestic or international environment.

EDUCATION

UNIVERSITY OF ××, Philadelphia, PA

Bachelor of Arts degrees in Economics Major, **20...**

Course work included International Trade and Monetary Economics.

Research Project: Export Sector of the Chinese Economy.

Overseas Study: Intensive Far Eastern program.

Honors and Activities: Dean's List; International Relations Undergraduate Student Association.

×× HIGH SCHOOL, Rockville, Maryland

College preparatory, honors, and advanced placement study, **20...**

Honors and Activities: Dean's List.

EXPERIENCE

CHAIRMAN OF THE BOARD, UNIVERSITY OF ××: HILL COLLEGE HOUSE, Supervised 550 student residents; payroll manager: expanded staff from 50 to 125 to increase involvement and activities, dispensed over $150,000 in wages and salaries.

August **20..**–June **20..**

W&D, INC., Research Department: assisted in financial analysis, economic trending, and other statistical work; established and followed up company contacts in CAD/CAM, machine tool, and robotics industries; provided information to account executives in field, supplied investment data for corporate, pension, and other major accounts of firm.

Summer **20..**

PERSONAL

Born: August 11, **20...** Traveled through the U.S., Greece, Israel, Caribbean, Taiwan, Hong Kong, and Singapore. Familiarity with French. Willing to relocate and/or travel in the U.S. and abroad. References available upon request.

Example 24.2.3　A Résumé 3　履歷表 3

CURRICULUM VITAE

NAME: James W. Clinton

ADDRESS: No. ××, Lane 13, Sec. 1, Neihu Rd., Neihu Dist., Taipei, Taiwan

DATE AND PLACE OF BIRTH: May 25, **20..**－Burlingame, CA, U.S.A.

MARITAL STATUS: Single

EDUCATION: Foothill × × College

Cupertino, CA, U.S.A.

Graduated: August **20..**, with honors

Degree: A.S. Business Administration

× × University

Overall Grade: Point Average (4.0 Scale): 3.72

ENGLISH TEACHING AND GENERAL WORK EXPERIENCE:

The Church of Jesus Christ

Taipei, Taiwan

Position: English Teacher

June **20..** to August **20..**

And High Air Aviation Inc.

×× Airport, CA, U.S.A.

Position: Parts Manager for ×× Aircraft

       Tasks included bookkeeping, purchasing, and distribution of materials.

OTHER EXPERIENCE AND ACHIEVEMENTS:

Worked for two years, from **20..** to **20..**, as a missionary in Taiwan.

Example 24.2.4　A Résumé 4　履歷表 4

CURRICULUM VITAE

Mary Tobin

No. ××, Lane 120, Dengshan Road, Beitou Dist., Taipei

(02) 2891-××××

B.A., ×× University at Albany, New York (**20..**) Anthropology Regent's Scholarship

W&D Foundation **20..–20..** (Fairfax, California)

Administrative Consultant: Development of curricula for seminars; coordination between classes; personnel development; bookkeeping; development of funding sources.

V&J Arts Institute **20..–20..** (Boulder, Colorado)

Teacher: Taught classes in General Business Practices.

Albany City, Inc. **20..–20..** (Albany, New York)

Counselor: Worked with six professors.

⑵ Autobiography　自傳

中英文自傳的寫法類似，雖並不一定要完全逐字地翻譯過去，但重點一定要把握住。寫自傳的方式有二種：一為傳統式，二為功能式。

1) 傳統式的自傳 (Traditional Autobiography)

依照自己的本身資料、家庭資料、教育背景、能力、嗜好、未來計畫與抱負等依序寫下來。是把所有的資料都列入了，但皆千篇一律，較平淡無奇。傳統式的自傳細節如下：

① 對自己做簡短的說明 (briefing)：如姓名、性別、生日、出生地。如果姓名已寫在標題旁或下面，文中可不必再提。

② 家庭資料 (family information)：家中人數，對每個家庭分子作個簡介。

③ 教育背景 (educational background)：從小學開始寫起直到最後教育階段。看情況，可略縮短，或由中學開始等。

④ 能力 (abilities)：描述在最後教育階段所學的各種技術與能力，包括專業能力、語言能力、人際關係等。

⑤ 嗜好 (hobbies) 及個性 (character)：描述出自己參與的活動及平日所做的休閒活動，由此可看出一個人的個性。個性方面可表明積極、活潑、文靜、負責等。

⑥ 未來計畫與抱負 (future plan)。

2) 功能式的自傳 (Functional Autobiography)

即針對所應徵工作的性質來寫。由自己相關的優點開始寫，配合學歷與經歷，到最後使自己的優點、學歷、經歷能符合所應徵工作的需求。

這是比較具有特色的寫法。因為它具有目標，功能式的自傳頗能留下深刻印象。

Example 24.3.1　A Traditional Autobiography 1　傳統式自傳 1

AUTOBIOGRAPHY

Lily Lee

I was born on October 29, **19..**, in Taipei, Taiwan. My father is a businessman. I have two brothers and two sisters. We enjoy a very harmonious family life.

At the age of six, I entered elementary school at a neighborhood school. Six years later, in September **20..**, I was at × × Junior High School. There, I studied very hard, which enabled me to enter the famous Taipei First × × High School in **20...**

After graduation from senior high school in **20..**, I participated in the annual test for Universities and Colleges. Fortunately, I was admitted to the Department of Anthropology, National × × University. The four years of undergraduate study there was fruitful. In addition to academic study, I was also engaged in field work and completed a paper on the "The Influence of Cosplay in Taiwan." I received a bachelor's degree in

June **20...**

To further my working experience, I wish to submit my qualifications and am sure that I will do my best if being employed.

Example 24.3.2 A Traditional Autobiography 2 傳統式自傳 2

AUTOBIOGRAPHY

Leo Wang

I was born on March 21, **19..**, in Yuanlin, Changhua County, Taiwan. There are four members in my family, including my parents, my elder brother and me. My father is an honest businessman; my mother is a housewife.

I was sent to school when I was six years of age. I lived up to my parents' expectation, as my records always showed a distinguished achievement at school, beginning from the elementary school to the university.

After six years of secondary education, I was successfully admitted to the Department of Chemistry, ×× University. I have always had a burning desire for Chemistry, and I hope to be an expert in applied Chemistry. Therefore, I took more than the normal amount of credits in the optional subjects and did a lot of outside reading and laboratory work. In summer, I worked at the ×× Pharmaceutical Co., Ltd., to earn tuition fees for the following semester and to obtain experience and knowledge in field work.

Now that I have completed the military service, × × months after graduation from the university, it is time that I find a suitable job to develop my potential and to put my career goal into practice.

Example 24.3.3   A Traditional Autobiography 3   傳統式自傳 3

AUTOBIOGRAPHY

Jenny Chang

I was born in Taipei, Taiwan on July 11, **19...** My father is a civil servant at the Department of Health, Taipei City Government. My mother is a school teacher in a junior high school downtown. Both of them are residents of Taipei.

Although I am the only child of my parents, I am by no means a spoilt girl. I am very independent and responsible.

Upon graduation from junior high school, I became a student of Taipei First × × High School. At school, I participated in some extracurricular activities, in which I developed interest in music, swimming and folk dancing. I even tried to join the school band; I can play many musical instruments, such as the clarinet and the French horn.

In **20..**, I entered ✕✕ University, and took international trade as my major. In view of the fact that Taiwan is an island with limited natural resources, our country must depend on export and import. International trade has become not only an act of transaction but also a way of life.

During four years of college training, I learned a great deal about the trading business. Before graduation, I was employed as a part-time clerk in a small trading corporation, responsible for computer operation and typing, which are my specialities.

I have been working in the present company for ten months now. The working condition here is good and my boss is very kind, but I wish to work in a large company where I can take on heavy responsibilities and develop my potentiality.

Example 24.3.4 A Traditional Autobiography 4 傳統式自傳 4

AUTOBIOGRAPHY

Tina Ro

On June 1, **19..** I was born in the suburbs of Changhua City. My father was a government official and was transferred his position for several times so our home moved from place to place. My father was retired in **20..**, when we moved to Taichung.

I am the fourth of my parents' five children. I have two elder brothers, one elder sister and one younger sister. My eldest brother handles a trading company. The second brother is a lawyer in Taipei. My elder sister is working on her Master of Business Administration degree at the University of ××. My younger sister is a junior in the Department of Economics of ×× University.

I entered ×× Elementary School when I was six. I was one of the top two among 50 classmates. Then I entered ×× High School in **20...** In **20..**, I was admitted into the Department of Foreign Languages of National ×× University. I shall be graduated in June as I hope to be employed right after graduation.

Thank you very much for your kind attention to my autobiography.

Example 24.3.5　A Functional Autobiography　功能式自傳

AUTOBIOGRAPHY

May Cheng

"Words without actions are of little use," is my motto.

I was born on December 27, **19..** in Taipei. I have three younger sisters and one brother. They are all students. My father is a businessman. He runs a hardware store. My mother is a nice housekeeper. They are kind, friendly, and conservative.

Since I was a little girl, I have been interested in business career. That is the reason why I entered National × × University and majored in Business Administration. During school days, I studied hard for all my lessons and learned ACCOUNTING, TIME MANAGEMENT, FINANCIAL MANAGEMENT, HUMAN RELATION, MARKETING, and so on. As to my professional skills, I am good at operating computer. My typing speed is 65 WPM.

Concerning personality, I am easy-going, active, initiative, and adaptable. As I am the oldest daughter, I am independent. I think that to be a competent SECRETARY, the most important elements are being responsible and open-minded. Being a clerk in our store for more than ten years, I understand how to deal with others and get along well. Customers are always right.

As I know, your company offers good working environment and good promotion system for your staff. It will be my pleasure if I have a chance to work for you. I will try my best to do my duty, help my colleagues, and create good working atmosphere.

⑶ Application Letter　申請工作函

申請工作函又稱應徵函。在某一方面來說，它又像是一封推銷函 (sales letter)，因為去找工作等於是去推銷自己的資歷、能力、訓練、經驗等。推銷函寫作的四個原則是：

1) 引起注意 (Cause attention)

2) 產生興趣 (Arouse interest)

3) 激發慾望 (Create desire)

4) 刺激行動 (Prompt action)

申請工作函的寫法亦相同。即要以資歷引起雇主的興趣，然後以過去的經驗記錄以獲得信心，最後促使雇主採取行動來安排面談，並予聘用。

Example 24.4.1　An Application Letter 1　申請工作函 1

Dear Sir,

I have read with interest your advertisement in today's "China Times" for a sales representative in your company. I feel that it is just the kind of post that I have been looking for.

I enclose my résumé and autobiography, and shall be obliged if you will give me a personal interview.

Yours truly,

Enc.

Example 24.4.2　An Application Letter 2　申請工作函 2

＊ 應徵經理女祕書職位：

Dear Sir,

In reply to your advertisement in today's "China Times" regarding a secretary to manager, I wish to apply for the position.

I am confident that I can meet your special requirements indicating that the candidate must have a good knowledge of English and accounting. I graduated in Business Administration from ×× University last year.

In addition to my study of Business English and Accounting while in the university, I also have had the secretarial experience for two years in W&D Trading Co., Ltd. The main reason for changing my job is to gain more experience with a superior trading firm like yours. I believe that my education and experience will prove useful for the work in your office.

Enclosed please find my curriculum vitae, certificate of graduation, letter of recommendation from the Dean of Business Administration of the University, and one recent photo. I shall be much obliged if you will give me an opportunity for a personal interview.

Sincerely yours,

Enc.

---

*履歷表：

CURRICULUM VITAE

Name in Full: Sandy Wang

Date of Birth: December 7, **19..**

Family Relation: Eldest daughter

Permanent Domicile: No. ××, Sec. 2, Neihu Rd., Neihu Dist., Taipei

Present Address: Same as Permanent Domicile

Educational Background: Entered National Hsinchu ×× Senior High

School in September **20..**, finished in July **20...**
Studied business administration at ×× University in September **20..**, finished in September **20...**

Working Experience: As stated in the letter of application.

Rewards: Won a prize for three years' regular attendance at the National Hsinchu ×× Senior High School. Won the second prize in the Intercollegiate English Speech Contest sponsored in **20...**

Personal details: Age: 23 Height: 165 cm

Weight: 54 kgs

Marriage: single

Hobbies: reading, stamp collection, and sports.

I hereby declare upon my honor the above to be a true and correct statement.

⑷ Unsolicited Letter　自薦信

自薦函即應徵者自己主動發信向公司機關詢問是否有人才之缺；此種信尤其具主動之精神，頗受企業界歡迎。

Example 24.5　An Unsolicited Letter　申請工作自薦函

＊應徵祕書職位：

Dear Mr. Williams,

Someday in the future you may have need for a new secretary.

Here is why I should like to offer myself for the job, and here is why I am so much interested in obtaining it. For one thing, I know that you do an enormous variety of work very fast and very well. This offers a real challenge to whoever works for you. It is the kind of challenge I'd like to meet because I have trained myself in secretarial work.

As to my mechanical abilities, I can operate computers very well and type at the rate of 70 words per minute.

I cannot think of any job in which I would be so useful in working as a secretary to you. I hope I could work for you.

Yours truly,

4. Interview

應徵者在寄出申請工作函或已填好申請工作表後，雇主公司開始審核工作。在審核工作後，便挑出資格符合者參與面談。所以，應徵者能參與面談，表示申請工作函及履歷表所列的資歷已被接受了。面談的目的不僅使雇主公司機構有機會瞭解應徵者，而且應徵者也可順便瞭解工作的性質及公司機構的狀況。

本節可分三部分來探討：

> 一、面談前及面談時
> 二、準備面談時之應對
> 三、面談檢討

一、面談前及面談時

A. 面談前

在應徵前，應徵者必須先有充分的準備，以便在面談者面前，有最佳的狀況表現。面談前的準備可分三方面：

> (一) 建立信心
> (二) 收集資料
> (三) 整理儀容

(一) 建立信心

　　首先要建立信心。要知道，大部分人只要有面談的經驗，就有失敗的經驗，萬一失敗還有其他的機會等著，心情放得開，自然容易建立信心。

(二) 收集資料

　　1. 雇主公司的狀況：

　　　信心建立在知識，而知識建立在準備之上。孫子曰：「知己知彼，百戰百勝。」對提供工作的公司要有一徹底的研究，對於面談必有助益。

　　2. 專業知識：

　　　面談時可能會問到的專業知識，必須收集，並予溫習。

(三) 整理儀容

　　面談的第一印象很重要。服裝要事先選定，以美觀大方為主。衣服的厚薄要與氣候相配合；顏色、樣式要適合求職時的場合。注意以整齊清潔合宜為原則。

B. 面談時

面談時需注意的事項分三個部分：

> ㈠ 到達
> ㈡ 在面談時
> ㈢ 面談結束

㈠ 到達

可早十分鐘，或更早些到達，以便先認識一下環境，並有助於自己定下心來面對面談的挑戰。

記得面帶笑容，對於接待的人員的服務，多予致謝，以留下好印象。

㈡ 在面談時

在聽問題時，要小心聽，並盡量精簡地回答。面談時要注意看面談者。面露微笑，坐姿要自然，讓人有很好相處之感。

㈢ 面談結束

面談者把文件收起，請應徵者等候消息，並問有沒有問題，或僅僅從椅子上站起來，這表示面談已結束。

二、準備面談時之應對

面談時的話題，大部分會環繞在面談者所問的問題上面，而這些問題的內容也跟面談者的層次有關。比如說：當人事主管問問題時，內容會比較廣泛而普遍。這是因為人事主管在整個雇用程序中是居於前段篩選的階段。但到了愈高層次的面談，問題就可能較專業化與細部化。

本小節分七項目來舉例：

(一) 認識自己

(二) 自己的學經歷

(三) 對方公司

(四) 專業知識及業務

(五) 認識應徵的職位

(六) 一般性問題

(七) 機智性的問題

(一) 認識自己 (About Yourself)：

1. 你是誰？你的家庭狀況如何？What's your name? What's your family background?

2. 你的個人人生目的是什麼？What's your goal in life?

3. 你的個人事業目標是什麼？What's the goal of your career?

(二) 自己的學經歷 (Educational and Experience Background)：

1. 你的教育背景如何？What's your educational background?

2. 你畢業於那所學校？What school did you graduate from?

3. 你有工作經驗嗎？Do you have any work experience?

4. 你認為你最喜歡的工作有那些？What are the jobs you like to do?

5. 你認為你有那些特殊優點和特殊能力？What's your major? What's your specialty?

6. 為什麼你認為你適合此工作？Why do you think you are qualified for the job?

(三) 對方公司 (Company)：

1. 你對本公司瞭解多少？How much do you know about our company?

2. 你如何知道本公司？How do you know our company?

3. 你知道本公司的特色有那些？What do you think are the features of

our company?

4. 你知道本公司的商譽如何？What do you think about our reputation?

5. 你如果成為本公司的一分子，會有何感想？ What do you think if you become a member of our company?

㈣ 專業知識及業務 (Professional Knowledge)：

專業知識及業務的問題因各行各業而異。

以下為祕書方面的問題：

1. 你認為如何才能作個成功的祕書？ Please tell me how to be a successful secretary.

2. 祕書的功能如何？What is the function of a secretary?

3. 那些是作個好祕書的條件？ What are the requirements of a good secretary?

4. 現代的祕書必須負那些責任？ What are the responsibilities of a modern secretary?

5. 你對於電腦的認識如何？How much do you know about computer?

㈤ 認識應徵的職位 (About the Job)：

1. 你知道在此職位上你的責任有那些？Do you know what responsibilities are on this job?

2. 你對於這個職位瞭解多少？How much do you know about the job?

3. 如果聘用你，你何時可來上班？ If we employ you, when can you start working?

4. 你對此職位的發展潛力知道那些？What is the prospect of the job?

㈥ 一般性問題 (General Matters)：

1. 你是否關心時事？Are you concerned about current events?

2. 你常說實話嗎？Do you always tell the truth?

3. 加班會影響你的家庭生活嗎？ Do you think working overtime will affect your family life?

4. 你要多少待遇？What's your expected salary?

(七) 機智性的問題 (Wits)：

1. 你承擔得了壓力嗎？Can you stand any pressure?

2. 要你做五年，你感覺如何？What's your idea on a five-year contract?

3. 為什麼想離開目前的工作？ Why do you plan to quit your present job?

4. 為何辭去上一個工作？Why did you quit your last job?

三、面談檢討

本小節分二部分來探討：

(一) 面談檢討 (Interview review)
(二) 寫一封後續感謝函 (A follow-up thank-you letter)

(一) 面談檢討 (Interview review)：

面談之後，回想一下自己的表現如何，回答下面問題，用 1 到 5 來代表你曾做到的程度：

1. 我讓自己的外表看起來舒服嗎？

2. 面談後我對這家公司的瞭解與先前的瞭解，相符合的程度有多大？

3. 我是否保持輕鬆並對談自如？

4. 我在回答問題時，是否在強調三件事：我的能力，我的意願與我對工作的適合性？

5. 我是否專心傾聽面談者說話？

(二) 寫一封後續感謝函 (A follow-up thank-you letter)：

在面談後約一、二天左右，可寫封後續函以感謝面談者撥空來處理
應徵之事。如果能再寫一封信給曾參與甄選事務，並曾幫忙接待的
祕書小姐，必可收到意外的效果。

Example 24.6 A Follow-up Thank-you Letter 英文後續感謝函

April 22, **20..**

Mr. Amy Lin
General Manager
V&J Trading Co., Ltd.
No. ××, Sec. 2, Nanjing E. Rd.,
Songshan Dist.,
Taipei

Dear Mr. Lin,

I just wanted to write to tell you how pleased I was to meet with you last
Thursday. Thank you for considering me for the position as your
assistant. The job is just what I am looking for, and I think that I would
be able to fit into your company very well.

I am looking forward to hearing from you soon.

Sincerely yours,

✎ Exercise

A. Questions 問答題

1. What are the common references required for job applications?
2. Give five examples of interview questions.

B. Business Insight 實務探討

◆ 找工作

找工作，一般而言，主要來源有三：一為推薦，二為自薦，三為由各種來源，如報紙、雜誌、人力銀行等。找工作有如推銷產品，所以在寫自傳、履歷表、應徵函時，就有如在寫推銷函一樣，必須注意推銷函的四個要素：

(1) To cause attention (引起注意)

(2) To arouse interest (產生興趣)

(3) To create desire (激發慾望)

(4) To prompt action (刺激行動)

在未見到人之前，用人單位只能由所獲得的資料，來判斷一個人的可適用性。所以，外表上應徵寄出的資料要美觀、大方、乾淨、整齊、齊全。在審核這些資料後，用人單位才會決定是否要請應徵者來面談。有些公司還強調應徵者要親筆書寫資料，其目的即在看應徵者的字體是否工整。俗話說：字如其人。能寫字工整的人，做事必能井井有條，也必能為用人單位所欣賞。

C. Grammar Practice 文法練習

★副詞 (Adverbs)──關係副詞 (Relative Adverbs)：

關係副詞兼有副詞與連接詞的作用。主要的關係副詞有 when, where, why, how, whenever (無論何時), wherever (無論何處), however (無論如何) 等。

種類	例　　　句
when (何時)	I remember the day when Roger came here.
where (何處)	This is the office where we work.
why (何故)	This is the reason why Wilson left.
how (如何)	Can you tell me the way how you did it?
whenever (無論何時)	You may come whenever you are free.
wherever (無論何處)	He may go wherever he likes.
however (無論如何)	We will do our best, however hard the job is.

Selection：選出最適當的答案

_____ 1. Vienna is the place _____ the musician was born.

(A) where　　　(B) which　　　(C) what　　　(D) wherever

_____ 2. This is the reason _____ the airplane was delayed.

(A) which　　　(B) that　　　(C) why　　　(D) how

_____ 3. _____ there is a will, there is a way.

(A) What　　　(B) Which　　　(C) That　　　(D) Where

_____ 4. The sooner we start, the _____ we will finish it.

(A) early　　　(B) earlier　　　(C) more earlier　(D) earliest

_____ 5. We are always busy _____ the president comes.

(A) whenever　(B) however　　(C) whatever　　(D) that

_____ 6. Tell me the time _____ you will arrive in New York.

(A) which　　　(B) when　　　(C) why　　　(D) where

_____ 7. We will ask the guide _____ the museum is.

(A) when　　　(B) which　　　(C) what　　　(D) where

D. Pattern Practice 句型練習

★其實：

> In fact...
>
> As a matter of fact...
>
> Actually...

1. 其實，我們早已於 3 月初將你們所訂購的 1,000 支熱水瓶運出。

_____

2. 其實，我們所報的電動價格是市面上最有競爭性的。

_____

E. Letter-writing 書信寫作

When applying for the position as a secretary, write your letter of application along with your autobiography and résumé.

商業知識

No. 27 金融：套匯與套利 (Arbitrage)

　　Arbitrage means a profit from the simultaneous purchase and sale of an asset. People make a profit from price differences of similar financial instruments on different markets or in different forms. Arbitrage exists owing to market inefficiencies. It provides a mechanism to ensure that prices do not deviate considerably from fair value for a long time.

定義

即時購買和出售資產，以賺取利潤。這是一個貿易利潤，在不同市場或不同形式，利用價格差異的相同或類似的金融工具。因此套匯與套利存在低效率的市場，它提供了一種機制，以確保價格在長期的時間下不會大幅偏離公允價值。

實務

實務上，套匯為利用各國貨幣匯率間的變化賺取差額利潤；套利則為利用銀行利率變化的差額賺取利潤。

Chapter Twenty-Five

Social Letters in Business

商業社交信

Outline

1. What is a Social Letter?

A social letter is a letter written, for some social purpose, to express feelings or to inform some personal matters.

社交信為社會交際信函，為表達個人情感或通知某些私人事物而寫。

2. The Characteristics of a Social Letter

The characteristics of a social letter are:

社交信的特色如下：

(1) Tone: Friendly and personal　語調：親切而友善

(2) Style: Informal and simple　形式：不正式及簡單

   1) Handwriting　　　　　　　親筆寫

   2) Format　　　　　　　　　格式

Heading 信頭：	可有可無
Inside Address 收信人地址：	可省略
Salutation 稱謂：	較親切，如 Dear Jim, Dear Lisa
Body of the Letter 信文：	用句較短，較親切
Complimentary Close 結尾敬語：	依交情而有不同之用語
最正式	Faithfully yours,
正式	Sincerely yours,
親切	Best wishes,
朋友親戚	With love,

3. The Kinds of Social Letters

(1) Letters of Introduction 介紹信

   介紹信的寫作要領如下：

   1) 提到與被介紹人之關係。

   2) 請求給予協助。

   3) 表示有機會樂於回報。

Example 25.1　　A Letter of Introduction　　介紹信

June 5, **20..**

Dear Sirs,

This letter will be handed to you by Mr. Tony Lee, our sales manager, who in April and May will be visiting Germany and France, where we are anxious to extend our interests.

If you should kindly help him get in touch with the people concerned or give him any help he may need, we would be very grateful.

We will always be happy to reciprocate any favor you may render to Mr. Tony Lee.

Sincerely yours,

信文中譯：

敬啟者：

　　此信將由李東尼先生──我們的業務經理，轉交給你。他將於 4 月及 5 月拜訪德國及法國。我們正渴望拓展我們的業務到此兩國。

　　如果你能幫他與當地相關人士取得聯絡或給予他可能需要的任何協助，我們將非常感激。

　　對於你給予李東尼先生的任何幫助我們將非常樂意來回報。

謹上

(2) Letters of Recommendation　推薦信

推薦信的寫作要領如下：

1) 提到與被推薦者之關係。

2) 被推薦者之優點，如能力、品德、個性、潛力、適職性、可塑性等。

3) 希望被推薦者能被接受或任用。

Example 25.2　A Letter of Recommendation　推薦信

July 1, 20..

Dear Sirs,

I take pleasure in recommending Ms. Linda Wu, a good friend of mine, who is applying for the vacancy as a secretary in your company.

I have known Ms. Wu since she graduated from National ×× University when she came to work as a secretary for me. She is responsible and open-minded. English is her specialty. She is well qualified for being a capable secretary. Your favorable consideration of Ms. Wu's application would be highly appreciated.

Sincerely yours,

信文中譯：

敬啟者：

　　我很榮幸推薦吳琳達小姐給你們。她是我的好朋友,現在應徵貴公司的祕書職位。

　　我認識吳小姐是當她在國立政治大學畢業後來作我的祕書。她是很負責而且心胸開闊的。英文是她的專長。她是非常有資格來作一位有能力的祕書的。我將非常感激你們能惠予考慮吳小姐的應徵。

謹上

---

(3) Letters Informing a Visit　通知訪問函

　　通知訪問函的寫作要領如下：

　　1) 告知要訪者之名、職稱。

　　2) 訪問之日、時、地、班機等。

　　3) 期待見面或惠予接機。

Example 25.3　A Letter Informing a Visit　通知訪問函

January 20, 20..

Dear Sirs,

I am pleased to inform you that Mr. Brown, our vice president, and I are scheduled to arrive in Taipei on January 25 at 18:20 by CAL flight 877.

We will contact you on arrival in Taipei and look forward with pleasure to seeing you and all your colleagues at your company.

Sincerely yours,

信文中譯：

敬啟者：

我很高興通知你，布朗先生——我們的副董事長和我預定於 1 月 25 日下午 6:20，坐華航 CAL 班機 877 號，抵臺北。

我們在到達臺北時將會跟你們聯絡，並很高興期待能見到你及貴公司的同仁們。

謹上

⑷ Letters of Thanks　感謝信

感謝信的寫作要領如下：

1) 感謝對方所給予的幫助。

2) 提到所受到的協助，收穫良多。

3) 希望關係能更加密切。

Example 25.4　A Letter of Thanks　感謝信

February 23, **20..**

Dear Sirs,

We would like to express our sincere thanks for the courtesy and assistance you have kindly extended to Mr. Tim Smith and me during our stay in your country.

This time we had the pleasure of visiting your factory and had the opportunity of discussing with you the possibility of promoting our new products. We appreciate your cooperation in this matter.

We expect we will have closer business relationship with you soon.

Sincerely yours,

信文中譯：

敬啟者：

　　我們感謝你們對史密斯提姆先生及我在貴國停留的期間所給予的幫助。

　　這次我們有榮幸參觀你們的工廠，並有機會與你們討論促銷我們產品的可能性。我們感激你們對此事的合作。

　　我們預期會跟你們建立親密的商業關係。

謹上

(5) Letters of Invitation　邀請信

邀請信的寫作要領如下：

1) 可分正式與非正式兩種。

2) 列出人、地、時與場合。

3) 希望能接受邀請。

Example 25.5　A Letter of Invitation (Formal)　邀請信 (正式)

Mr. Mike Lin

Vice President of

WATSONS IMPORTS, INC.

And Mrs. Lin

request the honor of your pleasure

at a reception

on Saturday, January 2, **20..**

from six to seven o'clock

at Garden Hotel, Taipei

to meet

Mr. Peter Wang, Chairman of

PIZA, INC.

and Mrs. Wang

R.S.V.P.

Miss Lisa Lin

信文中譯：

　　華生進口公司的副總林麥克先生和林夫人很高興邀請你們參加招待會，於 **20..** 年 1 月 2 日星期六晚上 6:00 到 7:00 在臺北花園飯店舉辦，與皮賽公司的董事長王彼得和王夫人會面。敬請回覆。

林麗莎小姐

Example 25.6　Accepting an Invitation　接受邀請信

Mr. and Mrs. David Liu

accept with much pleasure

the kind invitation of

Mr. and Mrs. Mike Lin's

reception

on Saturday, January 2, **20..**

from six to seven o'clock

at Garden Hotel, Taipei

to meet

Mr. Peter Wang, Chairman of

PIZA, INC.

and Mrs. Wang

信文中譯：

　　劉大衛先生和夫人很高興接受林麥克先生和夫人的邀請，於 **20..** 年 1 月 2 日星期六晚上 6:00 到 7:00 在臺北花園飯店與皮賽公司的董事長王彼得和王夫人會面。

Example 25.7　A Letter of Invitation (Informal)　邀請信 (非正式)

December 1, **20..**

Dear Sirs,

Our president, Mr. Soong, is giving a dinner party in honor of Mr. Mike Jackson at Garden Hotel on Thursday evening, January 2, **20..**, six o'clock.

We would be pleased to have you join us at that time and look forward to the pleasure of your company.

Sincerely yours,

信文中譯：

敬啟者：

我們的董事長宋先生於 **20..** 年 1 月 2 日星期四晚上 6:00 在花園飯店舉辦晚宴歡迎傑克遜麥克先生。

我們將很高興歡迎你居時能參加並期待光臨。

謹上

Example 25.8　Reply to an Invitation (Informal)　回邀請信 (非正式)

December 7, **20..**

Dear Mr. Soong,

Thank you for your kind invitation to the reception on Thursday evening, January 2, **20..**, six o'clock at Garden Hotel.

I shall be honored to attend.

Sincerely yours,

信文中譯：

親愛的宋先生：

　　感謝你的誠懇邀請參加於 **20..** 年 1 月 2 日星期四晚上 6:00 在花園飯店舉辦的招待會。

　　我將很榮幸參與。

謹上

⑹ Letters of Congratulations　祝賀信

祝賀信的寫作要領如下：

1) 以直接法破題，高興得知可賀之事。

2) 表示賀意。

3) 祝生意興隆。

＊寫作技巧：

一般書信寫作有兩個主要寫作方法：直接法及間接法。

　　1. 直接法：即把所要講可喜的事，開始及直接了當的表明，一目了然。在傳達喜訊或表達令人滿意之訊息時用之，如祝賀函等。

　　2. 間接法：即把想要講不如意的事，在開始時並未明白地表明，以免引起對方不良情緒反應，而以漸漸切入的方法，使對方較易接受，使用此法的有討債函等。

Example 25.9　A Letter of Congratulations　祝賀信

November 23, **20..**

Dear Sirs,

It is a great pleasure to learn that you have been appointed General Manager of your company. On this special occasion, we would like to send you our sincerest congratulations on this honorable appointment, wishing you every success in the future.

We hope that with your friendly cooperation, the relationship between our two companies will be further intensified in the years to come.

Sincerely yours,

信文中譯：

敬啟者：

　很榮幸得知你已被任命為貴公司總經理。在此特別的場合，對於你的榮任，我們願致上我們誠懇的祝賀，祝福你萬事皆順利。

　我們希望有你的全力合作，我們兩家公司的關係往後將更親密。

謹上

⑺ Letters of Sympathy　慰問信

　慰問信的寫作要領如下：

　1) 直接寫出慰問的原因。

　2) 表示難過，希望保重。

　3) 祝福。

Example 25.10　A Letter of Sympathy　慰問信

October 12, **20..**

Dear Mr. Clinton,

We were very sorry to learn from your e-mail of October 11, **20..** of your recent illness. We do hope that you will be on the road to recovery when this letter reaches you. My colleagues join me in sending you our warmest regards and best wishes.

Sincerely yours,

信文中譯：

親愛的克林頓先生：

　　我們非常遺憾從你 **20..** 年 10 月 11 日信中得知你最近生病了。我們都希望你在收到此信時，已漸康復。我的同仁們皆一起與我致上我們最溫暖及親切的問候與祝福。

謹上

---

(8) Letters of Condolences　哀悼信

　　哀悼信的寫法要領如下：

　　1) 對所得到的不幸消息表示遺憾。

　　2) 請節哀順變。

　　3) 保證繼續合作。

Example 25.11　A Letter of Condolences　哀悼信

September 5, **20..**

Dear Sirs,

We were deeply grieved to learn from your letter of September 1 of the death of Mr. Carl Lee, your President.

We fully realize how much the loss of Mr. Lee will be felt by all of you and would like to extend you our deepest condolences.

We assure you of our close cooperation in the future.

Sincerely yours,

信文中譯：

敬啟者：

　　我們非常遺憾從你們 9 月 1 日的來信中得知你們的董事長李卡爾先生的去世。

　　我們完全瞭解你們失去李先生的感受；我們願對於李先生的去世，致上我們最深沈的哀悼。

　　我們向你們保證以後仍會緊密的合作。

謹上

4. Certificate

A certificate is generally brief and to the point. For the salutation, it usually uses "To Whom It May Concern." The contents of the letter usually start with "This is to certify..." The certificate ends with a signature and a position, without a complimentary close.

證明書以簡單扼要為主，稱謂常用「敬啟者」，信文開場白為「在此證明……」，結尾敬語常省略。

(1) Certificate of Employment 在職證明書
(2) Certificate of Experience 經歷證明書
(3) Health Certificate 健康證明書

＊ 寫作技巧：

1. 對於職位，如果現仍在職，用現在式表示；如已不在職，則用過去式表示。

   e.g. He is a teacher.

   She is an assistant.

   Lisa was a secretary.

2. 如果現仍在職，用現在完成進行式以表持續動作。

   e.g. He has been working with the company since 20...

   She has been teaching in the school since 20...

3. 如果現已不在職，用過去簡單式以表職位、工作、動作及時間。

   e.g. He worked in our company from 20.. to 20...

   She was employed as a manager in our department from 20.. to 20.., totalling...years.

Example 25.12　Certificate of Employment　在職證明書

To Whom It May Concern:

This is to certify that Ms. Lisa Lin, born on May 1, **19..**, has been working as a secretary with the company since August 1, **20...**

　　　　　　　　　　　　　　　　　　W&D CO., LTD.

　　　　　　　　　　　　　　　　　　John Tsai

　　　　　　　　　　　　　　　　　　General Manager

信文中譯：

敬啟者：

　　在此證明林麗莎小姐，生於 **19..** 年 5 月 1 日，從 **20..** 年 8 月 1 日起擔任本公司祕書迄今。

　　　　　　　　　　　　　　　　　　W&D 有限公司

　　　　　　　　　　　　　　　　　　蔡約翰

　　　　　　　　　　　　　　　　　　總經理

Example 25.13　Certificate of Experience　經歷證明書

TO WHOM IT MAY CONCERN:

This is to certify that Mr. Peter Wang, born on July 12, **19..**, was an assistant engineer in our Machinery Department from June 1, **20..** to June 1, **20..**, totalling 5 years.

PIZA CO., LTD.

Richard Lin

President

信文中譯：

敬啟者：

　　在此證明王彼得先生，生於 **19..** 年 7 月 12 日，從 **20..** 年 6 月 1 日起至 **20..** 年 6 月 1 日止，共 5 年，擔任本公司機械部門的助理工程師。

皮賽有限公司

林理查

董事長

Example 25.14　Health Certificate　健康證明書

To Whom It May Concern:

Mr. William had a physical examination today. He was found to be in good health and is free of any disease.

Health Hospital

David Chou, MD

＊MD: Medical Doctor; Doctor of Medicine 醫師；醫學博士

信文中譯：

敬啟者：

　　威廉先生本日來健康檢查。陳先生身體健康，沒有疾病。

　　　　　　　　　　　　　　　　　　　　　健康醫院

　　　　　　　　　　　　　　　　　　　　　周大衛醫師

✎ Exercise

A. Questions 問答題

1. What is a social letter?

2. What are the characteristics of a social letter?

3. What are the kinds of social letters?

B. Business Insight 實務探討

◆ 社交信

　　在日常生活中有婚喪喜慶，在國際貿易上亦同樣會有如此狀況，只是其禮節必須依照國際慣例，不依本地習俗。在國際上，一般慣例，只以一張卡片來表達祝賀情意即可。如果是很親密的朋友，有時也送禮物，但很少送禮金。社交信，在國際貿易上用的機會很多，尤其在與對方公司做生意久了，關係較密切後，時常會用到；如對方成立分公司、新產品發表、經理高升職位等，皆有機會用到社交信。

C. Grammar Practice 文法練習

★副詞 (Adverbs)──疑問副詞 (Interrogative Adverbs)：

包括用以發問之 When, Where, How, Why 等副詞。

種類	例　　　句
when (何時)	When did you see our vice president?
where (何處)	Where does the buyer live?
how (如何)	How can I get to your office?
why (何故)	Why do you come to Taiwan?

疑問副詞亦可用於間接問句：

> S. + V. + when/how/where/why + S. + V.
>
> e.g. Tell me when you saw our vice president.
>
> 　　Do you know where the buyer lives?
>
> 　　Let me know how I can get to your hotel.
>
> 　　I'd like to know why you come to Taiwan.

Selection：選出最適當的答案

_____ 1. Ask the buyer where _____ from.

(A) does he 　　(B) he does 　　(C) he comes 　　(D) comes he

_____ 2. Ask Bob how old _____

(A) is he. 　　(B) he is. 　　(C) is he? 　　(D) he is?

_____ 3. Do you know why _____

(A) is he late? 　(B) he is late? 　(C) he is late. 　(D) is he late.

_____ 4. I don't know where _____

(A) he lives. 　　　　　　(B) does he live?

(C) he lives? 　　　　　　(D) does he live.

_____ 5. Nobody knows how _____

    (A) did he do it?   (B) he did it.   (C) he did it?   (D) did he do it.

_____ 6. Will you tell me where _____

    (A) is she.   (B) she is?   (C) she is.   (D) is she?

D. Pattern Practice 句型練習

★遺憾抱歉：

We regret...

We are sorry...

We apologize for...

We would like to make an apology for...

1. 我們抱歉收到你們 4 月 5 日來信，關於所運出的 5,000 件成衣。

   _____

2. 我們遺憾收到你們 7 月 1 日的來信，提到我們運出的羽毛球拍與樣品不符。

   _____

E. Blank-filling 填充練習

Dear _____,

I take _____ in recommending _____, who is a good _____ of mine and is _____ for the _____ as a _____ in your company.

I _____ known Ms. Wu since she was _____ from university and came to _____ as a secretary _____ me. She is _____ and

_____.

Your _____ consideration of her _____ would be _____
_____.

　　　　　　　　Sincerely _____,

F. Letter-writing 書信寫作

As a president of a trading company, write a letter of introduction for your secretary, Lucy Chang.

No. 28 金融：環球銀行金融電信協會
(SWIFT)

　　The Society for Worldwide Interbank Financial Telecommunication ("SWIFT") operates a worldwide financial network which exchanges messages between banks and other financial institutions.

　　環球銀行金融電信協會 (Society for Worldwide Interbank Financial Telecommunication, SWIFT) 運營著世界級的金融網路，銀行和其他金融機構透過它與同業交換訊息而完成金融交易。

參考資料：

外交部 NGO 雙語網站

NOTE

Chapter Twenty-Six

E-mail

電子郵件

📖 Outline

1. What is E-mail?

E-mail is a kind of communication through electronic equipment. It is one of the quickest ways of communication. With the facilities of computers, people can communicate with one another through e-mail. Speed, economy, and convenience are the features of e-mail.

電子郵件是一種經由電子設備的溝通方法。它是最迅速的溝通方式之一。有了電腦等設備，人們可以互相經由電子郵件聯絡。速度、經濟、方便為其特色。

2. The Characteristics of E-mail Writing Are:

電子郵件寫作的特色：

⑴ informal style　非正式的形式

⑵ simple structure　單純的架構

⑶ easy patterns　簡易的句型

Example 26.1.1　Advertisement (A)　廣告 (A)

廣告中譯：

擴展你的視野

歐洲十四天

金龍旅行社提供最好的黃金歐洲假期！你有機會欣賞歐洲——法國、
比利時、德國、荷蘭、義大利及英國的美妙風景。

想獲得更多詳細資料，請用滑鼠按此一下。

報價包含高級飯店的住宿與膳食，房間皆有衛浴設備。

價格：每人美金 2,000 元

出發：每星期六

折扣：團體有折扣

其他細節，請與我們聯絡。

Example 26.1.2   Advertisement (B)   廣告 (B)

廣告中譯：

> **家具王國**
>
> 價廉物美
>
> 馬可孛羅家具公司供應價廉物美的古典與現代家具。眾多金屬與木質家具展示。請用滑鼠按此。
>
> 本公司亦提供「自己動手」家具。詳細資料，請與我們連絡。

Example 26.2.1   Enquiry (A)   詢問 (A)

To: service@goldendragon.com

From: Andrew Sun

Subject: Golden Europe Holidays

Dear Sir/Madam,

We are interested in your Golden Europe Holidays. Please send us details of your prices and brochures available.

Yours sincerely,

Andrew Sun
General Manager

信文中譯：

敬啟者：

我們對你們的「黃金歐洲假期」有興趣。請寄來你們價格細節及現有的小冊子。

謹上

Example 26.2.2　Enquiry (B)　詢問 (B)

To: service@marcopolo.com.tw

From: Mike Lewis

Subject: Classical Oak Furniture

Dear Sirs,

We imported large quantities of wooden furniture and would like to see the details of your classical oak furniture.

Please send us the above reference soon.

Sincerely yours,

Mike Lewis

Import Manager

信文中譯：

敬啟者：
  我們進口大量的木質家具，想看看你們古典橡木家具的詳細資料。
請盡速寄來上述的資料。

謹上

Example 26.3.1　Reply (A)　回函 (A)

✉　　　　　　　　　　　　　　　　　　　　　　　－ □ ×

To: Andrew.Sun@startrade.com

From: Tony Wang

Subject: Golden Europe Holidays

Dear Mr. Sun,

Thank you for your e-mail asking about our Golden Europe Holidays.
We are pleased to attach herewith a leaflet for your reference.

Look forward to hearing from you soon.

> Tony Wang
> Sales Manager

信文中譯：

> 親愛的孫先生：
>
> 　　謝謝你的電子郵件，詢問我們的「黃金歐洲假期」。我們高興在此附上單頁的小冊子以供參考。
>
> 　　期待很快得到消息。
>
> 　　　　　　　　　　　　　　　　　　　　　　　　　　　　謹上

Example 26.3.2　Reply (B)　回函 (B)

To: Mike.Lewis@ranes.com

From: Bob White

Subject: Classical Oak Furniture

Dear Mr. Lewis,

Thank you for your e-mail. We are pleased to attach the required catalogues and price lists for your kind reference.

We expect to hear from you again soon.

Sincerely,

Bob White

Manager

信文中譯：

親愛的路易士先生：

謝謝你的電子郵件。我們高興附上所需的目錄與價目表以供參考。我們期待再度很快得到消息。

謹上

Example 26.4.1 Order (A) 訂單 (A)

To: Tony.Wang@goldendragon.com.tw

From: Andrew Sun

Subject: Golden Europe Holidays

Dear Mr. Wang,

We are writing in connection with your offer for Golden Europe Holidays and would like to inform you that a group of twelve persons from our company will join the holiday trip departing on Saturday, August 1. Details are attached.

Please confirm the booking soon.

Yours sincerely,

Andrew Sun

General Manager

信文中譯：

親愛的王先生：

　　關於你們所報的「黃金歐洲假期」，我們公司有一團十二位將會參加此一假日旅行，於 8 月 1 日星期六出發。細節附上。

　　請確認訂位。

謹上

Example 26.4.2　Order (B)　訂單 (B)

To: Bob.White@marcopolo.com.tw

From: Mike Lewis

Subject: Classical Oak Furniture

Dear Mr. White,

With reference to your price list dated March 18, we are glad to attach herewith our Order No. FT-021 for twenty items of your furniture.

Please confirm the order soon.

Sincerely yours,

Mike Lewis

Import Manager

信文中譯：

親愛的白先生：

關於你們 3 月 18 日的價目表。我們很高興在此附上我們的訂單 FT-021 號，訂 20 項你們的家具。

請盡快確認此訂單。

謹上

Example 26.5.1　Payment (A)　付款 (A)

To: Tony.Wang@goldendragon.com.tw

From: Andrew Sun

Subject: Golden Europe Holidays

Dear Mr. Wang,

Thank you for your e-mail of yesterday in which you confirmed the booking of our group tour of 12 persons.

For your information, as instructed, today we remitted US$24,000 in payment of the expenses and charges of the tour.

Yours sincerely,

Andrew Sun

General Manager

信文中譯：

親愛的王先生：

　　謝謝你昨天的電子郵件。在你的郵件上，你確認我們 12 人團體旅遊的訂位。

　　讓你參考，如所指示，今天我們已經匯上美金 24,000 元，支付旅遊的費用與價目。

謹上

Example 26.5.2　Payment (B)　付款 (B)

To: Bob.White@marcopolo.com.tw

From: Mike Lewis

Subject: Classical Oak Furniture

Dear Mr. White,

We have received your Sales Confirmation No. MP-011 and have today opened a L/C in your favor.

Please make sure shipment to be made in the middle of June.

Sincerely yours,

Mike Lewis

Import Manager

信文中譯：

親愛的白先生：

我們已收到你們的銷售確認書 MP-011 號，且於今天已開出以你們為受益人的信用狀。

請確認注意於 6 月中出貨。

謹上

Example 26.6.1　Complaint (A)　抱怨 (A)

To: Tony.Wang@goldendragon.com.tw

From: Andrew Sun

Subject: Golden Europe Holidays

Dear Mr. Wang,

Thank you for your careful arrangement which has made our tour to Europe very pleasant.

However, we have to point out that shopping in France took so much time. We would be grateful if you should improve this next time.

Yours sincerely,

Andrew Sun

General Manager

信文中譯：

親愛的王先生：

　　謝謝你細心的安排，使得我們的歐洲之旅非常愉快。

　　然而，我們必須指出在法國逛街採購佔了太多的旅遊時間。下次如能改進，我們將非常感激。

謹上

Example 26.6.2　Complaint (B)　抱怨 (B)

To: Bob.White@marcopolo.com.tw

From: Mike Lewis

Subject: Classical Oak Furniture

Dear Mr. White,

Please be informed that the furniture on Order No. FT-021 has arrived today. However, on opening the cartons, we found that 10 oak chairs, Item No. OK-09, were badly damaged.

The damage may be caused by poor packing or rough handling. Please send us the 10 replacements soon.

Sincerely yours,

Mike Lewis

Import Manager

信文中譯：

親愛的白先生：

我們通知，訂單 FT-021 號所訂的家具，本日已到達。然而，在開箱時，我們發現有 10 張橡木椅子，編號 OK-09，已嚴重損壞。

此損壞可能是由於包裝不良或粗魯搬運所引起。請立即寄來 10 張更換品。

謹上

Example 26.7.1　Adjustment (A)　調整 (A)

✉ ━ ▢ ✕

To: Andrew.Sun@startrade.com

From: Tony Wang

Subject: Golden Europe Holidays

Dear Mr. Sun,

We thank you very much for your e-mail of yesterday and would like to inform you that we will review the tour schedules this week for further improvement.

Thank you again for your kind suggestions.

Sincerely,

Tony Wang

Sales Manager

信文中譯：

親愛的孫先生：

　　我們謝謝你們昨天的電子郵件。我們想告訴你們本星期我們將檢討旅遊行程，以便作進一步改進。

　　再度謝謝你們的建議。

謹上

Example 26.7.2　Adjustment (B)　調整 (B)

✉　　　　　　　　　　　　　　　　　　　－ □ ✕

To: Mike.Lewis@ranes.com

From: Bob White

Subject: Classical Oak Furniture

Dear Mr. Lewis,

We are sorry for the damage in shipment of your Order No. FT-021 and have today sent 10 replacements of oak chair No. OK-09 by airfreight.

Please keep the damaged chairs for us or have a survey report made so that we may claim a compensation from the shipping company.

Sincerely,

Bob White

Manager

信文中譯：

親愛的路易士先生：

很遺憾你們訂單 FT-021 號的貨物發生損壞。而今天已由航空貨運運出 10 張，編號 OK-09 的橡木椅子更換品。

請為我們保留損壞的椅子或申辦公證報告，以便我們向船務公司申請理賠。

✎ Exercise

A. Questions 問答題

1. What is e-mail?

2. What are the features of e-mail?

3. What are the characteristics of e-mail writing?

B. Business Insight 實務探討

◆ 電子科技

人們只要有一部電腦或平板等，經過連線後，可與世界上任何地方有電子設備連線的人交談，同時並可經由網際網路 (Internet) 上網讀取資訊，與下載 (download) 列印出所需要的資料；尤其，又可經由 e-commerce (電子商務) 作商業活動。由此可知，電子科技所帶來的「震撼」與「影響」是無遠弗屆的。

C. Grammar Practice 文法練習

★倒裝句 (Inversion)：

英文中，有時為了強調句子某些字與詞，有時為某些字的習慣用法，常將句法倒裝，次序變更，稱為倒裝句。

種類	用法
1. 否定副詞與副詞片語	Never, hardly, scarcely, seldom, little, rarely, not until, no sooner...than, not only, by no means, in no way, on no occasion e.g. Never has he been there before. 　　（他以前未曾到那裡。） 　　Scarcely had she opened the box when she cried out. 　　（她一打開盒子就大叫。）
2. Only...	e.g. Only by working hard can he earn more money. 　　（只有努力工作，他才能賺更多錢。）
3. So...that...	e.g. So excited was he that he jumped on the ground. 　　= He was so excited that he jumped on the ground. 　　（他是如此的興奮，以致於在地上跳躍。）
4. so do I	e.g. Jack likes music, and so do I. 　　（傑克喜歡音樂，而我也是。） 　　Mark is a student, and so am I. 　　（馬可是個學生，而我也是。）

Selection：選出最適當的答案

_____ 1. Hardly _____ arrived when I heard someone call me.

　　(A) I had　　　　(B) did I　　　　(C) had I　　　　(D) I have

_____ 2. On no account _____ be dishonest.

　　(A) a man is to　　　　　　　　(B) should a man

　　(C) a man should　　　　　　　(D) is a man

_____ 3. Rarely _____ met such a strange person.

　　(A) I have　　　(B) have I　　　(C) I didn't　　　(D) did I

_____ 4. No sooner _____ left the hotel than it began to rain.

(A) had I   (B) did I   (C) I had   (D) have I

_____ 5. Never _____ heard of such a big buyer from New York.

(A) had I   (B) have I   (C) did I   (D) I have

_____ 6. Only when one loses health _____ its importance.

(A) does one know   (B) one knows

(C) one doesn't know   (D) knows one

D. Pattern Practice 句型練習

★你將有機會……

> You will have a chance to...
>
> You will have an opportunity to...
>
> You stand a good chance of...

1. 你將有機會在月底贏得此銷售競賽。

_____

2. 你將有機會建立你們在商場的優良名譽。

_____

★瞭解到／希望：

> ...on the understanding that...
>
> ...in the hope that...

1. 我們下此訂單時，瞭解到你們會在 8 月底前把此批網球拍訂貨運出。

_____

2. 我們已報給你們最低的價錢，瞭解到你們會在 9 月底前下一張 5,000 臺電風扇訂單。

_____

E. Letter-writing 書信寫作

You are an importer of furniture. After seeing an exporter's advertisement on the Internet, write an e-mail to the exporter to enquire about his products.

No. 29 金融：金融證照
(Business and Banking Licenses)

主要金融證照由台灣金融研訓院負責辦理。

其中主要的金融證照如下：

1. 初階授信人員專業能力測驗
2. 初階外匯人員專業能力測驗
3. 信託業業務人員信託業務專業測驗
4. 理財規劃人員專業能力測驗
5. 銀行內部控制與內部稽核測驗 (一般金融)
6. 銀行內部控制與內部稽核測驗 (消費金融)
7. 金融市場常識與職業道德
8. 金融人員風險管理專業能力測驗
9. 外匯交易專業能力測驗
10. 債權委外催收人員專業能力測驗

參考資料：

台灣金融研訓院

索引 INDEX

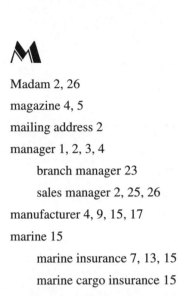

附錄一

世界時刻對照表

使用說明：橫排指同一地區之連續24小時。直排指同一時間各地不同的時刻，日期則依所在位置而定，如：臺北時間早上10點(2月1日)紐約約為晚上9點(1月31日)，南非則為清晨4點(2月1日)。夏令時間必須將當地的時間加快1小時，直到夏令時間結束即可恢復原本的標準時間。

地區																								
臺灣、香港	24	1	2	3	4	5	6	7	8	9	10	11	12	13	14	15	16	17	18	19	20	21	22	23
日本、韓國	1	2	3	4	5	6	7	8	9	10	11	12	13	14	15	16	17	18	19	20	21	22	23	24
澳洲(雪梨、墨爾本)	2	3	4	5	6	7	8	9	10	11	12	13	14	15	16	17	18	19	20	21	22	23	24	1
紐西蘭	4	5	6	7	8	9	10	11	12	13	14	15	16	17	18	19	20	21	22	23	24	1	2	3
太平洋區(舊金山、西雅圖、溫哥華)	8	9	10	11	12	13	14	15	16	17	18	19	20	21	22	23	24	1	2	3	4	5	6	7
山區(丹佛)	9	10	11	12	13	14	15	16	17	18	19	20	21	22	23	24	1	2	3	4	5	6	7	8
中部地區(芝加哥)	10	11	12	13	14	15	16	17	18	19	20	21	22	23	24	1	2	3	4	5	6	7	8	9
東部地區(紐約)	11	12	13	14	15	16	17	18	19	20	21	22	23	24	1	2	3	4	5	6	7	8	9	10
委內瑞拉	12	13	14	15	16	17	18	19	20	21	22	23	24	1	2	3	4	5	6	7	8	9	10	11
巴西、烏拉圭	13	14	15	16	17	18	19	20	21	22	23	24	1	2	3	4	5	6	7	8	9	10	11	12
摩洛哥	16	17	18	19	20	21	22	23	24	1	2	3	4	5	6	7	8	9	10	11	12	13	14	15
歐洲主要地區	17	18	19	20	21	22	23	24	1	2	3	4	5	6	7	8	9	10	11	12	13	14	15	16
南非	18	19	20	21	22	23	24	1	2	3	4	5	6	7	8	9	10	11	12	13	14	15	16	17
伊朗、沙烏地阿拉伯	19	20	21	22	23	24	1	2	3	4	5	6	7	8	9	10	11	12	13	14	15	16	17	18
印度	21	22	23	24	1	2	3	4	5	6	7	8	9	10	11	12	13	14	15	16	17	18	19	20
印尼	23	24	1	2	3	4	5	6	7	8	9	10	11	12	13	14	15	16	17	18	19	20	21	22

附錄二
世界國碼及重要城市區碼

國家／城市名稱	國碼	區碼
AFGANISTAN　阿富汗	93	
Alaska	1	907
ALBANIA　阿爾巴尼亞	355	
ALGERIA　阿爾及利亞	213	
Algiers		2
ANDORRA　安道爾	376	
ANGOLA　安哥拉	244	
Luanda		2
ANGUILLA　安圭拉	1	264
ANTARCTIC BASES 南極基地	672	1
ANTIGUA　安地卡	1	268
ARGENTINA　阿根廷	54	
Buenos Aires		11
Cordoba		351
La Plata		221
Mendoza		361
Rosario		341
Santa Fe		342
ARMENIA　亞美尼亞	374	
ARUBA　阿盧巴島	297	8
ASCENSION　亞森欣島	247	
AUSTRALIA　澳洲	61	
Brisbane		7
Canberra		6
Melbourne		3
Perth		9
Sydney		2
AUSTRIA　奧地利	43	

國家／城市名稱	國碼	區碼
Graz		316
Linz		70
Salzburg		662
Vienna		1
AZERBAIJAN 亞塞拜然	994	
BAHAMAS　巴哈馬	1	
Freeport		242
George Town		242
Nassau		242
BAHRAIN　巴林島	973	
BALEARIC ISLAND 巴里亞利群島	34	71
BANGLADESH　孟加拉	880	
Chittagong		31
Dhaka		2
Khulna		41
BARBADOS　巴貝多	1	246
BELARUS　白俄羅斯	375	
BELGIUM　比利時	32	
BELIZE　貝里斯	501	
BENIN　貝南	229	
BERMUDA ISLAND 百慕達群島	1	
Hamilton		441
BHUTAN　不丹	975	
BOLIVIA　玻利維亞	591	
La Paz		2
Oruro		52
Santa Cruz		3

國家／城市名稱	國碼	區碼
Tareja		66
BOPHUTHATSWANA 波布那	27	
Garankuwa		146
Mmabatho		140
Phokeng		14653
BOSNIA and HERZEGO 波士尼亞與赫塞哥維納	387	
BOTSWANA 波札那	267	
BRAZIL 巴西	55	
Brasilia		61
Maceio		82
Manaus		92
Rio de Janeiro		21
Salvador		71
Sao Paulo		11
BRITISH VIRGIN ISLAND 英屬處女島	1	
BRUNEI 汶萊	673	
Bandar Seri Begawan		2
Gadong		2
Mandaly		2
Seria		3
BULGARIA 保加利亞	359	
Bougas		56
Plovdiv		32
Rousse		82
Sophia		2
Varna		52
BURKINA FASO 布吉納法索	226	
BURUNDI REP. 蒲隆地共和國	257	
CAMBODIA 柬埔寨	855	

國家／城市名稱	國碼	區碼
Phnom Penh		23
CAMEROON 喀麥隆	237	
Douala		42
Victoria		33
Yaounde		22
CANADA 加拿大	1	
Edmonton		403, 780
Montreal		514
Ottawa		613
Quebec		418
Toronto		416, 905
Vancouver		604
CANARY ISLAND 加納利群島	34	
Las Palmas		28
CAPE VERDE ISLAND REP. 維德角共和國	238	
CAYMAN ISLAND 開曼群島	1	345
CENTRAL AFRICAN 中非共和國	236	
CHAD 查德	235	
CHILE 智利	56	
Concepción		41
Iquique		57
Santiago		2
Valparaiso		32
CHINA 中國大陸	86	
CHRISTMAS ISLAND 聖誕島	61	91+ 64
CISKEI 希斯凱	27	
Mdantsane		431

國家／城市名稱	國碼	區碼
Zwelitsha		401
COCOS ISLAND 可可島	61	91+ 62
COLOMBIA 哥倫比亞	57	
Barranquilla		5
Bogota		1
Cali		2
Cartagena		53
Maicao		54
Medellin		4
COMOROS 葛摩	269	7
CONGO 剛果	242	
COOK ISLAND 庫克群島	682	
COSTA RICA 哥斯大黎加	506	
CROATIA 克羅埃西亞	385	
CUBA 古巴	53	7
CYPRUS 塞普勒斯	357	
Larnaca		4
Limassol		5
Nicosia		2
CZECH REP. 捷克共和國	420	
Brno		5
Ostrava		69
Prague		2
Plzen		19
DENMARK 丹麥	45	
DIEGO GARCIA 迪亞哥加西亞島	246	9
DJIBOUTI 吉布地共和國	253	

國家／城市名稱	國碼	區碼
DOMINICA 多米尼克	1	767
DOMINICAN REP. 多明尼加共和國	1	809
Santiago		809
Santo Domingo		809
EAST TIMOR 東帝汶	670	
ECUADOR 厄瓜多	593	
Ambato		3
Ibarra		6
Quito		2
EGYPT 埃及	20	
Abdin		2
Alexandria		3
Benha		13
Cairo		2
Damanhur		45
EL SALVADOR 薩爾瓦多	503	
EQUATORIAL GUINEA 赤道幾內亞	240	
ERITREA 厄利垂亞	291	
Asmara	291	1
ESTONIA 愛沙尼亞	372	
Talline		–
ETHIOPIA 衣索匹亞	251	
Addis Ababa		1
Dire Dawa		5
FALKLAND IS. 福克蘭群島	500	
FAROE ISLAND 法羅群島	298	
FIJI 斐濟	679	
Suva		–

國家／城市名稱	國碼	區碼
FINLAND　芬蘭	358	
Helsinki		0
Imatra		54
Turku		21
Tampere		31
FRANCE　法國	33	
Bordeaux		–
Lyon		–
Marseilles		–
Paris & Suburbs		1
FRENCH GUIANA 法屬圭亞那	594	
FRENCH POLYNESIA 法屬波里尼西亞	689	
GABONESE REP. 加彭共和國	241	
GAMBIA　甘比亞	220	
GEORGIA　喬治亞	995	
GERMANY　德國	49	
Chemnitz		371
Dresden		351
Gera		365
Leipzig		341
Berlin		30
Bonn		228
Essen		201
Frankfurt Main		69
Hamburg		40
Koln		221
Munich		89
GHANA　迦納	233	
GREECE　希臘	30	
Athens		1

國家／城市名稱	國碼	區碼
Chios		271
Sparti		731
GIBRALTAR　直布羅陀	350	
GREENLAND　格陵蘭	299	
GRENADA　格瑞那達	1	473
GUADELOUPE ISLAND 瓜得魯普島	590	
GUAM　關島	1	671
Agana		–
GUATEMALA 瓜地馬拉	502	
GUINEA　幾內亞	224	
GUINEA-BISSAU REP. 幾內亞比索共和國	245	
GUYANA　蓋亞那	592	
George Town		2
HAITI　海地	509	
Cap Haitien		–
Gonaives		–
Les Cayes		–
Port Au Prince		–
HAWAII　夏威夷	1	808
HONDURAS　宏都拉斯	504	
HONG KONG　香港	852	
Hong Kong		–
Kowloon		–
New Territories		–
HUNGARY　匈牙利	36	
Budapest		1
Gyor		96
Miskolc		46
Saigotarian		32
ICELAND　冰島	354	

國家／城市名稱	國碼	區碼
Akureyri		–
Reykjavik		–
INDIA　印度	91	
Bombay		22
Calcutta		33
New Delhi		11
INDONESIA　印尼	62	
Bali		361
Bandung		22
Djakarta		21
Medan		61
Surabaya		31
Timor		390
IRAN　伊朗	98	
Mashhad		51
Shiraj		71
Tehran		21
IRAQ　伊拉克	964	
Baghdad		1
Basra		40
Karble		32
Najaf		33
IRELAND　愛爾蘭	353	
Cork		21
Dublin		1
ISRAEL　以色列	972	
Haifa		4
Jerusalem		2
Telaviv		3
ITALY　義大利	39	
Genova		10
Milan		2
Roma		6

國家／城市名稱	國碼	區碼
Venezia		41
IVORY COAST 象牙海岸	225	
JAMAICA　牙買加	1	
Kingston		876
JAPAN　日本	81	
Hiroshima		82
Kobe		78
Kyoto		75
Nagoya		52
Naha		98
Osaka		6
Tokyo		3
Yokohama		45
JORDAN　約旦	962	
Amman		6
Aqaba		3
Irbid		2
Zerka		5
KAZAKHSTAN　哈薩克	7	
KENYA　肯亞	254	
Kisumu		35
Nairobi		2
Nyeri		34
KIRIBATI REP. 吉里巴斯共和國	686	
KOREA NORTH　北韓	850	
Pyongyang	850	2
KOREA SOUTH　南韓	82	
Daegu		53
Gwangju		62
Inchon		32
Pusan	82	51

國家／城市名稱	國碼	區碼
Seoul		2
KUWAIT　科威特	965	
KYRGYZ REPUBLIC 吉爾吉斯	996	
LAOS　寮國	856	
Vientiane		21
LATVIA　拉脫維亞	371	
Riga		2
LEBANON　黎巴嫩	961	
Beirut		1
LESOTHO　賴索托	266	
Maseru		–
LIBERIA　賴比瑞亞	231	
LIBYA　利比亞	218	
Tripoli		21
LIECHTENSTEIN 列支敦斯基	423	
Vaduz		75
LITHUANIA　立陶宛	370	
Vilnius		–
LUXEMBOURG 盧森堡	352	
MACAO　澳門	853	
MACEDONIA REP. 馬其頓共和國	389	
MADAGASCAR 馬達加斯加	261	
MALAWI　馬拉威	265	
Blantyre		–
Lilongwe		–
Mangochi		–
Mbabzi		–
Zomba		–
MALAYSIA 馬來西亞	60	

國家／城市名稱	國碼	區碼
Ipoh		5
Johor Baru		7
Kelang		3
Kota Kinabaru		88
Kuala Lumpur		3
Kuching		82
Penang		4
MALDIVE IS. 馬爾地夫	960	
MALI　馬利	223	
MALTA　馬爾他	356	
MARIANA ISLAND 馬里亞納群島	1+ 670	
MARSHALL ISLAND 馬紹爾群島	692	
MARTINIQUE ISLAND 馬丁尼克島	596	
MAURITANIA 茅利塔尼亞	222	
MAURITIUS　模里西斯	230	
MAYOTTE ISLAND 馬約特島	269	
MEXICO　墨西哥	52	
Leon		47
Mexico City		5
Merida		99
Mexicali		65
MICRONESIA　密克羅 尼西亞	691	
MOLDOVA　摩爾多瓦	373	
MONACO　摩納哥	33	
All Points		92, 93
MONGOLIA　蒙古	976	

國家／城市名稱	國碼	區碼
MONTENEGRO 蒙特內哥羅	382	
MONTSERRAT 蒙哲臘島	1	664
MOROCCO 摩洛哥	212	
Casablanka		2
Rabat		7
MOZAMBIQUE 莫三比克	258	
Maputo		1
NAMIBIA 納米比亞	264	
Windhoek		61
Tsumeb		671
NAURU REP. 諾魯共和國	674	
NEPAL 尼泊爾	977	
Kathmandu		1
NETHERLANDS 荷蘭	31	
Amsterdam		20
Rotterdam		10
NETHERLANDS ANTILLES 荷屬安地列斯群島	599	
Curacao		9
NEW CALEDONIA 新喀里多尼亞	687	
NEW ZEALAND 紐西蘭	64	
Auckland		9
Christchurch		3
Hamilton		7
Timaru		56
Wellington		4
NICARAGUA 尼加拉瓜	505	

國家／城市名稱	國碼	區碼
NIGER 尼日共和國	227	
NIGERIA 奈及利亞	234	
Ibadan		22, 2
Kaduna		62
Lagos		1
NIUE ISLAND 紐鄂島	683	
NORFOLK ISLAND 諾福克島	672	3
NORWAY 挪威	47	
Narvik		–
Bergen		–
Drammen		–
Oslo		–
OMAN 阿曼	968	
PAKISTAN 巴基斯坦	92	
Islamabad		51
Karachi		21
Peshawar		521
Quetta		81
Sukkur		71
PALAU 帛琉	680	
PALESTINE 巴勒斯坦	970	
PANAMA 巴拿馬	507	
PAPUA NEW GUINEA 巴布亞新幾內亞	675	
PARAGUAY 巴拉圭	595	
Asuncion		21
Concepcion		31
Encarnacion		71
Sanlorenzo		22
PERU 秘魯	51	
Lima		1

國家／城市名稱	國碼	區碼
Callao		14
Piura		74
Trujillo		44
PHILIPPINES　菲律賓	63	
Cebu		32
Davao		82
Iloilo		33
Manila		2
POLAND　波蘭	48	
Gdansk		58
Krakow		12
Lodz		42
Warsaw		2, 22
PORTUGAL　葡萄牙	351	
Braga		253
Evora		266
Lisboa		1
MADEIRA　馬德拉	351	
Miguel		96
Pico		92
Sanjuan		91
Terceira		95
PUERTO RICO 波多黎各	1	787
San Juan		787
QATAR　卡達	974	
RUSSIA　俄羅斯	7	
Moscow		95
REUNION ISLAND 留尼旺島	262	
ROMANIA　羅馬尼亞	40	
Bucharest		1
Cluj		64

國家／城市名稱	國碼	區碼
Constanta		41
Craiova		51
Timisoara		56
RWANDA REP. 盧安達共和國	250	
SAMOA (American) 美屬薩摩亞	684	
SAN MARINO 聖馬利諾	378	
St. Kitts and Nevis 聖克里斯多福及尼維斯	1	869
SAO TOME & PRINCIPE 聖多美及普林西比	239	
SAUDI ARABIA 沙烏地阿拉伯	966	
Damman		3
Jeddah		2
Makkah		2
Riyadh		1
Taif		2
SNEGAL　塞內加爾	221	
SERBIA　塞爾維亞	381	
SEYCHELLES　塞席爾	248	
SIERRA LEONE 獅子山	232	
Bo		32
Freetown		22
Lungi		25
SINGAPORE　新加坡	65	
SLOVAK　斯洛伐克	421	
Bratislava		7
SLOVENIA 斯洛維尼亞	386	
SOLOMON IS. 索羅門群島	677	

國家／城市名稱	國碼	區碼
Honiara		–
SOMALIA　索馬利亞	252	
Mogadiscio		1
Kisimaio		3
SOUTH AFRICA　南非	27	
Bloemfontein		51
Cape Town		21
Durban		31
Johannesburg		11
Port Elizabeth		41
Pretoria		12
SPAIN　西班牙	34	
Barcelona		93
Granada		958
Las Palmas		928
Madrid		91
Valencia		96
SPANISH NORTH AFRICA 西班牙北非屬地	34	
Ceuta		56
Melilla		52
SRI LANKA　斯里蘭卡	94	
Colombo		1
ST. HELENA 聖赫勒拿島	290	
ST. LUCIA　聖露西亞	1	
Castries		758
ST. PIERRE & MIQUELON IS. 聖皮埃及密克隆群島	508	
ST. VINCENT & THE GRENADINES　聖文森島及格瑞那丁	1	

國家／城市名稱	國碼	區碼
Kingstown		784
SUDAN　蘇丹	249	
Khartoum		11
Omdurman		11
SURINAM REP. 蘇利南共和國	597	
SWAZILAND 史瓦濟蘭	268	
Manzini		–
SWEDEN　瑞典	46	
Gavle		26
Goteborg		31
Stockholm		8
Sundsvall		60
SWITZERLAND　瑞士	41	
Basel		61
Bern		31
Geneva		22
Zurich		1
SYRIA　敘利亞	963	
TAIWAN　臺灣	886	
TAJIKISTAN　塔吉克	992	
TANZANIA　坦尚尼亞	255	
Arusha		57
Dar-Es-Salaam		51
THAILAND　泰國	66	
Bangkok		2
Chiang Mai		53
Pattaya		38
TOGOLESE REP.　多哥共和國	228	
TONGA　東加	676	

國家／城市名稱	國碼	區碼
TURKMENISTAN 土庫曼	993	
TRANSKEI　川斯凱	27	
Butterworth		4341
Umtata		471
TRINIDAD & TOBAGO 千里達及托巴哥	1	868
TUNISIA REP. 突尼西亞	216	
Tunis		1
TURKEY　土耳其	90	
Ankara		312
Istanbul		212, 216
Izmir		232
TURKS AND CAICOS ISLAND　土克斯及開科斯群島	1	649
TUVALU　吐瓦魯	688	
UGANDA　烏干達	256	
Entebbe		42
Kampala		41
UNITED ARAB EMIRATES　阿拉伯聯合大公國	971	
Abu Dhabi		2
Ajman		6
Al Ain		3
Dubai		4
Fujarah		9
Ras Al-Khaimah		7
Sharjah		6
Umm Al-Quwain		6
U.K.　英國	44	

國家／城市名稱	國碼	區碼
Birmingham		121
Edinburgh		131
Glasgow		141
Leeds		113
Liverpool		151
London		20
Manchester		161
Nottingham		1159
UKRAINE　烏克蘭	380	
MYANMAR (BURMA) 緬甸	95	
Yangoon	95	1
U.S.A.　美國	1	
Atlanta (GA)		404
Austin (TX)		512
Baltimore (MD)		410
Boston (MA)		617
Buffalo (NY)		716
Chicago (IL)		708, 312
Cincinnati (OH)		513
Cleveland (OH)		216
Dallas (TX)		214
Detroit (MI)		313
Honolulu (HI)		808
Houston (TX)		713
Las Vegas (NV)		702
Los Angeles (CA)		213, 714 310, 818
Memphis (TN)		901
Miami (FL)		305

國家／城市名稱	國碼	區碼
Minneapolis (MN)		612, 651
New Orleans (LA)		504
New York (NY)		212, 718, 646, 347
Philadelphia (PA)		215
Pittsburgh (PA)		412
Portland (OR)		503, 971
San Francisco (CA)		510, 415
Seattle (WA)		206
Washington D.C.		202
U.S.A. VIRGIN IS. 美屬處女群島	1	
Charlotte Amalie St. Thomas		340
Christiansted St. Croix		340
Frederiksted St. John Is.		340
URUGUAY　烏拉圭	598	
Montevideo		2
UZBEKISTAN REP. 烏茲別克	998	
VANUATU　萬那杜	678	
VATICAN　梵帝岡	39	
VENDA　溫達	27	
Thohoyandou		159
VENEZUELA 委內瑞拉	58	
Caracas		2
Maracaibo		61

國家／城市名稱	國碼	區碼
Valencia		41
VIETNAM　越南	84	
Hochiminh		8
WAKE IS.　威克島	1	
WALLIS & FUTUNA ISLAND　瓦里斯及富都拿群島	681	
WESTERN SAMOA 西薩摩亞	685	
YEMEN　葉門	967	
Hodeidah		1
ZAMBIA　尚比亞	260	
Kitwe		2
Livingstone		3
Lusaka		1
Ndola		2
ZIMBABWE　辛巴威	263	
Harare		4

附錄三
常用商業縮寫字

@	at, to, from	單價、至 (航)、從 (航)
A.A.R.	against all risk	擔保全險
a/c, A/C	account	帳、帳戶
acc.	acceptance, accepted	承兌、承諾 (已)
ackmt	acknowledgement	承認、收據
a/d, A/D	after date	出票後限期付款 (票據)
ad, advert	advertisement	廣告
ad val.	ad valorem (according to value)	從價稅
AIG	American International Group	美國國際集團
AM, a.m.	ante meridiem (before noon)	上午
amt.	amount	額、金額
AN	arrival notice	到貨通知
AP	accounts payable	應付帳款
A/P	Authority to Purchase	委託購買證
a.p.	additional premium	附加保費
APEC	Asia-Pacific Economic Cooperation	亞太經濟合作會議
APROC	Asia-Pacific Regional Operation Center	亞太營運中心
A.R.	all risks	全險
Art.	article	條款、項
A/S	account sales	承銷清單
A/S, a/s	after sight	見票後限期付款
ASEAN	Association of Southeast Asian Nations	東南亞國家協會 (簡稱東協)
assn.	association	協會
asst.	assistant	助理、助手
att., attn.	attention	注意

av., av	average	平均
a/v	a vista (at sight)	見票即付
Ave, Av.	Avenue	街道

B

B/一, b/一	bale, bag	包、裝
bal.	balance	餘額
bbl.	barrel	桶
B/C	bill for collection	託收票據
B/D	bank draft	銀行匯票
b/d	brought down	承前頁
b'dle, bdl.	bundle	束、把
B/E	bill of exchange	匯票
b/f	brought forward	承前頁
bg	bag	袋
BIS	Bank for International Settlement	國際清算銀行
bkrpt	bankrupt	破產
B/L	Bill of Lading	提單
B/N	bank note	銀行紙幣
bot.	bottle	瓶
BOT	Build-Operate-Transfer	建造，營運，移轉 (如高鐵等)
B/P	bill purchased	買入票據、出口押匯
B/P	bills payable	應付票據
B/R	bills receivable	應收票據
B/S	balance sheet	資產負債表

C

C/一	case, currency	箱、通貨
c.	cent, centimes	分 (美)、分 (法)
CAD	cash against documents	現金交單
CFR	cost and freight	運費在內價

cat.	catalogue	貨品目錄
C.B.	clean bill	光票
CBM	Cubic meter	立方公尺
c.c.	carbon copy, cubic centimeter	副本、立方公分
C/C, C.C.	Chamber of Commerce	商會
CCCN	Customs Cooperation Council Nomenclature	關稅合作理事會稅別分類
CEO	Chief Executive Officer	執行長
c/f	carried forward	過次頁
CFR	cost and freight	運費在內價
CFS	container freight station	貨櫃集散站
CIA	cash in advance	預付現金
CIF	cost, insurance, and freight	運保費在內價
CIF&C	cost, insurance, freight and commission	運費、保險費、佣金在內價
CIS	Corporate Identity System	企業識別體系
ck., ck, cks.	cask	樽
C/N, C.N.	credit note, covering note, consignment note	貸項清單、保險承保單、發貨通知單
CNS	Chinese National Standards	中華民國國家標準
C.O.	certificate of origin	產地證明書
c/o	care of, carried over	煩轉、過次頁
Co.	company	公司
COD	cash on delivery	貨到付款
corp.	corporation	法人、公司
C/P	charter party	租船契約
cr.	credit	貸方、債權人
cs	case	箱
CSA	Canadian Standards Association	加拿大標準協會
Cu. ft., CFT, CUFT	Cubic feet	立方英尺 (才積)
c.v.	Curriculum Vitae	履歷表
CWO	cash with order	訂貨付現
cwt.	hundredweight	英擔 (英制質量單位)
CY	container yard	貨櫃集散場

D/A	documents against acceptance, documents for acceptance, documents attached, deposit account	承兌後交付單據、備承兌單據、附有單據、存款帳戶
d/a	days after acceptance	承兌後⋯⋯日付款
DAP	delivered at place	目的地指定地點未卸貨價
DAT	delivered at terminal	目的地指定港站或地點已卸貨價
D/D, D.D.	demand draft, documentary draft	即期匯票、跟單匯票
d/d	day's date (days after date)	出票後⋯⋯日付款
d.f., d. fet.	dead freight	空載運費 (船)
DM	direct mail	直接郵寄
D/N	debit note	借項清單
D/O	delivery order	小提單
do.	ditto (the same)	同上
D/P	documents against payment	付款後交付單據
DPU	delivered at place unloaded	目的地卸貨後交貨價
Dr.	debit, debtor	借方、債務人
d/s., d.s.	day's sight (days after sight)	見票後⋯⋯日付款

ea.	each	每、各
ECFA	Cross-Straits Economic Cooperation Framework Agreement	海峽兩岸經濟合作架構協議
e.e., E.E.	error excepted	錯誤除外
EEC	The European Economic Community	歐洲經濟組合 (共同市場)
e.g.	exempli gratia (for example)	例如
enc., encl.	enclosure	附件
E.&O.E.	errors and omissions excepted	錯誤或遺漏不在此限
Esq.	Esquire	先生 (信內尊稱)

ETA	estimated time of arrival	預定到達日期
etc.	et cetera	等等
ETD	estimated time of departure	預定離開日期
EU	European Union	歐洲聯盟
euro	European currency	歐元 (簡寫為€)
ex	out of, without	自、無、交貨
ex.	example, executive, exchange	例子、執行官、外匯交換

 F

F.A.A.	free of all average	全損才賠
FAQ	fair average quality	良好平均品質
FAS	free alongside ship	船邊交貨價
F.B.E.	foreign bill of exchange	國外匯票
FCC	Federal Communications Commission	聯邦通信委員會
FCL	full container load	整貨櫃裝滿 (整裝)
f.d.	free discharge	卸貨船方不負責
FDA	Food and Drug Administration	美國食品藥品監督管理局
f.i.	free in	裝貨船方不負責
f.i.o.	free in and out	裝卸貨船方均不負責
f.o.	free out	卸貨船方不負責
f.o., f/o	firm offer	規定時限的報價；穩固報價
FOB	free on board	船上交貨價
f.o.c.	free of charge	免費
FOR	free on rail	火車上交貨價
FOS	free on steamer	輪船上交貨價
FOT	free on truck	卡車上交貨價
F.P.A	free of particular average	單獨海損不保 (平安險)
fr., f	franc, from, free	法朗、從、自由
f.p.	floating policy	流動保單
FTA	Free Trade Agreement	自由貿易協定
FX	foreign exchange	外匯
FY	fiscal year	會計年度

Ｇ

g.	good, goods, gramme	佳、貨物、公克
G/A	general average	共同海損
GATS	General Agreement on Trade in Services	服務貿易總協定 (服貿) 是世界貿易組織 WTO 的條約
GATT	General Agreement on Tariffs and Trade	關稅貿易總協定
gm	gramme	公克
g.m.b.	good merchantable brand	品質良好適合買賣之貨品
g.m.q.	good merchantable quality	良好可售品質
GSP	Generalized System of Preference	普遍優惠關稅制度
g.s.w.	gross shipping weight	裝輪總重量
gr. wt.	gross weight	毛重

Ｈ

h.	hour, harbour, height	時、港、高度
H.O.	Head Office	總公司
h.p.	horse power	馬力
hr.	hour	時
HS	The Harmonized Commodity Description and Coding System	國際商品統一分類制度

#

IATA	International Air Transport Association	國際航空運輸協會
ICC	International Chamber of Commerce	國際商會
id.	idem (the same)	同上
i.e.	id est (that is)	即是
IMF	International Monetary Fund	國際貨幣基金
inc.	incorporated	有限責任公司 (組織)

Incoterms	International Commercial Terms	國貿條規
inst.	instant (this month)	本月
int.	interest	利息
inv.	invoice	發票
IOP	irrespective of percentage	不論損害大小
IOU	I owe you	借據
ISIC	International Standard Industrial Classification	國際產業標準分類
ISO	International Organization for Standardization	國際標準化組織

J

JIS	Japanese Industrial Standards	日本工業規格

K

k.	carat	卡拉 (純金含有度)
kg.	keg, kilogramme	小、公斤
K.W.	Kilo Watt	千瓦

L

lbs.	pounds	磅
L/C	letter of credit	信用狀
LCL	less than carload lot less than container load	不足一輛貨車載量 不足貨櫃裝載 (併裝)
L/I	letter of indemnity	賠償保證書
L/G	letter of guarantee	保證函
l.t.	long ton	長噸
Ltd.	Limited	有限責任

m.	mile, metre, mark, month, minute, mille (thousand), meridiem (noon)	英里、公尺、記號、月、分、千、中午
m/d	month after date	出票後……月付款
memo.	memorandum	備忘錄
Messrs.	messieurs	先生多數
MFN	Most Favored Nation	最惠國
MI	misery index	痛苦指數 (一種總體經濟指標，等於通貨膨脹與失業率總和)
M.I.P.	marine insurance policy	海上保險單
MIS	Management Information System	管理資訊系統
misc.	miscellaneous	雜項
M/L	more or less	增或減
Mme	Madame	夫人
MO	Money Order	撥款單、匯款單
Mr.	Mister	先生
MR	Mate's Receipt	大副收據，收貨單
Mrs.	Mistress	太太、夫人
m/s	months after sight	見票後……月付款
m.s.	mail steamer, motor ship	郵船、輪船
M.T.	metric ton, mail transfer	公噸、信匯
m.v.	motor vessel	輪船

NATO	North Atlantic Treaty Organization	北大西洋公約組織
N.B.	nota bene (take notice)	注意
NO.	number	號碼
n.o.p.	not otherwise provided for	無其他規定者、未列名者
n.o.s.	not otherwise specified for	無其他說明 (規定) 者
n/p	non-payment	拒付

Nt. Wt.	Net Weight	淨重

O.	order	訂單、定貨
O.B/L	order bill of lading	指示式提單
O.C.P.	Overland Common Point	通常陸上運輸可到達地點
o/d	overdraft, on demand	透支、要求即期付款 (票據)
OECD	The Organization for Economic Cooperation and Development	經濟合作暨發展組織
OEEC	Organization for European Economic Cooperation	歐洲經濟合作組織
OEM	Original Equipment Manufacturer	原廠委製、原廠設備代工
OK	all correct, approved	無誤、同意
O/No.	order number	定單編號
o.p.	open policy	預約保單
OPEC	Organization of Petroleum Exporting Countries	石油輸出國組織
o/s	on sale, out of stock	廉售、無存貨
o.t.	old term	舊條件
oz	ounce	盎斯

P/A, p/a, pa	particular average, power of attorney, private account	單獨海損、委任狀、私人帳戶
p.a.	per annum (by the year)	每年
p.c.	per cent, petty cash	百分比、零用金
per pro, pp., p.p.	per procurationem (by proxy, on behalf of)	代理
P/I	pro forma invoice	預估發票；形式發票
p.l.	partial loss	分損
P. & L.	profit and loss	損益
p.m.	post meridiem (afternoon)	下午

P.M.O.	postal money order	郵政匯票
P/N	promissory note	本票
PNTR	Permanent Normal Trade Relations	永久正常貿易關係
P/O	purchase order	訂單
P.O.B.	postal office box	郵政信箱
p.o.d.	payment on delivery	交貨時付款
P/R	parcel receipt	郵包收據
pro forma	for form's sake	形式的；估價單
prox.	proximo (next month)	下月
PS	postscript	再啟
pt.	pint	品脫
P.T.O.	please turn over	請看後面
Pty	proprietary limited	有限責任之公司 (澳)

qlty	quality	品質
qr	quarter	四分之一
qty	quantity	數量
quotn	quotation	報價單
qy	quay	碼頭

recd	received	收訖
recpt	receipt	收據
ref	reference	參考、關於
REIT	Real Estate Investment Trust	不動產投資信託 (即不動產證券化)
remit.	remittance	匯款
rm	ream	令
r.m.	ready money, ready-made	備用金、現成的
R.P.	reply paid, return of post	郵費或電費預付，請即回示

R.S.D.	receiving, storage and delivery	裝卸費用
R.S.V.P.	répondez síl vous plaît	請回答
R.T.	rye term	裸麥條件
rt.	rate	率

S.A.	Statement of Account	帳單
s.a.	subject to approval	以承認 (贊成、批准) 為條件
S/D	sight draft	即期匯票
S/D	sea damage	海水損害
sig.	signature	簽名
SITC	Standard International Trade Classification	國際貿易標準分類
S/N	shipping note	裝運通知
S.O., s.o.	shipping order, seller's option	裝船通知書、賣方有權選擇
SRCC	strike, riot, civil commotions	罷工暴動險
S/S, s/s, ss, s.s.	steamship	輪船
s.t.	short ton	短噸
st.	street	街
s.v.	sailing vessel	帆船
SWIFT	Society for Worldwide Interbank Financial Telecommunication	環球銀行金融電信協會
SWOT	Strengths, Weaknesses, Opportunities, Threats	企業競爭態勢分析 (強弱危機分析)

TAITRA (CETRA)	Taiwan External Trade Development Council	中華民國對外貿易發展協會
TLO	total loss only	只擔保全損 (分損不賠)
T.R.	trust receipt	信託收據
T.Q.	tale quale	現狀條件 (運輸途中損害買方負擔)，裝船條件
TPND	theft, pilferage, and non-delivery	盜竊遺失險

UCP	Uniform Customs and Practice for Documentary Credits	跟單信用狀統一慣例
ult.	ultimo (last month)	上月
uos	unless otherwise specified	除非另有規定
u/w	underwriter	保險業者

VAT	Value Added Tax	附加值稅
v., vs	versus	對於
viz	videlicet (namely)	即是
voy.	voyage	航次
VP	Vice President	副總
V.V.	Vice Versa	反之亦然

W.A.	with average	水漬險 (單獨海損賠償)
W/B	way bill, warehouse book	貨運單、倉庫簿
wgt	weight	重量
whf	wharf	碼頭
W/M	weight or measurement	重量或容量
w.p.a.	with particular average	單獨海損賠償
W.R.	War Risk warehouse receipt	兵險 倉單
wt	weight	重量
WTO	World Trade Organization	世界貿易組織
w.w.	warehouse warrant	倉單
w.w.d.	weather working day	良好天氣工作天
WWW	World Wide Web	網際網路

x	ex (out of without) exclusive	除外、無
x.d.	ex divident	除息
XX	good quality	良好品質
XXX	very good quality	甚佳品質
XXXX	best quality	最佳品質

yd.	yard	碼
yr.	your, year	你的，年
Yr. B.	year book	年鑑

附錄四

我國所得稅協定一覽表──(全面性協定)

簽約國 (地區) Country/Jurisdiction	簽署日期 Date of Signature	生效日期 Effective Date
新加坡 * | Singapore*	1981/12/30 (70 年)	1982/01/01 (71 年)
印尼 * | Indonesia*	1995/03/01 (84 年)	1996/01/12 (85 年)
南非 | South Africa	1994/02/14 (83 年)	1996/09/12 (85 年)
澳大利亞 * | Australia*	1996/05/29 (85 年)	1996/10/11 (85 年)
紐西蘭 * | New Zealand*	1996/11/11/ (85 年)	1997/12/05 (86 年)
越南 * | Vietnam*	1998/04/06 (87 年)	1998/05/06 (87 年)
甘比亞 | Gambia	1998/07/22 (87 年)	1998/11/04 (87 年)
史瓦帝尼 (原「史瓦濟蘭」) | Eswatini	1998/09/07 (87 年)	1999/02/09 (88 年)
馬來西亞 * | Malaysia*	1996/07/23 (85 年)	1999/02/26 (88 年)
北馬其頓 (原「馬其頓」) | North Macedonia	1999/06/09 (88 年)	1999/06/09 (88 年)
荷蘭 | The Netherlands	2001/02/27 (90 年)	2001/05/16 (90 年)
英國 | UK	2002/04/08 (91 年)	2002/12/23 (91 年)
塞內加爾 | Senegal	2000/01/20 (89 年)	2004/09/10 (93 年)
瑞典 | Sweden	2001/06/08 (90 年)	2004/11/24 (93 年)
比利時 | Belgium	2004/10/13 (93 年)	2005/12/14 (94 年)
丹麥 | Denmark	2005/08/30 (94 年)	2005/12/23 (94 年)
以色列 | Israel	2009/12/18 2009/12/24 (98 年)	2009/12/24 (98 年)
巴拉圭 | Paraguay	1994/04/28 (83 年) 2008/03/06 (97 年補充協議)	2010/06/03 (99 年)
匈牙利 | Hungary	2010/04/19 (99 年)	2010/12/29 (99 年)
法國 | France (French text)	2010/12/24 (99 年)	2011/01/01 (100 年)
印度 * | India*	2011/07/12 (100 年)	2011/08/12 (100 年)
斯洛伐克 | Slovakia	2011/08/10 (100 年)	2011/09/24 (100 年)
瑞士 | Switzerland	2007/10/08 (96 年) 2011/07/14 (修約換函)	2011/12/13 (100 年)

德國 ｜ Germany (German text)	2011/12/19 2011/12/28 (100 年)	2012/11/07 (101 年)
泰國 * ｜ Thailand* (Thai text)	1999/07/09 (88 年) 2012/12/03 (101 年議定書)	2012/12/19 (101 年)
吉里巴斯 ｜ Kiribati	2014/05/13 (103 年)	2014/06/23 (103 年)
盧森堡 ｜ Luxembourg	2011/12/19 (100 年)	2014/07/25 (103 年)
奧地利 ｜ Austria (German text)	2014/07/12 (103 年)	2014/12/20 (103 年)
義大利 ｜ Italy	2015/06/01 及 2015/12/31 (104 年)	2015/12/31 (104 年)
日本 ｜ Japan	2015/11/26 (104 年)	2016/06/13 (105 年)
加拿大 ｜ Canada (French text)	2016/01/13 及 2016/01/15 (105 年)	2016/12/19 (105 年)
波蘭 ｜ Poland	2016/10/21 (105 年)	2016/12/30 (105 年)

(* 新南向政策國家 / The destination countries of the "New Southbound Policy")

參考資料：

我國所得稅協定一覽表——(全面性協定) (民 109 年版)。取自財政部全球資訊網。

附錄五

我國所得稅協定一覽表——單項 / 海空運輸協定

簽約國 (地區) Country/Jurisdiction	內容 Shipping/Air Transport	簽署日期 Date of Signature	生效日期 Effective Date
加拿大｜Canada	空運 A	1995/07/10 (84 年)	同左 Same as left column
歐聯｜EU	海運 S	1990/08/01 (79 年)	同左 Same as left column
德國｜Germany	海運 S	1988/08/23 (77 年)	同左 Same as left column
日本｜Japan	海空運 S&A	1990/09/04 (79 年)	同左 Same as left column
韓國｜Korea	海空運 S&A	1991/12/10 (80 年)	同左 Same as left column
盧森堡｜Luxembourg	空運 A	1985/03/04 (74 年)	同左 Same as left column
澳門 (2017/12/31 以前)｜Macau(before 2018/1/1) 澳門 (2018/1/1 以後)｜Macau(beginning on or after 2018/1/1)	空運 A	1998/12/18 (87 年) 2015/12/10 (104 年)	1999/02/26 (88 年) 2017/12/29 (106 年)
荷蘭｜The Netherlands	海運 S	1989/06/07 (78 年)	1988/01/01 (77 年)
	空運 A	1984/05/28 (73 年)	1983/04/01 (72 年)
挪威｜Norway	海運 S	1991/06/07 (80 年)	同左 Same as left column
瑞典｜Sweden	海運 S	1990/09/05 (79 年)	同左 Same as left column
泰國 *｜Thailand*	空運 A	1984/06/30 (73 年)	同左 Same as left column
美國｜United States	海空運 S&A	1988/05/31 (77 年)	同左 Same as left column

(* 新南向政策國家 / The destination countries of the "New Southbound Policy")

參考資料：

我國所得稅協定一覽表－單項／海空運輸協定 (民 109 年版)。取自財政部全球資訊網。

10堂課練就TED Talks演講力

溫宥基　編著
車昀庭　審定

掌握TED Talks 演講祕訣，
上臺演講不再是一件難事。

★ **為你精心挑選的演講主題**
全書共10個主題，別出心裁的主題設計，帶出不同的學習重點，並聘請專業的外籍作者編寫每一課主題的文章，讓你輕鬆融入TED Talks演講主題。

★ **為你探討多元的關鍵議題**
涵蓋豐富多元的議題教育融入課程，包括生命、資訊、人權、環境、科技、海洋、品德、性別平等之多項重要議題，讓你多方面涉獵不同領域題材。

★ **為你培養敏銳的英文聽力**
每堂課的課文和單字皆由專業的外籍錄音員錄製，提升你的英文聽力真功夫。

★ **為你增強必備的實用單字**
每篇課文從所搭配的TED Talks演講影片精選出多個實用單字，強化你的單字庫。

★ **為你條列重要的演講技巧**
搭配精采的10個TED Talks演講影片，傳授最實用的演講技巧，並精準呈現演講的常用句型。

★ **為你設計即時的實戰演練**
現學現做練習題，以循序漸進、由淺入深的教學引導，將每一堂課所有的演講技巧串聯並整合即完成一場英文演講，練就完美的演講力。

新多益黃金互動16週：
基礎篇／進階篇

李海碩、張秀帆、多益900團隊　編著

依難易度分為基礎篇與進階篇，教師可依學生程度選用。

★ 本書由ETS認證多益英語測驗專業發展工作坊講師李海碩、張秀帆
　 編寫，及多益模擬試題編寫者Joseph E. Schier審訂。

★ 涵蓋2018年3月最新改制多益題型。每冊各8單元皆附聽力音檔及
　 一份多益全真模擬試題。

50天搞定新制多益核心單字
隨身讀

三民英語編輯小組　彙整

嚴選單字：主題分類新制多益高頻單字，五十回五十天一次搞定。

紮實學習：多益情境例句和字彙小幫手，補充搭配用法一網打盡。

四國發音：英美加澳專業外籍錄音員錄音，四國口音都一併聽熟。

易帶易讀：雙色印刷版面編排舒適好讀，口袋尺寸設計一手掌握。

免費下載：獨家贈送英文三民誌2.0APP，單字行動學習一點就通。

子彈筆記：學習歷程與單字扉頁小設計，學習進度管理一目了然。

國家圖書館出版品預行編目資料

商用英文／黃正興編著.－－修訂五版二刷.－－臺北
市：三民，2022
面；　公分

　　ISBN 978-957-14-6899-0 （平裝）
　1. 商業英文 2. 讀本

805.18   109011440

商用英文

編 著 者	黃正興
發 行 人	劉振強
出 版 者	三民書局股份有限公司
地　　址	臺北市復興北路 386 號 (復北門市)
	臺北市重慶南路一段 61 號 (重南門市)
電　　話	(02)25006600
網　　址	三民網路書店 https://www.sanmin.com.tw
出版日期	初版一刷 1996 年 4 月
	修訂五版一刷 2020 年 8 月
	修訂五版二刷 2022 年 3 月
書籍編號	S801190
I S B N	978-957-14-6899-0

三民書局